ChangelingPress.com

Outcast/Player Duet

Hounds of Hell MC Romance

Jamie Targaet

Outcast/Player Duet

Hounds of Hell MC Romance

Jamie Targaet

ISBN: 978-1-60521-958-5

Publisher:
Changeling Press LLC
315 N. Centre St.
Martinsburg, WV 25404
ChangelingPress.com

Printed in the U.S.A.

Editor: Treva Harte
Cover Artist: Bryan Keller

The individual stories in this anthology have been previously released in E-Book format.

Table of Contents

Outcast (Hounds of Hell MC 7)
A Hounds of Hell MC Romance
Jamie Targaet

Anna's his captive, but she's always been mine. I'll burn their empire to the ground to bring her home.

Anya -- I never forgot Jackson -- not when the foster system chewed us up and spit us out. Not when I was dragged into the nightmare world of Sebastian Six. Jackson was the one bright spot in my past, the only person who ever tried to save me. Now, trapped as Six's captive, I've lost hope... until I see him again. Jackson isn't just a memory anymore; he's a badass biker called Outcast. He fights the brutal champion in Six's underground ring, just to win a night with me. He's risking everything to get me out. This time, I'm not letting him go.

Outcast -- She was everything to me once. The only thing that ever mattered. I tried to save her when we were young and failed. But when her photo turned up on a soldier tied to a fake gun deal, I knew I'd been given another chance. I tracked her to Louisville, to the syndicate, to the monster who owns her. If she had been safe and happy, I would've walked away. But she wasn't. So I fought their champion in a cage match just to get close. Now I'm running with her again -- only this time, I'm ready to kill anyone who gets in my way for her. No one is taking Anya from me. Not now. Not *ever* again.

Chapter One

Outcast

Player scrolled through his phone in the passenger seat next to him, killing time while they waited in the Jeep for the Red Scourge MC's soldiers to show. In the back, Crash sat silent, his usual restless energy contained -- for now. Malachai's illegally modified rifles were tucked in the back, behind the rear seats, ready for the deal. Snow and the twins were positioned in the woods nearby, out of sight but primed to strike if things went sideways. Everyone was in place and ready.

Well, the Hounds were ready. The other MC was new to this part of Virginia, and the fact that they'd reached out about guns right away had sent up an immediate red flag for Outcast. Now they were running late, testing his patience as he ran through all the ways this deal could turn bloody if the buyers decided to play dirty. Yeah, the club needed the money, but with so many unknowns surrounding this crew, Razor had made sure they were prepared for everything. *Probably.*

The late February sky loomed heavy with dark clouds as the wind howled through the trees, whipping past them in the Jeep. Outcast killed the engine, powering down his driver's side window just an inch or two. He was vigilant, keeping an eye on all the vehicle's mirrors. He listened, trying to tune out the sounds of the wind and the occasional vehicle driving by on the highway behind them. For the meeting place, they'd selected a remote area between Mercy and Oak Grove. Outcast had picked it out -- a stretch with no houses or businesses -- in case things went south.

Player shoved his phone back into the pocket of

his leather jacket, his attention now on Outcast. "You sure you're feeling up to this, brother?"

Outcast nodded, shutting down any chance of a drawn-out conversation about his well-being. It was bad enough dealing with Deva every day, her constant hovering after his recovery from the beating Victor Grayson's men had handed him. And where Deva went, Razor followed -- especially now that they were together. His club president was a hell of a lot harder to shake than his sister.

"I'm fine," Outcast said, and for the most part, it was true. Mornings were rough, and by night, the lingering pain crept back in -- especially after a long day. But each day, it dulled a little more. Still, the slow recovery gnawed at him. Pushing forty or not, he should've been back to full strength by now, and the frustration of it sat heavy on his shoulders.

"They're here." Snow's rough whisper came over the walkie talkie Outcast had positioned in the cupholder of the center console.

Sure enough, a huge black Hummer turned off Route 221 onto the narrow dirt road where they waited. Player pressed the button on the transceiver and said, "Copy that."

Outcast watched the other vehicle move closer. Player grinned at him from the passenger seat, itching for a fight Outcast hoped they could avoid. "It's showtime," he said. Crash's gaze met Outcast's in the rearview mirror, and he nodded.

"Focus," Outcast told them, watching the Hummer rumble to a stop on the other side of the road. He counted four heads but there was plenty of room in that behemoth of a vehicle for more to be hiding. A bad vibe twisted in his gut. Just now he was really fucking grateful for Razor's command that they take backup.

It was ten minutes until five, and Outcast knew the sun was sinking toward the horizon, though the thick storm clouds kept it hidden. He slowly opened the door and stepped out of the Jeep, the wind biting against his skin. Crash climbed out at the same time, moving with his usual measured calm. Player, on the other hand, damn near rocked the whole vehicle as he jumped out of the passenger side, his boots hitting the ground hard. Moving too fast for Outcast's liking, Player strode around to stand beside him, his massive frame coiled tight, ready for a fight before one had even started.

The smell of rain and the acrid tang of cigarette smoke from the four men who exited the Hummer hung in the cold evening air. Outcast's weight shifted casually and every muscle he had tensed. This was far from his first deal, but something about this particular group set his nerves on edge.

Four men stood across from them, their faces partially obscured by the fading light and shifting shadows of the storm. Their leather cuts were crisp, their jeans too clean, and not one of them carried the rough, road-worn edge Outcast expected from outlaw bikers. Something about them felt off -- like they were playing a role rather than living the life. And considering none of the Hounds had ever heard of Red Scourge MC before now, that didn't sit right with him. Whoever the fuck they were, he didn't like the vibes they were giving off.

"Appreciate you boys coming all this way," the taller of the four drawled, lighting up a cigarette. Outcast recognized Hawk's voice from speaking with him on the phone. "Been hearing good things about the Hounds' hardware. Guess you need something to do out here in the middle of Bumfuck, Virginia."

Outcast nodded, holding Hawk's gaze as the other man sized him up. "Guess so."

Hawk took another step closer, studying Outcast. A challenge. After a minute, the man nodded. "Well, they were right about *you*. Outcast, right? You got some cold, motherfuckin' eyes."

Outcast never took on personal comments, just waited, staring the man down. Hawk, they were told, was a VP in his club. He had none of Snow or Razor's authoritative presence and his insecurities were as obvious as a Halloween mask. Hawk squared his shoulders, but the slight twitch in his fingers and the way he shifted his weight from foot to foot told a different story. The man wasn't as fearless as he wanted everyone to believe.

Player's posture radiating confidence. Towering over most, his broad frame made him an imposing presence -- only Beast outweighed him in the club. His voice was smooth, almost lazy, but the edge beneath it was unmistakable. "Money's what matters," Player said, flashing a grin that didn't quite reach his eyes. "If you've got that, we've got your hardware."

Hawk nodded to the younger man standing to his left who pulled a thick envelope from his jacket and handed it to him. Holding it up for the Hounds to see, he said, "Here's our end of the deal. Now, we'd like to see what we're paying for."

Without taking his eyes off the Red Scourge soldiers, Outcast said, "Crash."

It was the cue for Crash to climb into the back of the Jeep and haul out one of the two heavy plastic totes, each packed with rifles. He lowered it to the ground, unlocking the padlock that secured the lid to the body of the bin. Crash pulled out a sleek, fully-automatic rifle. Its dark wood grip and black metal barrel looked ominous in the dim light. Malachai, the newest patched member of the Hounds, was Goddamned good at what he did, illegally modifying weapons himself to make them more lethal. His skill with high-powered firearms was one of the reasons the prospect had earned his cut.

Crash moved with deliberate ease, stepping toward Hawk and extending an unloaded rifle. At the same time, Hawk handed over the thick, bulging envelope -- supposedly filled with cash. The exchange happened smoothly. *Too smoothly.* Outcast kept his eyes locked on the Red Scourge leader.

Hawk gripped the rifle, turning it over in his hands like he knew what he was looking for. Crash, on the other hand, tore open the envelope and thumbed through the stack of bills inside. Outcast caught the barely perceptible glance his brother-in-arms shot him.

I fucking knew it.

Before Outcast could call it out, Hawk's expression twisted into something sharp and satisfied. "Nice piece," he said, fingers tightening on the grip. "Real nice. Too bad we're takin' 'em for free."

Motherfucker.

A tense beat passed. Then all hell broke loose.

Hawk's men moved fast, hands going to their jackets. But they weren't fast enough. The first shot rang out as Player fired from the hip, dropping one of Hawk's men before the bastard could clear his weapon. Four more men spilled out of the Hummer, Red Scourge reinforcements armed and ready, their boots hitting the dirt with the confidence of men who thought they had the upper hand. Crash lunged back toward the Jeep, using it for cover as gunfire exploded around them. Outcast and Player followed his lead, ducking low as they dashed around the front of the

Jeep for cover. Yanking his pistol from its holster, Outcast fired off a shot that clipped one of the Scourge in the shoulder, sending him sprawling to the ground.

Snow and the twins emerged from the tree line like Goddamn wraiths, silent and deadly, their weapons lighting up the gray evening with muzzle flashes. Axel and Ryder moved in perfect sync, splitting off without a word -- Axel flanking left while Ryder pushed right. Their coordinated assault tore through the ambushers with ruthless efficiency.

Snow, ever the tactician, remained in the cover of the trees, picking his shots with terrifying precision. Each time his rifle fired, another body dropped, clean and lethal. The bastards never saw it coming. Axel fired off a burst, dropping a man who had been scrambling for cover behind a fallen log. Ryder, fluid and relentless, put a bullet through another's knee. The man was howling in the dirt when he took a second shot to the head. The Hounds moved fast as they weaved through the chaos like reapers in the night.

The would-be buyers hadn't expected this kind of resistance. They were outmatched, outgunned, and scrambling to get the hell out of there.

"Hawk's running!" Crash bellowed over the gunfire.

Snow turned sharply, tracking the movement. "Not for long," he said, lining up a shot -- but Outcast was already moving.

Outcast's shot missed, but Snow hit Hawk's arm as he made it to the driver's side of the Hummer and jumped behind the wheel. The only other Scourge left standing ran around the huge vehicle to climb in the back just as its engine roared to life. Hawk cast Outcast one quick, murderous glare as he hit the gas and hauled ass out of there.

That left Outcast and his crew standing there in the fading light, six bodies scattered on the dirt road all around them. Player watched with him as the twins searched through the dead Scourges' pockets. "Let's see what our friends brought to the party," he said.

Wallets, phones, IDs… all were dumped into a pile.

"Was there any money in that envelope?" Snow asked Crash as they watched the twins inspect the bodies, looking for identification and anything else they could use.

"A couple of hundred-dollar bills bundled with a bunch of paper in between." Crash confirmed their suspicions.

When Axel checked the last man, he sputtered where he lay, still alive. Blood bubbled up from his throat and ran down the sides his mouth as Axel pulled the man's wallet from his jacket, tossed it into the pile. He quickly searched his pockets, pulling something from inside the man's jacket -- a folded photograph.

"What are we doing with them?" Player asked, hands on his hips as he surveyed the carnage.

"Outcast." There was urgency in Axel's voice.

Outcast walked over to Axel who gazed at the worn photo from the man's pocket. "This looks like the photo at your shop, doesn't it?"

Taking the photo, Outcast just stared at it in stunned silence. It wasn't a copy of the same photo, but it *was* the same tattoo. The intricately designed phoenix tattoo stood out on the white skin of its wearer. It was distinct. He'd stared at it a million times. His fingers had traced over those lines in bold ink that stained her back. Just her jawline and chin appeared in the corner; a lock of her titian hair ran along the top of the picture.

It was her. Anastasia. His Anya.

When the owner of the photo coughed, a rattling wet sound, Outcast shoved Axel aside, grabbing the dying man's jacket and roughly hauling him off the ground to get in his face. "Where is she?" Outcast demanded.

Fear flashed in the man's dark eyes as he struggled to speak. Outcast held up the worn photograph of the woman he'd been seeking for years, shoving it at the man's face. Why did this random asshole have *his* Anya's picture? "Where is she?"

The light faded from the man's eyes as he choked, his entire body convulsing. One last spasm and he went limp. Dropping him to the ground, Outcast checked for a pulse but there wasn't one. The man was gone and all he had was a photo, the first sign of her he'd had in a long damn time. Rage and frustration sent his fist flying into the man's jaw, blood splattering with the blow. Outcast punched him again, then once more. Player finally pulled him back, holding onto him as he tried in vain to reach the dead son-of-a-bitch on the ground so he could keep pounding him.

"Hey, man," Player's low voice was by his ear. "He's gone. He's done."

His friend held onto him, but he kept swinging. When Snow appeared in front of him, concern flashing in his gray eyes, he stopped, trying to slow his breathing down.

"I'm not judging you, man," their club VP said. "But the sun's going down and we got to do something with these bodies."

"And we need to do a fucking good job of it," Ryder said. "Margot's still in hot water over the warehouse incident."

Focusing on his breathing, Outcast tried to quell the rage threatening to consume him. Snow was right; they needed to take care of the evidence. Picking up the precious photo where he'd dropped it, he tucked it into the inside pocket of his leather jacket.

Pointing to the pile of wallets and phones, Outcast looked to Axel. "Where's his wallet?"

Axel fished a beat-up brown leather wallet from the pile, handing it to him. Tucking it into his jacket, he tried to focus on what was before them right now -- the gun sale that had gone south, the dead soldiers they needed to deal with right away.

"Hold up," Crash said, pushing up the sleeve of the man who had Anya's photo. "Look at this."

On the inside of the man's forearm was a small black tattoo. Three snakes looped together in a very familiar logo. Outcast remembered it from *Sinister Skin Studios*, the tattoo shop Grayson had tried to set up in town when Grayson went after Outcast and Deva's tattoo shop, *No Mercy Ink*. They'd also crudely spray painted that fucking mark inside their tattoo shop when they trashed it.

"They're with fucking Grayson," Outcast said. A quick check of the other bodies revealed that they all had the same mark.

Snow called Razor, quickly giving him the story of what happened. When Snow mentioned that they were Grayson's men, he could hear the deep rumble of Razor's voice from where he stood. Snow explained they had several dead at the scene, nodding at whatever instructions their Prez gave him.

"There's bags in the back of the Jeep," Snow told them, ending the call. "Bag 'em up. Ryder, bring our truck around."

"Where are we going?" Player asked as the twins

hustled to go get the truck.

"Your father's farm," Snow explained.

Player nodded. "Yeah, yeah, you got it." Player's father, a retired Hound, had a pig farm a few miles away. It was a convenient way to get rid of the evidence.

Crash and Player grabbed bags to carry out Razor's orders. Outcast started to help them, but one look at the man who had Anya's picture had him seeing red, his fists clenching at his sides.

"We got you." Crash's hand on his shoulder pulled him out of his thoughts and the onslaught of emotions he couldn't control. "Stay here."

Pulling open the door, Outcast sat in the driver's seat, his emotions spiraling. Instinct had warned him this meeting would be a huge clusterfuck. They hadn't made a sale; they had six dead soldiers who turned out to be Grayson's men. Even worse, Hawk got away. They'd be back looking for payback sooner or later.

And to top it all off, one of the fuckers had Anya's picture. Why the fuck did he have *her* picture? How? Rage coiled tight in Outcast's chest, slowly spreading and burning through his veins. The man with her photo was one of Grayson's. Did that mean she was in *that* world?

If she was, Outcast was willing to burn it down just to get to her.

* * *

Anya

Anastasia Montgomery stood just outside Sebastian Six's office, her back pressed against the cold, smooth surface of the wall as she strained to catch every word filtering through the heavy oak door. The long hallway leading to the office was lined with sleek marble floors, their reflective surface amplifying the chill in the air. Expensive artwork hung on the walls, with a few small sculptures added to strategic places. But the muted tones and abstract designs felt as lifeless as the space itself. The glow of recessed lighting cast deep shadows, making the space seem sharper, more foreboding. The interior of the mansion reflected its owner's temperament -- opulent but soulless, a shrine to wealth devoid of warmth.

Through the cracked door, Anya could see part of his office -- a sprawling room dominated by a massive ebony desk with sharp, angular lines. The desk was immaculate, save for a stack of papers, his laptop, and a glass decanter of bourbon with a half-full tumbler next to it. Behind it, floor-to-ceiling windows framed the city skyline. She knew that view, but it was so vast and impersonal. It never failed to make her long for the wooded mountains and bright summer gardens of the small towns where she'd grown up.

The office furniture matched the vibe of the mansion: black leather chairs with chrome accents and a plush black rug that seemed to absorb the space instead of softening it. The only sound was the low murmur of Sebastian's voice, clipped and precise, his tone as frigid as the room around him. Anya shivered, not just from the chill but from the unmistakable aura of control and menace that clung to the walls of this place.

"It was a simple gun run," Sebastian's voice raised. "What the fuck happened?"

While he listened to the explanation of whomever he was on the phone with, Sebastian drummed his nails on the desk. As she listened, her heartbeat picked up, locking with the cadence of his impatient fingers. Anya hung on every word, hoping to hear that Sebastian was leaving. For a day, or a week. Hell, she'd even settle for a few hours.

Would he take CJ with him? CJ was just a soldier in Sebastian's sprawling criminal network who sometimes served as a driver for those at the top of the pyramid or acted as backup personal protection. It was how she'd met him. All she needed was a couple of hours with CJ, who looked at her like she was the damsel in distress he dreamed of rescuing. And didn't she need rescuing? She could talk to him, convince him to help her.

"I'm disappointed, Hawk." Sebastian's tone was chilling. Anya knew that tone very well. "Sounds like it was really fucking sloppy. Which six did you lose? Gale, Jeb, Curt… Who else?"

Anya's heart clenched, a jolt of shock and dread coursing through her. Was CJ among the dead? Killed on the mission Sebastian sent him on? Her mind reeled, rejecting the words even as they echoed in her head. *Please don't let CJ be one of them.* He couldn't be gone. He was supposed to be her chance -- her way out of this nightmare. A flicker of hope she had clung to in the darkness. Her chest tightened, breath catching as she fought the rising tide of panic. CJ, with his nervous smiles, had been the only one who treated her like she was more than a pawn in Sebastian's world.

"Roddy and CJ too?" Sebastian asked angrily.

"No," she whispered, her voice trembling. But the silence around her offered no denial, no solace, just the weight of a truth she wasn't ready to accept.

Blinking back tears, she tried to pull herself together as he ended the call. She needed to sneak back up to the bedroom before Sebastian noticed. Turning to head back up the hallway, Anya moved carefully, silently. She'd almost made it to the end of the hallway, when she heard him.

"Anya." He made her name sound ominous in the quiet of the corridor.

Her heart slammed in her chest as she stopped and gathered her courage. She had no idea what was coming because Sebastian was nothing if not unpredictable. Slowly, she turned to face him, a soft smile on her lips as she prayed the coming conversation wouldn't turn violent tonight. The blow of losing CJ was bad enough.

"Sebastian," she said as she sauntered back in his direction.

He stood just outside his office, his tall frame casting a long shadow. The glow from the crystal light fixture above highlighted the sharp angles of his face -- high cheekbones, a strong jaw, and eyes like shards of dark green glass that reflected nothing. His expression was impossible to read, a mask of cool detachment that made her stomach churn with unease. Dressed in his usual tailored slacks and crisp white shirt, he looked every bit the predator he was, composed and dangerous. His lips curled at the corners in a way that might have been a smirk or a sneer -- she could never tell. Anya prayed he was in a good mood, though deep down, she knew better. With Sebastian, good moods were fleeting, and bad ones could be deadly.

"Was there something you wanted?" he asked, his voice smooth and measured, offering no hint of his mood. His unreadable gaze pinned her in place, a silent challenge she couldn't afford to lose.

Anya stepped forward, masking her nerves with her practiced smile. As she closed the distance between them, his scent -- sandalwood and deep green woods, rich and expensive -- wrapped around her like an unwelcome embrace. It was the scent of power, control, and something darker that made her skin crawl. She pushed the revulsion deep down, reminding herself that survival was the only thing that mattered. With careful ease, she tilted her head slightly.

"I was lonely waiting for you," Anya purred, striking a pose in the champagne-colored peignoir set she wore. "It's late."

Her heart beat so loudly as she waited for a reaction that she wouldn't have been surprised if he could hear it. That assessing gaze looked her up and down, his powerful hand closing over her hip and sliding up the side of her body to her breast. Anya let her eyes slide closed and let her mouth fall open as if she spent every moment aching for his touch, craving it. When he pinched her nipple sharply, she fought the impulse to react. Her captor liked pain, and if she even gave him a hint it was too much, he'd double down. His kind of "loving" would leave her bruised and aching for days.

"I don't think it's *me* you're lonely for," he said in a low voice as he pulled the sash of her peignoir set to open the robe, revealing the gown underneath.

He grabbed her face in his hand, a cruel viselike grip, while she absorbed the blow of having been caught in a lie. Sheer panic had her trying to pull herself free of him. But fighting him was pointless as he dragged her to his office. Sebastian roughly slung her into the office before slamming its door shut and locking it so no one could make it in to help her no matter how loudly she screamed. Not that they would. His men were likely as terrified of him as she was.

Like a beast, he chased her down in his office. Sebastian cornered her easily enough; her back was to one of those floor-to-ceiling windows. She shook violently with terror. His eyes were pools of cold anger as Sebastian got in her face, but he wasn't touching her yet. "Which one were you fucking, Anya?" he asked in a tight, bitter voice.

She was already shaking her head in denial. "No one," she managed. "I belong to you."

His open-handed slap to her face stunned her. "You have a lot of free time on your hands," he said through his teeth. "Don't you? Which one was it? Who were you fucking?"

An image of CJ flashed in her mind, and she cringed with guilt. No, she hadn't fucked him or anyone else while she'd been in Sebastian's clutches. She would have fucked CJ if she thought he could have given her a chance to escape her opulent prison. She would have convinced him that she loved him, anything, if she could just regain her freedom. Not only that but she had the world's worst poker face. Would Sebastian read the guilt on her face and take it as confirmation of what he was accusing her of?

"Wasn't fucking anyone," she murmured as tears leaked from the corners of her eyes. Her ears still rang from the blow, and she stayed still, hoping some miracle would happen and he'd be drawn away by business that was far more important than her. But it was late, almost midnight. No one would dare disturb him at this time unless a catastrophe was in progress.

"But you *were*." Again, he grabbed her chin, yanking her head roughly to make her look at him. "It was CJ, wasn't it? Is that who you were spreading your legs for?"

"No," she managed even with the punishing grip he had on her face.

"The stupid fucker was ogling you every chance he got," Sebastian growled. "Don't lie to me!"

"I'm not," she said, her breath coming fast. "I wouldn't."

"Too bad," he said, lowering his head until they were nose to nose. "Your little boyfriend is dead."

Releasing her, he violently grabbed the back of his huge leather office chair and shoved it across the room. Grabbing her by the back of the neck, he shoved her toward his desk, bending her over it. One of her elbows landed on a neat stack of papers, the other almost knocking over his bourbon. Sebastian hauled up the back of her garments, ripping off the delicate thong that matched.

Gripping her even tighter, he pinned her to the top of the desk while he shifted behind her. The sounds of a buckle undone, a zipper pulled down. She knew what came next and she braced herself. She cried out because he liked that, he wanted to know he was hurting her. Each thrust felt a little less like being sliced open by razor blades as her walls stretched and tried to lubricate around him, trying to quickly adjust. Behind her he growled in anger, swearing at her under his breath as he fucked her mercilessly.

Anya just let the tears come. She just wanted it to be over. She had gotten somewhat good at mentally detaching herself from Sebastian's brutality, like the way he used her body now. Her gaze moved over the desk he held her to, returning to the laptop. A generic photo of the Antarctic with its icebergs and glaciers, showed on its screen in shades of white and pale blue.

Unbidden, an image of his eyes flashed in her memory. She tried not to think of Jackson too much because of the wave of regret and pain it brought. The night in Memphis seemed like a lifetime ago. Despite the violence that led to their reunion, she'd spent one amazing night with him. And like a fool, she'd left him there before dawn, letting her insecurities and the past prey on her mind.

While thinking about Jackson tore open the hole in her heart that never healed, it did temporarily dull the pain of Sebastian rutting into her like a beast. Gave her something to focus on besides fear and stinging loss.

Jackson. She'd give anything just to see him one more time before she died. And her death always felt close.

Chapter Two

Outcast

After spending a couple of hours taking care of the bodies at Player's family farm, Outcast went straight to his house. He wasn't worried about heading back to the clubhouse with the others to explain what happened. Snow and the twins would take care of that. The club's attempt to sell the guns they had ready had gone completely fucking sideways, the entire situation leaving him rattled on a few levels.

Killing, whether it was for the club or personal, wasn't something any of them took lightly. Outcast didn't have a high number of people he'd taken out, but he could remember each of their faces. Strange details stuck in his mind, showed up in his nightmares. The smell of whiskey and blood at the bar in Memphis, the stinging smell of disinfectant spray and old urine at the Lorrys' place. The way his knuckles split and bled the night at *Sackett's* last fall, how it felt like he was grinding glass into the wounds every time he hit someone.

He took his time in the shower, letting the hottest water he could stand wash over him. He stood under the spray while the dirt, blood, and smell of death washed away. All the while, he couldn't stop thinking about the photo of Anya they found on that man. On one of Grayson's fucking men.

It was the real reason he'd hurried home. The rest of them could talk about the deal that had gone wrong and the men they'd killed. Their ties to Victor Grayson were sure to strike a nerve with Razor every bit as much as it did him.

Or would have if not for Anya's picture. He just couldn't get her and the damn photo out of his mind as he dried off, then got dressed quickly. Nervous energy hummed through him as he headed for his living room, snatching that same photo from the coffee table where he left it.

Anya had been asleep or lying there with her eyes closed when it was taken, her bare back with that unmistakable tattoo highlighted in the picture. Printed photos just weren't that common these days and to find one of her on some random soldier's body meant what? Was CJ Stenberg the man she loved now? Is that why he had her picture? Or was it worse? The Hounds learned firsthand that trafficking was a big part of Grayson's operation. Was Anya being trafficked?

The thought turned his stomach, and he dropped onto his recliner, still staring at the image. Stenberg had no wedding band, but he knew it was foolish to get his hopes up over that. What if he and Anya had been together? Did she love him? Had he been able to see her smile? See *her* every single day?

Remembering that he had the man's wallet, he went to dig it out of his jacket so he could go through it again. It gave him a place to start. Because his gut told him that if he could track down CJ Stenberg, or at least where he'd been, just maybe he could find Anya herself. Had she been happy with CJ? Maybe. Maybe not. Either way, it was a question he had to answer. He needed to see her. He needed to know she was happy and safe, especially since he'd failed her so badly when it mattered the most.

His phone hummed, drawing his attention. His sister's name flashed on the screen. He knew if he didn't answer the call, she'd probably drive right over there. And he couldn't handle that tonight. "Yeah?"

"Are you okay?" Deva demanded.

"I'm fine," Outcast said, hoping she'd just let it

go.

He wasn't that lucky.

"Want to tell me about the photo?" Deva asked.

Here we go. So much for Hound business staying with just the members. "No, I really don't."

"Was it really her?"

The doubt in his sister's voice was understandable. What were the odds he'd find a picture of the woman he'd never forget on a random guy the Hounds shot dead on a failed gun deal? But it still happened, and the photo was undeniably Anya.

"It was." He didn't mean for sadness to creep into his tone.

"So that picture you've always kept at your station in the shop was her?" Deva asked. "That's her tattoo?"

"Yeah, it is," he explained. "I didn't do it. But I saw it firsthand."

"I know it's not your work," Deva said. "Did she have that tattoo when --"

"No." Outcast cut her off. "She was sixteen. She didn't get that until a few years later."

"Wait… you've seen her?" Deva asked. "Since that… night?"

Deva didn't remember much about the night he tried to run with her and Anya, to escape the nightmare that was Gene Lorry's so-called foster home. And he was grateful for that. He didn't want his younger sister knowing what the evil fucker had done to Anya, what he probably would have done to Deva too if given time and opportunity. Their escape attempt failed. An observant neighbor saw them sneaking out of the house and called the cops. Then CPS got involved. It got them away from Lorry and his terrified wife. Still, thanks to the Lorrys' lies, he and Deva had been separated for the next two years. And it was ten years after that before he found Anya again on that one random night in Memphis.

"Just once," he said. "Just one night."

"Razor says you said her name," Deva said slowly, "when you were in the hospital."

"I was pumped full of fucking pain meds," Outcast said in a lighter tone. "Probably mentioned my kindergarten girlfriend too."

For a moment, she was quiet. He just knew her mind was going a mile a minute. Finally, she asked, "You're going to look for her, aren't you?"

Yes.

"Don't worry about it, Deva," he said quietly.

"Snow said you were upset --"

"Snow's not supposed to be sharing club business," he reminded her.

"Whoa now," Deva said. He could hear the smile in her voice. "You being upset isn't exactly club business. And Razor is the president of the Hounds. I'm his old lady. That doesn't earn me something?"

"No!" Razor bellowed from the background on Deva's end. Outcast had to laugh when Deva yelled "fuck you!" back to him.

It also let him know he was on speakerphone.

"Yeah, I was a little upset to find that photo on the guy, but it was the heat of the moment." Outcast thought as an explanation it was good enough. "The deal went wrong, and we were upset about it. And that's all."

Another pause. Finally, Deva said, "Okay… You only had one appointment for tomorrow and they rescheduled for next week. Why don't you take tomorrow off? Rest?"

He thought he heard Razor say her name, trying

to get her to back off. Like that was ever going to happen.

"Sounds good," Outcast said. "I'll do that. You're okay at the shop on your own?"

"I'll be fine," Deva assured him, sounding happier now that he'd given her something. "Have a good night. Love you, bro."

"Love you too."

Outcast ended the call, scrubbing his hands through his hair after he put his phone down.

You're going to look for her, aren't you?

He *did* plan to look for her. He just had to.

A couple of shots of vodka took the edge off a long fucking day as he made himself supper. But no matter how hard he tried, he couldn't stop thinking about Anya. Again, he'd been about to get the man's wallet out of his jacket when the rumble of a motorcycle came up the lonely country road he lived on. Light from its headlight flashed through his living room windows. He didn't know who was visiting so late or why, but he waited patiently for whoever it was to come to the door.

It was Snow on his doorstep, the Hounds VP, standing there with his hands shoved into the pockets of his jacket. His breath plumed out like cigarette smoke in the cold air. His white hair was windswept, his gray eyes were sharp and assessing on Outcast.

"You got a minute?" Snow asked calmly.

Nodding, Outcast stood back and let him in.

"I brought you something," Snow said without preamble, handing him a smart phone with a cracked screen. "I used his fingerprint to get in it. I reset the pin. It's 4444."

Outcast took the phone but stared at Snow in confusion.

"Thought you might want to look through it," his VP said.

CJ Stenberg's phone? Oh, he certainly did.

"It's your responsibility to make sure the phone and his wallet disappear when you're done with them, okay?" Snow seemed to be struggling with what he wanted to say. "I don't need to know what all that was about today but… Do whatever you need to do, man."

"Thank you." Outcast meant it.

Snow headed back for the door and left without another word.

Outcast locked up his house, turned out all the lights. He took the photo, wallet, and phone with him as he headed for his bedroom. Climbing onto his bed, he didn't bother to turn on the TV, which was the first thing he normally did. Once again, he went through the wallet belonging to CJ Stenberg. There was nothing out of the ordinary there. The man's driver's license gave Outcast his address. There were a couple of credit cards, an insurance card. The three hundred dollars in cash would come in handy.

Thanks to Snow, he got into the man's phone easily enough but there wasn't much to find there at first glance. A few emails, the usual apps. But it was the photos on the phone that he was most interested in. And what he found in the gallery of photos on the man's phone grabbed his attention quickly.

Anya, *his Anya,* in so many of the photos on the man's phone. The majority of the photos weren't posed. There were candid shots of her walking, usually alone. His hungry eyes took in every detail of her. Anya in beautiful, expensive clothes, never seeming aware that someone was taking her picture. The photos showed her walking by the same expensive cars, in front of the same huge stone mansion.

After a few moments, he was pretty sure of a couple of things. CJ Stenberg may have been interested in her. Hell, given the number of photos he had on his phone of her, it appeared that he was fucking obsessed. But Anya wasn't *with* him. But then remembering the more intimate photo the man had of her, maybe she wasn't *supposed* to be with him. And why with all the photos he had of her did he carry a printed photo of her on him?

His mind spun out so many possibilities. Either she lived at that mansion, or she was a frequent visitor. Since Stenberg's photos all placed her at that mansion, it would suggest that the man was there often himself. He didn't appear to be anyone special. A soldier. Stenberg obviously didn't live there. But just maybe he worked there.

Grabbing his laptop, Outcast looked up the man's home address online. The street view showed Stenberg's house wasn't any bigger than his own, only it was in a poor neighborhood with houses crammed together on tiny lots. It sure as fuck wasn't a mansion. And when he used the man's phone to take one of the mansion photos and do a reverse-image search, nothing came up on the magnificent house. But instinct told him that he might find Anya there.

* * *

Anya

The next morning, she woke up tired and resigned. Sebastian was always up and gone before dawn. His early bird mentality was also demanded of her. She was to be up by six each morning, dressed -- because his "lady" would not be a whore who stayed in bed all day -- and ready to occupy herself in the mansion in a way that didn't cause any problems for him or his interests.

It was a somber morning, and her body ached after Sebastian's attentions last night. With CJ gone, she would have to start over on finding a way to escape Sebastian's clutches. Two years had stretched out like an eternity since Sebastian had declared her his. Each passing day chipped away at her sense of self, leaving her more afraid of disappearing into the cruelty that surrounded her.

Anya kept her head down as she moved through the dimly lit corridors of the mansion, making her way toward the library. The estate was sprawling, a labyrinth of expensive excess, but it always felt cold -- no warmth, no comfort, just pristine furniture and soulless design meant to intimidate rather than welcome. She barely made it past the grand staircase when Sebastian's voice cut through the silence like a blade.

"Anya."

Her stomach dropped, but she turned smoothly, schooling her features into polite indifference. He stood at the far end of the corridor, his dark green eyes locked onto her like a predator assessing his prey. With a flick of his fingers, he motioned her toward the living room.

The space was massive, designed more like an opulent throne room than a place for relaxation. A fire burned low in the wide stone hearth, casting flickering shadows across the dark wood-paneled walls. The ceiling stretched high, with intricate crown molding and a glittering chandelier that somehow managed to make the space feel colder rather than grand. Leather sofas, deep mahogany tables, and an oversized bar filled with expensive liquor completed the look -- power and indulgence wrapped in quiet menace.

She stepped inside, immediately noticing they weren't alone.

Near the bar stood a thickset man in a tailored gray suit -- Donovan, the ruthless handler of Sebastian's underground cage fighting operation. She'd met him at the first of two cage matches she'd attended with Sebastian. He carried himself with the quiet arrogance of a man who controlled lives with a single decision. Next to him, radiating sheer brute force, was one of his prized fighters.

Anya had seen her share of violent men, but this one was something else. He was a towering mass of muscle, with shoulders broad enough to block out the chandelier's light. His heavily tattooed arms were crossed over his chest, veins bulging beneath inked skin. His nose had been broken more than once, and a jagged scar ran down his left cheek, a testament to the kind of life he led. His knuckles were raw, split from too many fights, too many victories. His eyes, dark and void of emotion, flicked over her like she was nothing.

Unease coiled in her stomach, but she forced herself to meet Sebastian's gaze instead. Whatever this was, she had a bad feeling about it.

"Have a seat, Anya," Sebastian instructed. Coming to a stop behind the huge leather chair where he normally sat, he patted the back of the chair with his hand. "Sit *here*."

With all eyes on her now, she timidly walked into the room, perching on the edge of Sebastian's chair and fighting the urge to run screaming from the mansion. She glanced fleetingly at each of Sebastian's guests but otherwise kept her gaze down.

"Just to review," Sebastian said to the men. "You, Donovan, will have everything set for the weekend fights by noon on Friday, yes?"

Donovan nodded. "Everything is set, boss. The venue is secure, and the VIP area was cleaned up last night. All the fighter contracts are signed and finalized, just like you wanted."

"Good," Sebastian said, placing a hand on Anya's shoulder. "Anya, you've seen Goliath fight before, haven't you?"

Sebastian knew she had. Politely, she nodded, making brief eye contact with the enormous fighter who looked like he could snap her spine with one hand. "Yes, I have."

"He's undefeated," Sebastian went on. "And he's fighting again Saturday night. Do you want to see him fight?"

The last thing Anya needed was to get into deeper trouble with Sebastian. The rough sex session she'd endured last night wasn't enough to make up for the fact that, in Sebastian's mind, she'd been disloyal. In truth she hadn't been disloyal but if she thought she could escape, yeah, she would have been. The most important thing she could do right now was acting on her best behavior.

"Yes," she said, smiling. "I would."

The fighter's gaze landed on her then, his gaze cold. What puzzled her was why Sebastian wasn't putting a stop to him staring at her. Usually more than a quick glance from another man set him off. But right now, he was silent and behind her so she couldn't easily gauge his expression.

"So we have a deal?" Donovan asked Sebastian, his gaze moving back and forth between her and her captor.

Why were they looking at me like that?

"We do. Thank you for coming over," Sebastian said, announcing the end of the visit.

Donovan and his fighter rose from their chairs at that and so did she, out of respect. Both men walked past her to shake Sebastian's hand and make their exit. Before walking out of the room, Goliath stopped and glanced back at her, his gaze moving over her in a way that filled her with dread.

Was she missing something here?

Staying where she was, Anya waited for the other shoe to drop. She knew Sebastian too well. She knew there was something coming and that she wasn't going to like it. When Sebastian turned his attention back to her, it was all she could do to mask the fact that anxiety and fear were threatening to take her over.

"Do you like Goliath, Anya?" Sebastian asked in a calm tone. It was way too calm.

Her mind scrambled for the appropriate response to that, and Sebastian watched with a smirk on his face. It was like he could read her thoughts, and he was enjoying her anxiety.

"He's an impressive fighter," she finally said. It was the least offensive thing her mind could conjure in that moment.

"He is." Sebastian shoved his hands in the pockets of his slacks. "And no one has been able to beat him since he's been fighting for me. That's been five years."

She nodded, knowing it was to her advantage to play along. Words would only dig a deeper hole than she already had.

"On Saturday night, he'll still be undefeated," Sebastian went on. "It's a certainty."

Why was he telling her this? Why did he want her to go to the fight Saturday night? She'd gone a couple of times before, wincing at the brutality of the fights with every kick and blow. Was this punishment for her disloyalty in his head? Anya was confused because when it came to punishing her for many imagined slights, the consequences were usually immediate and terrible, leaving her scarred both physically and emotionally.

The sense of foreboding was beginning to eat her alive.

"Goliath's put on a show for me over the years," Sebastian went on, "and he's made me a lot of money. Today, they came to negotiate more money for him. And I agreed. He's *loyal*. Something *you* know nothing about. He'll get paid more money starting with Saturday's fight. I reward those who are loyal to me. Those who aren't…"

Anya was so afraid to ask where he was going with this. Fear froze her to the spot as she waited for an explanation.

Moving closer to her, Sebastian got in her space, staring directly into her eyes. "I'm still upset about your little fling with CJ."

Anya shook her head in denial. Sebastian grabbed a hand full of her hair and viciously yanked her head back, his lips were now pressed to her ear. "You were disloyal to me. And you know what I'm going to do about that? Huh? *You* are Goliath's bonus for winning Saturday night. You wanted to fuck someone else after all. And whatever is left of you after fucking him on Sunday better be Goddamned grateful when you come back here to me. And *loyal*. So loyal to me that you never look at another fucking man. Ever."

Anya shook in his clutches, at the venom in his voice. Horror at what he just said left her speechless. If that huge fighter won, Sebastian was just giving her to him for the night? How would she even survive that? As many times as Sebastian threatened her with what would happen if she were ever disloyal, she was struggling to accept that he would just pass her to another man, especially a vicious brute like that.

"Now, go to your room and figure out what you're going to wear to the fight," Sebastian said, releasing her hair and shoving her away from him, causing her to stumble. "I want it laid out on my bed for approval by the time I'm ready for bed."

"I will," she whispered. Tears spilled from her eyes and her shaking was worse now, reactions that she couldn't control. It brought a smile to his face. Nothing made Sebastian happier than seeing someone who wronged him suffer.

Not waiting for him to think of a way to make her situation worse, she scrambled out of the living room and headed for the bedroom to do his bidding. Somehow, she held herself together until she made it to the cold bedroom she shared with Sebastian. Once that door closed behind her, the sobs came on, fear threatened to consume her. Anya slid down the door, wrapping her arms around herself as she sank onto the floor.

A bigger realization hit as she sat there, crying her heart out. Yes, it was horrible that he was handing her to the cage fighter for a night as the man's "bonus." And Goliath *would* win. But just like with all of Sebastian's petty torments, she knew that it wouldn't be a one-time punishment. He'd do it again. Maybe he'd hand her off to one of his generals or one of his business alliances. Her value would go down in his eyes until she ended up being nothing more than another prostitute to him.

What could she do? How had she gone from the possibility of recruiting CJ to help her escape Sebastian's clutches to being whored out by the monster after CJ was killed? From the frying pan into the fire.

It was the theme of her entire fucking life.

How was she going to survive this?

* * *

Outcast

No matter how hard he tried, he couldn't stay asleep. His dreams started out normal, but every single one took a dark turn until he was left looking for Anya and unable to find her.

He finally gave up and got out of bed at four Friday morning, started packing a few things. He went through CJ Stenberg's wallet again, looking at the address. Louisville, Kentucky, huh? He could be in Louisville by noon if he hustled.

Outcast had to find her. He'd never forgiven himself for what happened the night they tried to run from Gene Lorry. If he'd been faster, smarter -- if he'd just been *more* -- they would have made it. The three of them could have started over, built the kind of life none of them had ever known. A family. Anya had adored Deva, and she loved him. The three of them could have been happy.

Instead, everything went to hell.

They'd taken Deva from him, ripped her away. Since he was also a minor at the time, there wasn't a damn thing he could have done to stop it. And Anya -- he'd lost her too. It had been ten years before he found her again, before fate or whatever cruel force ruled their lives put her back in his path in Memphis. One perfect night. The kind that should have meant forever.

And then he'd woken up the next morning, after finally finding her in the Bluff City, and she was gone.

He'd lost his mind searching for answers,

replaying every second of their time together, trying to figure out where he'd gone wrong. Maybe she didn't love him anymore. Maybe she never had.

But that wasn't it. He knew it in his gut.

There'd been something in her eyes that night. A flicker of fear she hadn't quite been able to hide, a shadow haunting every touch, every kiss. She played it off like it was nothing. Tried to, anyway. But he saw through it. And now, all these years later, it still clawed at him, ate at the edges of his sanity. Because whatever had scared her enough to run…

She hadn't trusted him to protect her. He'd failed her again.

Outcast had to know where she was -- had to know she was safe. Happy. Even if she belonged to someone else. It wasn't impossible that she'd really been with CJ Stenberg. The thought made his chest tighten, but if that was the truth? He was gone and she'd need someone when it all fell apart. She'd need a friend.

And if that's all he could be to her now? Then so be it. He'd be whatever she needed.

Stenberg's phone had been similar to his, so his charger worked to power it up. He'd gone through the device for a couple of hours last night and he almost tucked it into his pocket as he got ready to leave, thinking he'd seen all there was to see. But then he decided to give it one more look.

He scrolled through the man's search history. Porn, sports, news. Nothing unexpected. But then there were the gambling searches. Not betting sites -- no, Stenberg wasn't throwing money around on some online sportsbook. These were advice sites, strategy guides, tips on beating the odds.

That meant he wasn't just placing bets. He was

doing it somewhere that didn't operate by the usual rules. Somewhere off the books. Maybe even somewhere dangerous.

Outcast wasn't surprised. Grayson's world was a vast criminal network, with threads stretching into every vice imaginable. If Stenberg had been mixed up in something, it wasn't a question of *if* it was illegal -- just *how* illegal.

If Stenberg wasn't using an online betting site, that meant he had to keep track of his wagers another way. Outcast searched the phone again, this time paying closer attention to the details he'd skimmed over before. A basic notebook app -- something he'd disregarded at first -- caught his eye. When he pulled it up, the first file was just a grocery list. Nothing suspicious.

But when he scrolled further, other files told a different story. Notes on bets. Dollar amounts. Names. And one name stood out more than the rest.

Goliath.

Over and over again, tied to different figures, different wagers. Whoever Goliath was, Stenberg had been in deep with him. And that? That was worth looking into.

Strapping his bag to his bike, Outcast was ready to go to Louisville. He took a deep breath and started the engine.

Chapter Three

Anya

The air inside *Purgatory* was thick with sweat, blood, and the deafening roar of a crowd hungry for violence. Beneath the lurid red lights, the cage at the center of the underground venue gleamed like a steel monster waiting to devour its next victim. The scent of damp concrete, beer, and the unmistakable stench of brutality clung to every surface. Anya sat beside Sebastian, her pulse a wild drumbeat in her chest as she struggled to keep her fear from showing. He liked it when she was afraid, thrived on it. The bastard was in a good mood tonight, relaxed in his throne-like seat overlooking the pit, sipping whiskey as he waited for the inevitable. *When* Goliath won his match, she wouldn't be leaving with Sebastian. She'd be handed over as a prize. A punishment for her supposed betrayal with CJ.

It made her feel ill. She hadn't been with CJ. But the truth about her and CJ didn't matter. The truth had never mattered to Sebastian.

Dressed in a black silk slip dress that clung indecently to her curves, she felt more exposed than she ever had in her life. The thin straps dug into her shoulders, and the slit up her thigh promised easy access -- exactly as Sebastian had intended. He wanted her on display as a tantalizing reward for the monster about to win his fight. Her hands trembled, but she curled them into fists, nails biting into her palms. She wouldn't let them see her break.

"Excited about tonight?" Sebastian asked as he slid a warm hand over her knee.

The sick little grin he flashed her made her feel ill. Anya kept her mouth shut. What was she supposed to say? Lie and say, yeah, she wanted to fuck the bloodthirsty monster everyone came to see? That would only encourage him -- give him the idea that this should become a habit. But if she said no? That would be worse. He'd make her pay for it, find some new, twisted way to humiliate her. Maybe in front of everyone. Maybe in a way she'd never come back from.

His grip on her knee tightened, fingers digging in hard enough to leave bruises. *A reminder. A warning.*

"It didn't have to be this way," Sebastian murmured, his voice deceptively calm, laced with the kind of anger that terrified her. "All you had to do was be loyal, like you promised me in the beginning. But no, you had to go behind my back and spread your legs for someone else. Tell me, Anya… were you trying to make a fool of me?"

She shook her head, biting back the bile rising in her throat, hating the feel of his hand on her skin. He could feel her trembling. *Knew* she was afraid. And he loved it. It was a drug to him, an intoxicating high he never got enough of.

Sebastian leaned in, his breath warm against her cheek. "This is your only warning," he said, fury burning in those dark green eyes. "Disappoint me again, and you won't live to regret it."

The first fight was already underway, and Anya couldn't tear her eyes away, not out of interest, but out of morbid dread. Two younger fighters, wiry and hungry, tore into each other like rabid animals. Blood slicked the concrete beneath them, their bare knuckles already raw and split open. No gloves. No padding. Just flesh and bone, cracking and tearing under the relentless force of fists and elbows.

One of them -- a lean, tattooed kid who couldn't

have been more than twenty -- caught a brutal hook to the jaw that sent him stumbling back, spitting blood. His opponent, broader and meaner, didn't hesitate. He closed the distance, grabbing the kid by the back of the neck and driving a knee into his ribs with a sickening crunch. The crowd roared, fists pounding against the metal barriers.

Anya flinched as the tattooed fighter crumpled, gasping for breath, but he wasn't out. He surged forward, tackling his opponent to the ground, raining desperate, vicious punches down on his face. The other man bucked under him, one elbow catching the kid in the temple. The younger fighter went slack for half a second -- just long enough for his opponent to flip him onto his back and unleash a punishing barrage of blows.

Blood sprayed. The tattooed kid's head snapped with every strike. The crowd screamed for more. Sebastian, beside her, chuckled low under his breath, fingers still absently stroking her knee. The ref didn't stop it. There were no rules here. No mercy. The fight wouldn't end until one of them wasn't getting up.

Anya's breath hitched when her gaze drifted past the carnage in the cage -- and landed on *him*.

Goliath.

He stood just outside the cage, watching the bloodbath unfold with an expression of cold disinterest, as if it bored him. The low red lights barely touched him, leaving him half in shadow, but it didn't soften the sheer size of him. He was massive, a wall of muscle wrapped in dark, inked skin, his arms crossed over his chest like he was carved from stone. Scars crisscrossed his knuckles, old and new, testaments to the kind of damage he could do with his fists alone. He wasn't hyped up like the other fighters. He wasn't stretching or bouncing on the balls of his feet. He didn't need to. He knew he was going to win.

A cold knot formed in her gut when Goliath caught her staring at him. The weight of his stare settled on her, slow and deliberate, like he could already taste the fear coming off her in waves. Her skin prickled, her fingers going numb where they gripped the edge of her chair. A smirk tugged at the corner of his mouth, lazy and cruel, like he was in on a joke she hadn't yet figured out.

A fresh wave of screams erupted from the crowd as one of the fighters in the cage collapsed in a bloody heap. Anya flinched, her pulse hammering wildly, but she couldn't look away from Goliath.

Sebastian's hand slid higher up her thigh, his grip tightening. "Getting nervous, sweetheart?"

She swallowed hard, the bile rising in her throat. She wasn't just nervous. She was *terrified*.

* * *

Outcast

By the time Outcast found *Purgatory*, he was already running on rage and adrenaline.

It hadn't been easy. He hit the underground fight scene in Louisville as soon as he rolled into town Friday afternoon, starting with the usual haunts -- fight gyms, dirty backroom betting houses, bars where the bruised and broken nursed their wounds. He wasn't looking for *Purgatory* at first. He was looking for Goliath. And the bastard wasn't hard to find.

Everywhere Outcast asked, the name carried weight, like the guy was a Goddamn legend. "You want to see him fight?" One bouncer had laughed, eyeing him up and down like he didn't belong. "You'll have to get into *Purgatory* for that."

That was all he needed. From there, it was a matter of pressing the right people -- leaning on a low-level fighter who owed too much and had too little to lose. On Saturday night, Outcast was standing inside *Purgatory*, surrounded by a bloodthirsty crowd.

The place was everything he expected -- an illegal fight pit dressed up like an exclusive underground club. The stench of sweat, booze, and desperation filled the air, the steel cage in the center gleaming under dim, flickering lights. The fights were raw, brutal, and there were no rules except the unspoken one: *Don't stop swinging until the other guy stops moving*.

Outcast made his way toward the bar, eyes sharp as he took everything in. He wasn't just here for a drink. He was *hunting*. The bartender spotted him before he even sat down. She was young, dark-haired, and smirking like she saw something she liked. He let her look. It worked to his advantage.

"Beer," he said, tossing a bill on the bar.

She slid a bottle his way, leaning in with a teasing grin. "Haven't seen you here before. You fight?"

He took a swig, letting the question hang before giving her a slow smirk. "Not here."

She laughed, intrigued. "Well, maybe you should. You look like you could break someone in half." She draped an arm on the bar, lowering her voice just enough to feel like an invitation. "What brings you to *Purgatory*, then?"

He glanced at the cage, but Outcast didn't linger on the fight. He was already scanning the room, hunting for familiar faces. Instead, his eyes landed on something else. Near the cage, perched on an elevated platform like some kind of Goddamn king, was a man sitting in what looked like a throne. Dark wood, red velvet, positioned just high enough to make sure everyone knew exactly who ran the place. Next to it was another seat -- empty for now.

Outcast turned to the bartender, who still seemed very interested in talking to him. "Who's the guy with the throne?"

She followed his gaze, rolling her eyes as she wiped down the bar. "That's Sebastian Six. Owns *Purgatory*. Runs the fights, runs the money, runs the people stupid enough to owe him something." She smirked, but it didn't reach her eyes. "Scary as hell, even when he's in a good mood. And trust me, you don't wanna see his bad ones."

Outcast took a slow sip of his beer, filing that information away. Sebastian. If he ran this place, he knew everyone who fought here. And if Goliath was fighting tonight, Sebastian was the one pulling the strings. He was about to ask more when movement caught his eye.

A woman stepped onto the platform, walking toward the empty seat beside Sebastian. She moved like she was made of glass -- shoulders tight, steps careful, as if the wrong move would shatter her completely.

His grip tightened on his bottle as the dim lighting hit her face. *Anya*.

For a second, he couldn't move. Could barely breathe. She looked different. Thinner. Paler. That fire he'd always admired in her was dimmed, replaced by something that made his chest tighten like a vise. *Fear*. She was stiff, her hands curled into fists in her lap, her expression empty in a way that only meant one thing. She was barely holding it together.

He forced himself to stay still, to not react, even

as rage simmered under his skin. His grip tightened on his beer bottle. *What the hell had they done to her*?

The bartender followed his gaze, rolling her eyes. "Yeah. That guy thinks he's king of the damn world. Even thinks he gets to decide who his lady ends up with."

Outcast kept his expression neutral, but his pulse pounded like a war drum. "That so?"

"Oh yeah. That poor girl." The bartender shook her head, her voice lowering conspiratorially. "She's his, but he's handing her off to Goliath tonight. *When* he wins." She made a face, disgust curling her lip. "Like she's a Goddamn victory prize."

Fury coiled tight in Outcast's chest, but he forced himself to stay relaxed, to keep the easy smirk on his face. "That a regular thing?"

"Not that I've seen. But he's pissed at her for something." She shrugged, swirling a rag inside a glass. "If Goliath wins, she's his for the night from what I'm hearing. And we *all* know Goliath's gonna win."

Outcast swallowed down the fire rising in his throat. He gave the bartender a slow nod, tipping his beer toward her. "Good to know."

Then he turned back toward the pit, his hands curling into fists.

Because if Sebastian thought he could give Anya away like she was some trophy to be passed around? He was about to learn the hard way that he'd made the wrong fucking call.

* * *

Anya

The moment the announcer stepped back into the cage, the crowd surged forward, hungry for the carnage they'd been promised. A sick energy pulsed through *Purgatory*, a tension that thickened the air, making it hard to breathe. Anya's hands twisted in her lap, pressing deep into her thighs as she forced herself to keep still.

Goliath entered first, stepping into the cage like he *owned* it. And maybe he did. The crowd roared his name, their voices a deafening mix of cheers and jeers. He didn't acknowledge them. He didn't need to. His massive frame, the way he rolled his shoulders with slow, deliberate ease, the absolute calm in his dead-eyed stare -- it all told the same story. *He knew he was going to win.*

His opponent followed. A beast of a man, tall and broad, covered in tattoos. *A real fighter.* The kind that would send most men running. He threw a few test punches in the air, muscles flexing beneath scarred skin, his expression a mask of sheer determination. The kind of man who had probably won plenty of fights. Who might have even thought -- stupidly -- that he stood a chance tonight.

The bell rang.

And it was over before the crowd even settled in.

Less than a round.

Goliath didn't just beat him, he *destroyed* him. The man barely got in two swings before Goliath's massive fist collided with his jaw, sending him staggering. A brutal uppercut followed, snapping his head back with a sickening crack. He went down hard, hitting the mat with a thud that sucked the air out of the room. He twitched once, then didn't move again.

Silence fell. Then, a heartbeat later, *chaos*.

Boos. Outrage. A few cheers, but mostly frustration. This wasn't what the crowd had come for. They wanted *blood*. A real fight. And Goliath had ended it too fast, too easy. Beside her, Sebastian cursed under his breath. His hand formed a fist, his face twisting with irritation. He hadn't wanted this, either. People had paid good money for a show, and *this* wasn't going to keep them satisfied.

Anya barely heard him. Her pulse pounded, her chest tightening as reality closed in on her. *Goliath won*. And that meant *her*.

She felt Sebastian shift beside her, waving a hand toward the announcer who rushed over. The suited man leaned down as Sebastian spoke low, his words drowned out by the restless roar of the crowd. But Anya didn't need to hear. She already knew how this was going to go.

A moment later, the announcer stepped forward, bringing the mic to his lips.

"Ladies and gentlemen, seems like our champion isn't even breaking a sweat tonight!" The crowd's restlessness grew. "So how about we raise the stakes?" He let the question linger, stirring the room into a fever pitch. "Is there anyone in the house who thinks they can take on Goliath? Any man bold enough to step in the cage?"

Anya barely registered the murmurs around her, the shifting bodies as men considered their chances. None of them would be that stupid. None of them would --

Then she saw him. A figure moved through the crowd, stepping forward into the light. Broad shoulders, a familiar stance, that unmistakable confidence in the way he carried himself. Her breath hitched. *No.*

Jackson. Why was he *here*? What was he doing?

Their eyes met. For a second, everything around her faded. The noise, the lights, the smell of blood and sweat. Everything disappeared under the weight of that single moment. Hope swelled in her chest so fast it hurt. But it was chased by something colder, sharper -- *terror*. Her fate with Goliath had been bad enough. The thought of him *winning her* had made her stomach turn. But now… now she might have to watch him kill Jackson too.

She wouldn't survive that.

Next to her, Sebastian was too pissed to notice that her fear had escalated. She couldn't breathe as she watched Jackson step into the cage, as the announcer hyped up the crowd, spinning this into an unexpected bonus fight. The man grinned, obviously relieved he had a taker, and approached him with the microphone. "Who is challenging Goliath tonight? Where are you from?"

"Jackson," was all he said as he continued to stare Goliath down.

It felt like her heart would beat out of her chest. What was Jackson thinking?

Goliath didn't react immediately. He stood there with a blank expression, watching Jackson the way a wolf watches prey it doesn't consider a challenge. He rolled his massive shoulders, the faintest smirk tugging at his lips like this was nothing more than an inconvenience.

In horror, she watched as Jackson started moving with calculated precision. He stepped forward, shrugged out of his jacket. Then he pulled his shirt over his head, tossing it to the side, revealing a body honed from years of hard-earned strength. Thick muscle, chiseled like granite, but lean enough that every flex and shift showed his control. His torso was covered in ink, an intricate tapestry of black and gray tattoos -- some detailed and elaborate, others crude and jagged. Stories of dark times and longing written in ink and scars.

The crowd noticed. A few murmurs rippled through the air. Whoever they thought he was, they were starting to second-guess.

But Goliath? He barely spared Jackson a glance. He just cracked his knuckles, waiting for the bell.

Anya's hands clenched. *Please don't do this. Just walk away.*

Then the bell rang, and there was no stopping it. The steely look on Jackson's face told her no one could have pulled him out of that ring and live to talk about it.

The fight began with some of the crowd willing to give it a go, the rest heading for the bar or the bathroom. The fighters circling each other didn't seem to notice or care.

Goliath lunged first, massive fists swinging in brutal, bone-crushing arcs. But Jackson was fast. Faster than the crowd expected, faster than Anya had even dared to hope. He dodged the first swing, ducked under the second, pivoting smoothly to the side as Goliath's knuckles cut through empty air.

The crowd that remained around the cage roared, sensing something different. *This wasn't going to be like the last fight.* Others who had wandered off, looked back from their place around the bar or restrooms in interest, the cheering getting their attention.

Jackson stayed light on his feet, circling, waiting. He had to know he wasn't stronger. Beating Goliath wasn't going to come from brute force -- it had to be skill. *Strategy.* He landed the first real hit. A sharp jab to Goliath's ribs, quick and precise. It wasn't much, but it was a warning shot. Goliath barely reacted.

It was hard for her to watch.

The fight picked up, the crowd drifting back to the cage. Jackson kept slipping away from Goliath's devastating swings, striking back with sharp, tactical hits wherever he could. He was quick, controlled, and focused, his movements like a predator that knew it couldn't take the beast head-on but could bleed it slowly.

Goliath was massive, but he wasn't slow. He moved with surprising speed for his size, his fists swinging through the air with lethal intent. The crowd flinched with every near miss, each one powerful enough to shatter bone if it landed.

But Jackson was a ghost. He ducked, weaved, sidestepped -- his body twisting just enough to let the punches graze past, but never truly land. And when the opportunity came, he struck. A sharp jab to the ribs. A brutal hook to the side. A fast, snapping strike to the kidney.

Goliath didn't flinch. Not once. The crowd was in it now. Chants of "Goliath!" rose as they cheered their champion on. He took the hits like they were nothing. No stagger, no change in expression, no hesitation. Just pure, relentless forward motion. It was like trying to cut down a tree with a pocketknife.

Jackson's fists had to ache. His knuckles looked raw from slamming into muscles and bones that refused to give. He looked steady, controlled, but Anya could see the first signs of fatigue creeping in -- the slight tension in his shoulders, the fraction of a second longer it took him to reset after each hit. He needed an opening, a weakness, *something* to make Goliath react.

And then -- just for a split second -- he did. A body shot landed just right, a sharp strike to the liver. Goliath grunted. It wasn't much, but it was *something*.

A crack in the armor. A sign that the monster was a normal man after all.

Jackson pressed in, shifting his strategy. More body shots, hammering at the same spot, testing if Goliath would start to favor his side, *anything* to give him a real opening. The problem? Goliath wasn't just a brute -- he was smart. He let Jackson think he was gaining ground. Let him throw those sharp, precise hits. Let him get just close enough to feel like he was in control.

And then Goliath struck. It was fast. Too fast. A brutal feint with his left, baiting Jackson into dodging right -- right into the *real* hit. A right hook that came from nowhere. And it *landed.*

The impact sent a sickening crack through the air, snapping Jackson's head to the side. Blood sprayed from his mouth, and for the first time, he lost his footing, his legs buckling as he staggered back. The crowd *exploded,* sensing the shift, the moment the fight turned in Goliath's favor.

Jackson barely caught himself before hitting the mat, his body swaying as he fought to stay upright. Anya couldn't breathe, her nails digging into her palms as she watched him blink hard, trying to shake off the brutal hit. He wasn't moving fast enough. She could see the way his vision wavered, the slight hesitation in his stance, the way his breathing had turned ragged. *He's hurt.*

Terror coiled around her ribs like a vise. If he didn't recover -- if he didn't do something -- Goliath was going to end this. And she would have to watch him die.

Goliath grinned. He knew that shot hurt. He moved in fast, throwing another devastating blow -- one that would end the fight right there. Jackson *barely* dodged it, rolling away, but he was slower now. The hit rattled him. The second he found his balance again, Goliath was already on him. He landed a crushing elbow to the ribs. A knee drove into his gut. A second hit to the same spot, knocking the breath from his lungs.

Anya's heart was in her throat. Jackson was losing.

And Sebastian was already smirking next to her, pleased at the spectacle the new challenge match created. The crowd was rabid. "Put him down," he muttered under his breath, leaning back in his chair, completely at ease now.

Goliath shoved Jackson hard, sending him stumbling against the cage. The crowd screamed, demanding the knockout, the kill shot.

But Jackson wiped the blood from his mouth, rolling his shoulders. He looked like he was hurting, but he wasn't out. Goliath charged, aiming to finish it, his massive fist swinging for the knockout punch.

At the last second, Jackson dodged. Not back -- forward. He ducked low, throwing his entire body weight into an explosive uppercut, his fist crashing into Goliath's jaw with *everything* he had left. The sound was deafening. Goliath's head snapped back. His entire body swayed. And then -- to the absolute shock of the crowd, he went down. Goliath toppled to the mat, twitching for a second before all motion stopped.

The arena went silent. For half a second, no one moved. Then the entire place exploded into cheers and applause.

Sebastian shot up from his seat, his drink slamming onto the table. "What the *fuck* --"

But Anya wasn't looking at him anymore. Her

wide, disbelieving eyes were locked on Jackson, bloody and battered, standing over the unconscious monster that was never supposed to fall. Hope and fear crashed through her at once. Because he'd won.

But what happened now?

* * *

Outcast

His knuckles throbbed, his ribs ached, and blood dripped from the corner of his mouth -- but none of it mattered. The only thing he saw, the only thing that mattered, was her.

Anya.

She was frozen in her seat, eyes wide, her face pale beneath the dim red glow of *Purgatory's* overhead lights. Her hands were clenched so tightly in her lap that her knuckles were bone white, her lips slightly parted in shock. She wasn't relieved. She was terrified.

His heart dropped at the sight, but there was no time to process it because the crowd was going crazy, a deafening roar shaking the underground arena. The announcer grabbed his arm, yanking it up into the air like he was some kind of conquering gladiator. "Your winner -- Jackson!"

The noise surged, fists pounding against the metal barriers, bodies pressing forward, hungry for the next spectacle. Some cheered, others cursed, and Outcast barely heard any of it over the blood still rushing in his ears. He wasn't here for their damn entertainment. He wasn't here for a fucking victory lap. He let them celebrate, standing there in the middle of the cage while Goliath remained sprawled on the mat, unconscious. The crowd could have their moment, let the shock settle.

Then the announcer's grip loosened, and Jackson

was ushered out of the ring. Straight to *him*.

Sebastian Six sat on his throne, still looking irritated as hell, but beneath that, Outcast caught something else. Calculation. Typical businessman, always spinning shit to his advantage.

"Well," Sebastian drawled, swirling his fresh drink, expression shifting from anger to something more amused. "That wasn't what I expected. But I can admit when something is good for business."

Jackson didn't say a damn word, just wiped the blood from his cheek with the back of his hand. He could feel Anya's gaze locked on him, but he didn't dare meet it yet. Not until this was done.

Sebastian smirked. "A rematch would be a hell of a draw." He leaned forward. "You game?" At Jackson's nod, he said, "Name your price."

Outcast didn't hesitate.

"I'm not interested in money."

Sebastian arched a brow, intrigued. "No?"

Outcast turned his head, gaze landing on Anya.

"I want her."

The amusement in Sebastian's face faltered for just a second before his grin widened, slow and shark-like. He leaned back, tapping a finger against his glass. "The prize promised to Goliath if he won."

Anya sucked in a sharp breath beside him, her body visibly tensing. Outcast saw her hands tremble, saw the way she fought to hide the raw horror that bled into her expression. Sebastian noticed too. And for him, that was enough. She looked properly terrified now. Properly punished.

"Fine," Sebastian said with a lazy wave of his hand. "She's yours for the night."

Outcast kept his face unreadable, cold as ice, a slow-burning fire spread through him at the casual way the bastard handed her over to someone he didn't even know. Like she wasn't a person -- just another bet settled.

Sebastian snapped his fingers at one of his men. "There's a suite ready for the occasion," he said with a smirk. "Fancy place, good view, champagne in the room. I like to keep my investments happy." His gaze slid back to Outcast. "You'll be accompanied by two of my men. Can't have the goods getting damaged."

His blood boiled, but Outcast forced a slow nod, his voice just as cold. "That's fine."

A man he didn't recognize gestured for him to move, and Outcast fell into step beside Anya, his pulse steady and controlled. She walked stiffly, her entire body wound tight like a wire about to snap.

Outside, two men were waiting. It was dark in the parking lot but not so dark he couldn't get a good look at the two guards Six sent with them. He was keeping a sharp eye out for the two survivors from the failed gun deal because they would recognize him. The men led him and Anya to a sleek black limo -- the one meant for Goliath. Outcast held back as Anya hesitated for just a second before stepping inside. Then he followed, sliding in beside her.

The guards went to the front of the limo, one driving. The engine started, a soft purr in the quiet cabin where they sat. Pushing the button as soon as he located it, Outcast put the darkened privacy glass between them and the guards. As they pulled away from *Purgatory*, Outcast finally let himself breathe.

The first part was over, and it had been hard.

But now came the real fight.

Chapter Four

Anya

Jackson had been about to speak in the limo once they were on their way, but she met his gaze, silently shaking her head. She wasn't willing to take any chances with his safety or put him in more danger than he'd already put himself in by speaking in front of Sebastian's men.

The moment the hotel door shut behind them, Anya felt like the world was tilting beneath her feet. Her breath came shallow, hands clenched at her sides as she stared at the man who had just fought for her -- literally stepped into a bloodstained cage and risked everything to get her out of Goliath's grip tonight. Jackson. *Her Jackson.*

All she could do was stare at him in the dimly lit hotel room, dressed in jeans and a leather jacket that was as black as his hair. He was no longer the boy she had loved all those years ago. That boy had been full of fire, full of reckless hope. The man standing before her now was harder, colder, carved from something unbreakable. But when she looked into his eyes, she still saw the boy who had tried to save her. The boy who had whispered, *We're getting out of here, Anya. I swear it.*

The soft, muted conversation outside the enormous luxury suite was a reminder that two of Sebastian's thugs were outside the door. Anya wrapped her arms around herself. Jackon's blue-eyed gaze watched her every movement intently. She had no idea what to say. Anya had spent a decade trying to forget the sound of his voice, the way he made her feel like she was someone worth saving.

And yet, here he was again, risking his life for

her without hesitation. Shrugging out of his jacket, Jackson wrapped it around her shoulders and guided her into the suite, steering her to the posh cream-colored sofa in the spacious living room. The warmth of his body and the scent of him were heavenly as she snuggled into it and took a seat on the couch. Jackson prowled around the room until he found the mini bar, pouring himself vodka. Pulling out another tumbler, he filled that with brandy and carried both glasses back to where she was sitting. Handing her brandy, he took a seat next to her.

In the well-lit space, Anya got a good look at Jackson -- his knuckles were shredded and a fresh cut sliced through his brow. Blood dried in streaks down his arm from underneath the sleeve of his black T-shirt, stark against the ink that covered his skin. He was hurt. Considering Goliath's size, skill and brutality, it wasn't lost on her how easily Jackson could have been killed. Taking a small sip, from her glass, she felt it burn its way down her throat.

"You shouldn't have done that," she whispered, her gaze taking in all his wounds.

His brow furrowed, those intense ice-blue eyes studying her. "Done what?"

She watched him gulp down his own drink, struggling to find the words. "Goliath." She shook her head. "You could have been killed."

His gaze on her was intense as he dropped his glass on the coffee table in front of him, his eyes lit up in determination, conquest, and something else she couldn't identify. The corner of his mouth curled up in a half-smirk.

"How did you even find me?" He'd just shown up in *Purgatory*. Shouldn't he have forgotten about her by now?

"Why were you hiding from me?" His voice was a shade deeper than she remembered. "It's been ten years."

That had her cringing in shame. Yes, she had been hiding from him. For a couple of different reasons.

"Ten years," she repeated. "You could have been happy in those ten years, you know. You don't owe me anything, Jackson."

His expression hardened. "The hell I don't."

A lump lodged in her throat. This Jackson was older, darker -- fierce, relentless, impossible to shake. And just like before, he wasn't going to walk away. She just didn't know if she had the strength to tell him the truth. Not yet. Not when her heart still ached with what they'd lost all those years ago.

"I'm sorry," she whispered, knowing he had to be hurting from the fight as she tried to down more of her brandy with shaking hands.

He hid the pain from his many injuries well. Next to her, Jackson's presence crackled with barely contained energy, even after the horrific match against Goliath. He looked anything but tired -- his posture tense, his broad shoulders rigid, every muscle coiled like a predator waiting to pounce. His sharp gaze never left her, dark and unreadable, making her feel as if she were the only thing anchoring him in the moment. There was a restlessness about him, like a caged animal pacing the edges of its confinement, daring the world to challenge him again.

Trying to be brave, Anya drained her glass, welcoming the slight numbness, the warmth it lent her. With her gaze on his bloody knuckles, she said, "I'm sure there is a first-aid kit somewhere. We should take care of your wounds."

Shifting on the couch, the full force of his attention was on her. "Later," he said, his gaze sweeping her over with a hunger that surprised her. "You were Goliath's prize tonight?"

Shame flooded her entire being. She didn't know how he found that out, but she nodded.

"Did you *agree* to that?" Jackson asked.

"No." How could he ask that? What woman who had a choice would agree to *that*?

"Has he ever given you to anyone else?" Jackson was dead serious, studying her as he waited for an answer.

Anya shook her head. "No. That was the first time."

"And then he gave you to me, someone he didn't even know." His tone was laced with anger. Jackson shifted just a little closer to her. "Who is Sebastian Six to you?"

How did she answer that? "I'm… I'm his."

Her hesitation and fear seemed to be enough of an explanation for him. He ran an impatient finger down the side of her face, tracing a path from the apple of her cheek down the slim column of her neck. He had to have seen the finger bruises Sebastian left on her. The skimpy dress he'd made her wear didn't hide a lot.

"Who is CJ to you?" he asked in a softer tone.

How did Jackson even know about CJ? Anya sensed her answer to that question was important to him. Placing her glass on the coffee table by his, she swallowed hard. "He worked for Sebastian," she said quietly. "He was a friend… He's dead."

Jackson moved just a little closer, now backing her into the corner of the sofa. "A friend? He was *very* interested in you. He had a picture of you on him. A picture of your back. That's actually how I found you."

That left her even more confused. *What photo*? She shrugged because she didn't know the answer to that.

Anya pulled Jackson's jacket tighter around her, breathing in the worn leather and the faintest trace of him. It was too big, swallowing her up, but the warmth was a comfort she hadn't known for years. Jackson reached into the inner pocket and pulled out something small, something folded. He smoothed the creases with calloused fingers before holding it out to her. The moment she saw it, she saw herself and the phoenix tattooed on her back from the grainy, dog-eared photo -- her blood turned to ice. She barely recognized the version of herself captured there, looking away as if she hadn't known the picture was being taken. But she remembered that moment and how naive she'd been. She remembered when it was taken, right before Jackson found her in Memphis.

Why did CJ have it? Her breath hitched, her fingers trembling as she reached for the photo, her mind reeling with questions and fears she wasn't ready to face.

"He was interested in me," she admitted. "I'm not proud of it, but I was hoping he'd could help me… leave here."

His gaze searched hers, his rough palm slid along the side of her face. It was like he was trying to decide if she was real or not. His touch was careful, but his hand was trembling. Nerves? He didn't have a nerve in his body. Not after watching that fight. Was it restraint?

That's when the realization hit her. Did Jackson kill CJ? As the question floated through her head, Anya's mind drifted -- unbidden -- back to that night in Memphis, the last night they had been together. That night had been a happy chance meeting until another violent man tried to ruin it. Jackson had snapped and stopped him. He had done it for *her*. And she had felt… what? Gratitude? Horror? Love? Maybe all of it, tangled into something she hadn't been able to unravel then, something she still didn't know how to name.

Tonight? He'd done that for her too.

Now, she sat across from him, the weight of that memory pressing against her ribs as she asked, "Did you kill CJ?" The words were quieter than she intended, but they carried the full weight of everything she was afraid to know.

Jackson stayed where he was, his breath coming fast as his hand framed her face with care. After a moment, his gaze locked with hers. He nodded. Leaning in, he brushed a kiss over her forehead. "You had nothing to do with how we crossed paths," he whispered, taking the photo from her hand and placing it on the table. "You weren't the reason he died."

Why had Jackson been there when CJ died? What kind of life had Jackson been living that put him in the middle of all this? She hadn't seen him in ten years. But the boy she had known wasn't the same man who had taken down Goliath tonight like it was just another fight. That kind of power, that kind of control, didn't come from nowhere. It was earned, hardened by experience, sharpened by survival. Had he always been this dangerous? Or had the years apart turned him into something darker, something even more lethal?

The scent of him reached her through layers of leather, sweat, and blood. She shivered when he dropped another kiss on her cheek, her jaw. One long arm wrapped around her, pulling her into him and out of his jacket as his lips teased hers. It was a tentative kiss, before his lips blazed a warm trail across her face.

"Haven't seen you in ten years, Anya," he whispered by her ear. "I looked for you."

"I'm sorry I wasn't there the next morning." She was. Gasped as he trailed kisses down her neck, his passion gaining steam. Anya pressed into him, enjoying the heat of his kisses, his touch. "I was --"

"Later." Pressing his face into her neck and hair, Jackson breathed her in. "You smell so good."

Anya had never really let herself hope that they'd ever be together again. Now that she was here in his arms, she melted into him. Her heart flew in hope even as the fires broke out in her body. She didn't have to pretend to enjoy his touch because she wanted it, craved it. When their lips danced together, her arms slid around him, trying to be careful of his injuries.

Jackson didn't just kiss her, he took possession of her mouth. She wanted him to claim every part of her. His mouth crashed over hers, rough and unyielding, stealing her breath, her thoughts, her everything. His hands gripped her hips, pulling her flush against him, like he needed to feel every inch of her, like he was branding her with his touch. The heat of him, the sheer dominance in the way he kissed her, sent a shudder through her that had nothing to do with fear. This wasn't a kiss, it was a raw, possessive vow that no matter how much time had passed, no matter how much distance had separated them, she was still his. And God help her, she *wanted* to be.

Jackson scooped her off the couch and carried her like she didn't weigh a thing to the huge bed at the heart of the suite. He'd barely set her down on the edge of the bed when his restraint started to slip. He was a storm all around her, capturing her mouth in a searing kiss as his hands skimmed possessively over her body. She wasn't gentle when she urged him to pull off his T-shirt so she could explore all those muscles and tattoos with her fingers. He wasn't careful when he pulled the thin straps of her dress off her shoulders to reveal her breasts, to palm them in rough hands as his lips feverishly tasted hers. Her nipples tightened to hard points against his hands, and she pushed herself at him, wanting more.

He rolled them until she was beneath him and in a frenzy, she helped shove his jeans down and off to reveal all of him. He winced once when her arm brushed a huge bruise forming over his ribs, but he didn't pause. When they rolled again, Anya straddled his slim waist while Jackson greedily pulled her down to him, feasting on her nipples with lips and tongue until she was panting above him. Her panties were a thin barrier between the heat of his cock and her weeping pussy as her excitement climbed. When she worked herself wantonly against his erection, he groaned. When her fingers slid into the black locks of his hair and tugged, he rolled his hips beneath her making her want more, making her crave him.

Easing a hand between their bodies, Anya pulled the crotch of her panties aside. It was an invitation for Jackson to push into her and give her what they both wanted. Instead, his grip tightened on her hips, and he slid down the bed under her. When he held her just above his face, she gasped at the sight. When he pushed her down so he could take her apart with his mouth, Anya cried out in the silence of the hotel room.

His moan sent currents of pure desire racing through her. Her hands clutched in his hair as he teased her clit with a clever tongue, over and over until she shivered and melted above him. Her thighs quivered around his face as he traced her opening with a finger, the laps of his tongue never ceasing. It was an intoxicating, sensual act that sent her heart flying even as she danced on the tip of his tongue. The walls of her pussy clenched in desire as her body wept on his face. The intimacy of the act wasn't something she'd experienced before. The heat in his incredible blue eyes led her to know that he wanted to claim her in every way he could. The past had taught them both that every moment was precious. What if they never saw each other again?

Anya wailed when her orgasm slammed through her. She ground herself onto his face, too lost in the moment to remember his injuries. Jackson didn't seem to care; he worked her through her release.

Faster than she could keep up with, Jackson rolled her under him and this time, he took himself in hand and pushed into her, fast and hard. He slid in with ease on the slick of her passion and she hung onto him, never wanting to let him go as her walls stretched around him. When he couldn't go any further inside her, they just held each other for a long moment. Anya felt their hearts beating in unison and wrapped herself around him like she'd never let him go.

She didn't want to let him go *ever* again.

Slowly, with care, he began to move in her. He took her hands in his and pinned them to the bed on either side of her head, the gesture loving as much as it was dominant. Jackson wanted her to be his and he'd never made a secret of it. From the way his cock slid in and out of her passage to the way he dropped heated kisses over her face and chest, Jackson finally claimed her as his.

He loved her carefully at first, but desire was quick to hound her again. Her walls clenched him in greed, her arms and legs wrapped around him in a possessive plea. Her nipples ached, brushing against his chest. Her pussy wept as release rode her down. Jackson knew it too, sliding a hand between their bodies to tease her clit with gentle strokes of his fingers, a counterpoint to the sharp thrusts that rocked her beneath him. When she went sailing over the edge, she screamed his name, riding the waves of an orgasm unlike anything she'd known before. The world faded away, his own cries faded into the background, until all that was left was the pleasure she was drowning in with him as her life raft, the only thing that could save her.

Jackson was right behind her, thrusting into her harder and faster until he couldn't breathe. When he reached his end, he pulled free of her, and she felt the warm spurts of his release on her thighs and the outer lips of her pussy. His breath rushed through her hair as he dropped to her side, keeping her in his arms as he did.

Anya wanted to savor every moment she had with him as her heart pounded away. The way he held her and made her feel cherished; she wanted those burned into her memory. It didn't matter that they'd never had the luxury of time to be together. It only mattered that she was here with him now, a stolen night she never expected to have. She wouldn't ask for anything else. Her heart knew this was where she belonged; her body just proved it. She even fought sleep for him, not wanting to miss a single moment.

* * *

Sebastian

The morning light barely penetrated the thick curtains of Sebastian's study, but the dim glow of the massive screen in front of him was enough to illuminate his sour mood. He leaned back in his chair, swirling a crystal tumbler of whiskey he hadn't touched, eyes locked on the recording of the previous night's fight.

Goliath lay sprawled on the bloodstained canvas, motionless. And standing over him, victorious, was Jackson.

Sebastian scowled, rewinding the footage for the third time. Frame by frame, he analyzed every move, every strike, every calculated shift in stance. Goliath was an animal. Yet this man, this nobody who called himself Jackson, had put him down like it was nothing. Maybe Goliath was overpaid, going soft. He needed to consider what he was going to do about that.

The fight should have been a spectacle. Instead, it had been an execution.

Sebastian shook his head at the frozen image on the screen, rubbing his jaw as frustration ran through him. Who the fuck was this guy? Some nobody with the balls to step into his ring and take down Goliath. Sebastian's goals were still met. The fight had been spectacular, and excitement around a rematch was already all anyone tied to *Purgatory* could talk about.

And Anya… Anya was the real prize. Handing her over saved Sebastian a substantial sum of money, but more than that, it was a lesson in obedience. She needed to understand loyalty -- his loyalty came at a price, and her defiance had made him look weak. That couldn't stand.

He had sent two of his men along to ensure she was returned exactly as she was when she left, unmolested and unharmed. From a certain perspective, it was the harsher punishment. At least with Goliath, she had known what to expect.

But something wasn't sitting right. The fight had been too fast, too precise. Goliath was a brutal, seasoned fighter, yet Jackson had dropped him with a level of skill Sebastian hadn't expected. Maybe a rematch could rake in some real money, but his instincts screamed that this wasn't just about the fight. Something bigger was at play, and he damn well wasn't going to ignore it.

The man didn't want the money. He wanted *Anya*. His mind couldn't let it go. Yeah, maybe word got around the club that she'd be given to Goliath when he won and that is why the victor demanded her. Anya was a beautiful woman. That's why she belonged to *him*. But Sebastian had never seen Jackson before in *Purgatory*.

His jaw clenched as he downed the whiskey in one gulp, the burn doing little to calm the anger simmering beneath his skin. Control. Precision. Power. These were the cornerstones of everything he had built, the foundation of the empire he had painstakingly crafted from the shadows. Every deal, every favor, every threat was all orchestrated with purpose. He had spent years pulling strings in the dark, moving the right people like chess pieces, always five steps ahead, guaranteeing that when he wanted something, he got it. No one disrupted his plans.

Until last night.

And yet, here he was, watching the aftermath of a situation that didn't *feel* controlled. Jackson. The name curled through his mind like poison. Maybe he'd underestimated him. Maybe he'd have to correct that oversight. Soon.

Right now, he was stuck waiting for that useless bastard, Hawk. Shot or not, Sebastian had demanded he haul his ass here personally. He'd given Hawk money to buy him guns with specific mods and he'd failed to do that. And Hawk got six of his men killed. *Useless fucker.* Something about Hawk's story just didn't add up.

The door creaked open, and Hawk limped into his study, his arm in a black sling. His face was a mix of pain and frustration, but Sebastian really didn't give a damn.

"Tell me," Sebastian said coolly, keeping his gaze on the frozen frame of Jackson on the screen. "Why the fuck am I out several thousand dollars without the guns I wanted? And why are six of my fucking men dead?"

Hawk exhaled sharply, like he had a dozen things he wanted to say but knew better than to interrupt.

Sebastian didn't wait for a response. "You assured me the Hounds weren't an issue anymore. You said the shitshow in Mercy had been handled. Instead, we lost nearly two dozen bodies to the cops and Grayson's entire investment is in the gutter. Now I'm out a lot of money and I don't have the guns I wanted."

Hawk shifted on his feet. "Look, boss, I get it, but you --"

"Do you?" Sebastian snapped, setting the empty tumbler down so hard it nearly shattered. "Do you really? Because I don't think you do."

Leaning back in his chair, Sebastian drummed his fingers idly against the polished mahogany of his desk. He let his gaze turn sharp and calculating, and it pinned Hawk in place as he considered what to do with the man. Hawk droned on, his pathetic attempts at explaining how the gun deal had gone to hell getting more annoying. But there was one glaring problem with his story. His money was still missing.

Hawk swallowed hard, shifting on his feet. "Boss, I -- I had the money. I swear. But when everything went south, I had to ditch it. The Hounds --"

Sebastian slammed his hand onto the desk, the sharp sound making Hawk flinch. "The Hounds?" His voice dropped into something eerily calm. "You're telling me they took my money? Because it sounded like you handed over something they *thought* was cash, told the Hounds you were taking the guns for free, and all hell broke loose. Did I miss something?"

Hawk's eyes widened comically.

"That's right," Sebastian went on, "I talked to Ronnie and that's how he explained it."

Hawk's mouth opened, but no words came. His bravado had vanished, leaving nothing but panic in his dull, beady eyes.

Sebastian rose to his feet, adjusting the cuffs of his pristine button-down. "Loyalty, Hawk," he murmured, stepping around the desk. "It's a simple concept. I reward those who serve me well. I elevate them, give them power, money, women. But disloyalty?" He tsked, shaking his head. "That, I won't tolerate."

He leaned in close, his voice dropping to a near whisper. "You thought you could steal from me? Line your own pockets with my money and walk away unscathed?" A slow, cruel smile stretched across his lips as Hawk took a stumbling step backward. "Let me tell you something about men like me. I don't lose money. And I sure as hell don't let rats keep it."

Hawk's lips parted, a last-ditch effort to plead his case, but Sebastian had already decided his fate. And in his world, there was only one way to deal with a traitor.

Sebastian had to give the guy credit; he stood there stoically watching him return to his desk to press the silent alarm. Some men begged for their lives, others tried to run or to charge him. None of them had ever escaped. No one ever did. Hell, Hawk didn't move even when two of Sebastian's soldiers came to take care of him. But just as he was being dragged out, something caught Hawk's eye.

"Wait!" Hawk said, digging in his heels to try and stop the two men from dragging him off. "Look at the screen, boss!"

What the fuck was this?

"That's one of them!" Hawk yelled frantically. "That's one of them Hounds. The one they call Outcast. Look at his eyes!"

Holding up a hand, he signaled to his men to stop. Marching up to Hawk, Sebastian said, "Who?"

"That man standing in the cage on your TV," Hawk exclaimed. "Is that the one that beat Goliath last night?"

Sebastian's blood ran cold as he slowly turned back to the screen. The frozen image of Jackson, raised fists, eyes sharp and burning with purpose, stared right back at him. He remembered the name Outcast from brokering the deal with the Hounds for the guns. Outcast. From Mercy. From the same MC that had obliterated Grayson's foothold in town, ruined their operations, and cost them millions.

They'd been the ones to stop it all. The Hounds of Hell MC.

Sebastian's white-hot rage threatened to boil over. "You didn't fucking realize this last night?" His voice thundered through the study.

Hawk clenched his jaw, shook his head. "I wasn't there. I felt like shit."

Sebastian let out a slow, trembling breath, fingers curling into fists as his mind raced. Yes, he remembered Hawk'd told him he wouldn't be attending. The coward had been trying to avoid him as long as he could because he knew he was dead. But this?

First, Grayson lost Mercy. Now, they waltzed into *Purgatory* like they owned the place. Took his fighter down? Took his woman?

No. *No.*

This wouldn't stand.

"Take him out," Sebastian growled to his men, turning his back on Hawk as he snatched his phone off the desk. "Now."

Without hesitation, his men took Hawk out to deliver his justice. Sebastian just stood there, seething, heart pounding with unfiltered rage. Then, with a sudden, explosive motion, he grabbed the empty whiskey glass and hurled it at the wall, watching it shatter into a thousand pieces.

Breathing hard, he ran a hand through his hair, forcing himself to think. To act.

Jackson -- no, Outcast -- thought he could just walk into his world, humiliate his fighter, steal from him? He gritted his teeth, pressing a number on his phone.

"Lock them down," he ordered his men at the hotel guarding Anya, his voice deadly calm. "No one in, no one out. I want them waiting in that hotel suite until I get there."

The only way this ended was with blood.

Chapter Five

Outcast

The quiet hum of his phone vibrating on the bedside table pulled him from the depths of dreamless sleep. He stretched, wincing as pain shot up his legs -- a brutal reminder of the fight he'd barely walked away from the night before. His gaze landed on the glowing screen, Deva's name staring back at him.

Sunday. By now, his sister knew he was gone. Razor knew too, and he'd be pissed as hell that Outcast had taken off solo again. But at least Deva would understand. She might not like it, but she'd know why he had to go. She remembered those dark days in Gene Lorry's house. Even as a child, she'd seen too much. And she remembered more than he wished she did.

Just after six in the morning, and he really didn't want to move. The room was quiet, the early light struggling against the heavy curtains, casting everything in shadow. Lying on his side, he held Anya against him, her head tucked against his chest, her steady breathing a soft rhythm against his skin. She was sound asleep, and for once, he was the one awake.

After that night in Memphis -- after she vanished without a word -- he didn't trust sleep. Didn't trust that when he woke up, she'd still be there. He wasn't letting her slip away again. Pressing a slow kiss into her hair, he exhaled. He still had no idea how the hell he was going to get them out of this hotel, out of Louisville, out of Sebastian's reach. But her tearful words from the night before still echoed in his head, driving him forward.

I was hoping he'd could help me… leave here.

Outcast had only seen Anya with Sebastian Six for a couple of minutes, but that was all it took to know she was terrified. The way she kept her head down, the tension in her posture -- she was trapped, and she knew it. How long had she been in his clutches?

The bastard had planned to hand her over to that fucking bruiser he'd bested in the cage last night -- just to punish her for disobedience. For what, he didn't know. He didn't need to know. That was bad enough. And when Goliath lost, Sebastian had tossed her to some random guy from the crowd, like she was a prize to be claimed. If he was willing to do that, it was only a matter of time before things got far worse. He refused to let himself imagine just how bad it could get.

The night they'd spent together had been far too short, but every second of it was burned into his memory. The way she looked at him, the way she touched him -- it felt like she needed him as much as he needed her. Maybe she'd given in to the one man she knew loved her. Maybe she'd just been seeking comfort in the only familiar thing she had left. Outcast didn't care what the truth was. Not now. Not when he had her back in his arms, not when he had a chance to do what he should have done all those years ago. He'd found her, and he was going to free her. He'd rip her out of this gilded prison, drag her from the shadows of whatever hell Sebastian kept her locked in, and set her free.

If she wanted to be with him, he'd never ask for another Goddamn thing as long as he lived. If she wanted to go her own way, it would gut him -- but he wouldn't stop her. But he sure as hell wouldn't stop trying to convince her that she belonged with him. That he loved her.

He should've saved her back then. Should've been stronger, faster, smarter. If he had, they could've built a life somewhere. A family. She wouldn't have been tossed around like a flower in a storm, broken and scattered by forces bigger than her. He would have kept her safe, just like he had Deva.

But he hadn't. And now, he had one chance to make it right.

What the hell was he going to do?

Carefully, he slid out of bed, somehow managing not to wake Anya as he reached the edge of the massive mattress. Running a hand over his face, he glanced down at his knuckles -- still raw and bruised from the fight. His ribs ached like hell, his cheekbone throbbed, but pain was the least of his problems. He'd taken worse. What really gnawed at him was time. Or the lack of it.

Sebastian Six and his men would figure it out soon. Maybe they already had. Two men had survived the shootout that set all of this in motion -- Hawk and another. If either of them had been at the fight, they would have seen him. One or both would have recognized him. And he'd known that risk going in. The fight had been recorded. The moment Sebastian's men reviewed the footage from *Purgatory* -- the second someone put two and two together -- Sebastian would know. He'd realize Outcast wasn't just some random brawler looking for a payday. He was there for something far more dangerous.

And he was a Hound -- one of the men who'd helped burn Grayson's empire to the ground. One of the men at that ill-fated gun deal who put six of Sebastian's men in the dirt. If they caught him, they'd bury him so deep no one would ever find his body.

But none of that mattered. Outcast wasn't worried about what would happen to him -- he'd made peace with that kind of risk a long time ago. But if Sebastian got his hands on Anya… No. He wouldn't even let the thought take shape. He wasn't going to let anything happen to her. Not again. Anyone who tried wouldn't live long enough to regret it. All that mattered was getting her out.

Pulling on his jeans, Jackson headed for the door. Looking through the peephole, he saw the shoulder of one man still standing guard. He didn't see the other man, but it didn't mean he wasn't out there. Taking a deep breath, he considered what they needed to do. The two men had been out there all night without the benefit of sleep. If he could get Anya up and ready, figure out a quick and quiet way to take out the two thugs on the other side of the door, they could get the hell out of there.

Whatever he did, he had to do it quickly. They were on the clock.

Behind him, Anya shifted in the bed, hand searching the bed next to her where he'd just slept. Not finding him, she blinked like a sleepy owl, looking around the room. His heart clenched at the fear that crept into her expression.

"I'm here," he said quietly, walking back to her. Her eyes widened as he sat on the edge of the bed next to her, reaching out a hand to stroke her hair. Anya lay there on her side, gazing up at him with such hope, and a modicum of trust. How could she look at him with such hope? With even a sliver of trust after what had happened? After how he'd let her down?

But not today. Today, he was making up for all of that.

"What happens now?" Anya said so quietly he almost didn't hear her.

"Do you want to stay where you are?" And he sure as fuck hoped the answer to that was no. "Or do you want to come with me?" More hope, more trust in her eyes. It was all he could do to hold her gaze. His heart pounded in fear as he waited for her answer.

"I want to go with you," she whispered, her eyes shiny with building tears. "But I'm so scared. Sebastian is…"

Outcast pulled her into his arms with passion, with need. She wanted to go with him. She trusted him. That's all he needed to know. Anya clung to him, in his arms where she should have been the whole fucking time. It felt right. It *was* right. She was his.

"We have to move fast," he whispered into her hair. "I need you to get dressed and I need you to be ready to run when I say."

Her gaze drifted over the pool of the skimpy black dress Sebastian had made her wear, the high strappy heels.

"Don't wear the heels," he said quickly. "You'll wear my jacket over your dress. Once we get out of here, I'll find you something else, okay?"

Her gaze was back on him, a swirl of fear, doubt, and hope. Slowly, she nodded. "Where are we going?"

"I'm taking you home with me," Outcast told her, hoping she could read the sincerity on him.

Anya was already shaking her head. "Sebastian will find us," she whispered, hope fading from her face. "He's powerful. He's -- He'll find us. The family will find us."

Outcast understood her fear. Yeah, the bastard was powerful, had connections. Victor Grayson had also been part of his criminal network and they'd taken him down. He wasn't going to fucking tuck tail and run from Sebastian Six just because he was higher up the food chain.

"I have a family too," Outcast told her. "And they're strong enough to fight for us. We're strong enough to keep you safe."

Her mind had to be going a hundred miles a minute, but they'd have to talk later. Sebastian could show up any minute now. Grabbing his shirt from the floor, he pulled it on before opening the curtains to reveal a beautiful view of the dawn. All the pretty shades of orange and pink were lost on him as he unlocked the door to the balcony and walked out.

Just as he thought. They were a good seven floors up. As an escape route, it wasn't an option. Behind him, Anya climbed out of the bed, pulling on her clothes with shaking hands. Marching back to the door, he looked out the peephole again. He still just saw the one guard. Where did the other one go? Or was he there and out of sight?

Once he had Anya wrapped up in his jacket, he motioned her to the door. Whispering, he explained what he needed her to do. It broke his heart a little how scared she was, but she didn't hesitate. Staying behind the door, Outcast waited as she opened the door of the suite to address the guard he saw. Maybe both of them.

Anya hesitated only for a second, masking her nerves behind a carefully neutral expression. The man standing in the hall was slouched against the wall, rubbing a hand over his tired eyes, a deep yawn cracking his jaw.

"Can I go home now?" she asked, her voice laced with just the right amount of irritation to make her request sound routine. "I've got things to do."

The man blinked at her, sluggish and unbothered. He pulled his phone from his pocket with one hand while the other scratched at the scruff on his jaw. "Yeah, yeah. Hold up. Gotta text Sturge to come up."

That was all Outcast needed. The moment the

guy's focus shifted to his phone, Outcast lunged from behind the suite door, silent and precise. His left hand clamped over the thug's mouth, muffling the startled grunt that barely made it past his lips. His right arm was wrapped around the man's throat in a brutal, crushing chokehold.

The guard thrashed, phone slipping from his fingers as his hands clawed at Outcast's arm, desperate for leverage. Too late. Outcast had already cinched it tight, cutting off both air and blood flow. The struggle was over in seconds. The man's body went limp, deadweight against him. Outcast carefully lowered him to the carpet without a sound, keeping his grip firm until he was certain the bastard was out cold.

Straightening, he glanced at Anya. She stood frozen in the doorway, eyes wide, breathing fast.

Outcast grabbed the phone from the floor and shoved it into his pocket. "We've got maybe two minutes before Sturge gets here," he muttered, already dragging the unconscious man into the suite.

He turned to Anya, his voice sharp but calm. "We need to move. Now."

She nodded, swallowing hard, and followed as he yanked open the suite door. The hallway was empty -- for now. Anya kept close, her breathing unsteady, as Outcast led her down the corridor in her bare feet, his eyes scanning for their next move. They took the back stairwell, descending six flights before slipping onto the main floor where the valet parking desk sat near the grand entrance. It was a sleek, open space, all polished marble and towering chandeliers. Guests in designer suits and designer casual wear milled about, waiting for their rides.

Outcast watched for a few seconds, finally spotting a valet who had been distracted by a celebrity guest and had just returned to his post. The man's valet jacket hung loosely on his shoulders. The perfect mark.

"Stay behind me," he murmured to Anya before moving in.

Like a shadow, he slid up behind the valet, grabbing the guy's shoulder and wrist in a firm, practiced grip. Before the man could react, Outcast twisted just enough to be able to knock him out cold with one blow, catching his body before it hit the floor. "Jacket," he muttered, slipping the red-and-black uniform off the guy. Anya looked stunned but helped him pull it on over his bloody, sweat-streaked shirt.

Outcast lifted the electronic valet scanner off the unconscious guy's belt. It beeped softly as he scrolled through the list of parked vehicles. "Got it," he said, eyes narrowing at a recently dropped-off Ferrari 812 Superfast -- sleek, black, and built to outrun whatever hell Sebastian might throw their way. They needed a miracle to get out of this mess and by God, he found it. Handing Anya a pair of oversized sunglasses from the valet stand, he said, "Put these on. Act normal."

She slid them on, taking his offered hand and playing along as they strolled toward the Ferrari like a couple waiting for their ride. A valet attendant barely glanced at them, too busy dealing with a drunk guest arguing over his Lamborghini. Outcast scanned the ticket, and the Ferrari's taillights flashed in response.

Anya's hand shook in his. "Please tell me you know how to drive this thing."

"I can drive it," he said before pulling open the door and shoving her inside. "Buckle up and hang on."

The moment he climbed in behind the wheel and the doors shut, Outcast fired up the engine. The deep, throaty roar of the V12 turned heads, but he was already shifting into gear.

That was when he saw the second thug Sebastian had sent with them running out of the lobby. Sturge moved to the valet lane, frowning as he scanned the waiting cars -- and then his eyes locked onto Outcast through the windshield.

"He sees us," Anya breathed.

Sturge reached for his gun.

Outcast floored it. The Ferrari's tires screeched, leaving a thick black streak of rubber across the valet lane as they tore onto the boulevard.

"Hold on," he growled as he jerked the wheel, narrowly missing a Rolls-Royce pulling up to the entrance. Behind them, a black SUV peeled away from the curb, its headlights cutting through the morning peace like twin daggers. Sebastian had already sent backup and they were in pursuit. The chase was on.

The Ferrari tore through the Louisville streets, its tires shrieking against the pavement as Outcast pushed its V12 engine to its limits. The city blurred past in streaks of blue sky and skyscraper, but his focus was razor-sharp. The black SUV thundered forward, right behind them, its grille in clear view in the rearview mirror.

"Hold on!" Outcast barked.

Anya gripped the edge of her seat, knuckles white, eyes wide behind the sunglasses he'd made her put on. A deep gasp escaped her when a loud popping sound erupted behind them. Gunfire.

One of Sebastian's men leaned out the passenger window, a pistol flashing in his hand. Bullets ripped through the peaceful morning, one shattering the Ferrari's side mirror, another pinging off the metal just inches from Anya's door. She shrieked, twisting in her seat.

Outcast gritted his teeth. "Stay down!"

Taking a hard left, he nearly clipped the corner of a parked truck. The rear of the Ferrari fishtailed, skidding on the pavement before regaining traction. Behind them, the SUV overshot the turn, smashing into a row garbage cans, buying them mere seconds. And they fucking needed every second they could possibly get.

"There's an alley to the right!" Anya yelled, pointing in that direction.

Outcast's jaw locked to see how tight it was. Too tight for the SUV to follow. It wasn't meant for cars like the one they were escaping with either. It was barely wide enough for a regular sedan, let alone a multi-million-dollar, high-powered sports car. But the alternative was getting shot to hell.

He yanked the wheel hard. The Ferrari whipped into the alley, the narrow passage rushing toward them like a collapsing tunnel. Metal screamed as the sides of the car grazed the brick walls, sending up a shower of black dust and sparks. The driver's side mirror snapped clean off, leaving him only the rearview now to navigate. Anya ducked in her seat and looked like she was praying.

The SUV tried to follow -- and slammed to a stop. The vehicle was too wide. He heard metal grinding and furious shouting behind them, but they were already out the other side.

Anya's head was back up, twisting in her seat to look behind them. "There's more of them!"

Outcast kept going until the Ferrari roared onto an open street, but the moment of victory was short-lived. Another set of headlights flared behind them -- a second SUV. *Fuck*! Sebastian's men were ready.

Scanning the road ahead, Outcast realized that

Downtown was coming to an end. They were approaching the edge of the city. Just past those warehouses at the next intersection, he had his bike stashed behind an old industrial lot. If he could just ditch the car and get to his bike, they could disappear.

But that was easier said than done. The SUV behind them gunned its engine.

Outcast spotted another shortcut -- a loading dock ramp leading to what looked like a deserted warehouse lot. "Shortcut or straight shot?" he growled.

Anya's eyes flicked between the road and the SUV. "I don't know this road well enough to say."

He made the choice. Outcast yanked the wheel hard and stepped on the gas. The Ferrari shot up the loading dock ramp like a Goddamn missile, launching off the edge.

For a terrifying half-second, the car hung in the air -- no pavement, no tires on the ground, just dead space, fear, and adrenaline. When the car smashed down onto the cracked asphalt of the warehouse lot, tires screeching, suspension groaning in protest, Anya screamed. The impact slammed them into their seats, and Outcast struggled to regain control of the car. The Ferrari swerved, fishtailed, but then held steady.

The SUV with Sebastian's men wasn't as lucky. In a desperate attempt to keep up, the driver gunned it up the ramp, misjudging the angle and speed. The front wheels clipped the edge, sending the massive vehicle tilting forward mid-air. For a split second, it hovered at a sickening angle before gravity took over. It slammed down nose-first, the impact crumpling the hood like paper, before momentum carried it into a violent roll. The SUV flipped onto its roof, metal shrieking as it skidded across the pavement in a shower of sparks. Windows exploded outward, tires bounced uselessly, and the final, bone-jarring crash left it lying still -- a smoldering wreck of crushed steel and broken glass.

Outcast barely spared it a glance.

"Out," he ordered. They ditched the Ferrari, Outcast leaving the valet jacket in it, and ran across the darkened warehouse lot. Outcast's bike was right where he'd left it, behind a rusted-out dumpster -- a matte-black Harley-Davidson Nightster that was built for speed and stealth. Fast as he could manage, he yanked his Hounds jacket out of his bag and pulled it on. Pulling out his two half shell helmets, he quickly put one on Anya before getting them on the bike. He could tell from the terror in her eyes that she'd never been on a bike before.

"Just hang on," he said. "Close your eyes if you need to."

Engines revved in the distance. Sebastian's men were coming.

Outcast twisted the throttle, tires peeling out as they tore away from the wreckage and into the dark Kentucky morning. The roar of the engine was deafening, but he could still feel Anya's grip tightening around his waist, her fingers clutching at his jacket like a lifeline. Outcast sucked in his breath. His ribs were sore, but he'd handle it. Anya's body tensed at every turn, every slight shift of momentum. But she held on, pressing close, trusting him with her life.

They had to make it to Mercy, and every second counted. Sebastian wouldn't wait long to retaliate. The moment his men failed to check in, hell would be coming for them. Worse, Sebastian likely now had a name to put to the man who'd stolen from him -- not just some nameless fighter from *Purgatory,* but a Hound. And that meant every road between Louisville and Mercy could be crawling with men ready to collect on Sebastian's rage.

Outcast leaned low over the handlebars, pushing the bike faster. The cold wind sliced through his jacket, but adrenaline burned hotter. He couldn't afford to stop. Couldn't afford to think about what would happen if they didn't make it. Anya was a warm weight against his back, a shaky reminder of why he had to keep going.

The road stretched ahead, empty for now, but Outcast knew better than to trust the silence. He'd been hunted before, traveling fast, light, and solo. This time, though, he wasn't running alone.

Chapter Six

Outcast

As they pulled into Big Stone Gap, Outcast cut the engine beside a small, dimly lit thrift shop tucked between an old gas station and a rundown diner. The ***OPEN*** sign flickered weakly in the window, casting a pale neon glow onto the cracked sidewalk. It wasn't much, but it would do. It was approaching noon.

Anya shivered against the chilly air as she climbed off the bike, her bare feet vulnerable against the pavement. She looked like a ghost of herself, still wrapped in the skimpy dress from fight night. His nondescript jacket provided her upper body warmth, but her lower body wasn't as well protected. The adrenaline from their escape had probably gotten her this far, but now reality was setting in. Outcast didn't say a word, just reached for her hand and led her inside.

The bell above the door jingled as they stepped in, the warm air hitting them like a wave. Rows of worn-out clothes, boots, and other forgotten relics of past lives cluttered the space, the scent of moldering fabric and dust lingering in the air. The old woman behind the counter barely looked up, her attention on a video playing on her phone that was propped up next to the vintage cash register.

Outcast walked them to the ladies' section and stayed by her side as Anya looked through racks of jeans and slacks for something that would fit. Once she found a pair of faded jeans that looked to be in decent shape, she moved on to the shirts, looking around nervously every few minutes even though Outcast never left her side. She found a hoodie, then looked at him with a nod.

"We're not done yet," he told her. They picked out thick socks for her, new but inexpensive. They found a pair of flat, black boots in her size. With his plain jacket, she would be warm enough. But there were a couple of other items they needed before they were done. She followed him as he looked through hats, looking confused. But he found what he was looking for -- a gray cap, which he handed to her.

"Your hair," he said simply. "It's too recognizable."

Anya swallowed hard but nodded, disappearing into the cramped fitting room. As she changed, Outcast paced, jaw tight, scanning the street outside through the dusty front window. They had to keep moving, but she couldn't run like this -- vulnerable, exposed, in nothing but that dress. When Anya stepped back out, bundled in new layers of anonymity, something in his chest eased. She looked smaller but stronger, the oversized hoodie swallowing her frame, the beanie pulled low over her ears. She was still Anya. But now, she'd be a lot harder to spot.

She met his gaze, her voice softer now. "How do I look?"

"Like we might actually make it out of this," he muttered. They approached the counter, and Outcast plucked a pair of cheap sunglasses off a small rack of them before handing over the tags from their purchases and a few crumpled bills to the cashier before leading her back out into the warm Virginia morning.

Anya didn't look as vulnerable as she pulled on the helmet and climbed on the back of his bike. But he had no idea when she'd last had a meal. Maybe a short break wouldn't be a bad idea. He knew just where to go that might offer them a little protection and they reached it in ten minutes.

Outcast eased the bike into the parking lot of a roadside bar nestled between the towering mountains of Big Stone Gap. The neon sign flickered *Two Wheels Saloon*, a known neutral ground where bikers from all clubs could drink in peace without politics turning the place into a war zone. Gravel crunched beneath the tires as he rolled up to a spot near the entrance, the familiar sight of patched men loitering outside, smoking and shooting the shit. A couple of them glanced up at him, clocking his patch, but there was no tension in their gazes.

His first priority wasn't the crowd. It was Anya. As soon as he killed the engine, Anya again loosened her grip on him, her hands trembling slightly as she unclenched them from his jacket. She'd held on for a couple of hours, and he knew she was running on nothing but fear and adrenaline. He turned slightly, his hand coming up to rest against her knee.

"You good?" he asked, voice low, meant only for her.

She nodded, but it wasn't convincing. Her face was pale, her lips pressed into a tight line.

He exhaled. "Come on, let's get inside. I'll get you some food. You can stretch your legs."

Anya didn't argue, but her movements were sluggish as she slid off the bike. He caught her elbow when she stumbled, steadying her. "Easy."

"Sorry," she muttered, shaking her head.

"It's not your fault." Outcast gave her a reassuring squeeze before leading her inside.

Outcast felt Anya stiffen the moment they stepped inside the bar. He didn't blame her. The place had a reputation -- one he was counting on to keep them off Sebastian's radar, at least for a little while. The air was thick with the scent of beer, sweat, and fried food. The low hum of conversation punctuated by the occasional clatter of pool balls or sharp bark of laughter.

He didn't miss the way heads turned as they entered, some curious, some wary. A woman like Anya -- delicate, beautiful, and out of place -- drew attention. She shrank slightly under the weight of all those eyes, her grip tightening on the hem of her jacket. She didn't belong here. Not in a place like this. Not in his world. Even so, he had no intention of letting her go.

Keeping his stride slow and deliberate, Outcast placed a possessive hand on the small of her back, guiding her deeper into the room. His presence alone was enough to keep anyone from asking the wrong kind of questions. No one wanted to pick a fight with a man who had blood on his knuckles and the look of someone willing to spill more. He caught sight of a familiar face at the bar -- he couldn't remember the man's name. The guy was trouble, but the right kind of trouble today.

Outcast leaned in close, his lips brushing Anya's ear as he murmured, "We're safe here. Just stay close to me."

A jukebox played an old country song in the corner, and the low murmur of conversation filled the space. Bikers, truckers, and locals occupied the mismatched tables and barstools. He found them a booth near the back where he could keep an eye on the door and the parking lot. Anya slid into the seat across from him, her hands gripping the edge of the table. After a moment, she realized she was still wearing sunglasses and slid them off her face.

"The clothes make you feel better?" he asked.

She nodded, her gaze meeting his. "Are we

getting closer to Mercy?"

"Halfway there," he assured her. "But we need a break. You need to eat something. And I need to figure out how to keep us from getting ambushed before we get there."

She swallowed hard. "Sebastian --"

"Won't touch you again," he cut in firmly. "Not now, not ever."

Her expression wavered, like she wanted to believe him, but he knew the weight of her past said otherwise.

"I don't just mean me, Jackson," she whispered. "What about you? The people you care about in Mercy? If he finds out where we're going…"

Outcast leaned forward, his forearms resting on the table. "I'm pretty sure he already knows who I am. And if he knows that much, he knows where I come from. He's coming for us. But the Hounds don't scare easy. You've got no idea what you're walking into, sweetheart. If he follows us, he's the one in for a fight."

"The Hounds?" Her brows bunched together in her confusion. "Is it… like a biker gang?"

He nodded. "Club. But yeah, the Hounds of Hell has a chapter in Mercy. I've been patched for a few years now."

Outcast leaned back in his seat, watching Anya process everything. Still, there was a glint of hope in her light green eyes. He exhaled, running a hand through his hair before leveling her with a steady look.

"MC life -- it's not just some weekend biker club," he said, his voice low but firm. "It's brotherhood. Loyalty. We take care of our own, we protect what's ours, and we don't back down from a fight." He let that sink in before continuing. "When I patched in, I found a family I could trust. Men who would bleed for me, and I'd do the same for them. That means if someone comes for us -- or for *you* -- they'll have the whole damn club to deal with."

Outcast studied her, trying to read her reaction. Yeah, she was probably just going along for now. But he was hoping she'd want to be part of his world once she got to know it. It wasn't just him she could rely on, but all his brothers. All their women. Particularly Deva. If he knew his sister, she'd beat someone's ass to protect Anya.

"You're with me now. That means you're under Hound protection. No one's touching you without going through me and my brothers first."

A cute blonde waitress stopped at their booth, bringing them glasses of water with paper-covered straws and a couple of laminated menus. Telling them she'd give them a minute and come back for their order, she dashed on to her other customers while Anya studied him, looking unsure of what to say.

"What do you do for a job?" she asked quietly. "Do you work for the club or --"

"I own a tattoo shop," he explained. "Well, Deva and I own it. We're the artists there."

Some of the anxiety bled out of her expression. "Deva? How is she?" A small smile played about her lips. "I was told that they separated you and her after…"

Outcast didn't want to speak Gene Lorry's name any more than she did. But he nodded. "They did separate us for a while. We went to different homes. At least they sent her to a decent home. I turned eighteen a couple of years after that and by the time I reached that birthday, I had a job, and some money saved up. As soon as I got an apartment, I petitioned the court to get custody of her. She's been with me ever since."

The caring in her expression as he talked about his sister warmed his heart. Anya was as kind as she was beautiful, and Deva had loved her back in the day.

"Will I get to see her?" Anya asked with a thread of hope in her tone.

"You will," he said as their waitress returned. Outcast ordered burgers, fries, and beers for them. "Deva lives in Mercy, and not too long ago, she started up with Razor. He's the president of our chapter of the Hounds."

"Razor?"

"It's his road name," Outcast explained. And he just knew the next question he was going to ask.

"What's your road name?"

"Outcast," he admitted.

"You just got through telling me about your club and your brothers," she said. "An outcast is someone who really doesn't belong anywhere."

That was true enough. "You're not wrong. I get myself into trouble going off on my own sometimes. But so far, they always have my back."

"Do they know where you are now?"

Anya had always been quietly observant, bright. That hadn't changed about her.

"Deva does," he explained. "Which means Razor knows too. And he's probably threatening to kick my ass right now. But if I need him, if I need *them*, they'll be there."

Before she could argue, the air around them shifted. A presence loomed at the edge of their table.

"Didn't expect to see a Mercy boy all the way out here," a familiar voice drawled.

Outcast looked up, his gaze locking onto a tall, lanky man with dark eyes and an easy smirk. His cut announced he was a Cottonmouth from Abingdon, not

Oak Grove. The Cottonmouth leaned against the edge of the booth, arms crossed over his chest.

Outcast had met him a couple of times, always in passing, but there was no bad blood between them.

"You're the one they call Outcast," the man said.

He saw fear rise in Anya's expression before he nodded to their guest. "I am. You?"

"Vendetta."

The other biker nodded back, then flicked his gaze to Anya. She shrank slightly under the weight of his attention, but Vendetta just arched a brow before returning his focus to Outcast. "Not speaking of the lady here, but *you* look like shit. Rough night?"

Outcast snorted. He could just imagine what he looked like after Saturday night's fight. "Something like that."

Vendetta jerked his chin toward the empty seat next to Anya. "Mind if I sit?"

Outcast hesitated for half a second before nodding. Vendetta wasn't a threat, and right now, he needed intel from someone who knew these roads better than he did. Vendetta slid into the seat, stretching out like he had all the time in the world. "So, what's got you holed up in here?"

"Passing through," Outcast said vaguely.

"Uh-huh." Vendetta wasn't buying it. He glanced at Anya again, taking in her clear distress. His dark eyes flicked back to Outcast, sharper now. "Trouble?"

"You could say that."

Vendetta tapped his fingers against the table, studying him. "Heard about a gun deal going sideways a few nights back. Some poor bastards got wiped the fuck out."

Outcast sighed. So, the news was already

spreading. *Fuck.*

Vendetta leaned in slightly. "Word on the street is, someone important lost a lot of men in that mess. And he ain't happy."

"Sebastian Six," Outcast said flatly.

Vendetta let out a low whistle. "Shit. That's a name I don't like hearing." He shook his head. "If he's after you, man, you've got problems."

"No shit," Outcast muttered.

Vendetta exhaled, rubbing his jaw. "You need a clean route out of here?"

Outcast nodded, wondering what the man wanted. He wasn't just being a good Samaritan here. "Yeah. And maybe a distraction to keep them looking the wrong way."

Vendetta thought about it for a moment, then grinned. "I can work with that."

Anya finally spoke, her voice soft. "Why would you help us?"

Vendetta's expression darkened. "Because I've got my own reasons for wanting to piss off the right people." His smirk returned, but there was a dangerous glint in his eyes. "And because fucking over Oak Grove's Cottonmouth chapter is a pastime of mine."

There it was. He almost hoped to get this story. It wasn't a common thing for a biker to have beef with his own club, even if it was a different chapter.

Vendetta met his gaze, nodding.

"Then let's make a deal."

"All right, Mercy boy," Vendetta said. "Let's get you and the lady the hell out of here."

Getting their waitress's attention, Outcast asked to get their order to go, handing her a fifty as they got ready to go with Vendetta.

* * *

Anya

The low rumble of a passing eighteen-wheeler rattled the thin walls of the mobile home as Anya sat gingerly on the edge of the worn-out mattress. The place smelled faintly of old wood, cigarette smoke, and motor oil -- a scent that clung to everything like a second skin. The small bedroom had nothing but a bed, a scratched-up dresser, and a single window with half-broken blinds that let in slivers of the setting sun. She wouldn't have said she felt completely safe there. No. But she felt safer than when they'd been on the open road, exposed.

Her entire body ached. The events of the last two days drained every ounce of energy from her, yet she still couldn't seem to relax. Jackson sat on the edge of the bed, scrolling through his phone. He was exhausted too, but she knew better than to think he'd actually try to rest or sleep.

Vendetta had given them the spare room without much fuss, tossing Jackson a set of keys to the trailer before heading out with nothing more than a vague, *"Got some things to set up. You're safe here for now."*

That was the part that unsettled her -- *for now.*

Her fingers curled into the threadbare blanket, her stomach twisting as doubt seeped in. Could they really trust Vendetta? Sure, he seemed to hate Sebastian and the Oak Grove Cottonmouths enough to want to help, but she'd seen how quickly people changed when the right pressure was applied. A man like Vendetta wasn't doing this for charity. He had his own reasons, and she wasn't sure if they were the kind that worked in their favor or the kind that would turn on them when it suited him.

Glancing over at Jackson, she noted the tension in his shoulders, the way his fingers flexed as if he were itching to grab a weapon even in supposed safety. He hadn't said much since Vendetta left, and that made her more nervous than anything. She hated to even ask the question that she'd been harboring for the last couple of hours, but she really didn't have a choice.

"Do you trust him?" she finally asked, her voice barely above a whisper.

Jackson exhaled through his nose, lifting his head to meet her gaze. His pale blue eyes were sharp, calculating. She recognized it as the same look he had when they'd planned to escape Gene Lorry's house. No doubt he was weighing the risks in his head as much as she had. But she knew very little about his life, his world.

"I trust that he wants something," he admitted. "Just gotta figure out what that is before it bites us in the ass."

Anya nodded, the exhaustion in her bones deepening. They had a temporary reprieve, but the fight wasn't over. Not even close.

Jackson rubbed the back of his neck, his fingers dragging over the rough stubble on his jaw. His gaze met hers, hesitation flickering in those sharp eyes before he let out a heavy breath. "I know you don't trust me," he murmured, his voice rough, edged with something bitter. "Not after what happened all those years ago."

Anya's heart clenched. Even after everything they'd just survived together, he still thought she held that night against him. That he had been the one to let *her* down. The guilt in his voice cut her deep, sharper than any blade Sebastian or his men could have wielded.

She sat up straighter, ignoring the aches in her body, and reached for his hand. He didn't pull away, but he didn't meet her eyes either.

"You're wrong," she said softly. "Jackson, I *do* trust you."

His fingers twitched beneath hers, as if her words physically shook him. His posture was still rigid with doubt.

"I ran from you," she admitted, squeezing his hand. "That wasn't because I didn't trust you. It was because I was scared. Because I thought if you knew everything, you'd…" She swallowed hard, her throat tight. "You'd leave. That you wouldn't want me anymore."

His head snapped toward her, his gaze darkening with something fierce, something unreadable.

"I never would have left you," he ground out, voice low, heavy with conviction. "I *never* wanted to lose you."

She felt the burn of unshed tears behind her eyes. The past had stolen so much from them -- time, love, choices. But at this moment, she wouldn't let it steal this second chance they had too. Jackson still held her hand, his thumb brushing over her knuckles absentmindedly, but there was something unreadable in his gaze now.

"What did you mean by that?" he asked, voice quiet but firm. "If I knew everything… What didn't I know, Anya?"

Her stomach dropped. She'd known this moment would come, but now that it was here, the words tangled inside her like thorned vines, cutting deep. She exhaled slowly, steadying herself before meeting his eyes. "There's a lot you don't know," she admitted. "Things I should have told you years ago. But I was afraid. And once I ran, it felt impossible to go back."

Jackson didn't rush her. He just waited, his patience more unnerving than his temper would have been.

"I was pregnant." The words felt like stones falling from her lips, shattering in the silence between them.

Jackson didn't move at first. Didn't breathe. His grip on her hand tightened just slightly, but his expression didn't change. It was like he was bracing himself, waiting for her to say it was a mistake, a misunderstanding.

"When?" His voice was rough, like gravel scraping against pavement.

Anya swallowed hard. "Back in the Lorrys' house. Before we planned to run. I didn't tell you because I thought we'd get out, and then I'd tell you when we were safe. But we never got that chance."

Jackson's hand suddenly pulled away from hers, and for the first time in all the years she'd known him, she couldn't read his expression. "What happened?" he asked, his voice eerily calm.

Her throat tightened. She already knew what he was asking. "I told myself it was yours because I needed to believe that," she admitted. "But… I couldn't know for sure."

The muscle in Jackson's jaw jumped, and for a long moment, he didn't speak. His eyes were dark, unreadable, but the tension in his body was palpable. They'd never talked about the fact that Gene Lorry had been having her since she arrived at his home months earlier, before they took him and his sister in. They didn't talk about how his scared mouse of a wife knew what was happening and did nothing. *Nothing*. Jackson knew that. He'd offered to confront the man himself, but she begged him not to. She knew they wouldn't be believed or worse, they'd blame Jackson for her pregnancy. They'd be separated. It was then they planned to escape and take Deva with them.

The three of them made it out. But the police and CPS were called, and they didn't make it far.

"After we were separated, the social workers realized I was pregnant." She cut off, glancing away. "When I got sent to my room to get my things… He punched me. Here," she barely got the words out, gesturing to her midsection.

Anya pressed on, knowing she couldn't stop now. The next part was the worst, and her heart cracked in fear and despair, but the truth had to be known. An investigation was to take place and all three of them were sent to collect their belongings. Gene Lorry had found a way to sneak up to her room, to confront her. To blame her for everything. To protect himself and his horrible deeds, the bastard had punched her in the ribs, in the stomach *hard*. It took her breath away. The CPS agents suspected something was wrong but ultimately decided it was the trauma of being caught and fear of what would happen next. It wasn't until hours later when the bleeding and cramping came on, bad enough to make her want to die, that they realized she'd been pregnant. Lorry apparently told them it was Jackson's to cover his guilt.

Jackson exhaled sharply, standing abruptly and pacing the small space like a caged animal. His hands went to his hips, fingers digging in as if he were physically holding himself together.

"You were pregnant," he repeated, almost to himself.

"I was."

He turned, and this time, she could see devastation, rage, and grief all crashing together behind those stormy ice-blue eyes. "And they believed that I --" He cut off, shaking his head as if the thought itself was too much.

"Lorry lied," Anya said, firm. "He lied to keep his dirty little secrets, to keep us apart, Jackson. I know that now… I never stopped thinking about you. I never stopped missing you."

Jackson let out a bitter breath, running a hand over his face. "Jesus Christ."

Anya stood then, moving toward him hesitantly, unsure if he would even let her touch him right now. "I didn't tell you to hurt you," she said softly. "I told you because I don't want to keep running from the past. And because I don't want you to carry the weight of it alone anymore. You tried to help me. You did everything you could. I never blamed you for what happened."

Jackson's gaze snapped to hers, something unreadable shifting in his expression. "You think I'm the only one carrying the weight?"

He exhaled, closing the distance between them in one stride. His hands cupped her face, his touch firm but careful, like she might break apart if he held her too tight. "You survived all of it. And you're still standing," he murmured, voice thick with emotion. "You fought. Just like you always have."

His gaze searched hers, his eyes glassy with unshed tears. "There's something else," he said. "I know you. What is it?"

After all this time, he could still read her so easily. It was as if their time apart had never happened. Finding the strength to finish it seemed impossible and now, at this moment, he would tell her that he understood. He'd promised her it was okay. But down the road she knew there was a chance that if they stayed together, this last piece of the truth could part them…

"Jackson, I…" *How do I tell him this*? "There was damage from the… miscarriage. I can't have… any more children."

He didn't let her go, holding her there with her face in his hands. "I'm so sorry," he whispered. "I'm so sorry for all you've been through… You have to know… if you want children one day, we can always adopt. All I've ever wanted was *you*."

… we can always adopt…

She didn't know what the future would hold, but his words were enough for now. It was enough to lift some of the weight and sorrow from her heart. Just maybe it did the same for him. Jackson's throat bobbed as he swallowed, his eyes searching hers for something unspoken. Then, with a slow exhale, he finally let his shoulders relax just enough for her to see the man she'd always known beneath the hardened edges. He lifted her hand to his lips, pressing a kiss against her knuckles, lingering there for just a second longer than necessary.

"I'll always come for you," he murmured. Anya believed him.

She didn't know who started the kiss. It was whisper-soft, a promise. His hands slid down from her face, skimming down her body. When he pulled her firmly against him, her heart hammered in her chest, locking to the rhythm of his as the seconds stretched out. She let him deepen this kiss, her hands sliding up into the sleek black locks of his hair. The taste of him, the feel of him in her arms pushed all the angst of the past and uncertainty of the future aside as he steered them to the bed and not-too-carefully dropped her onto it, following her down.

Desire and need had them plucking at each other's clothing. Jackson pressed her onto her back beneath him and tears slid from the corners of her eyes as he hovered over her. Jackson's heated gaze locked with hers as he slotted a muscular thigh between hers. Her hands found their way back into his hair as he nudged up into her melting center, building a delicate ache that felt so good.

His kisses went to her head like good whiskey, sending ripples of heat and growing euphoria racing through her bloodstream. Her thighs clamped around his as his lips danced against her own in a kiss that was gentle but demanding all the same. When his weight eased onto her, she vined her limbs around him, wanting more. Her hands clutched in his hair as his lips blazed a trail across her jaw to seek out all the places that made her tremble. She'd pretty much disappeared beneath him, and she loved it. Loved the chorus of sounds he pulled from her as his mouth trailed down her neck to her chest.

Jackson stripped off the hoodie with haste, his lips surrounding one of her nipples a beat later. He left her gasping as his lips and tongue teased the aching peak, causing the ache deep in her body to grow. Anya's back arched, a wanton plea for more. It gave him easier access and he took it. Her thighs clamped around his in desperation, needing relief. The intensity of her need was climbing. His hot mouth moved to her other breast as his hands worked the front of her jeans, to quickly to push them and her panties down.

He still loved it when she tugged his hair. She pulled a groan from him by pumping her hips against him, begging him without words to give her release. She felt that raw sound throughout her body, gasping as he moved further down. Sliding a hand down to the swollen, soaked flesh between her thighs had him licking his lips, watching how she worked her clit to help put out the fire.

"No, you don't." Jackson's voice was low and rough.

Batting her hands away, he got his mouth on her. Hips, lips and tongue on that tender flesh had her climaxing in seconds, wailing in the quiet of the bedroom. His hands wrapped around her thighs, holding them open as he went to work, teasing her through the powerful orgasm in a way that kept her flying. She couldn't move her lower body, couldn't get away from the onslaught of pleasure Jackson was subjecting her to.

Anya writhed wildly on the bed, knowing the sight of his black hair brushing against her thighs as his mouth took her apart would forever be seared into her memory. He teased her relentlessly until she came a second time with the world spinning around her, her back arching wildly as he worked her through it.

As she lay trembling on the bed, Jackson scrambled to peel off his T-shirt and shove down his jeans while she watched him with a hungry gaze. As soon as his cock was freed, she got her hand on his heated erection, warm velvet in her grasp. Jackson came back up to her, his shadow swallowing her again as he kissed her lips, giving her a taste of her own need. It only pushed her desire higher, making her wind herself around him again.

"See how good you taste?" he asked.

Taking himself in hand, he slid himself through her slippery folds, back and forth. Each pass was a flagrant brush against her clit, sending shots of pleasure racing through her. When he started pushing into her, his breath was a warm rush against her face. He filled her, had her sucking in a breath as her pussy walls stretched around him. All the while, his gaze with those ice-blue eyes stayed on her, watching for any signs of distress. By the time he reached the end of her, she was already on the edge again. The only thing that prevented it was the fact that he'd stopped moving to let her body adjust.

Anya was ready to go. Her hands slid down to the firm globes of his ass, squeezing. "Move," she whispered. "Ride me." She was burning from the inside, her lower body stretched around his cock, quivering in need. When she raked her nails up his back, she hoped he'd take the hint and destroy her.

Jackson started moving, slowly, and it was everything she craved. His cock hit places inside her that left her breathless. His muscular body pressed her into the mattress, and it was all she could do to hang on as his thrusts sped up. He wasn't fucking her. He was *claiming* her. It was in the tender possession of his hands that skimmed over her body. It was in the sweet caress of his lips over her face and shoulders. He made her take his cock, filling her again and again with thrusts that punched the air from her lungs. When her inner walls began to quiver around him, she braced herself for one last release that had her heart hammering against his.

Jackson sped up. "Be a good girl and come all over my cock," he purred in her ear.

Anya didn't have a choice. Burying her face in his chest to muffle the scream, she let go. And he kept going as she rode him, pleasure pulsing through her body as he began chasing his own end. Her name was a prayer on his lips as his movements quickened, desperate now instead of careful. When he came, he growled, looking beautiful above her as he was lost to the same pleasure he'd just drowned her in.

Anya felt like a tremendous weight had been taken off her shoulders tonight. All the secrets she'd held onto to avoid hurting Jackson had worked through her over the years like slow poison. She never thought she'd see him again, but he'd found her. And none of the terrible things she'd worried about had happened when she finally shared the secrets she had held for so long. Jackson hadn't hated her or blamed her. He listened. He had no way of knowing that just by listening, loving her, he was *healing* her.

It would take time and there would still be scars from the past. But it was more than she ever dared hope for.

Wrapped up in his arms in the quiet of the bedroom, Anya allowed herself to drift off to sleep. She couldn't remember the last time she'd been able to let her guard down.

Chapter Seven

Outcast

The scent of burnt coffee lingered in the cramped kitchen, mixing with the acrid staleness of cigarette smoke. Outcast sat at the rickety table, arms crossed, foot tapping impatiently against the tile floor. The morning light filtered through the dingy blinds, casting striped shadows across the small space.

Vendetta leaned against the counter, sipping from a chipped mug like they had all the time in the world, while Anya sat beside Outcast, silent but tense. He could feel the weight of her unease in the way she curled her hands around the cup of coffee she hadn't touched.

Enough waiting.

"Why are you helping us?" Outcast finally asked, voice low but firm.

Vendetta smirked but didn't look up right away. Instead, he took another slow sip of his coffee, like he was savoring the moment before dropping a bomb. Then, finally, he exhaled and met Outcast's eyes.

"You know the Oak Grove Cottonmouths?" Vendetta asked, voice rough from years of smoke and bad decisions.

Outcast gave a slow nod, already not liking where this was going. "I know 'em."

"Well," Vendetta said, setting his mug down with a quiet clink, "they've been making moves. Big ones. And it's all tied to your boy Sebastian Six."

Anya stiffened beside him, fingers tightening around her cup.

"The hell does that mean?" Outcast demanded.

Vendetta's grin faded, and for the first time he looked completely serious. "Means Sebastian's setting up shop throughout Virginia, just like he tried to do in Mercy. He's using the Oak Grove Cottonmouths as his in. Same business, same filth. Trafficking, extortion, the whole nine yards. And you wanna know the worst part?"

Outcast didn't speak, but he had an idea where this might be headed.

"They're using a tattoo shop as a front. A place called *Sinister Skin Studios*." Vendetta's gaze met Outcast's. "I'm sure that sounds familiar, doesn't it?"

Anya looked at him in confusion, her face paling. "What happened?" she whispered.

Outcast shook his head, his chuckle bitter and humorless. "The bastard doesn't quit," he growled. "Tried to use *No Mercy Ink* to do the same damn thing in Mercy using someone named Victor Grayson. We stopped him."

Vendetta nodded. "Grayson is just one of his dogs. Yeah, now he's moving on to Oak Grove to expand his empire instead. They're giving him a stronghold in the state, and they ain't shy about who they step on to make it happen." His gaze darkened. "A bunch of our guys in Abingdon moved over there, wanted me to be part of it. When I spoke out, they made sure I knew I wasn't welcome anymore."

Vendetta tipped up his chin. The scar around Vendetta's neck was harsh, wrapping around his throat like a ghostly noose, a deep, uneven band of discolored skin. Darker in some places, lighter in others, where the flesh had been stretched and torn. The texture was rough, slightly raised, the kind of scar that didn't just fade with time. It had the unmistakable look of a ligature mark, a brutal imprint left behind by rope or wire, something that had bitten in too deep, held too long.

The faint purplish hue at its edges suggested it had only been a few months since the injury, and the way he occasionally rolled his shoulders, stretching his neck as if trying to shake off an invisible weight, told Outcast Vendetta still felt it. It wasn't just a scar; it was a statement, a mark left by someone who had fully intended to see him dead. But Vendetta had survived. And the way his dark eyes burned beneath the shadow of his cap told Outcast that whoever had done it wasn't nearly as lucky.

Outcast let it all sink in. Vendetta wasn't just pissed about some personal score he wanted to settle; he was a man who'd been cast out by his own brothers because he refused to be part of the filth they were building.

"So, what?" Outcast asked. "You help us, and we help you clean house?"

Vendetta shrugged. "Eventually. But first, we need to get you two to Mercy in one piece."

Anya finally found her voice. "How?"

Vendetta pushed off the counter and folded his arms. "Not the easy way, that's for damn sure. Sebastian's got eyes everywhere. Roads, motels, probably half the damn truck stops from here to Mercy." He nodded toward Outcast. "You're a dead man walking the second they figure out who you really are."

Outcast's mouth twisted into a smirk. "They already know."

Vendetta huffed. "Yeah, well, that makes shit even trickier." He leaned in, voice dropping slightly. "We go the backroads. No highways, no main drags. We stop in Wytheville at an old industrial park I know -- neutral ground. We grab gas, burner phones, anything else you need to stay off the radar."

Outcast nodded, his mind already working through the logistics.

"Speaking of," Vendetta pulled a phone from a drawer by his sink. "Use this if you need to get word out to your people. Should have some juice left in it."

Tucking the burner phone away, Outcast focused on their situation.

Vendetta wasn't wrong. With Sebastian's network crawling through the state, it wasn't going to be as simple as just riding through town unnoticed. They needed to be smart. But smart didn't sit well with him when Anya was still at risk.

He turned to her, taking in the tension in her frame, the way her hands trembled just slightly as she finally lifted her coffee for a sip. She was scared. And she had every reason to be.

"Anya," he said, voice softer now. She looked at him, and for a moment, he saw the girl he'd lost all those years ago. The girl he'd promised to protect. The girl he'd failed.

"Can you do this?" he asked, not out of doubt, but because he needed her to know she had a choice.

She set her coffee down, straightened her shoulders, and met his gaze with steel in her eyes. "I can."

Outcast exhaled, then nodded once. "Then we move out in twenty."

Vendetta grinned. "Atta boy."

They had a plan. Now, they just had to survive it.

Motioning for Anya to follow him, he led her back to the bedroom they'd shared last night. As soon as he disconnected his phone from the charger, the screen lit up with Deva's name. When he checked notifications, he saw he had a dozen calls from her and even more texts. He wouldn't have put it past his sister to send the cavalry after him, so he needed to tell her something.

Using the burner phone Vendetta gave him, he typed in Deva's number.

Unknown: *I'm okay. I plan to be home by tonight.*

His gaze met Anya's as she nervously perched on the side of the bed with her mostly full coffee cup. Deva was typing.

Deva: *Did you find her*?

Outcast had to smile at that question. Deva knew what mattered to him.

Unknown: *She's with me.*

While Deva was typing, Anya asked, "Do you really trust this guy?"

Her tone was sincere. She wasn't questioning his judgment. "I don't know him," he admitted. "You saw his neck, right?"

Anya swallowed, nodded at the memory of the brutal mark on their host.

"I don't know him to trust him," Outcast explained. "But I trust the man's need for vengeance. His own brothers did him wrong and he'll be expecting me to return the favor."

"Will you?" she whispered, watching him so closely for a reaction.

Outcast nodded. "I will. My MC might want to jump in too. There's no love between us and the Cottonmouths in Oak Ridge. You'll hear a lot of stories when we get home. Believe me."

The remark was meant to make her feel better, but Deva was still typing and within seconds, Anya's face crumpled, and the tears came on. Outcast could deal with just about anything but that. In a flash, he was next to her on the bed, wrapping an arm around her. He wasn't surprised. She'd been so brave the last couple of days and he had no idea what she'd been through in the hands of the heartless bastard who had been keeping her.

"I'll keep you safe," he whispered, pressing a kiss into her hair. "I promise."

Swiping at her tears with her fingers, her gaze met his. "It's not that," she said. "It was when you said home… It's not something I feel like I've ever had."

The soft words broke him more than any threat could. He held her tighter, let her work through the emotion. Until he and Deva had found Mercy, and the Hounds, he hadn't known what home meant either, hadn't understood its true meaning.

Home wasn't a town or a city. It wasn't a mansion or a shithole apartment. No, home was the people you loved and who mattered to you. Deva had been the only home he had until he found his brothers. And even then, he always felt that his home was incomplete. The missing piece was the woman in his arms. They'd make it back to Mercy and with her, he'd be happy. He'd finally be complete.

The burner phone vibrated in his palm, cutting off Deva's typing mid-response. The number on the screen made his stomach clench.

Razor. *Shit.*

Outcast exhaled through his nose, rubbing the tension from his forehead with his free hand before tapping the answer button. "Yeah."

"Yeah?" Razor's voice was sharp enough to cut. "That all you got to say to me right now?"

Outcast ran a hand through his still-damp hair. "Knew you'd be callin' sooner or later."

"Yeah, well, I'd rather it be sooner than after I have to dig your dumb ass out of a grave," Razor snapped. "You think I don't know when one of my guys is runnin' off on a Goddamn suicide mission?"

Outcast clenched his jaw, but he didn't argue. Razor had every right to be pissed. "You done?" he asked flatly.

"Oh, I ain't even started," Razor bit back. "You think you're the only one with skin in this game? You think you don't have people who give a shit whether you live or die? Deva's been a fucking wreck since late Friday night."

Outcast rubbed the back of his neck, his fingers grazing the fading bruises along his jaw. He glanced over his shoulder at Anya, who began stuffing what little they had into his old backpack.

"I'm gettin' her out, Razor," he said, voice firm but low. "And I'm sorry as hell I'm bringing a shitstorm down on all of us, but… I failed her when it really mattered. I had to do this. I had to make this right."

Anya stopped what she was doing, eyes wide with emotion as she listened.

A heavy sigh crackled through the line. Razor wasn't an emotional man, but Outcast knew that sound well. It was the same deep, measured breath the man took before a fight, the same restraint he had before he made a hard call.

"Yeah," Razor finally said, voice quieter. "I know, brother. And I ain't here to tell you not to. Just tell me you got a plan."

Outcast blew out a breath. "I've got an ally helping us. You're not going to like it… or *him* for that matter. But he's got his own reason for wantin' to take down Six."

Razor grunted. "He's gotta be a fucking Cottonmouth? Damn. Really?"

That had him grinning. Razor'd guessed

correctly. He was nothing if not perceptive.

"Who the fuck is Six?"

"Same group as Grayson except he's higher up the food chain," he said. "That's why I'm glad to have someone who knows a little about him. And he's got some intel to share. Later. If we get through this mess."

"Well, hope you trust him," Razor said. "Because while you've been playin' ghost, this someone sent men to Mercy. Must be this Six you're talking about."

That sent a shock of adrenaline through Outcast's veins. He stood up, pacing toward the window. "What?"

"We haven't figured out what they want yet," Razor admitted. "But they're watchin', pokin' around. My guess? Lookin' for leverage. If Six's crew thinks they can take you off the board, they're gonna try. And if they can't? They'll go after what you love."

His stomach clenched. "Deva --"

"She's fine," Razor assured him quickly. "She's with us at the clubhouse. Nobody's gettin' near her. But you need to get your ass home, Outcast."

Outcast exhaled sharply, dragging his hand down his face. "We're on our way. Just hold things down till we get there."

"Always do," Razor said. There was a beat of silence before he added, "And, Outcast?"

"Yeah?"

"Deva's told me a little about the situation," Razor said in a kinder tone. "I'm not happy with how you went about it, but I get it. Bring her home."

A lump formed in Outcast's throat, but he forced it down. His grip tightened around the phone.

"I will."

* * *

Anya

The industrial park sat on the edge of Wytheville's wilderness, a skeleton of its former self. Cracked asphalt stretched between rusting warehouses, their windows shattered and doors hanging open like yawning mouths. Overgrown weeds pushed through the concrete, and the husks of forgotten machinery sat abandoned in the shadows, collecting dust and decay. A distant train horn echoed through the desolation, a reminder that civilization wasn't too far away -- but out here, in this forgotten place, they were alone.

They took an old, beat-up pickup truck Vendetta had stashed for emergencies, its faded paint and rusted edges blending, drawing less attention on the road. It matched the vibe of the forgotten industrial sprawl. The truck bed held Jackson's bike, carefully concealed beneath a weathered tarp secured with bungee cords. It wasn't ideal, but rolling into Wytheville on a loud Harley could easily have been a death sentence. This way, if things went sideways, they still had an escape plan -- one that relied on speed, maneuverability, and Jackson's ability to ride like hell. The truck rumbled over pothole-riddled pavement as they neared the meeting spot, tension thick in the cab. They were running on borrowed time, and every second counted.

Vendetta guided the truck down an uneven service road, his expression unreadable. He drove carefully around the potholes, heading toward a rusted-out semi-trailer covered in graffiti before sweeping toward a structure that looked one strong gust of wind away from collapsing. It was the last place anyone would think of searching for anything valuable, which made it perfect.

Jackson barely waited for the truck to stop before

hopping out, scanning the area. The place was quiet -- too quiet -- but nothing about Vendetta's demeanor suggested alarm. This was a known place to him. A safe house.

Anya had sat between them in the truck and now she carefully climbed out the passenger side while Vendetta went in the opposite direction. A chill ran down her spine even though it was a warm day for March. Some sense of foreboding gave her pause. Did they really need to stop here? She'd seen firsthand just how brutal Sebastian and his followers were. She didn't want to waste a minute more than they had to because she knew he was watching and waiting.

"This way," Vendetta grunted, leading them toward the warehouse.

Anya hesitated, gripping Jackson's sleeve. "We're really going in there?"

He glanced down at her and she knew he recognized her fear. Guilt flashed in his pale blue eyes. "Five minutes. We refuel, grab what we need, and go."

Inside, the place was organized chaos -- a stash house disguised as rubble. Against one of the reinforced walls sat old military surplus crates, stacks of water bottles, gas cans, and even an aging but functional generator. In a corner, covered in a tarp, sat an old but reliable sedan and a couple of dirt bikes. The scent of oil and dust lingered in the air.

Vendetta cracked open a locked metal cabinet, tossing Jackson a burner phone and loading a shotgun. "Food, first aid, fuel. Take what you need. You need any ammo?"

"Yeah," Outcast replied. "I've got a .45."

Vendetta passed Anya three small white boxes that were surprisingly heavy. Fast as she could, she passed them off to Jackson like they were burning her fingers. Guns and everything to do with them scared her.

Jackson stopped then, his gaze on her. "You don't have a phone on you, do you?"

"Well, that's a shit time to ask," Vendetta's voice raised in anger, thinking she might've had a phone on her that could be traced by Sebastian and his men.

"No," she said looking from Jackson to Vendetta and back. "Sebastian didn't allow me to have a phone."

A muscle in Jackson's jaw twitched but he didn't say anything. Vendetta, however, was still interested in the direction the conversation just took.

"Hold on," Vendetta said, placing the now loaded shotgun on the bench next to him and studying Anya. "What exactly is Six after the two of you for?"

"Me," Anya told the man before Jackson could speak. "I've been his… for a couple of years now."

Their host's face darkened in anger, and she started trembling hoping she hadn't just set him against them too.

"The fucker sold you around?" Vendetta asked.

Anya shook her head. "No, I was just his." The shame of being such an evil man's captive weighed less when she admitted to that and the feel of Jackson's supportive hand at the small of her back helped as the man who'd been her first love quietly showed his support.

Vendetta's intent gaze moved from her to Jackson. "I grew up in Abingdon," he said. "Back when my best friend and I were prospects, his little sister fell in with the wrong crowd. She was just in high school, you know. She disappeared for a few months and honestly, we thought she ran off with a boyfriend that nobody liked. But no, she ended up being in that mess. By the time they got her back, and she still wasn't twenty yet, she looked like a fucking skeleton. She was addicted to drugs, had had two abortions they made her do. It was almost a year of hospitals and programs before she got around to being anything close to normal. And she's never going to be the same. I hate the fuckers. I'm glad you got your woman out of there, man."

Jackson's gaze was on her. "Me too."

Vendetta went back to grabbing what he needed. Jackson pulled a huge handgun from the holster he wore, loading it from one of the ammo boxes. "You have a small handgun?"

"For her?" Vendetta nodded. From a drawer behind him, he pulled out a gun smaller than Jackson's, handing it to him handle first. "It's a 9mm Glock. It's got a kick, but she should be able to handle it. And that generation really doesn't have a safety so…"

Anya sucked in a breath as Vendetta handed him a couple of boxes of ammo for the Glock. She'd never fired a gun. She wouldn't even know what to do. Jackson read the apprehension in her eyes, pulling a worn black clip holster from the shelf in front of him. All she could do was watch him load the gun before he yanked up the hem of her hoodie and fastened that holster to her jeans. When he slid the gun into it, his gaze locked with hers.

"Be aware of it," he told her. "Handle it carefully."

"Jackson --"

"Just keep it," he said, "for me. If we get separated or something happens, I don't want you to be completely defenseless."

She didn't like the idea at all, but he'd risked so much for her. She just nodded while the two of them grabbed everything they thought would be needed to get for the rest of the trip to Mercy.

Jackson grabbed a gas can and stepped toward the truck, but before he could even reach the door, Vendetta cursed under his breath.

"We got company."

They froze. Engines rumbled in the distance. Jackson shoved Anya toward cover, hand already going for his gun. Vendetta crept toward the loading dock, peering out a broken window. The sun glinted off the chrome of a side mirror of a muscle car and several black SUVs tore into the lot, kicking up gravel, forming a blockade.

Then came the first gunshot. The explosive crack of a rifle split the silence, sending shards of glass raining down as a bullet tore through one of the high windows.

"Stay down!" Jackson barked at her, drawing his gun just as another shot slammed into the metal shelving nearby, sending sparks flying.

Sebastian's men were everywhere. Engines revved, tires skidded across gravel, and the warehouse doors shuddered violently as someone tried to force their way inside. Through the jagged gaps in the walls, Outcast spotted at least a dozen men moving in, weapons drawn, fanning out to cut off every possible escape.

"They brought a Goddamn army," Vendetta growled, shotgun in hand as he ducked behind an overturned workbench. He fired off a shot, the boom echoing through the warehouse as one of the gunmen went down, his body crumpling onto the cracked concrete.

More shots rang out, bullets shredding through the decaying walls, ricocheting off rusted machinery.

Jackson pivoted and fired, dropping a man as he tried to sneak around the side. He winced and she knew he was still hurting from the beating he'd taken when he fought Goliath. For *her*. His phone fell out of his pocket as he moved and she scrambled to grab it, to keep it safe for him.

A voice cut through the chaos. "Anya!" The shout was laced with cruel amusement.

Anya's blood ran cold as she saw one of the bastards standing just outside through a hole in the wall where she hid. The man gripped a rifle, his grin wide as he scanned the warehouse.

"Sebastian wants you back," the man called out. "Come on out now. Don't make this harder than it needs to be."

Anya stiffened from where she hid behind the crates, her breath shallow. She felt Jackson's gaze on her before his expression became one of pure rage. Without a moment's hesitation, he was moving. Darting from cover, he emptied his clip, hitting the man in the center of his chest. The bastard staggered, a shocked gurgle escaping him before he collapsed into the dirt.

But that was all it took. A chorus of gunfire erupted, forcing Jackson to dive for cover behind a rusted metal cabinet as bullets whizzed past.

"Jesus Christ, Outcast!" Vendetta shouted over the chaos. "You got a death wish?"

If Jackson heard him, he didn't acknowledge it. Fury darkened his face. Someone tried to rush him from behind as she watched. He spun, slamming the butt of his gun into the man's jaw before shooting him point-blank. The man dropped.

But there were too many of them.

Vendetta cursed, fumbling for his keys. "We

need to move. Now!"

Anya pushed herself up from behind the crates, realizing they had to go. She barely made it a step before rough hands clamped around her wrist, yanking her back. Anya let out a startled cry.

Jackson crossed the distance in two strides, tackling the guy and slamming him into the wall. He delivered a vicious punch to the bastard's ribs, then another to his throat. The man sagged, choking, but Jackson wasn't done. He grabbed the man's own knife from his belt -- and drove it deep between his ribs. The guy gasped, blood bubbling on his lips as he slid to the ground.

Vendetta was already at the truck with the engine roaring. Jackson grabbed Anya's hand and hauled her toward the vehicle, throwing open the cab door and shoving her inside. She watched with her heart in her throat as he dove in after her. Vendetta floored it, tires screeching as they peeled out of the warehouse. Her stomach lurched as they gained speed, flying down the narrow country road. She couldn't look out the windows. Sebastian's men would be behind them. They were taking the winding road way too fast. And Sebastian's men knew exactly what vehicle they were in.

A humming from the pocket of the leather jacket she wore had her fishing out the burner phone. Notifications lit up the screen. Mostly from Razor but the latest one was from Deva.

Deva: *Jackson, where the hell are you? Are you close? If you can let us know where you are, we can get some help there.*

Blowing out a breath, Anya tried to focus on anything but the fact that they were flying down the road. Another message from Deva came through.

Deva: *For fuck's sake, Jackson. For once in your damn life, let someone help you. At least for her.*

Deva. Anya remembered the bright young girl who was Jackson's younger sister. She'd been ten the last time she saw her and Anya recalled the time they spent together in Lorry's house. She'd been so protective of the child. Her greatest fear had been that Lorry would do something to Deva, just like he had to her. It was the biggest reason she'd agreed to Jackson's plan to get them out of there.

Deva was grown now and with Razor who was apparently the leader of the Hounds. They wanted to help and she and Jackson needed that.

Jackson turned in his seat to glance out of the truck's back window, not looking at her. "I just see one heading this way," he said.

"There will be more," Vendetta said as he kept on driving. "I'm hoping to lose them here in the next mile or so. I'm going to hit 100 and we can just take that all the way into Mercy."

Anya made up her mind. She couldn't fight and she was scared as hell to have a gun clipped on her body. She hit reply to Deva's last message.

Deva, it's Anya. We need help. We're in Wytheville. We're going to get on 100 soon and take that to Mercy.

Deva was typing instantly.

Deva: *Are you two okay?*

Anya typed back quickly.

We're okay. Thank you.

Anya just prayed that they all stayed that way.

* * *

Deva

Phone in hand, Deva ran from Razor's bedroom at the Hounds clubhouse to his office, pushing her way in past the men gathered around her man's desk. Her heart hammered in her chest in relief and fear. Her brother was alive. He was getting closer. Anya was with him and so far, safe.

Hero, Crash, and Player were in the office around Razor's desk, the mood pure tension.

"I heard from them," she said, giving Razor her phone. "I heard from *her*."

Razor read the text conversation on Deva's phone intently. "At least one of them has a damn brain," he said. Handing the phone back to her, he looked at each of his men. "Outcast and his lady are in Wytheville," he told them. "They're going to pick up 100 and come into Mercy that way. We have a location and a timeframe. Let's make a plan."

"I'll go get Snow and the twins," Hero said, dashing around her to leave the office and find them.

Razor's gaze returned to her. "Thank you," he said to her, trying to sound reassuring. "We're on it."

It sounded like she was being dismissed, and her brother was in play. No way in hell she was just going to dutifully go back to the bedroom like a good woman. Neither of the office chairs were occupied so she took a seat in one of them, folding her arms across her chest. She wasn't going anywhere.

Razor blew out a sigh, but he didn't say anything. When Hero returned with Snow, Axel, and Ryder, they all got to work.

Chapter Eight

Anya

The fluorescent lights above the gas station buzzed, the bright evening sun casting a dull, orange glow over the pavement as it sank into the horizon. The old station was little more than a couple of pumps, a rundown convenience store, and a dimly lit payphone that looked like it hadn't worked in a decade. Beyond it, the Virginia twilight stretched in all directions, dense woods pressing in around them like a trap waiting to spring.

Anya clenched her arms around herself, trying to ward off the cold -- not from the night air, but from the ice creeping into her bones. Jackson sat on the tailgate of Vendetta's truck, his face tight with pain as he stripped off his jacket, revealing the blood-streaked gash along his forearm.

"You were shot?" Anya moved closer to inspect his wound. It wasn't deep, but it looked bad. The bullet had grazed him during the ambush at the industrial park, leaving a nasty tear in his skin. Blood dripped from his elbow, painting dark streaks along his forearm.

"It's fine," Jackson muttered. "Just a scratch."

Vendetta snorted, filling the gas tank on the other side of the truck. "Yeah? Well, you're still bleeding all over my damn tailgate."

Anya ignored them both, grabbing the first-aid kit Vendetta had found in the truck when they stopped to get gas. She ripped it open, hands shaking as she pulled out a bottle of antiseptic and some gauze. "Hold still," she ordered, voice sharper than she meant it to be.

He didn't flinch when she pressed the soaked

gauze to the wound, but his jaw clenched.

Anya's hands moved with steady precision, her fingers deftly cleaning the wound without hesitation. She'd done this before -- too many times. The coppery scent of blood mixed with the sharp burn of antiseptic, but it didn't faze her. She knew the sting, the raw pain, the way flesh tore and healed. Years of patching herself up after Sebastian's punishments had taught her exactly how to handle wounds like this. Her vision stayed clear, her stomach steady, as she focused on stopping the bleeding and making sure the injury wouldn't slow him down.

She was so damn tired. Tired of running. Tired of being hunted like an animal. Tired of feeling like no matter how far they went, Sebastian would always be a step ahead. Her breath hitched, and suddenly, she was crying. It hit her all at once -- the exhaustion, terror, the helplessness. Tears slipped down her cheeks before she could stop them, her hands trembling as she wrapped the bandage around his arm.

"I can't do this anymore," she choked out. "I can't keep running, Jackson. It never stops. No matter where I go, who I become, it always catches up to me."

Jackson went still, his pale blue eyes locking onto hers. "Why weren't you there the next morning? You never told me."

"The night you found me in Memphis was supposed to be my first night," she said trying to speak through tears of fear and frustration, "as a high-end escort. That man you killed? He was supposed to take me to Sebastian. I just didn't know it yet. That's why you didn't see me the next morning. I ran. I ran from Sebastian for *years*. It wasn't until a couple of years ago that he finally caught up with me. I expected he was going to kill me… You know, for making him look bad.

No, it was worse… Men want what they can't have."

"I can't fault him for wanting you," Jackson told her, his voice rough but steady. Before she could pull away, he caught her wrist and tugged her toward him. "But it's not going to save him. We're almost there. Just a few more hours and we'll be in Mercy."

Anya shook her head, chest tight with fear. "And then what?" she demanded. "You think Sebastian's just going to let this go? You think he's not already planning his next move?"

"No," Outcast admitted. "But he's gonna find out real quick that the Hounds don't play defense. We end this." His grip on her tightened, not in restraint, but in reassurance. "You're not alone in this, Anya. You never were."

Anya closed her eyes, pressing her forehead against his. She wanted to believe him. She *needed* to.

A low throat-clearing interrupted them, and they turned to see Vendetta watching, arms crossed. "Hate to break up the moment, but we may want to split up," he said. "Sebastian's men are still on our asses."

Jackson straightened immediately, already shaking his head. "No."

Vendetta held up his hands. "Look, I get it. But Sebastian's looking for the two of you together. If we split up, we buy more time. You two take the bike. I'll keep the truck, lead them in the opposite direction. I'll veer off 100."

"Right now," Jackson told him, "You're the only backup I've got."

Anya's stomach dropped. "That's not necessarily true." Pulling out Jackson's phone, she handed it to him. Would he be angry with her for interfering? Had she just messed everything up?

Jackson skimmed the texts between her and

Deva. His blue-eyed gaze was on her in a second. "I'm sorry," she said.

"Don't be," Jackson told her, with something like relief crossing his features. To Vendetta he said, "The Hounds are on the way for us."

"All right then," Vendetta told them. "I'll draw 'em off. You two head on to your brothers."

"Thank you," Anya told him. She knew he'd expect their help in the future when the time was right. But she was still grateful.

Vendetta nodded to her. To Jackson, he said, "I'll be in touch."

Jackson nodded, a silent agreement. "Thanks, man." They shook hands before getting Jackson's bike out of the truck bed. They needed to get back on the road and fast. "Be careful."

Anya swung her leg over the bike behind Jackson, wrapping her arms tightly around his waist as the engine rumbled to life beneath them. The road stretched ahead, dark and uncertain, but at least they were moving -- no more hiding, no more waiting for the next blow to land. As Jackson pulled out onto Route 100, she felt him shift slightly, his hand pulling his phone from his pocket for the briefest second. A message. The tension in his body eased as he read it, but he didn't say a word. Instead, he slipped the phone away, revved the throttle, and took off down the highway, leaving nothing but the roar of the engine and the question burning in her mind.

* * *

Outcast

The night stretched ahead of them, endless and cold, the highway a black ribbon cutting through the Virginia wilderness. Outcast's hands tightened on the handlebars as the wind whipped past them, sharp enough to sting. Anya held onto him, her body pressed against his back, and he could feel the slight tremor in her arms. She was exhausted. Hell, they both were. But they weren't far now.

His phone buzzed again in his pocket, a reminder of the text he'd read minutes ago. Safe house secured. Coordinates sent. Hounds would be waiting. He hadn't told Anya yet -- not because he was keeping her in the dark, but because every mile between them and the industrial park ambush felt like another breath of relief, another step toward keeping her out of Sebastian Six's grasp for good.

A few more miles. Just a little longer.

The bike's headlight cut through the darkness, illuminating the worn asphalt as they approached the outskirts of a small town. Outcast spotted a flickering neon sign up ahead -- *Dino's Gas & Go*. It wasn't much, just a single pump and a rundown convenience store, but it was enough. They needed to stop, to warm up, to regroup.

Easing off the throttle, he pulled into the lot, the gravel crunching under his tires. The place looked abandoned, but the faint hum of lights inside the store told him otherwise. He killed the engine, the sudden silence almost deafening after hours of riding.

Anya hesitated behind him before climbing off, rolling her shoulders like she was trying to shake off the cold. "Are we stopping for long?" she asked, her voice quiet but steady.

"Just long enough to get gas and check in," Outcast said, swinging his leg over the bike. "We're close now."

She nodded, rubbing her hands together for warmth as he pulled out his phone. He checked the address again, committing it to memory before sending a quick text back to let the Hounds know they were almost there.

Once they'd gassed up, they got back on the road stretching out before them and winding through the Virginia countryside, dark and desolate. The only sound was the steady hum of the engine. Outcast kept his eyes on the road, scanning the tree line on either side. Too many places for someone to hide out here. Too many ways this could go sideways.

Anya's arms were tight around his waist, her cheek resting against his back, her body warm despite the cold. He could feel the tension in her grip, the way her fingers curled into his jacket. She was holding on, not just to him but to the hope that this safe house was exactly what they needed it to be -- safe.

The miles blurred together in the darkness, the moon occasionally breaking through the thick clouds overhead, casting pale light across the landscape. The town had long since faded behind them, replaced by dense woods and open fields, the occasional farmhouse set back from the road, windows glowing like distant beacons.

At last, Outcast spotted the turnoff. A narrow gravel road cut through the trees, nearly invisible if you didn't know to look for it. He slowed the bike, tires skidding slightly as they hit the loose rock. The path was lined with gnarled oaks, their bare branches reaching overhead, forming a tunnel of shadows that swallowed them whole as they made their way deeper in.

Then, up ahead, the house came into view. A modest, two-story structure, its wooden siding weathered by time. A single porch light burned, casting a dim yellow glow over the steps. Two bikes were parked out front -- Ryder's and Axel's. A dark SUV was pulled off to the side, half-hidden by the trees. The place wasn't much, but it had been reinforced. Heavy blackout curtains covered the windows, and a new security camera perched just above the front door, its red light blinking. Likely Snow's handiwork.

Outcast cut the engine and let the silence settle around them. He felt Anya shiver behind him, but she didn't move to climb off. For a moment, neither of them did. The weight of the past twenty-four hours hung between them, thick and heavy. The front door creaked open. A figure stepped out onto the porch, broad and imposing. Razor.

Outcast exhaled slowly. They'd made it. Helping Anya off the bike, he kept her close, knowing she was cold. "Long day?" Razor asked with a tired grin, his gaze moving from him to Anya who stiffened next to him.

"Sure the fuck was," Outcast told his Prez. "Razor, this is Anya."

Razor nodded to her. "Glad to finally meet you. Glad you both got here in one piece."

Something occurred to him. "Deva's not here, is she?"

Razor chuckled. "Better get your asses in there."

As soon as Outcast and Anya stepped inside, the warmth of the safe house wrapped around them like a blanket, but they barely had a second to take it in before a blur of motion in black clothes with purple hair came flying toward them.

"Jackson!" Deva slammed into her brother, nearly knocking him off balance, her arms wrapping around him so tightly it was like she was trying to merge into his skin. Outcast barely had time to brace himself before she buried her face in his chest, her breath hitching with emotion.

"Jesus, Deva," he muttered, arms coming up to return the embrace. "I'm fine."

She pulled back just enough to glare at him, her eyes flashing. "You are not fine! You disappeared without a word -- again! And I had to hear from Razor what kind of mess you got yourself into! Do you have any idea how worried I was?"

Before Outcast could answer, Deva shifted her attention to Anya, her expression softening as relief flooded her face. Without permission, Deva pulled the cap off her head to reveal her coppery hair. "Anya?" Anya barely had time to process before she was wrapped up in Deva's arms, the smaller woman hugging her fiercely. "You're okay. God, I was so scared for you."

It took Anya a second to react, but when she did, she hugged Deva back, unshed tears making her eyes shine. No hesitation, no judgment -- just warmth and relief.

"I can't believe you're here," Deva continued, pulling back just enough to get a good look at her. "I didn't know if I'd ever see you again."

Anya swallowed hard. "Me either. You're all grown up. You're so beautiful."

"I'm pretty well looked after. You will be too." Deva's gaze flicked between them, her sharp mind already piecing things together. "You guys have a hell of a lot to catch up on." She shot her brother another glare before shaking her head. "But first, you're sitting down, and I'm getting you both something to eat."

Outcast let out a heavy sigh but didn't argue. There was no point -- Deva was like a force of nature when she got like this.

Razor, who had been leaning against the doorframe, arms crossed, smirked. "Told you she wouldn't take no for an answer."

Anya glanced up at him in time to see him roll his eyes, even while he let Deva lead them further into the house. For the first time since they'd made their escape, Outcast felt something settle in his chest. They weren't safe yet. But they weren't alone either.

"Hey, man!" Axel flashed him a smile as he took a seat at the kitchen table, next to Anya. Ryder, his identical twin, came up behind him, relief showingin his steely blue eyes as he looked them over.

"Anya, this is Axel and Ryder," Deva explained. "Guys, this is Anya."

Deva served them takeout burgers and fries while Razor passed everyone cold bottles of beer. Once they all sat around the table, Anya almost looked too tired to eat but she went through the motions, listening as they talked. Considering everything she'd been through, he was proud of the way she was holding up.

"What happened to your face?" Ryder asked before taking a swig of his beer.

Outcast let out a low grunt, pausing mid-bite as he wiped the corner of his mouth with the back of his hand. "Ran into a door."

Axel snorted from where he sat, arms crossed over his chest. "Yeah? Door have fists?"

Outcast smirked, but he knew the bruises on his jaw and the dried cut along his cheekbone made it look more like a wince. "Something like that."

Anya glanced his way before turning toward Axel. "It was an underground fight club run by a psychopath. That's what happened to his face."

Ryder's brow shot up as he glanced between Outcast and Anya, putting the pieces together. "Jesus.

That was your way of getting her out?"

Outcast set his burger back on the plate. "It worked, didn't it?"

Razor, quiet up until now, exhaled sharply, giving Outcast a measured look from across the table. "Barely."

Anya swallowed hard, burger in hand hovering over her plate, fingers tense. She looked up, her voice steady despite the exhaustion in her eyes. "If he hadn't done what he did, I'd still be there."

Ryder let out a slow whistle. "Shit." He shook his head, rubbing a hand over his jaw. "You really did go full berserker mode, huh?"

Outcast smirked. "Did what I had to."

Razor leaned back in his chair, his expression unreadable. "And now we have to deal with the fallout."

Silence stretched between them, heavy with unspoken weight. Anya's hand trembled as she put the burger down. Outcast reached out, placing his hand over hers.

Deva broke the moment with a sigh, pushing away from the table. "Well, that explains why you look like hell." She met Anya's gaze, softening. "But you're here. Both of you. That's what matters."

Anya gave a small nod, as Outcast cut his president a look.

Axel cracked a smirk. "So… does this mean we get to hear about how you kicked some guy's ass in a cage fight?"

Outcast chuckled, shaking his head. "Eat your damn food, Axel."

Razor set his beer down, his hazel eyes locked on Outcast. "Now tell me -- who the hell is Sebastian Six, and what does he have to do with Victor Grayson?"

Outcast sighed, running a hand down his face. His knuckles were still raw from the fight, and the ache in his ribs reminded him of everything they had barely escaped. He didn't want to do this. Not right now. But Razor wasn't the type to wait for answers.

"Sebastian Six is higher up than Grayson," Outcast said finally, meeting his president's gaze. "Maybe the top. And he's worse. Grayson tried to build something in Mercy, on Six's behalf. Sebastian's the real thing -- wealthy, connected, ruthless. His operation runs through the South like a Goddamn disease."

"Trafficking?" Razor asked.

Anya, sitting stiff beside Outcast, flinched at the word. He could feel the tension radiating off her.

Outcast nodded. "Among other things. Cage fights, weapons, drugs, laundering. He's got his hands in everything dirty you can imagine. He backed Grayson when he came to Mercy, probably saw an opportunity to expand. When we burned Grayson's little empire to the ground, we didn't just piss off the men running it -- we pissed off the one funding it."

Axel exhaled sharply. "Jesus."

Deva, arms crossed, narrowed her eyes. "So what does this mean for us? For Mercy?"

Outcast shook his head. "I don't know. It's been weeks since we shut down Grayson's operation and we haven't heard a word."

"Except the gun deal," Axel pointed out. "Was that tied to this guy?"

Meeting his gaze squarely, Outcast said, "It was."

"So they *haven't* forgotten about Mercy." Razor scrubbed his hand over his beard. "They wanted to see what type of hardware we're peddling."

It was likely true. And if so, that meant they hadn't heard the last of Six and any henchmen like Grayson. Six would care about his losses. And Anya. He wouldn't let any of it slide. He'd come back for them. For *her*.

Out of the corner of his eye, he didn't miss the terror forming on Anya's face. Razor saw it too. For a moment he studied her, and she was just wilting under that intent stare. "Who are you to Six?" Razor asked her.

Dropping her gaze, she seemed to be struggling with what to say. He was about to answer for her, but she finally met Razor's gaze. "I ran from Sebastian for years, but he finally caught me. And for the last two years I --"

"It doesn't matter," Deva cut in forcefully, staring Razor down. "She's been our friend since I was a child. Jackson has been looking for her for years. She's with *us*."

Razor's hands went up defensively, trying not to crack a smile at the ferocity of his woman. "She *is* with us. That was never up for debate. I just needed to know." Then he did smile. "Took the man's woman out from under him, huh?"

"I was more like… property," Anya added, her gaze on the burger she'd stopped eating.

Wrapping an arm around her shoulders, Outcast pressed a kiss into her hair. Yeah, the evil fucker had put her through a lot, and she'd barely told him anything so far. To Six, she was property. To him, she was *everything*. And he didn't care who he had to fight to make sure she knew that.

Color rose in Deva's face. "I'll cut his fucking heart out."

Razor steepled his fingers, nodding slowly, still

grinning. "All right. That tells me where we stand. Now who was it that helped you, and what the hell he wants in return?"

Outcast smirked, rubbing the back of his neck. "That's the fun part."

Axel and Ryder exchanged looks. Even Deva leaned in a little.

"Vendetta's a Cottonmouth," Outcast started. "He's from the Abingdon chapter, and he's got a big fucking bone to pick with Eli Crizer and the chapter in Oak Grove."

"Who the fuck doesn't?" Ryder asked.

Razor's jaw ticked at the mention of Eli. The Oak Grove Cottonmouths had been a thorn in the Hounds' side for too long. Yeah, the Cottonmouths had helped them out against the mafia fucks that came to hit Mercy over Sadie, Axel's old lady. But they'd also put his daughter Jade in danger, then came after their chapter of the Hounds in their own clubhouse until Eli put a stop to it. Not one of them was worth a damn.

"According to Vendetta, the Oak Grove boys are in talks with Sebastian and his bunch to set up shop on their turf," Outcast continued. "They want to be part of his network. Probably already are."

Axel cursed under his breath. "Are you fucking kidding?"

Outcast shook his head. "Says he doesn't want to be part of an MC that sells people," Outcast said. "He got kicked out of their chapter a while back. They did a number on him. Can't say I blame him. But he doesn't have the numbers to take them on alone."

Razor's eyes darkened. "And what does he want from us?"

Outcast shrugged. "Support. When the time comes, he wants the Hounds to back him when he goes after Oak Grove. In return, he helped us get here. And he kept Sebastian's men off our backs for as long as he could."

Silence stretched over the table. Razor leaned back, drumming his fingers on the wood, deep in thought. Finally, he exhaled. "This shit just keeps getting deeper," he muttered. "But it's good to know where the pieces are moving."

Deva looked between them all. "What now?"

Outcast's grip tightened around his beer. "Now? Now we get ready. Because I guarantee you, Sebastian isn't done with us yet."

"When we get done with him," Razor said slowly, "he'll wish he was."

Chapter Nine

Anya

"I found some extra blankets," Deva called out before stepping into the bedroom, arms full of neatly folded fabric.

Anya had just finished drying her hair from the shower, the warmth of the water still lingering on her skin. Dressed in the fuzzy pajamas Deva had thoughtfully provided, she felt the comfort of something soft and clean for the first time in what felt like forever.

She hadn't seen Deva since she was a child, but Anya hadn't been lying -- she really had grown into a beautiful woman. Yet, with her bright purple hair framing her face in soft waves, Deva still had that youthful energy Anya remembered about her. Dressed in gray sweatpants and a black T-shirt, she could have easily passed for a teenager, but Anya knew better. Deva had to be close to thirty now.

A glimpse of ink peeked out from the collar of her shirt, a delicate web of butterflies curling around her left wrist in black and deep blue accents. Deva placed the small stack of blankets on the bed before giving Anya an approving once-over. "Those look great on you. I get too hot when I sleep to wear fuzzy PJs or flannel, but I'm glad someone can use them."

Her easy smile made Anya's chest tighten. This was a woman she had once considered a little sister. And now, here they were, meeting again in a way neither of them could have ever predicted.

"Thank you," Anya said, sitting on the edge of the bed as Deva settled beside her. The low hum of voices and occasional bursts of laughter drifted up the stairs from the men gathered downstairs.

Deva smirked, tilting her head toward the sounds. "He's down there telling a tall tale," she said. "Something about fighting some massive guy named Goliath and, at the end of it, you were handed off to him. Any of that true?"

"Every word," Anya admitted. "If he hadn't claimed me for the night, I would have been given to Goliath instead. That's why he did it."

All the humor drained from Deva's face, her expression tightening with a mix of anger and sympathy. "Jesus," she whispered. "Are you serious?"

Anya nodded. The truth was best.

Deva exhaled sharply. "This was the main guy? Sebastian Six?"

"That's him."

"Did he… do that a lot?"

"No," Anya replied, shaking her head. "That was the first time. It was a punishment. I'd been flirting with one of his men; just a guy who ran errands, drove cars, provided muscle when needed. I thought if I could convince him I loved him, maybe he'd help me get out. But then he got sent to meet the Hounds about a gun deal… and he was killed. Sebastian accused me of having something with him, so…"

Deva's jaw clenched. "That man had a picture of you," she said. "Of the tattoo on your back. Which, by the way, is beautiful. When Jackson saw it, he lost his mind. Snow -- he's our VP -- said Jackson had the guy's wallet and phone. That was all it took. He left Friday, no warning. I was scared out of my wits… But I get why he did it. He never forgave himself for what happened that night. At the Lorrys'."

That name sent an icy jolt through Anya's veins. Gene Lorry was dead -- he couldn't hurt her anymore. But trauma had a way of settling deep, no matter how many years passed. Jackson had been the one bright light in that house, the only real hope she'd had. He'd fought for her, and she'd given him her heart in the darkest time of her life.

"You know, he never talks about it," Deva admitted. "We've never talked about that night, not once. I can't say I remember everything, but I remember you. And Jackson? He never got over you."

Anya swallowed against the lump in her throat. "We were just kids," she murmured. "And he tried to help me. There's nothing he needs forgiveness for."

Deva gave her a knowing look. "Good luck telling him that."

"Good luck telling me what?" Jackson's voice surprised them from the doorway. He looked as tired as Anya felt.

Deva got up from the bed, giving Anya a hug. "I'll let you two talk about that," she said. She hugged her brother. "Goodnight. We're in the bedroom next door."

"Goodnight," Anya called as Outcast closed the door behind Deva as she walked out.

He looked exhausted, but she couldn't help but smile as he shrugged out of his jacket and walked toward the bed. "What will you need luck for?"

Jackson pulled off his T-shirt, and Anya's smile faltered. She winced at the sight of him. His torso was a canvas of deep bruises and healing cuts, the dark ink of his tattoos only making them look more menacing. The injuries, stark against his pale skin, added to the dangerous energy that already clung to him like a second skin. All she could do was stare as he sat down next to her.

"It looks a lot worse than it feels, okay?" Jackson cupped her face in one of his hands, his touch careful.

"It always looks worse when it's healing. Don't worry about it."

Carefully, she traced her fingers around the deep bruises at his ribs. How did that *not* hurt like hell?

"Did it feel good to get a shower?" he asked with a smile.

"It did," Anya told him, but her mind was still on her conversation with Deva.

"You didn't answer my question," he prompted softly. "What were you and Deva talking about?"

"The past," she admitted, shaking her head. "Look what you've put yourself through for me, Jackson. Look at *you*. You've been running for days with little sleep and covered in bruises and wounds. Now your club is involved, your friends and family. Sebastian is coming for us. No one steals from him or makes him look like a fool. *No one*. I'm not worried about myself… I think I'd always resigned myself to the fact that if I couldn't find a way out, well, he'd eventually kill me. But if something happens to you or to Deva or to anyone close to you, I don't know if I can live with that. I'd rather live on in your head as a bittersweet memory and know that you were happy and safe somewhere."

A tear escaped the corner of her eye as she talked; he brushed it away with a rough thumb. "You were never in my head. You've always been *here*." Jackson pointed to his heart. "I never stopped looking for you after Memphis. I've looked for you for years. And I thought, even if she hates me when I find her, even if she's found someone else, I have to make sure she's safe. Happy… I guess if you were running from him, I know why I couldn't find you."

"Why would I have ever hated you?" Anya didn't understand.

"You saw me kill that man." His gaze was intense on her, like he was willing her to understand. "Just for putting his hands on you. But that's who you are to me. I've loved you since the minute I met you in that hellhole we tried to escape from. It never went away for me, Anya. I need you to understand that. I would do *anything* for you."

Anya remembered that night so clearly. That last night she'd spent with him had been a sacred memory she'd clung to when life while running from Sebastian -- or being with him -- became a nightmare. Some nights, it had been all she had left to hold onto.

"You said you ran from him," Jackson said. "How did he know about you in the first place?"

It was a fair question. It wasn't lost on her that he hadn't yet asked what happened to her when they were taken from Gene Lorry's custody. Was he afraid her story would get worse? She didn't want him to shoulder more responsibility than he already had.

"I got lucky in my next foster home," Anya said slowly. "You remember Moira Downing? I think she tried to help me because of the… miscarriage. I didn't say anything about him attacking me at the time. I was afraid there was a chance I could be sent back there. To *him*. He denied doing anything to me. Said he was concerned because of how sexually active you and me were. I lost it a couple of days later and since I was still in the shelter, she came by to talk to me. I told her the truth then. I don't know if they went after him. I just know he's dead now. And I was sent to a nicer home with good foster parents. They were a little religious, but they were genuine. They were also fostering Lisa. I made friends with her."

Jackson listened intently, taking her hands in his as he did.

"She turned eighteen before I did," Anya went on. "She went all the way to Nashville because she wanted to be a singer. She was really talented. I didn't turn eighteen for a few more months. Once I did, she called me. She had a job and an apartment, so I went out there to live with her. At first, all I knew was that she made a lot of money, and she had a beautiful tattoo on her back -- a nightingale. For a few months, life was good."

Jackson didn't say anything, just listened.

"She said she was singing at a bar called *Inferno,*" she explained. "She said they were looking for bartenders and I should apply. So I did. I got hired on the spot and it came with one of those beautiful tattoos. There was a lot I didn't know." Taking a deep breath, her hands squeezed his. "My first night working there, I saw that Lisa was actually a stripper. I tried not to make a big deal of it because I didn't want to hurt her. I showed up for my training and I was just sitting at a table off to the side and I was so confused. I didn't know I was waiting to be taken to Sebastian. That's when I saw you."

A smile played around his lips as he shared her memory. The moment she spotted him was the first time she'd felt real happiness since the last time she saw him. It gave her hope.

"That night… at the *Inferno,* when I saw you again, it felt like fate. Like somehow, after everything, I was given a second chance. I was terrified, but for the first time in so long, I was happy." She swallowed hard, forcing herself to keep going. "Spending the night with you… Jackson, I can't even explain what that meant to me. But it didn't last."

She took a deep breath, bracing for the worst part. "Lisa called me sometime after midnight. She was frantic, begging me to come to her. I knew something was wrong, but I didn't realize how bad until I got there. Marco Santoro had been one of Sebastian's men, and someone told them he was dead. They didn't know who did it… but it wasn't hard to figure out. His job was to bring me to Sebastian, and I was with someone else that night."

She gripped his hands tighter. "They told me Lisa would die unless I gave up the name of the man who killed him." Her throat tightened, but she forced the words out. "I couldn't. I wouldn't. So, they killed her in front of me."

Outcast cursed under his breath, but she barely heard it over the pounding in her ears. The heartbreak of that memory broke over her, raw and painful.

"That's when I agreed to be Sebastian's to save my own life. And I know he thought he'd be able to get the name of the man who killed Santoro from me. Of course I knew that." She shook her head, her voice turning hollow. "It didn't even matter. I found a way out by sunrise. I'm still not sure how I pulled that off. I thought I had escaped him for good… but he never stopped hunting me."

Her voice broke, and for the first time in years, she let herself feel the crushing weight of it all. Of what had been stolen from her. Of the guilt that had never let her go. She had survived, but at what cost? Jackson held her while she cried, letting out all the fear and tears she'd kept at bay for literally years. There with him, the fear seemed to fade into the distance. It was just her and him. It felt like that's where she was always supposed to have been. It was like breathing again after being deprived of air.

Anya didn't know if she kissed him, or he kissed her. She didn't care. They were together in the moment, no longer alone. Deva was there, his MC brothers. For a night, they could hold back the storm. For a night they could let it all go.

Jackson's hands smoothed over her back and into her hair as she deepened the kiss, needing him closer. She was careful with her own hands because of his many wounds but if anything hurt, he didn't let on. His hands clutched at the hem of her fuzzy pajama top, pulling it up and off to get his hands and mouth on her breasts. Pulses of pleasure ran through her bloodstream as his lips and tongue teased one nipple while he teased the other with the rough pad of his finger. He made them tighten into points that ached and craved more of his attention. And he took his time with her, making her feel like she was the only thing in his world.

Her fingers slid into his hair, tugging because she knew he loved that. He moaned around the tight peak of her flesh, and she felt it all the way down to her core. Her panties were already soaked, her thighs clenching in need as he teased her and made her crave him even more. When he lifted his head to claim another kiss, Anya let him move her to the center of the bed. And he was everywhere.

Jackson peeled off her panties and pajama bottoms with haste and then dove for her with his mouth. It was all she could do to keep quiet as he lashed her clit with his tongue and twisted in her folds, tasting her, until her fists tightened in his hair, and her back arched off the bed. It was like her body couldn't decide if it wanted more of his attention or if it was too much. Honestly, she didn't care. It felt like her blood was heating up, flowing to her pussy where she needed relief from all the sensations in the worst way. She'd only been with Jackson a couple of times in bed, but she was quickly learning that he knew exactly how to take her apart, to shake her to her foundations until all she saw was him. All she needed was him.

Jackson moaned against her wet folds, and he almost made her come from that alone. There was heat in those ice-blue eyes as he glanced at her from between her thighs. She pawed at his head, the bedding, her own breasts as he pushed her closer to the edge. Tugging on his wrist, she tried to get him to relent because she wanted to feel him inside her, to be joined with him. But Jackson wasn't going to be deterred. He worked her with his mouth until release broke over her. The lusty high she was riding raced through her veins, had her covering her face with a pillow to keep his sister Deva next door from knowing what he was doing to her, how he claimed her.

His smile was wicked as he pulled the pillow away, settling himself on top of her. He'd shed his jeans at some point, and he took himself in hand, sliding the swollen head of his cock through her wet folds. It was just another tease, and he knew that, the smile he wore one that reminded her of the boy that was her first love.

"You ready?" he whispered as he began to push into her.

"Always," was all she could whisper.

He wasted no time, sliding home inside her. It took her breath away, but it was everything she needed and wanted. Taking her hands in his, he pinned them to the bed on either side of her and slowly started thrusting. Careful strokes at first with him circling his hips to hit all the pleasure points inside her. He was warming her up. He dropped heated, wet kisses over her face and breasts, gentle in a way that his hips weren't. His thrusts gained speed and strength until she was panting for him, moving her hips with him, wanting everything he could give her. Without words, she begged him for all of it.

His lips blazed a trail across her face to her ear and then he started whispering the most sinful things as pleasure began building again in her lower body. Her walls clenched around him with each stroke as he whispered into her ear.

"You should have come back to me that night," Jackson whispered. "I would have taken you away. Anywhere... Because you were never his to take. You're *mine*. You've always been mine... I'll fuck you in front of him to prove that point and then, I'm going to make sure he never sees or thinks of you ever again."

His tone was ominous, but it also pushed her desire higher. Jackson had been through so much for her. He'd looked for her for years. She *was* his. Whatever he wanted, she'd give it to him. He still loved her, was drowning her in desire even though she'd fled from him too. Tears stung her eyes to think they could have been together all this time, happy and safe from the cruel dark world of Sebastian Six.

His hand carefully slipped between their bodies, his fingers working her clit delicately, a counterpoint to the way his hips pistoned into her, punching the air from her lungs with every thrust. Orgasm was chasing her hard as he kept going, and a beat before it caught her, in that split second where she was reaching for the pillow, Jackson's hand covered her mouth roughly and then he fucked her hard. Anya screamed beneath that hand as he kept going, unholy pride lighting up those pale blue eyes as he claimed her, drew her release out until she thought she might pass out.

Jackson chased his own end, his movements

inside her just short of painful until he came. And he was so beautiful at that moment with his eyes closed, his face relaxed, his lips parted. Reaching up, she traced her fingers over the side of his face, her breath rushing out in time with his. Collapsing onto the bed next to her, Jackson wrapped his arms around her, pulling her close.

"You can get a good night's sleep," he whispered against her hair. "We're safe tonight. And I swear to you, I'll keep you safe every night after this one."

There in his arms, with her head on his chest, she believed him. The pounding of his heart by her ear soothed her, easing her into sleep.

* * *

Outcast

The quiet hum of a phone pulled him out of sleep, had him looking around for the source. He had two phones; his was on the nightstand but the sound wasn't coming from there. Anya's eyes were wide on his as he climbed out of bed, listening. Fishing his jacket from the floor, he noticed the hum came from one of his pockets. He pulled out the burner phone Vendetta had given him at the industrial park just before Six's men arrived, glancing at the unknown number flashing across the screen. He already knew who it was.

"Yeah," he said, his voice still rough from sleep.

"They found me," Vendetta said, his tone tight with frustration. "Six's men. Cut me off outside Abingdon, roughed me up a little, but let me go. They had a message they wanted me to deliver personally."

Outcast exhaled sharply. "What is it?"

"Six wants you to meet him at the site of the gun deal. Just outside Oak Grove," Vendetta went on, "where it all began. Tonight, just before midnight."

Outcast's grip on the phone tightened. That was now enemy ground. Not just because of Six but because of the Oak Grove Cottonmouths. They weren't Sebastian's men, but they were aligned enough to make this a serious trap.

"How many did he bring?"

Vendetta scoffed. "A lot, brother. You're walking into a warzone."

"You plan on being there?" Outcast asked.

There was a pause. Then Vendetta sighed. "Yeah. I'll be there."

Outcast hung up. His jaw clenched as he stared at the wall. The weight of what was coming pressed heavily on his chest. He turned, his gaze landing on Anya where she now sat on the bed, knees drawn up, arms wrapped tightly around herself. She hadn't heard everything, but she'd probably heard enough.

"He's coming for me." It wasn't a question.

Outcast nodded, watching fear rein her in, dim her light.

"You're going, aren't you?" she asked quietly.

"I have to."

"No, you don't." She shook her head. "This is a death trap, Jackson. You know that."

He crossed the room in a few quick strides, sinking onto the edge of the bed beside her. His hands framed her face, thumbs brushing her cheekbones. "I know. But it ends tonight."

Her breath hitched, her hands smoothing over his chest. "Promise me you'll come back."

Outcast leaned in, pressing his forehead to hers. "I will. No one's taking me from you again."

He kissed her, slow, deep, possessive. When he pulled away, her lips were trembling, but she nodded.

She understood.

Outcast dressed in record time, pulling on jeans and a clean shirt with sharp, efficient movements. Every muscle in his body was tense, coiled with the weight of what was coming. He slid on his cut, feeling the familiar weight settle over his shoulders like armor before striding out of the bedroom and downstairs, leaving Anya to shower and get dressed.

Razor was already waiting, leaning against the edge of the kitchen table, arms crossed over his chest. Axel, Ryder, and Crash stood nearby, their conversation cut off the second Outcast entered. Their expressions hardened as they read his face.

"Six made his move," Outcast said, getting straight to the point. "They caught Vendetta outside Abingdon and turned him loose to deliver a message to me."

Razor's hazel eyes darkened. "What message?"

"Six wants me to meet him where the gun deal went to hell," Outcast answered. "Outside Oak Grove."

Axel scoffed. "That's a Goddamn trap if I've ever heard one."

Outcast agreed. "V said Six has a lot of men with him. So probably not a fair fight."

Crash ran a hand through his hair, shaking his head. "Of course not."

Razor finally pushed off the table, walking up to Outcast. "You're doing this?"

Outcast met his gaze without hesitation. "Yeah. But not alone."

Razor gave a sharp nod. "Damn straight you won't." He looked at the others. "We hit him hard and fast. No more games. No more waiting."

"Let's end this," Outcast said, his voice steel.

"One way or another."

The room fell silent, each man weighing what that meant. "I'll call Snow to rally the troops back home. The rest of you get your asses in gear. We roll out in an hour."

Outcast took a breath, pushing down the lingering dread in his gut. This was it. The final stand.

And one way or another, it would end tonight.

Chapter Ten

Outcast

The full moon lit up the empty road in a cold, menacing glow, casting long shadows from the towering trees on one side and the tangled overgrown field on the other. The air was crisp with coming spring, and the rising wind swept through the trees and the field as the Hounds of Hell waited, still and silent, ready for the outbreak of violence at any minute.

Outcast placed himself at the vanguard of their formation. Crash and Player, the two men he trusted most in the world, had his back. Razor, ever the strategist, took the position to his right. His hazel eyes were sharp, difficult to read in the moonlight as he scanned the area around them. Closer to the tree line, Snow and the twins waited, weapons ready, with Malachai behind them, hidden by the trees, his confident hands gripping his latest modified rifle. Beast and the rest of the Hounds, including a couple of prospects on the fast track to getting patched, completed the lineup. Each one of his brothers waited, fully prepared for whatever shitstorm Sebastian Six planned to rain down on them.

It was eerily quiet all around them, the only sound the approaching hum of engines. Outcast's heart sped up. The Hounds had met Six's crew here before for the fake gun deal -- they just hadn't known it at the time. It would end in the place where it started. *Tonight*. One way or another.

Bright headlights cutting through the darkness had Outcast straining to look in their direction. Two black SUVs and a couple of muscle cars pulled up across from them on the other side of the road, their low rumble hitting his ears like a warning growl. The doors popped open in seconds, almost synchronized. Outcast was taken aback to see Six himself step out of the back of one of the SUVs, his movements slow and deliberate. He moved with the confidence and arrogance of a man with an army at his back. At least he'd dressed for the occasion. No suits tonight, just jeans, a collared shirt, and a jacket that would still stand out in their rural setting. The menace flashing in the man's dark gaze was hard to miss.

The men following him looked like mercenaries. There were at least twenty of them, spilling out from the vehicles, armed and vigilant. Outcast kept his hand at his side by a gun. Taking a deep breath, he steadied himself. He wouldn't allow impulse to put them all in more danger than they were already in.

Razor stepped forward, matching the controlled stance of Six and announcing himself as the Hounds' leader. "Let's get on with it," he called, his voice calm and steady.

Six smiled but it didn't reach his eyes. "Appreciate you boys meeting us here again," he said, his tone pure sarcasm. "Nice little reunion spot, don't you think? Brings back memories. Like how you took out several of my men."

"Memories, huh?" Razor scoffed. "Like setting up a fake gun deal to take out several of my men and steal hardware from us?"

"Look, I'm a reasonable man," Six said, gesturing at Outcast. "How about a trade? I want Anya back." The man's focus shifted to Razor. "And I want Jackson here. Or is it *Outcast*? I get the two of them, and the rest of your club walks away."

Outcast's fists clenched at his sides. He knew what the bastard *really* meant. Six wouldn't just kill him. He'd kill Anya too. Feeling the weight of the man's gaze, he blew out a breath. It was a quick and easy offer on the surface, but his gut told him it wasn't going to be that easy. Six was too calm. Too at ease. He'd come all the way out here to confront the Hounds, putting himself in potential danger. As far as Outcast knew, the man was near the top of the food chain in their organization, way above Victor Grayson. Men in his position usually didn't show up for the grunt work.

Then trees rustled behind them. *Son of a bitch.* There it was. They weren't alone. The Hounds had their backs to the forest. But Six already had snipers in position there. A gust of wind carried the scent of gun oil and tension. Outcast's gaze cut to the tree line just as a faint metallic glint caught the moonlight -- a sniper scope. *Damn it.*

"Razor," Outcast muttered, just loud enough for his president to hear.

"I see 'em," Razor replied, but there was no panic in his voice. "Malachai?"

Malachai had melted deeper into the woods like a phantom the moment they arrived, just in case. Just to be prepared for anything. And it looked like anything was starting now.

"I got 'em," Malachai whispered into the comm clipped to his vest. "There's two."

Then, like fate pulled the trigger itself, Six gave the slightest nod. The first shot rang out. One of Six's men dropped out of a tree behind them, Malachai's shot dropping the bastard before he ever got a shot off.

"Down!" Razor barked.

And then all hell broke loose. Gunfire erupted from both sides, muzzle flashes lighting up the night like the Fourth of July. The Hounds dropped and scattered behind their bikes and beat up vehicles, returning fire. Bullets thudded into bark and dirt, pinged off metal. Six's men advanced, using the SUVs for cover, unleashing controlled bursts as they fanned into formation.

The field became a Goddamn warzone.

Ryder and Axel worked together, picking off targets, covering each other with near-perfect precision. Snow knelt low just ahead of them, firing with brutal calm, firing his pistol in rhythm. He scanned the trees between shots, keeping an eye out for the second sniper Malachai warned them about. Crash and Player flanked Outcast, covering him as he charged forward, tracking a shooter crouched behind a rear wheel and dropping him with one clean shot.

Then came the sharp *crack* -- different from the scattered semi-auto gunfire around them.

"Shit!" Malachai's voice rang out through the comm just before it cut out. Outcast's stomach dropped. Turning his head toward the tree line, he watched Malachai fall from his perch, his brother's shoulder a mess of blood, the rifle coming down with him. He'd live if they could help him quickly enough -- but he was out of this fight.

It was just the beginning.

Beast's roar of pain echoed across the field as a bullet tore through his thigh, spinning him backwards, behind cover. One of their prospects, a young kid named Cueball, wasn't as lucky. He caught two rounds center mass and crumpled next to Beast. Razor rushed over, dragging the kid into partial cover with Ryder and Axel laying down suppressing fire. Blood soaked the dirt beneath the kid in seconds.

"We're losing ground," Razor growled into his radio. "Regroup. Now! We need to --"

But then --

"Hold your fire!" The shouted words rang out like a death knell, followed by an eerie, surreal silence. All eyes turned to the road. A familiar-looking, blacked-out pickup rolled in slow and steady. One headlight out. Mud splattered across its hood. The driver's door opened, and out stepped Vendetta. Outcast's blood ran cold to see the Cottonmouth from Abingdon who'd helped him and Anya make it back to Mercy once everything went to hell.

Only this wasn't a reunion. The fucker had Anya. His girl's hands were bound in front of her, clothes streaked with dirt. She'd been roughed up, but she was alive. Her eyes were wide with fury, with terror, but she was silent.

It was all Outcast could do not to lose his mind. How the fuck did he get her? He'd left her with Deva and Margot at the clubhouse. There were a couple of soldiers left there to help. No way the fucker should have been able to march his happy ass in there and come up with Anya to serve her up here to Six. But since he had, what did that mean for his sister? Was Deva okay? Margot and the others?

Outcast exchanged a look with Ryder, and concern flashed in his brother's eyes.

Six smiled like the devil himself. "Well look who it is," he said, spreading his arms as if welcoming home a runaway pet. "I gotta admit, I wasn't confident you'd bring her back in one piece, Cottonmouth. I sure as hell owe you a drink."

Vendetta said nothing. He shoved Anya forward, and Six's men grabbed her. The Hounds froze. No one breathed.

Six's voice dripped with triumph. "It's over. I've got the girl. Outcast, I've got *you*. And now, you're going to watch every last one of your brothers die. And then I'll shoot you my-fucking-self." He turned to his men, pointing out Outcast like a king giving commands. "Kill everyone -- except him."

Outcast's heart thundered in his ears as the barrel of a gun pressed to Anya's back. Their eyes met across the clearing. Maybe for the last time. *This can't be it.* He'd finally found her, the only one he'd ever loved, only for them to die here. He mouthed her name.

Anya nodded. She had no tears, she wasn't begging. Lifting her chin, she showed strength in these final moments. Her silent way of telling him: *Don't give up, Jackson. Don't you dare give up.*

And that's when Vendetta moved. Spinning fast and fluid, he grabbed the pistol from the man holding Anya, shooting him point-blank in the face. In the same motion, he shoved Anya to the ground and dragged her behind his truck for cover, firing on Six's men as he moved.

"Now!" Razor bellowed. "Light these fuckers up!"

The Hounds didn't hesitate. The twins led the surge forward, gunning down anything that moved. Snow pivoted, taking out a shooter behind the SUV. At his signal, Crash and Player flanked left, covering Vendetta as he and Anya sprinted toward the Hounds' side of the skirmish.

Outcast didn't go for cover. He went for Six. The two of them locked eyes as the battlefield burned around them. Six pulled a pistol, his expression twisted with rage. Outcast drew at the same time. Two shots rang out together and time seemed to stand still.

Six stumbled backward. Outcast stood still. In the span of a heartbeat, Six's knees buckled. He dropped to the ground, clutching his stomach, blood seeping between his fingers. Rage faded to disbelief as he fell, as blood spilled from his lips as he gagged and coughed.

Outcast wasn't done. He stalked forward, jaw tight, chest heaving, and pointed his gun at Six's face. "You'll never hurt her ever again," he said, then pulled the trigger.

The final shot rang out, echoing into the calm that followed. A few of Six's men remained -- leaderless and confused -- and they were no match for anyone there. Vendetta, Razor, and the Hounds closed in fast, finishing the fight with brutal efficiency. A few surrendered, others scrambled off like cowards or men who were there for the paycheck and not the loyalty. The rest were dropped where they stood.

After the last shot was fired, Outcast sprinted for Anya. She was already standing, Vendetta cutting through her bonds. When she saw him coming, she didn't move. Outcast pulled her into his arms, holding her like he might never get the chance again.

"I thought I lost you," he whispered into her hair.

"You didn't," she whispered. "You never will."

Vendetta stood nearby, gun still in hand, watching the road for movement. His gaze met Outcast's and he gave a nod in silent understanding.

"For a minute there, I thought you sold us out," Outcast told him.

"I don't work for cowards," Vendetta muttered. "I used her to get close. She didn't make it easy."

Anya glared at him. "Damn right I didn't."

A wry smile touched the edge of Vendetta's lips. "You had to *believe* it, angel."

Outcast was so happy to have her finally safe from Six that he'd let it go. For now. Anya was safe in his arms and that was everything to him. She was the rest of his life.

The low hum of an engine approached fast, and they froze, watching a familiar SUV pull up. Its LED headlights were blinding in the dark, the doors flew open. Both women looked pissed. Margot stayed by the vehicle, evaluating the scene through her experience in law enforcement. His sister didn't give a fuck. She stormed out, gun in hand.

"Where the hell is she?" Deva asked, wild-eyed.

Anya stepped out from behind Outcast, still shaken, but very much alive.

"I'm right here," Anya called out.

Deva's knees nearly gave out in front of them. "Jesus, girl." Shoving her gun in her holster, she ran to Anya, purple hair flying, throwing her arms around her in a quick, tight hug. "Don't ever do that to me again."

"Believe me, I *won't*," Anya said, her voice firm even though she was shaking. She cut Vendetta another glare.

Vendetta winked at her, trying not to laugh. Outcast shook his head. If he had to guess, Vendetta must have caught Anya trying to make it to the battle and went from there.

"Take her back," Outcast called to his sister.

Deva nodded, stopping to talk to Razor for a second, then to kiss him before turning back to herd Anya toward Margot's SUV. Anya ran back to Outcast instead.

"I don't want to leave you," she whispered, still scared and riding high on adrenaline.

Pulling her close again, he pressed a kiss into her hair. "I won't be long. Go with Deva."

"We've got wounded," Razor called as Anya reluctantly did what he wanted and headed for

Margot's SUV. "Let's get everyone out of here. Cueball needs evac now."

Snow was already on the radio calling the clubhouse for backup.

The fight was over and Six was dead.

Anya was, at last, *his*.

The first light of dawn was heading for the horizon and Outcast joined in the effort to get his brothers the help they needed, to deal with the dead.

But the war? That wasn't over yet. Not by a long shot.

* * *

Anya

The next morning, she woke up in bed alone. Checking Jackson's phone on the bedside table, she saw it was afternoon. Where was Jackson?

The sun was bright, filtering through the window by the bed. She hadn't had much of a chance to look around Jackson's house when they'd arrived early this morning. Now in the light of day, she looked around the room. Stretching, Anya got up. She'd wore one of Jackson's shirts to bed, pulling on the sweatpants he found for her last night.

Jackson's bedroom was quiet. As if it had been waiting. The space was simple, masculine, and like the man himself, deliberate. Heavy, dark wood antique furniture anchored the room. It was the kind of furniture that had seen years but held its own. The wide, sturdy bed she'd just emerged from had a black quilted coverlet and sat against one wall, no unnecessary pillows or frills. Just enough for comfort.

On the other side, a tall chest of drawers stood beside a nightstand topped with a minimalist lamp and a weathered book on the art of tattoos. A framed black-

and-white photo of his old bike sat beside it, edges curled a little with time. The floor was clean, his boots lined neatly by the door, the faint scent of leather, soap, and something warm -- like cedar and ink -- lingered all around.

The walls were bare except for a few pieces of framed artwork -- tattoo flash sketches he'd done years ago. No awards. No photos of the club. Nothing flashy. Just pieces of his craft. Pieces of his soul.

It was the mirror above his dresser that stopped her in her tracks. Tucked into the frame, almost hidden if you weren't looking, were bits of the past he'd never let go of. As she took a closer look at them, she stared in wonder. Jackson and Deva had arrived at Lorry's house a few months after she ended up there. They'd lived there together for six months. She'd treasured the memories of that time, even with Lorry abusing her and showing interest in then ten-year-old Deva. Aside from the night she found him -- and left him -- in Nashville, Anya had always assumed that he'd probably moved on from her a long time ago.

The memorabilia he'd tucked into that antique mirror told a different story. There was a faded photo of her laughing with the sun in her hair, and she remembered that day. A movie ticket stub from the time they'd snuck away from the library club in high school and went to see a movie. She didn't even remember the film. She just remembered that they held hands the entire time. A tiny scrap of a napkin with her handwriting -- just her name and a heart. Old, sun-bleached, but kept safe behind the edge of the glass. A dried wildflower, delicate but intact.

Anya reached out, fingers brushing the edge of the photo, and her throat tightened with all the emotions she felt crashing in.

Jackson never said it. Not really. Not after all that time. But he didn't need to. It was still here. Every piece of her. Every memory.

He'd only ever loved one person.

And it had always been *her*.

"She's up," he said quietly from behind her. She'd never heard him approach.

And he'd caught her there, staring at the treasured items in the mirror, and tears threatened to spill from her eyes. Happy ones this time. For a moment, when his gaze met hers, he looked startled. When he followed the line of her gaze, the concern in his expression faded.

"After I left you in Nashville," she said, turning to face him, "I assumed you'd move on from me. And I'd wished that for you. I pictured you with a wife, maybe a couple of kids… I didn't exactly see you becoming a biker."

Jackson chuckled at that. He stood near the window, the morning light slanting across his bare chest, highlighting every single bruise, every scar. The sun didn't soften him; it revealed him. All of him. His fair skin showed deep purple bruises from the cage match with Goliath -- an angry welt along his ribs, a split knuckle wrapped in gauze. There were fresh cuts across his shoulder from last night's fight, raw and red against the ink that marked his skin like armor. The long, healing gash across his side still looked like it hurt. The story of everything he'd endured to keep her safe was there, marked on his body in ink and blood.

And it wasn't just his body that showed the toll. His eyes, pale blue but steady, held deep shadows. Jackson wasn't someone who showed pain easily, but she could see it so clearly now, in the set of his jaw, the slight hitch in his breath when he moved. It was all there in the way he stood, never resting, never relaxed -- just bracing.

And still, he looked at her like she was the only thing in the world that mattered to him. That would ever matter. Not the bruises. Not the blood. Not the broken parts inside him. Just *her.*

He was battered and worn to the bone. But he *was* standing. Still her protector. Still *hers.* And he always had been.

"A tattoo artist, yes. But more than that," Swiping at her tears with her fingers, she looked him over. "I remember your drawings. You used to draw when you couldn't sleep. They were so beautiful. I always pictured you working in some studio, displaying your works for small, snobby crowds. You were always so talented."

When she mentioned his drawings -- those quiet afternoons when he'd sketch, pretending not to watch her -- he didn't say anything at first. Something shifted in his expression. A flicker of raw emotion behind those tired eyes. He stepped closer, slow and quiet, reaching around her. His fingers curled around the worn handle of the bottom drawer, pulling it open with a low scrape. He fished a sketchbook out of it -- leather-bound, edges worn with time, the elastic band holding it together all frayed.

Without a word, he opened it and began flipping through its pages. Anya's breath caught. It took her a moment to realize that they weren't all drawings *of* her. The sketches were how he *saw* her. One showed her curled up on a couch, laughing at something unseen. In another, she sat cross-legged, lost in thought. She stood by a window in another, sunlight across her shoulders. One gave the perception of movement -- like she was caught mid-turn, hair swept up, eyes shining like she was about to say something important.

Anya had never posed for a single one. She glanced at the dates in the corners. Most were after Nashville. After she'd left him.

"You kept drawing me," she whispered.

Jackson nodded once. "I never stopped seeing you." His thumb paused on one sketch. She was sleeping in that one -- peaceful, soft, wrapped in sheets and just how she looked now.

"I drew that the night after Mercy," he said quietly, eyes on the page. "Didn't sleep. I just needed to remember you were really here."

Her throat tightened, eyes burning. She looked up at him. "How long have you been doing this?"

Jackson's gaze was so open it almost hurt. "Since you left that night in Nashville. Guess I just never figured out how to let you go."

She reached out and touched the edge of the page. Her likeness. His love. Still there. It had always been there.

"You never had to."

Carefully taking the sketchbook from his hands, she placed it on the top of the chest of drawers. Wrapping her arms around his neck, Anya kissed him, trying to pour every ounce of love, every measure of gratitude into that kiss. Their hearts beat in unison when he returned her kiss. There was no passion or seduction there. Just reverence, a promise of a future stretching out before them.

Finally, together, as they always should have been.

Player (Hounds of Hell MC 8)
A Hounds of Hell MC Romance
Jamie Targaet

I've played every game there is. But this time, it's for keeps.

Heather -- Brick promised me a good paying job. I didn't know he was working for a cartel. When their money goes missing, I'm hunted along with him, used, and finally left with the Hounds of Hell MC in Mercy to answer for *his* crimes. If not for Player, I would have wound up dead -- or worse. He claims me as his old lady to keep me from being turned over to the cartel. He shields me, fights for me. And somehow, I'm starting to believe I matter again. The cartel is still gunning for me, but Player's not backing down. He says I'm his, and I *want* to be. If we can survive this.

Player -- I'm called Player for a reason. My life's been a string of one night stands and bad decisions. Until Heather. She's scared and in over her head, but there's something about her I can't shake. When Brick leaves her in Mercy, running from the cartel he stole from, I make a choice. I don't care what she's done or what they think she knows. Heather's under my protection now. If anyone wants her, they'll have to go through me -- and every single brother I've got.

Chapter One

Player

The Hounds of Hell clubhouse sat at the far end of Main Street, past the reach of the twinkling lights and holiday carolers who'd turned Mercy's annual tree lighting into a full-blown event last night. Normally, the Hounds didn't bother with Christmas decorations because they were too much trouble, too much cheer. But this year was different.

Deva, Razor's old lady, made it clear even if the club wasn't going to feel like home, the place could at least look the part for the holidays. No one was going to tell the president's lady no. So now mismatched strands of blinking lights clung to the porch, a half-hearted apology, and the scent of pine fought to cut through layers of leather, smoke, and liquor. Inside, the mood was anything but festive.

Since Player had lost a bet, one he still claimed was rigged, he'd earned the honor of decorating the Christmas tree Deva had dropped off at the clubhouse the night before. The tree was still boxed in Razor's office, fake pine branches and all, along with a tub of lights, ornaments, and exactly one glitter-covered star Snow refused to touch.

Player had his hand on the doorknob, figuring he'd grab the box and let Razor know he was making good on his punishment. But then he paused, hearing Razor and Snow talking in low and clipped voices, the kind of conversation you didn't interrupt unless invited. Whatever was going down in there, it wasn't about garland or tinsel.

He heard the rumble of a bike pulling in out front. Curiosity made him let go of the doorknob and head for the front of the clubhouse to see who'd come calling.

The bike now parked out front belonged to Brick, a patch from the Mississippi chapter in Biloxi. From what he remembered, the guy was all swagger and no spine. Player didn't like him, but Brick had never been dumb enough to test anyone here directly. He'd visited Mercy a couple of times in the past, but he always had the good sense to fly under the radar.

A second rider dismounted, swinging one long leg over the back of the bike. A woman. No, not just a woman. A *vision.*

Her dark jeans clung to her, her boots dusted with grit from the road. A leather jacket hung too heavy on her slender frame. When she pulled off the helmet, she shook loose long, glossy dark spirals of hair. She turned her head enough for Player to catch a flash of wide green eyes and a full mouth. A woman who looked like *that* should be all sass and fire, but there was a wariness about her. Her gaze moved over the front of the clubhouse as though being there filled her with dread. She expected trouble.

Was she with Brick? How had he gotten a woman who looked *that* good? Brick looked like he'd crawled out from under a busted oil pan and hadn't changed his shirt since. He had a thick neck, and a gut stretching the bottom of his cut. He wore his hair slicked back, as if he thought he still had a full head of it. The man's nose was twisted from too many fights he probably hadn't won, and a mouth that curved like he was about to lie.

Brick turned and spoke to her. She nodded and followed him. There was a subtle shift in her posture. Her shoulders were tight. She was bracing for a fight.

Player wasn't buying those two as a couple. She didn't belong on the back of Brick's bike or in his bed unless money was involved. Staying in the shadows near the main entrance, he folded his arms and watched as Brick swaggered toward the clubhouse.

The main door opened, and Brick walked in with the woman, in time to see Razor and Snow walk back to the front of the house.

"Brick," Razor said, voice flat. "Didn't expect to see you."

Brick gave Razor a lazy grin. "I'm calling in that favor, brother. Need a place to crash for a while. Lay low."

Favor, huh? Player stepped toward the front door. Razor didn't do favors. Anyone who knew the man knew that. But Player had a pretty good idea what favor Brick was talking about.

Back when Sadie had first showed up in Mercy, before becoming Axel's old lady, they'd found a tracker on her car, put there by the abusive Mafia boyfriend she'd been running from. To throw him off, Ryder, Axel's twin, had driven the vehicle all the way to Mississippi. The Biloxi Hounds had been the ones to help him make the tracker disappear without a trace.

If that was the "favor" Brick meant, it wasn't much of one. Ryder wouldn't have needed a lot of help to lose the tracker. If Brick was desperate enough to stretch the truth about something like that, there was a lot more to why he'd shown up here with a woman on the back of his bike.

Razor's stare was ice cold. Apparently their president didn't like Brick any more than Player did. Player leaned against the wall, letting his presence be known. Brick's gaze moved toward him and back. Player smiled.

Razor looked Brick over like he was already sorting out the lie. "Funny," he said. "I don't remember owing you shit."

Brick tipped his chin up. "You don't, huh? What about when Ryder came down to Mississippi with that tracker you needed gone? Who do you think helped him ditch it in the bayou, so no one found it?"

Razor's gaze didn't so much as flicker. "I remember Biloxi helping him out. Didn't know that meant you specifically."

Brick gave a shrug meant to look casual. "I was there. Helped ditch the thing myself. Figured that kind of help might buy me a place to breathe for a few days."

"You think you're in the right place for that?" Razor's voice was low, dangerous.

Snow shifted beside him, arms crossed. Player watched the way Brick's gaze bounced between them, like he couldn't decide who'd swing first.

"You want a roof? I want answers," Razor went on. "Why you're here. What kind of heat's chasing you." Razor's hazel-eyed gaze shifted to the woman standing behind him. "And her? She yours?"

Brick gave a one-shoulder shrug. "Yeah. She rides with me."

"Didn't ask if she rode in with you. I asked if she's *yours*."

"Heather's with me," Brick said, a little more force in his voice now. "You don't need to worry about her."

"If she's under this roof, she's my business," Razor told him. "You want her here, then I need to know she's not a problem."

Brick chuckled without humor. "She won't be. She knows how to stay quiet."

Snow's jaw muscle moved. Their VP didn't like men who talked about women as if they were property. Not in his clubhouse. Not since he met his little blonde baker, Emily.

Snow remained silent, his gaze locked on Brick like he was already considering the consequences of dragging the fucker out by his dirty collar. Player felt the same way, and not only because Brick was an asshole. They'd all seen worse. What bothered him was the way the young woman with him stood behind him. She *was* keeping quiet, and she didn't look down or even move. Seemed she didn't want to draw attention. Was she afraid of something? The only thing he knew for sure about her was she didn't belong with a man like Brick. Player couldn't decide if that made her more interesting or more dangerous.

Brick's smile slipped. "Nothing big. Got caught in some noise down south. Figured I'd lay low for a bit. Okay with you?"

Razor stared at him for a long second, then tipped his head slightly. "That the best you've got?"

Brick chuckled. "Just a little heat. Wrong place, wrong time. A meet went bad, and one of their guys got in my face about her." He tipped his head toward Heather. "I handled it, but you know how it is… words get twisted."

Snow's expression didn't change, but Player caught the flash in his eyes -- *bullshit*. From the way Razor's jaw flexed, he'd heard enough too.

"Right," Razor said flatly. "We'll talk inside in my office. You'll tell me *everything*. And if I find out you left anything out…" He didn't need to finish the sentence.

"Understood," Brick said finally.

Their president stepped aside, but not because he trusted the man. Razor never made a move without knowing every angle first.

Brick slowly started walking down the hall toward Razor's office. The woman made no move to follow him. She stood near the door, hands at her sides, her eyes down. She didn't look afraid now. No, she simply waited. Like she was used to being left behind.

Snow glanced at Razor. "You want me to hang back?"

Razor shook his head. "Nah. Get over to the bakery and try on the damn Santa suit before Emily starts calling. If she has to chase you down again, we're all gonna hear about it."

Snow's jaw flexed as he gave the woman one last look. He nodded before walking out the door.

Razor turned to Player. "You're here to put the damn tree up, right?"

Player arched a brow. "Yeah. Why?"

"Go get all of everything out of the office." Razor said dryly. "Our guest can keep you company while you take care of that. Make sure she doesn't wander."

Player's gaze slid back to her. "Want me to entertain her?"

Razor's stare hardened. "I want you to *watch* her."

The president stayed out front, keeping their unplanned guest company with a silent, watchful presence while Player slipped down the hall to Razor's office. The artificial Christmas tree and the two overstuffed bins Deva had dropped off were stacked inside the door. He ignored Brick, who sat in one of the chairs like he owned the place, casually flipping through a magazine. Player grabbed the tree box and both bins, carrying them back through the hall. As he stepped into the common room again, Razor gave him a nod and headed for his office without a word.

For a long moment, the woman didn't say

anything and neither did Player. But she surprised him by looking directly at him, catching him off guard with her steady gaze. She looked so tired.

Player gave her a slow grin as he walked with the box that held the fake tree. "So. You got a last name, Heather?"

She hesitated long enough to make it clear she was deciding whether or not to answer. "Lynch."

He let the name roll through his head. Didn't sound like a club girl's name, or the name of someone who followed guys like Brick across state lines, either. Sounded like the name of someone who used to have roots, used to have something solid, before the road ripped everything up.

"All right, Heather Lynch," he said, while setting up the bottom of the tree. "You a runner? Or are you simply bad at picking men?"

Heather *really* looked at him then, with no smile or attitude. The same tired calm he'd read in those soft green eyes since she got off the bike. "I guess that depends," she said softly. "Which answer keeps me out of trouble?"

Player let out a whistle. "Damn. All right. You got a little bite under all the silence."

Heather didn't reply, but the corner of her mouth twitched as if she wanted to smile but hadn't done so in a long time.

"You planning to stay with *him* long?" Player asked, pulling out the middle section of the tree and snapping it onto the base.

"I wasn't planning to be here at all."

Her answer confirmed his suspicions. Watching her for a second longer, Player reached into the box for the top of the tree and locked it in place. "Looks like you're stuck with me for a little while."

"Lucky me," she said with no sarcasm, a soft murmur like she hadn't decided if he was a threat or a reprieve.

For the first time in a long damn while, Player wasn't sure either. He reached for the tub with the lights, grateful he had something to do besides stare at the little lady. She seemed uncomfortable enough. "So… if you weren't planning to be here, where were you headed?"

Heather's gaze moved to the door Brick had disappeared through. "Somewhere else."

"Not much of an answer."

"It's all I've got right now."

Player studied her. She wasn't giving him attitude, or defiance. All he saw was exhaustion that went deeper than the ride from Mississippi, and deeper than whatever excuse Brick was trying to feed Razor right now.

"You don't talk much," he pointed out, keeping his tone casual.

"But you do," she replied without missing a beat.

He grinned. "Yeah, but I've got a reputation to maintain. Part of the charm."

Heather looked at him again, those green eyes magnetic. "That what you're doing now? Being charming?"

He shrugged. "Nah. Just making conversation while I decorate this Christmas tree. Razor said to watch you, not interrogate you."

She surprised him by not letting the silence sit. "You're not doing either."

Her words weren't flirty or smart. She was being honest, and he liked that in a woman. She wasn't *his* woman. She might not even be an available woman. But Player shifted, intrigued. "You always this blunt?"

he asked.

"Only when I'm tired," she replied, watching him walk around the tree, wrapping the line of lights around it. "And surrounded by strangers."

"Brick's not a stranger though, right?" Player wanted to know the relationship there. She couldn't be with that guy.

Heather's jaw tensed. "No." Then she went quiet.

Player paused as he finished the first string of lights, his voice softer this time. "You scared of him?"

That got a reaction. Her gaze locked with his like she hadn't expected the question. Was it confirmation? A denial? Instead, she said, "Why are you asking?"

He shrugged again, reaching back into the tub for the rest of the lights. "I'm not great with sitting quiet when something doesn't feel quite right."

Heather's gaze lingered on him for a second longer than before. Was she trying to decide if she could trust him? Or did she see him as another wolf in a different leather cut?

"You're not what I expected," she murmured.

Player smirked. "Most people say that right before they fall for me."

This time, she did smile. Small, and barely there, but real, and her beauty came through like a flash of sun on a cloudy day. *Damn, she's a knockout.*

The door opened down the hall. Razor's boots echoed across the floor.

Heather's smile disappeared as if it had never been there. Something twisted in Player's chest. She'd only let her guard down for thirty seconds, and already she pulled it back up. He hated understanding exactly why. Whatever life she'd been living with Brick had taught her showing too much was dangerous. She'd learned smiles could be taken as invitations, words could be twisted and used against you. Better to stay neutral, unreadable, until you knew exactly where you stood.

Brick reappeared a moment later, nodding toward her like she was an afterthought. "C'mon."

Heather followed him toward the door without a word, her steps quiet, her face a mask again. Player stood there with a string of lights in his hands, watching as Brick led her out to the bike to grab their bags.

A shadow shifted behind him. Razor came up, silent as ever, stopping at Player's side. Together, they watched through the window as Brick swung a duffel off the back of his ride and barked something over his shoulder at Heather.

Razor's gaze didn't leave the scene. "You see what I see?"

Player sighed. "Yeah. And I don't like it."

Razor stood beside him, arms loose at his sides, eyes fixed on the pair outside. "Brick says they had a run-in with a rival MC down south. One of their boys got sweet on Heather, wouldn't take no for an answer. Brick stepped in, said he killed the guy, and now the other club is out for blood."

"What other club?" Player asked.

"Chrome Savages," Razor replied, cutting him a look.

Player didn't look away from the scene. Brick yanked his duffel closer, talking over his shoulder. Heather stood a few feet back, still as stone. "That what you believe?" he asked.

Razor sighed. "Not for a second. Clubs don't go to war over women unless she's someone's old lady or she's tied to someone in their leadership. Chrome Savages aren't about to spill blood over some girl they met at a bar."

Player grunted. "You think he's feeding you a line."

"I know he is. If he'd really put one of their guys in the ground, they wouldn't be letting him take a scenic ride across three states. They'd be on his ass before he left Mississippi. My guess? He's hiding something bigger, and she's part of the cover."

That, in Player's mind, was far more likely.

Razor's mouth flattened. "He says she's his old lady. If that was true he was justified in defending what's his. But there's something else going on. If he *did* kill a Savage, there would be bodies chasing him all the way up here."

"She's *not* his old lady." Player huffed.

"I think his story sounds just true enough to keep me from throwing him out on his ass until I know what he's really running from," Razor said. "Chrome Savages aren't a problem for us yet, but if they become one, I want them both where I can see them."

That sounded right. "You're letting them stay here?"

His gaze stayed on Heather. She stood like she was waiting for a cue, not an equal partner in whatever Brick was selling. Yeah… there was more to this. If Razor's plan meant keeping her close and under watch, Player was all for it. Smartest move they could make. If she really was in trouble, maybe the only chance she had.

Razor nodded slowly.

"And me?"

"You're gonna make sure she doesn't wander while I dig into what really happened." Razor finally looked at him, his eyes cold. "She's not our problem yet. But the second she is, I want to know first."

Player laughed. "You do see the comedy here, right? You're asking me, the club's pussy hound, to keep an eye on the little lady."

Razor didn't blink. "Figured you'd enjoy the work."

"Sure," Player said with a smirk. "But you sure you're not worried about me moving on her?"

"If she's really in with the Hounds, she's already been warned about you," Razor said, turning back toward his office. "I don't care if you charm your way into her pants, Player. But don't turn this into a bigger mess than it already is."

Player watched him go, still grinning. "Yeah, boss. I'll babysit your maybe-problem."

Turning back to the window, he saw Heather still out there with Brick, her hands stuffed in the pockets of her jacket. Her head was turned away like she was somewhere else entirely.

* * *

Heather

Heather had stopped keeping track of the states. The miles blurred together, each one decorated half-heartedly for a holiday she didn't feel. The only reason she knew it was December was the gas stations playing Christmas music and flashing plastic reindeer lined the rooftops and yards in every small town they passed. She hadn't planned on being here in Mercy, Virginia, and definitely not with him.

When she met Brick back in Mississippi, he'd been the kind of man who got noticed when he walked in a room. He had a loud laugh, easy smile, and the patch on his back got people's attention. He'd come into the bar where she worked, ordered a drink, and treated her like she was the only one worth talking to.

After months of scraping by and keeping her head down, his attention was hard to turn away from, especially when he started talking about cash.

Brick had said he'd take care of her. He had, at first. In the beginning she thought he was trying to fuck her for money. But he actually had little jobs he sent her on.

He had "little favors" for her to run. She'd pick up envelopes and drop off packages. Nothing heavy or shady on the surface. Brick told her it was club business for the Hounds of Hell in Biloxi, and she didn't ask questions. The money was better than anything she'd been making at the bar, and she told herself she was finally part of something solid. Maybe she could finally make a decent living.

Until the night he came back from a big delivery empty-handed. The package he'd been carrying, a shipment she'd unknowingly helped move, had been stolen. So had a large sum of money which wasn't his to lose. Brick told a story of how he'd been held at gunpoint while meeting the intended buyer. The thieves had made off with both the package and the money.

The cartel he'd been dealing with didn't buy his story about the "robbery." They wanted their money, and they wanted it *now*.

That's when Heather learned the truth. She hadn't just been running errands. She'd been a clean face to move cartel product, illegal drugs, through places they didn't want to be seen.

When he told her he was hitting the road, she panicked. What was she supposed to do? Stay behind and wait for the cartel to find her? His terms were clear enough: if she shared his bed, she could come with him. He'd "keep her safe." She'd packed a bag, and they hit the road.

What choice had she really had? She hadn't ever found him physically attractive. Far from it. By then she'd seen Brick for what he *really* was. He was crude and sloppy, carrying himself like he was something special when he was anything but. She'd told herself their relationship was temporary, she'd find a way to slip out before the cartel caught up to them. But every mile they put behind them felt like another door closing, another escape route vanishing.

They'd been on the road for weeks now. "Safe" wasn't a word she believed anymore. There had been an endless string of cheap motels, side roads, and one-night stops until Brick told her they were making a stop here in Mercy. Club business, he said. He knew the president here, and Razor owed him a favor.

Heather wasn't sure she believed the story. Once she met the president of the Mercy chapter of the Hounds of Hell, she doubted Razor was the type to owe anyone *anything*. But Brick had a way of talking like he already was in charge of any room he walked into. He said the Mercy chapter had been through a war helping an ally take over another club. They'd be too busy patching themselves up to ask too many questions about why he needed a bed for a while.

Maybe that was true. But the way Razor eyed Brick when they walked in told her the man wasn't buying what Brick was selling.

Now, back outside with him, she stood beside the bike while he dug through the bag strapped to the back. It was midday and cold, and the air smelled of burning wood from a woodstove or fireplace. Heather noticed leftover banners from a tree lighting ceremony still flapping in the wind down the street. She paid attention to anything but the man rummaging beside her.

A movement caught her eye. Through the clubhouse window, the man she'd talked to leaned in the frame, broad shoulders filling the space. He was all relaxed posture and steady eyes, watching them like he had nothing better to do, but he missed nothing.

Heather had met plenty of men like him before. Mr. Right Now. The kind who smiled easily, charmed faster, and walked away as quickly when the night was over. Still, her gaze lingered.

He had a rough, dangerous look some women went weak for, with short sandy hair, a neat beard framing a hard jaw, and striking blue-green eyes that could pin you in place. He was strong and solidly built, with broad shoulders and long, muscular limbs that spoke of power even when he stood completely still. There was something in the way he carried himself, coiled and ready. He'd been in enough fights to know exactly how to finish one. He was maybe a little bit dangerous, in a way that made her pulse jump.

Heather had learned to keep her distance from men like him. But for some reason, she didn't look away. Something about the way he watched her, like he was reading more than she was saying, sent a ripple through her chest. Not fear, but something sharper and curious.

Brick muttered something under his breath and shouldered the bag. Heather grabbed her smaller bag and turned to follow him inside, but not before glancing over one last time.

The man still stood there, still watching her, and damn it, she was still looking right back at him. Heather followed Brick back into the clubhouse. The man from the window waited, closer now. His leather cut stretched across his shoulders and his intent gaze chased hers away. Heather focused on the floor instead, and he fell into step with them, leading them down a hallway.

"Got a room you can use while you're here," he said, his voice a quiet rumble. "Until Razor decides what he's doing with you."

Brick gave a tight smile. "Appreciate that, brother."

They reached a small guest room with a narrow bed, a dresser, and a bathroom big enough to turn around in. Their guide stepped inside first, flipping on the light. "Not much, but it's clean."

Brick lingered in the doorway. The other man leaned against the frame, casual but not moving aside. "So, what's the real story?"

"Told Razor already," Brick said. "A little heat back home; nothing to drag anyone else into. We'll keep out of your hair."

"Right," the man said, the word flat enough to scrape.

Brick's eyes narrowed slightly. "We're tired, man. Just wanna get my old lady settled."

Heather caught the way the other man's gaze slid to her for the briefest moment before he stepped back, letting them pass. He didn't believe Brick. She didn't know how she knew. Maybe the set of his jaw. His voice didn't change, but she felt it all the same.

Once the door shut behind them and he left them alone, Brick dropped his bag on the bed and turned to her. "That was Player."

"Player?" she asked.

"Yeah. Calls himself that for a reason." Brick's tone was sharp, dismissive. "You'll want to steer clear of him. He fucks anything that moves. Guys like that don't think twice about stepping on another man's toes."

Heather sat on the edge of the bed, running a thumb along the seam of her jacket. She didn't answer, but the image of Player leaning in the doorway, watching Brick with an unreadable look, stuck in her head. Stepping on another man's toes? That was funny. She wasn't Brick's old lady. Never had been. It was something he said because it suited him, made things simple for other people to understand.

Still, she hated when he told people that. But it really bothered her more that he'd said that to *him*. To Player. Like Brick was staking a claim where none existed and wanted to make sure the other man kept his distance.

Part of her hoped he wouldn't.

Chapter Two

Player

Sackett's was the same as always, crowded, loud, and smoky. The place smelled of beer and old wood, the kind of bar where the music never got so loud you couldn't hear a fight start. The bar had always been a Hounds hangout, and it taken one hell of a beating last summer. The Hounds, the Cottonmouths, and what seemed like half the damn Mafia had turned the place into a battlefield. Old man Phillips sold the bar after that, and now it had a new owner. They'd mostly cleaned the place up now, but the scars were still there. There were scratches on the bar top, a dent in the jukebox, and a couple of patched holes in the wall didn't quite match the paint.

Player occupied his usual spot, a cold beer sweating on the rail beside him while he lined up his next shot. He was kicking Beast's ass at pool, with Crash leaning on the next table over and grinning at every bad break. Crash had Helena with him tonight, her laugh cutting through the noise every so often. Outcast came out too, with Anya perched comfortably in his lap as if she'd been there all her life.

A couple of girls lingered by Player's table, all legs and long hair, pretending to watch the game but really watching him. He gave them a lazy grin between shots, keeping the conversation easy and suggestive enough to make them lean closer. The two of them appeared to be close friends who'd happily share. Taking them both home would be a hell of a way to end the day, and he'd never been one to turn down a good threesome.

He had Beast sweating over the last stripe when the door opened.

Brick walked in as if he owned the fucking place, and trailing behind him was Heather. Player's jaw clenched. *Christ.* Couldn't he get away from this asshole today?

Even in the dim light, Heather stood out. Her hair was a wild riot of dark curls, loose over her shoulders. She wore a jean jacket with painted on jeans and a low-cut top which didn't give too much away. Those wide green eyes scanned the room like she was taking note of every possible exit. She obviously wasn't there to kick back and enjoy a couple of hours at the bar.

Player straightened without meaning to, his pool cue resting loosely in his hand as he watched them weave through the crowd. Brick had his hand on her lower back, guiding her, but she didn't lean into him or even look at him. She didn't look like she wanted to be in the same zip code as Brick.

Player knew the feeling. He turned back to the table, but his focus wasn't on the game anymore. Brick didn't so much as glance at the pool table. He steered Heather to a small table along the wall, talking to her low and fast. Player couldn't make out what he said, but the man's tone was agitated. She didn't say much back, just nodded with her gaze fixed on the table like she was counting the wood grains. As soon as Brick moved off toward the back, a waitress swooped in to take her drink order. Heather gave a small, polite smile, rattled off something Player couldn't hear over the clatter of pool balls, and folded her hands in her lap.

He tracked Brick, more out of habit than anything else, until a flash of polished steel caught his eye. Brick, sitting in a booth in the back, hand on the table between him holding a revolver, and leaning toward a stocky guy in a leather vest. Player didn't recognize the other man, but even across the room, he knew those chrome-plated grips, engraved with the Hounds' emblem near the base -- Razor's custom .45 revolver. One of the pieces he kept under lock at the clubhouse, safer there than at his gun shop.

Brick was walking around like the piece was his to sell.

Player shook his head. Razor's .45, no doubt about it. Razor didn't lend his guns, not to anyone. He sure as hell wouldn't lend them to Brick. Whatever deal the fucker was here to make, it had crossed the line into club business.

Well, tonight got way more interesting. If Brick was dumb enough to be flashing the .45 here in Mercy, then Player would make sure the weapon didn't leave the building. He set his bottle down and drifted past Beast, clapping the bigger man once on the shoulder. "Back in a minute," he said under his breath.

Beast didn't need details. He followed Player's line of sight. Whatever he saw there had him paused at the pool table, scanning the room as if he was sizing up a fight. Crash had clocked it too by now. So would Outcast. All three of them were waiting to see what move Player was about to make when he reached the back booth.

Brick hunched forward, his voice low as he spoke to the guy in the vest sitting across from him, a man Player didn't recognize. Dropping himself into the booth beside the buyer, Player grinned as if they'd been saving him a seat. Brick's gaze moved up, the smirk he'd been wearing faltering for half a second before snapping back into place. A muscle ticked in his jaw, a little tell he was angry. But he wasn't stupid enough to start something there.

"Well, well," Player drawled, grinning at Brick. "You're out here peddling that beauty without letting me take a look first?"

Brick's eyes narrowed. "We're in the middle of something."

"Yeah," Player said, reaching for the gun. "I can see that. *In the middle of* making a really bad choice." He turned the .45 in his hands like a jeweler admiring a diamond, his thumb brushing over the intricate engraving. "Razor's piece, huh? You've got to admit, the man's got good taste."

The buyer shifted uncomfortably. "Razor's?" The man recognized the name, and he didn't want any trouble. "Or is it yours?"

Player looked up, grinning. "Is now." He reached into his pocket and tossed a folded wad of cash onto the table. "Here's a couple hundred for your trouble, Brick. You can buy Heather a nice dinner or a bus ticket. Whatever."

Brick's jaw worked, but with Beast posted at the bar now, watching like a hawk, and Crash watching intently from the pool table with Outcast, the man knew better than to make a scene.

Player stood, tucking the revolver into the back of his jeans. "Pleasure doing business," he said with a wink. "Next time, though? Don't try to sell me shit you stole."

Brick muttered something under his breath, but Player didn't bother asking him to repeat it. The man wasn't going to push this with three other Hounds already closing the gap. Player turned his back on both men without hurry, walking the gun right out of their reach. He could feel Brick's glare drilling into him the whole way.

By the time he reached the pool table, Beast had

returned, grinning like Christmas had come early. Crash shook his head, muttering. "You're an asshole," he said with pride in his voice.

Player shrugged. "Yeah. But I'm Razor's asshole."

He racked the balls again, but in the back of his mind, he knew this wasn't over. Brick wasn't stupid enough to forget what had happened. If the man was desperate enough to sell Razor's prized piece, then something bigger and badder was right on his heels.

* * *

Heather

Heather barely had time to finish her drink before Brick slid into the booth beside her, scowling. She'd seen him earlier, hunched over in a back booth with a guy she didn't recognize. Whatever they'd discussed hadn't gone well. His body language screamed tension, and now he looked like he'd swallowed broken glass. He didn't offer a word of explanation, just flagged down the waitress and ordered a beer in a voice edged with exhaustion.

They sat in a silence that felt heavier with each passing minute. Brick's fingers drummed once on the tabletop, then stilled. He kept glancing toward the other side of the bar, like something over there had its claws in his thoughts.

Heather sipped her drink and tried not to ask, but the tension rolling off him made her stomach knot. Her gaze wandered, catching on the pool table where some of Mercy's Hounds were gathered. Player lined up a shot, the cue stick steady in his hands. She watched the easy confidence in his stance, the quick, fluid motion as he sent the cue ball spinning across the felt. It cracked against its target, sinking two solids in one smooth move.

Glancing over his shoulder, he caught her watching him and winked, a flash of mischief in his blue-green eyes sent a jolt low in her belly.

Brick must have noticed, because he scrubbed a hand down his face, his stare narrowing like he could burn a hole through Player's back. After a few minutes, he pushed back from the table. "Let's go."

He'd barely touched the beer he ordered. "Don't you want to finish that?" She nodded at the bottle.

"Not in the mood tonight." Brick's sharp tone was obviously meant to keep her from arguing.

He paid their bill on the way out of *Sackett's*, and as he did, she looked back over at the pool table and found Player watching her before she followed Brick out the door. The cool night air jolted her out of the temporary lull she'd enjoyed from the bourbon. Brick hustled across the lot, walking fast enough she had to hurry to keep up.

The ride back to the clubhouse was too quiet, and she felt tension in his body as she clung to him on the bike. The steady thrum of the engine and the way his shoulders stayed locked tight, every muscle in his back telegraphed something was very wrong.

Heather kept replaying what she'd seen at the bar. Brick had met with another man in one of the back booths, leaning in close over the table, talking quietly. She couldn't hear a word, but the way he'd kept checking over his shoulder told her it wasn't casual conversation. Then Player had walked back there, sliding into the booth as if he'd been invited, his easy grin cutting into whatever Brick had been trying to do. The other man left not long after, when Brick came stalking back to her looking like he'd bitten into something rotten.

What had Brick done?

When they reached the clubhouse, she saw another bike parked out front. The sight made Brick hesitate for half a second before shoving open the door.

Razor waited inside, leaning against the bar with a beer in hand, but the way his gaze locked on Brick suggested he'd been waiting there a while. "Let's talk," Razor said, nodding his head in the direction of the office. "Both of you."

Brick shifted uncomfortably. "You don't need her for this. I know what you wanna talk about, but she's not involved."

Razor's expression didn't change. "She's standin' here, isn't she? Riding in with you, living under my roof? That makes her involved until I say otherwise." His tone left no space for argument.

Heather's pulse kicked up, but Brick only nodded. Razor jerked his head again toward the office. "Now."

"Sit," he said once they'd reached the office, not bothering to raise his voice. There were two chairs on the other side of his massive desk, and the intensity in the man's gaze had her legs moving before she could think better of it. Brick dropped into the chair beside her, tension rolling off him in thick waves.

Razor's gaze cut between them as he took a seat, cool and steady. "I'm gonna keep this simple. My .45 revolver, my *custom* .45 revolver, doesn't walk itself out of a locked cabinet, and it sure as hell doesn't end up in the back booth at *Sackett's* unless somebody decides to make it their payday."

Heather's stomach sank. *Brick had stolen the man's gun?* Her gaze moved to Brick, but he stared straight ahead, shoulders squared as if he could hold his ground by sheer will.

Razor leaned forward, forearms on the table. "So, tell me, Brick. Why are you *really* here in Mercy? 'Cause I don't buy the bullshit you've been feeding me."

Brick's laugh was thin and nervous. "Told you already. We're trying to give that little incident over my old lady here time to blow over. That's all."

"Since when does a brother putting a roof over your head justify stealing his property and trying to pawn it at *Sackett's*?" Razor asked.

Heather's head snapped toward Brick. *It was true then.*

Brick kept his eyes on Razor. "I needed some cash, brother. Not like I can hold down a job right now. No harm done. You got it back."

"That revolver stays locked up for a reason," Razor said, his gaze sharp enough to cut. "You don't *take* from me. And you don't bring your mess to my door without explaining why it's here."

"I told you --"

"You told me a story," Razor cut in. "Now I want the truth. Who's chasing you?"

Brick glanced at Heather, then back at Razor. "This ain't her business."

"Wrong," Razor said flatly. "If she's under my roof, everything that touches you touches her. So, unless you want her finding out the hard way, you start talking."

Brick leaned back, arms folding across his chest. "Look, I'm sorry about the gun. I'll be gone by morning."

Razor stared him down. "That's not an answer."

"Only answer you're getting." Brick's voice was flat, his eyes hard, but Heather caught something else there, a flicker of emotion she couldn't read.

Razor sat there for a long beat, beer bottle turning slowly in his hand, before he finally said, "Fine. You're gone by morning. But if you're still here when I wake up, we're going to have a much longer conversation."

Brick stood, dragging his chair back with a scrape. "Won't be a problem." He stalked out of the office without looking at her.

Heather's stomach sank. What was Brick doing?

Heather stayed seated for a beat, her pulse hammering. Razor still leaned forward, his gaze on her, weighing whether to say something. Her throat felt tight. Part of her wanted, *needed,* to tell him the truth, but fear got the better of her. She wasn't ready to hear whatever response would come out of his mouth.

They didn't deserve more of this man's mercy. Not for helping the cartel chasing them to peddle drugs.

Standing, she muttered something about catching up and slipped out into the hall.

Heather turned and followed Brick down the hall, quickening her pace until she caught up. "Brick, what was that about?"

"Nothing you need to worry about."

"Did you steal from him? That's not nothing."

Brick shot her a glare. "I told you what you need to know."

"You're not telling me anything," she replied, her voice sharper than she meant it to be. Ever since they'd rolled into Mercy, Brick had been quiet and cagey. The way he kept things close to his chest scared her, because if the cartel was catching up with him -- well, they were after her too, and if he wasn't talking, then she didn't know how bad the situation truly was… or how close danger might be.

He stopped at their door, shoulders tight, and slid the key into the lock. "Quit asking questions you don't want the answers to."

The door swung open, and he stepped inside without waiting to see if she followed.

Before following Brick into the room, Heather hesitated in the hallway. The walls were closing in on her, his silence pressing down heavier than anything Razor had said. Her mouth was dry, her thoughts racing. Maybe if she found some water before bed, she could calm down enough to think, to sleep.

She turned away from the door, scanning for a kitchen. Each creak of the floorboards seemed louder than the last, her pulse matching the beat. The panic clawed at her ribs, whispering that she was alone in this. Brick had stolen a gun from their host and tried to sell it. Yeah, money had been tight on the road, but something had shifted. Whatever Brick had gotten himself into tonight had put them both in even more danger.

* * *

Player

Player walked through the clubhouse doors after leaving *Sackett's*. He found Razor in his office, finishing off a beer. He recognized the look on his president's face. Something was up. Without a word, he set Razor's custom revolver down on the desk with a soft clunk.

Razor's gaze shifted to the gun, then back to him. "Brick's decided he'll be gone by morning," Razor said flatly. "Didn't want to tell me the truth. His choice." Taking the pistol, he slid it into a drawer.

Player didn't know whether to be relieved or pissed. Brick bailing before things got worse would be a great thing. Heather walking out of Mercy? He didn't look forward to the idea at all. His mind was already wandering to ways he could prevent that from happening even though he knew it was a bad idea.

"Far as tonight goes," Razor continued. "She had no idea. I saw it on her face. Still, keep your eyes sharp until they're out of town."

Player nodded. "Yeah." He hesitated, then asked, "You want one of us to hang around the clubhouse tonight? In case something else walks off... or..."

Razor leaned back in his chair, considering Player's offer. "I'm staying. I called Deva right before they got here to let her know. But it wouldn't hurt if you stayed too. I don't think Brick's stupid enough to try again tonight, but I wouldn't bet money on his self-control either. Keep your eyes open."

"You got it," Player told him. He'd text Crash, Outcast, and Beast to update them on the situation. Then he'd crash in one of the rooms.

Player wandered out of the office, his mind on *her*. Honestly, he regretted that Heather would be gone soon. There was a mutual spark. He caught the way she'd looked at him earlier, the subtle interest there. She felt it too.

As he headed into the main room, movement caught his attention at the corner of his eye.

He spotted her down the hall, her soft hair catching the dim light. Her steps were slow, heading in the direction of the kitchen. Player's steps were light on the worn floor as he followed, Razor's words were still running around in his head. *She had no idea.*

She filled a glass with water, not reacting to his presence yet.

"I hear you're gone by morning," he said casually, leaning against the doorway.

She froze, her hand on the tap. "That's what I heard too."

He shrugged, watching her closely, and reading every flash of emotion crossing her face. "Figured I'd hear it from you."

Weariness still clung to her. She clearly didn't know how to answer him. Turning the glass in her hands, she took a slow sip.

"What's going on, Heather?" Player asked. "And don't tell me nothing, 'cause I can see it all over you."

Her gaze drifted away, toward the dark window over the sink. Her lips pressed together as if she was holding back more than words. He caught the fear under the fatigue she wore like a heavy cloak. The kind of fear that sat deep and stayed quiet. He could read it as big as a road sign.

When her teeth sank into her full lower lip, he decided not to push further. Player had always been a sucker for a damsel in distress, and this little lady… well, his gut told him she was in bad trouble.

Switching gears, he put on what he hoped was a kind smile. "Hey, if you ever need something," he said, keeping his tone light, "you know where to find me. Doesn't have to be about Brick. Hell, doesn't have to be about anything at all. Just… don't try to handle everything all yourself. Not in this world."

Her green eyes came back to his, cautious but curious. "Why would you care?"

Player shrugged, as if the answer didn't matter much. "'Cause trouble is a whole lot easier to deal with when you've got backup."

Something he said got her attention. He saw the way her eyes grew shiny. Her hands were shaking as she set the glass down on the counter. That's when it clicked. She truly was afraid. Brick wasn't supporting her. Whatever trouble they were in, it hadn't started with her. Brick had gotten himself into something, and she'd been dragged along for the ride. But when the shit hit the fan, she'd be the one left standing in the blast zone, collateral damage to his mess.

He tilted his head, studying her. "You really with him? Or is that just what he tells people?"

Heather's gaze shifted toward the doorway, as if she was worried Brick was about to walk in. Then she shook her head slowly. "I've been… with him," she admitted, her voice barely above a whisper. "But not because I wanted to be. More for… protection." Her tone was flat.

Player got it then. Whatever demons were chasing them, Brick had fucking twisted the situation into leverage. Made her pay for "protection" in the only currency she had to offer. He wondered if he could even call the fucker's actions protection at all. From where he stood, it was probably a fucking miracle the two of them were still alive.

Something sharp curled in his gut. Yeah, that protective instinct had gotten him into trouble a few times. She wasn't his, but she wasn't Brick's either. None of that mattered. Heather was in trouble, and he wouldn't be able to live with himself if he stood by and watched her get swallowed whole. He kept his voice steady. "You ever decide you want out, sweetheart, you let me know. I'll make sure you walk away still breathing."

Her eyes met his for a heartbeat, and the flash of hope there had his heart skipping a beat. She didn't say anything, though, just looked away. Her quiet "thank you," was unexpected, but sincere.

Player pushed off the doorway, letting her have the space. No promises, no pressure. Just the truth. He left her there in the dim kitchen, the hum of the fridge the only sound between them.

* * *

Heather

Heather woke to silence the next morning.

For a moment, she thought Brick had gone to grab coffee or bum a smoke outside. It wasn't unusual for him.

But the other side of the bed was cold, the sheets smoothed flat as if they hadn't been touched. Her gaze swept the small room. *Empty*. His duffel bag was gone. His jacket, the one he never left behind, was nowhere in sight. She grabbed her phone from the nightstand, frantically checking notifications. No messages. No missed calls. A hollow feeling opened in her chest. Brick wouldn't leave without telling her.

Pushing back the covers, she pulled on her jeans with hands that felt clumsy and crossed to the window. The bikes out front were the same as last night, except Brick's was missing. Unease became growing certainty. Brick had walked out, left her there with no warning or explanation.

They'd been low on money for weeks, Heather knew. That was why he'd gotten the bright idea to stop in Mercy when they hit Virginia. "Free rent," he'd said, if they handled it right. Play their cards smart, make themselves useful, and they could ride out the lean patch without spending a dime.

Apparently, the money problem had been bigger than she'd realized. Bad enough to steal from their host and walk into a bar with the man's custom handgun.

Maybe bad enough to dump her here in Mercy as if she was garbage he no longer needed or wanted. Or maybe… Her blood ran cold. Or maybe it wasn't about wanting her gone at all. Maybe leaving her behind was his way of settling his debt with the cartel, payment in flesh instead of cash.

Her heart raced as she fought back panic. If that was his intention, then she hadn't been abandoned. She'd been traded. And the worst part? She couldn't even decide which possibility was worse -- either he'd left her to save himself, or he hadn't thought about her at all.

With a chest tightened by fear, Heather yanked on her boots and coat and headed for the hall. She needed answers, and only one person might have them and be willing to share them with her if he was still there.

She found Player out front. His head came up when she stepped onto the porch, surprise flickering across his face. "Heather?"

"You seen Brick?" she asked.

Player frowned. "Not since last night. Thought you were with him."

Her stomach dropped. "No. He's gone. His stuff's gone."

That got him on his feet, his blue-green eyes narrowing. "*Gone* gone?"

She nodded, crossing her arms to keep her hands from shaking. "Did he say anything before he left?"

Player shook his head slowly, still processing. "I was up around five. The bike was already gone. Razor and I figured you were too."

He'd left her. No note, no call, nothing but an empty bed and a louder silence than she'd ever heard. A numbing cold spread through her, making her shake where she stood. The realization hit like a gut punch. If Brick had left her behind, he'd done it for a reason, and none of the possibilities were good.

A faint hum drifted in on the morning air, so quiet she almost didn't hear it at first. The sound grew, layer by layer, turning into the steady growl of multiple engines. The sound crawled along her skin, setting every nerve on edge.

Player's gaze shifted past her, toward the road. "You hear that?"

She turned, squinting into the bright strip of daylight beyond the clubhouse driveway. The rumble sounded closer now, deep and deliberate, the kind of company that never needed to rush. Dust plumed up in the distance, sunlight winking off chrome.

Two black SUVs emerged first, moving in a tight line. A pair of bikes flanked them, the riders dressed in dark leathers, visors down. The cars slowed as they approached, the sound of engines filling every space around her until it felt like she couldn't breathe.

Player's voice dropped. "Stay behind me, Heather."

Just like that, she knew trouble had caught up to her.

The cartel had arrived.

Chapter Three

Player

Two dark sedans slowly rolled up the dirt drive, flanked by a pair of bikes, rumbling low and steady. Player shifted, planting himself between Heather and the open yard, his palm pressing lightly against her hip.

"Stay behind me," he said again without looking, his eyes locked on the convoy.

The cars stopped a dozen yards from the porch. Doors opened, and men stepped out. They wore dark jeans, button-down shirts, all of them with a sharp, polished look that didn't belong in a small town like Mercy. Even without colors, Player knew exactly what they were.

The lead man looked to be mid-forties, with black hair slicked back. His was the kind of thin smile that promised nothing good, and he stood with an easy, practiced posture that said he was used to being respected and obeyed. His dark, calculating eyes swept the porch as if he was taking inventory. When they landed on Heather, his mouth curved enough to suggest he had stumbled across a forgotten prize worth reclaiming.

"Where's Brick?" the man called. His voice was smooth, and his words held a Spanish accent.

"Why're you asking?" Player called back.

"He owes us a *substantial* amount of money."

Brick had always been a hustler, always working some angle. But owing a cartel money? This wasn't just bad. This was playing Russian roulette with a full chamber -- the kind of stupid that got people killed quickly, and not always the ones who deserved to die.

"I asked you a question," the man said, stepping

forward one measured pace. "Where. Is. Brick?"

"Not here," Player said, his voice even. "He left town before sunrise."

The man's smile thinned. "And left *her* behind?" His gaze slid past Player, landing on Heather again like a spotlight. "Interesting."

Heather shifted closer to Player's back. He felt the faint tremor in her touch, a shiver she couldn't quite hide.

The man's tone cooled. "We can use her to lure him back."

Behind Player, Heather stiffened.

A humorless smile tugged at Player's mouth. "I wouldn't count on that. If he valued her so much, he wouldn't have left her here."

The man's eyes narrowed, the faintest hint of a smirk playing at his lips. "Then she'll help me recover my expenses until he's brought to me."

Player stepped down one step, closing the gap by half. "Not happening," he said flatly.

The man's smirk deepened, as if he thought Player were bluffing. "Brick's not here to protect her."

Player's weight shifted forward, his stance widening. "She doesn't need Brick," he said, his voice low and even. "She's *mine*."

The cartel man's gaze flicked past him, sizing Heather up before returning to Player. "Yours?"

"My old lady," Player confirmed, the words dropping like a lock clicking into place. "Touch her, you're touching me. That's a problem you don't want."

Behind him, he felt Heather go still, the air between them suddenly tight. Razor's sharp inhale from the doorway said all Player needed to know. He'd crossed a line that would have consequences later, if they waited that long.

Well, it was done now. If Razor wanted to chew him out another time, so be it. Right now, keeping Heather out of the hands of the cartel mattered more than club politics.

The man stared him down. "Your old lady, huh?" His gaze slid over Heather like he was appraising stolen goods. "Funny. Brick swore she was *his*. Did this happen overnight?"

Player didn't move or blink. "No. She's always been mine."

The man stepped closer, studying them like a gambler sizing up a risky hand.

Behind him, Heather's fingers knotted in the back of his cut, the tremor in them telling him she knew exactly how bad this could get if he played the scene wrong.

Player shifted enough to block her from view. The man's grin widened, but never reached his eyes. "While your intentions are admirable, are you sure you want to put yourself and your club in danger by trying to shield her?"

The man's gaze stayed locked on Player for a beat too long before he gave a small nod to one of the bikers flanking the cars. The biker swung off his seat, slow and deliberate, as if he had all the time in the world.

"Talk is cheap," the man said. "Let's see if you've got something worth protecting."

Player bit back a smirk. *Jesus, did they practice in the mirror, or was it a natural gift*? His stance tightened. "Take one more step, and I'll show you how cheap your *life* can get."

The biker paused, his eyes narrowing. The man lifted a hand, halting him, but his expression didn't soften. "So, you *do* think she's worth more than Brick's debt to us. Interesting." He let that hang in the air, a challenge wrapped in mock curiosity, before glancing at Razor in the doorway. "Your president agree with this?"

The man's question hung in the air, his dark-eyed gaze shifting from Player to Razor as if he already knew the answer.

Razor stepped forward, his boots thudding against the porch boards, his gaze cutting to Player first, sharp and warning. "Depends," he said finally. "Are you here to talk business, or to start a war in my front yard?"

The cartel man's smile was thin. "Depends on your man here." He tilted his chin toward Player. "He's making claims. Claims that cost a lot of money. May cost you your lives."

Razor didn't look away from the man, but Player felt the weight of his president's silent message all the same. *We're going to have words later.*

"She's under our protection," Razor said, slow and deliberate, as if he wanted every word to register. "Which means any business with her, you bring to *me*. Not him."

The cartel man's smile didn't falter, but the air seemed too thin, sharp and dangerous. "Let's make this simple," he said. "You bring us Brick. *Alive*. He owes us, more than you can cover in good faith." The man's gaze drifted to where Heather still hid behind him, lingering long enough to make Player's fists curl. "Or maybe she helps work off the debt. All you have to do is give her to us, take some of the pressure off yourselves."

Stepping a fraction closer, the man's voice dropped to something that almost sounded like an introduction. "Luis Salazar. Some call me ,El Cuervo."

Player didn't know the name, but apparently Razor did. A flash of recognition crossed his president's features, there and gone. Enough for Player to catch it and know one thing for sure. This was *bad.*

Player shifted his stance, and every muscle was tight.

Razor's words were slow, deliberate, and laced with steel. "Not happening." He let the words hang, then took a measured step forward, crowding the porch space between them. "Brick owes you the debt, not her. She's under our protection. He may wear our patch, but he's not my brother and he's not part of my club. You want him? Hunt him down yourself." Razor's gaze didn't waver, even as the air seemed to charge with silent threat. "But the girl stays here."

"Then we wait." Salazar's tone was easy, but his gaze was filled with cold calculation. His smile never reached his eyes. He smoothed a hand over his jacket as if the matter were settled. "We'll be in touch."

Player didn't move until they were gone. His pulse hammered in his throat, every instinct screaming they'd stepped into something they couldn't fight their way out of cleanly. Behind him, Heather was a wreck, and Razor… Razor was about to raise hell. Holy shit, this wasn't just trouble. This was the kind of mess that got people buried.

* * *

Heather

Heather's hands wouldn't stop shaking. Her head was spinning, her stomach flipping as if she'd been yanked off one cliff and shoved toward another. She didn't know which was the worst scenario: being left in the crosshairs or watching Player throw himself into the line of fire for *her.*

Why would he do that? He didn't know her, and he sure didn't owe her anything.

Brick had left her in Mercy last night without a word and wouldn't likely look back. He'd left her standing there with her heart pounding and the air tasting like blood and danger. If it hadn't been for Player stepping in and Razor backing his play, the cartel would be getting ready to sell her to get back some of the money Brick took from them.

Heather froze when Razor's gaze cut past her to the street, tracking the slow crawl of a black SUV before it disappeared around the corner. The weight of his attention came back to her, sharper than before. "You got any idea who he was?" Razor's voice cracked through the air like a whip. The man's hazel eyes were wild as he raked a hand through his longer gray hair. "'Cause I *do*. You're lucky you ain't in a damn van halfway to Mexico right now."

Heather's throat went dry. She opened her mouth, but no words came out.

"That son of a bitch is cartel muscle. *Real* cartel. Did Brick bring you here knowin' that?"

She shook her head quickly, but Razor's stare cut through her as if he didn't believe her -- or maybe he didn't want to. "They call him *El Cuervo* -- the Crow. You know *why* they call him the fucking crow?" Razor didn't wait for an answer. "'Cause he circles over what's left when he's done. Picks you clean, leaves your bones for the sun."

He leaned in, his voice colder. "Back in Juárez, they say he put a whole family in the ground over a debt their boy couldn't pay. Then he packed the heads into a crate and shipped them to the debtor's boss like a fucking message."

Razor straightened, his fury barely leashed. "In

some places, *cuervo* can mean priest, as well. Fitting. 'Cause this guy doesn't stop at killing you, he delivers your fucking last rites. That's the kind of nightmare Brick dragged into my clubhouse."

Razor scanned the quiet street as if it might bite him back. "We're not doin' this out here," he said, jerking his chin toward the clubhouse.

Player hesitated only a second before following him inside and she scrambled after them. It was eerily quiet inside the Hounds' clubhouse, the muffled thud of their steps on the hallway floor the only sound. Razor pushed open a door to his office, motioning them through.

The office smelled faintly of cigarettes and leather. There were framed photos of guns on the walls with images of the men in the motorcycle club from different get-togethers and parties. Behind the desk a rack of shotguns caught the light. Plenty of things to look at instead of meeting the gaze of either man, because it was only a matter of time before they came to their senses and realized giving her up would save them a lot of trouble.

Razor shut the door behind them before marching around his desk to take a seat, staring her down.

"You better start talkin', sweetheart," Razor said. "'Cause my chapter got shoved neck-deep into cartel business thanks to that worthless piece of shit you showed up with."

Heather's chest ached like she couldn't get air. "I knew," she forced out, her voice shaking. "I knew it was a cartel. I was… a fresh face moving product for him. I didn't know who it was for. Not at first. Brick said it was nothing I had to worry about." Her eyes burned, shame and fear tangling in her throat. "But the night he came back empty-handed, I found out what he'd *really* done. Who he'd stolen from. We went on the run that night, and we haven't stopped."

Razor stared at her as if she'd spat in his drink. "You knew." His voice was low, but the rage in it could've rattled the walls. "You knew you were moving product, and you didn't think to ask whose?"

"I told you," she said, the words tumbling out. "He didn't tell me until --"

"Until what? Until it was too damn late?" Razor's voice cracked like a whip. "Do you even get what you've dropped into my lap? El Cuervo isn't some street thug you can pay off and walk away from. That son of a bitch will gut you for the thrill and smile while he does it."

Heather flinched, the heat of his words burning through her. Shame crawled up her throat, thick and choking, until she could barely swallow. Her hands twisted in her lap, nails digging into her skin to ground herself. She'd thought she understood what kind of danger Brick had put them in. Hearing it from Razor, hearing the name, made it real in a way that turned her insides cold.

Razor turned on Player, jabbing a finger at him. "And you -- claiming her as an old lady? You ever had an old lady before?"

Player's jaw worked, but he didn't answer.

"Didn't fucking think so," Razor snarled. "You'd have to stick with the same woman for more than a week. Now you've got the cartel thinking she's under our protection. Which means you've painted a damn target on the Mercy chapter. For *Brick*. For that coward's fucking debt."

Player's shoulders stayed squared, but Heather could feel the tension radiating off him.

Razor blew out a breath through his nose, sharp and angry. "You better pray I get to Brick before they do. 'Cause if El Cuervo thinks we're covering his debt, we're *all* dead men walking." He grabbed his phone. "Now, get the hell out of my office so I can make some calls."

Heather trailed Player out of Razor's office, her stomach still knotted so tightly she could barely breathe. "Who are you calling?" she asked, pitching her voice low, knowing speaking any louder might draw the wrong kind of attention.

"Snow," Player said, scrolling through his contacts. "The VP. Runs a security outfit here in Mercy. Knows how to make problems disappear before they hit the front door."

He put the call on speaker as they reached the conference room. Snow picked up on the first ring, his voice clipped. "Does this have to do with fucking Brick?"

Player's jaw flexed. "Yeah. Brick split this morning, left the woman, and a guy who calls himself El Cuervo showed up looking for them."

A beat of silence, then Snow's tone went harder. "I'm on my way. You keep her inside. Phone, laptop, tablet -- anything she's used since Brick brought her in, I want it waiting for me. Don't touch it after."

"Got it."

"And, Player? She doesn't leave your side."

The call ended, the quiet in the room suddenly heavy. Heather's pulse thundered in her ears.

Player didn't say much as they left the conference room, only a clipped "Come on," before heading down the hallway at a steady pace. After a beat, he added, "Snow is on his way. He wants anything they could've used to track you or leave a trail."

Heather nodded. Her brain had stopped working. Her legs carried her forward, but it felt as if she were moving through mud. The room she and Brick had been given wasn't far, but every step made her stomach twist harder.

She rubbed her arms. Her skin was too cold and too hot all at once. "Does Snow do simple security or cyber security?"

"Cyber security. Online surveillance. Tech wizard shit," Player said, glancing her way. "I work for him. He runs a business out here. Private sector contracts, sometimes corporate. He's real quiet about it, but Razor trusts him with our lives."

Heather swallowed hard. *Our lives*. She didn't deserve to be included.

When they reached the door, Player paused and looked at her, his expression gentler this time. "Need the basics. Your phone. Anything Brick gave you. If there's a laptop, smart watch, old SIM cards -- doesn't matter how small it seems."

Heather opened the door slowly, the air inside thick with memory and dread. Her side of the bed was unmade, the sheets still rumpled from a night that felt a thousand years away. Her small bag sat in the corner, slumped with the weight of what came next. Only *her* things remained, as if everything she touched had only been weighing him down.

She crouched beside the bag and unzipping it with shaking hands, dumping the contents out on the floor so he could see them. Her clothes. A half-used bottle of dry shampoo. Her phone charger. She reached into the side pocket and pulled out her phone, her fingers trembling. "I don't have much," she whispered.

Player took the phone and slid it into his back

pocket without commenting. "It's enough. Snow'll check it out."

Heather kept digging anyway, thinking maybe she'd missed something useful tucked between the seams of her T-shirts. All she found was a folded grocery receipt and a single earring she'd thought she'd lost two towns ago. Tears blurred her vision as she looked through her things carefully.

"I didn't mean for any of this to happen," she said suddenly, the words cracking as they escaped her. "I didn't know how deep Brick was in. I never wanted anyone to get hurt. I never --" Her voice broke off.

Player knelt beside her, his voice quieter now. "Brick left you here to face the music. Says more about him than it ever will about you."

Heather blinked hard, her eyes burning. The words struck something deep. She swallowed against the lump in her throat. "I was trying to keep up. I didn't know what we were walking into until…"

Player didn't say anything right away. He stayed next to her, close, but not crowding her, his presence steady in the silence. When he finally spoke, it wasn't harsh. "You're not the one who stole from the cartel, and you didn't bring them to our door."

Glancing up into his blue-green eyes, she shook her head. "But I came with him."

"And he left without you." The words cut but not cruelly. More lancing a wound already festering.

"You could've handed me over," she said. Her voice was raw. "That might've ended this mess for you and your club."

Player scrubbed his hand down his face. "Might've," he agreed. "Or it might've made things worse. We took Brick in. Gave him our roof. Cartel shows up, we give them you? Doesn't wipe the slate.

Just shows them we're willing to bend." He looked at her then, really looked. "Guys like Salazar? They don't stop at one bend. They keep pushing till you break."

Heather couldn't hold his gaze. Her hands twisted in her lap. "Then why say I was yours? Why would you put yourself on the line… for me?"

For a beat, Player didn't answer her. The silence stretched until she thought maybe he wasn't going to. "Look, you didn't deserve what he did to you, and I don't like fucking cowards. Especially the kind who throw someone else to the wolves to save their own ass." He leaned his elbows on his knees, voice low. "I couldn't stop the cartel from showing up. But I could make damn sure they didn't walk out with you."

Her throat tightened. She didn't know what to say. She didn't even know how to feel, but it seemed like the floor under her had cracked open and she didn't know what was solid anymore.

Player stood, giving her space. "Let's get Snow what he needs. He'll be here any minute. Then we figure out what the hell happens next."

* * *

Heather sat at the long table, her hands tightly clenched tightly in her lap. The room was crowded now with Razor at the head, Player beside her, and three new arrivals who looked as dangerous as they were handsome. The one who looked most intense had longer, nearly black hair they called him Outcast. Crash was smaller with dirty blond hair tied back and intense blue eyes. The third was a huge man appropriately called Beast. They were all clearly Player's friends. The way they looked at her, though -- not with distrust, but with concern, hit her harder than suspicion would have.

Snow showed up within minutes, marching in

with a sleek laptop bag slung over his shoulder and his phone pressed to his ear. She recognized him from yesterday with his white hair and pale eyes. His energy was different, more focused today.

"Tell me you've got the phone," Snow said as he hung up and took a seat across the table from her and Player.

Player nodded toward Heather. "She does. We left it in airplane mode till you got here."

Snow set his bag on the table and flipped open his laptop. "Good. Let's see what we're dealing with."

He held out his hand, not even asking for permission, and Heather passed it over, her stomach twisting.

"I thought of something," she said quietly. "When we hit the road, Brick made changes to my settings. He did something so we wouldn't lose each other if we got separated."

Crash snorted. "Yeah, or so he could track you."

"Not just that," Snow said, frowning as he navigated the phone's settings. "He turned on location sharing. And he didn't turn it off. Got him."

Everyone leaned in.

"I've got a live ping," Snow went on, holding up the phone. "Not a cached signal, real-time location sharing."

"You're kidding." Crash shook his head. "Dumb bastard really left the trail wide open."

"Looks like he's in Pine Hollow," Snow confirmed. "Moving slow. He might be hunkered down there or thinking he's lost the scent. But this?" He angled the phone so Razor and Player could see the screen. "This gives us a head start. At least until he remembers and shuts it down."

Player leaned back in his chair, arms folded.

"Let's make sure we're in position before that happens."

"Outcast, Crash -- you're with Beast," Razor said. "You three grab what you need and roll out now. I want eyes on Brick before sundown."

Outcast nodded, already heading for the door. Crash clapped Player's shoulder once on the way out in quiet, quick solidarity, and followed.

Heather watched them go, afraid to get her hopes up, to believe she might survive this. They were going after Brick. They knew where he was because of *her*.

Snow looked up at her as he continued setting up tracking. "You helped us find him, sweetheart."

But it didn't feel like enough. Not when men were walking into danger for mistakes she couldn't undo. Heather's arms wrapped tighter around herself as Beast, Crash, and Outcast disappeared down the hall. The silence that followed wasn't comforting. Shame and fear curled hot in her stomach.

But then something occurred to her, a horrible possibility.

She looked up, eyes wide. "Wait."

Player glanced at her from where he sat, his brows raised.

"Is that how they found us so fast?" Her voice was barely above a whisper. "When we got to Mercy. They showed up hours later, like they knew where we'd land. Could… be because of my phone too?"

Snow stiffened. Player's jaw ticked.

"You had location sharing on for Brick," Snow said slowly, piecing it together. "If he had it on for you too…"

"Then they could've been watching both ends," Player muttered, dark and low. "Salazar wasn't just sniffing around. He knew exactly where to fucking look."

Heather shook now. If he was right, that made this so much worse. "I brought them here."

Player's tone was gentler than she expected. "No. *Brick* brought them here. You didn't know you were the bait."

Why had Brick done this to her? She'd given him everything he wanted. Now, she was in the hot seat and so were his brothers in Mercy. Hearing it laid out so plainly, *you were the bait,* cut through her like a blade. Her anxiety had been escalating since the moment she realized Brick had left her here, making her chest hurt.

Yeah, she'd allowed Brick to drag her into this, and she'd known there was danger. She'd accepted that as penance for her own stupidity. But not like this. Not that her presence, her phone, her blind loyalty could have put other people in the cartel's crosshairs. So far, these men who had looked her in the eye and mostly spoken to her with respect. They stood their ground with that terrifying man and his cartel when they could've handed her over.

She'd never wanted to be someone's weapon or burden. Her voice caught as she whispered, "They came because of *me*."

Player didn't look away. "They came because of *him*. All you did was trust the wrong man. That's not a crime, Heather."

But it felt like a crime now. One that could cost lives. The guilt, raw and choking, had nowhere to go.

Snow rose from his chair, her phone still in hand. "I'll strip everything off, wipe it clean. But if they were using her signal, they may still think she's here." He looked from Razor to Player. "We might want to get her out now."

"Yeah, we sure as shit can't risk her staying *here,*" Razor said, eyeing Player. "We need a place that's locked down but not obvious." He pointed at Player for emphasis. "And she never leaves your sight."

Player gave a sharp nod. "I've got a place in mind."

As Snow walked out of the conference room, Razor patiently waited for Player to elaborate.

"Margot's parents' place," Player said in a low voice. "It's empty now. She moved in with Ryder, and she hasn't put it up for sale yet. Still here in town, but off the radar."

Razor nodded his approval. "Wait until dark. I'll bring my truck back here for you." That decided, Razor left the room in a hurry.

Heather was trying to keep up with the decisions being made. "Margot is someone's old lady?" she asked.

Player nodded. "She's also a deputy sheriff. We'll be good there."

But the knot in her stomach only twisted tighter. "*I* should be doing something," she said. "To make this right. Not hiding out like a coward while your friends walk into something because of me."

Player watched her like he already knew where she was going. "You think putting yourself in the line of fire fixes this?"

She opened her mouth, then closed it again. God, it sounded stupid when he said it. But the guilt was clawing at her ribs, and she didn't know where else to put it. "I… I don't want anyone to get hurt." She sighed. "Not for me."

"I get that." His voice was steady. Not soft exactly, but steady. "But this isn't about you making it right. You walking into danger won't fix a damn thing. It doesn't give Beast, Outcast, or Crash an edge, and it sure as hell won't make me feel better."

The last part got her attention, but she took it with a grain of salt. Yeah, he'd been her hero, saved her from the cartel by claiming she was his. The man was hot as hell. He'd be a ride she wouldn't mind taking.

But Brick had said the man would fuck anything that moved. His own president explained to him, to have an old lady, he'd need to spend more than a week with her. *Player*. It was probably for the best she didn't even think about him as anything more than the man who might get her out of this situation alive.

"Look, you didn't choose this," he went on. "Brick did. He's the one who made the mess. You just happened to be the piece he thought he could play."

She dropped her gaze, but he wasn't finished.

"Let us do what we do, Heather," he said, looking her in the eye. "I'll keep you safe until we get this resolved."

Heather nodded, swallowing the lump in her throat. She didn't deserve his protection or his brothers, but he was offering anyway. Right now, that was all she had left to hold on to.

Chapter Four

Heather

The ride through Mercy in the borrowed truck was too quiet. Every streetlamp felt like a spotlight on her, every shadow a threat waiting to unfold.

Heather sat rigid in the passenger seat with her hands clenched so tightly in her lap her knuckles hurt. The engine hummed beneath them, steady and unbothered, unlike her. Looking out the side mirror, she saw two motorcycles following them closely. Two dark figures in the night, rough outlines carved from shadows. Were they the same riders who rolled into Mercy with the cartel at the clubhouse?

She couldn't help it. Her chest tightened and her heart raced.

"They've been following us since we left," she whispered, barely trusting her voice. "Player --"

"They're Hounds," he said, as if that answered everything.

She couldn't believe how calm he was. "You're not worried?"

Player flashed her an easy smile. "Axel and Ryder. They're two of our enforcers. They're watching our backs tonight at Margot's place."

Enforcers? It wasn't until her ill-advised entanglement with Brick that she realized how little she knew about motorcycle clubs and their lingo. So they were muscle for the club then. He said they were watching their backs tonight, so there was that.

"I think I mentioned Margot, Ryder's old lady, is a deputy sheriff here in town," he added, as if that would somehow make all this less terrifying.

Heather swallowed hard, her gaze back on the mirror. The two riders moved in perfect sync flanking them like shadows with purpose. It felt more dangerous than protective. All things considered, she didn't *feel* worthy of protection.

"Her parents okay with us staying in their house?" she asked, wanting to be as prepared as she could for what she was walking into.

Player's sigh was a quiet sound in the cabin. "Honey, they're gone," he said. "Her mother, if I remember right, died in a car accident a while back. Her father was shot and killed last year at the gas station where he was working."

She knew she had to be staring at him in horror. "That's terrible."

"Yeah, it was," he explained. "It was Mafia. Long story. But we ran 'em off."

They ran them off? She realized he meant the Hounds had. But hell's bells, what dark, criminal underworld had she been dumped into here? *The Mafia*?

The silence in the cab was heavier this time. Every bump in the road made her pulse jump. The closer they got to town, the higher her anxiety level rose.

Player steered the truck off the main road and onto a quiet side street. The crunch of gravel beneath the tires was the only sound breaking the heavy silence. Heather leaned forward as they slowed in front of a modest one-story house, its porch light glowing like it had been left on for them.

"Here," Player said in a low voice.

Axel and Ryder pulled in behind them, their engines idling a moment before cutting off. In the rearview mirror, Heather saw them dismount in unison, scanning the street as if they expected trouble around every corner. It reminded her how serious her situation was. The kind of serious where people died.

Player opened his door and stepped out without hesitation. She followed, her fingers trembling slightly as she gripped the handle. The night air felt cooler here, quieter, as if it knew better than to make noise. Margot's parents' house sat just five miles from the sheriff's department according to Player, but it could have been in another world.

Heather stood at the edge of the walkway, looking up at the little white house with its green shutters. There was a mailbox shaped like a barn up front. A windchime stirred lazily from the porch. The residence was quaint and peaceful. Somehow, it was even more terrifying to her than the clubhouse.

"Keys are under the mat," Player said, bending to retrieve them. "Margot's been meaning to sell the place but hasn't gotten around to it yet."

"She pays to keep the power on?" Heather asked.

Player winked at her before unlocking the door and pushing it open, letting warm air and the faint scent of old wood and lemon cleaner drift out. "Nah, we know somebody at the power company."

She hesitated for a moment.

"Come on," he said gently. "It's safe."

Heather stepped inside. The house was still. Framed photos hung in the entryway from graduations and family holidays. A smiling teenager with warm brown eyes in a softball jersey smiled at her from a framed picture on the wall. A jacket still hung by the door. The kind of place where someone should've been waiting in the kitchen, offering her a cup of coffee and a warm smile.

Instead, there was only quiet. She stood there probably too long, but Player didn't rush her. He waited until she finally whispered, "Are you sure this is okay?"

"It's more than okay," he said, voice steady. "It's temporary, secure, and I'm staying here with you. You're not going to be alone here, okay?"

That landed like a stone in her chest. She didn't know what she was supposed to say. Instead, she nodded and walked in farther, trying not to cry.

Standing near the front window, Heather folded her arms tightly across her chest. The tick of an old-fashioned wall clock and the occasional creak of settling wood as Player walked through the living room were the only sounds. When the knock came, two short raps followed by the front door easing open, she nearly jumped out of her skin.

A man in a leather jacket stepped in first, followed closely by another man who looked exactly like him. Identical twins from their dark hair to their steely blue eyes. The only difference as far as Heather could tell was one had longer hair, just touching his shoulders. His brother had shorter hair and close-cut beard.

"Axel," Player said pointing to the man with longer hair. Then he pointed to his brother. "Ryder."

Player met them at the door. "All clear?"

Axel nodded. "Nothing moving on the street. No sign of a tail."

Ryder added, "If they're looking, they're not close. For now."

Player clapped Ryder on the shoulder. "Appreciate it. You good to rotate watch with Axel tonight?"

"Got it covered," Ryder said, then glanced toward Heather for the first time. His gaze wasn't cold, just cautious.

Heather straightened instinctively, managing a

small nod.

"Thanks… thank you," she said, hating the wobble in her voice as she spoke.

Player gave a short laugh. "She's been through enough, boys. Ease off the war faces."

That got the faintest smirk from Axel. Ryder gave Player a look that said, *you brought this home; we're just making sure it doesn't bite.*

The twins didn't linger. "We'll be outside," Axel said, already heading back out the door.

"Sleep if you can," Ryder added, his tone a little softer now that introductions were out of the way.

The door clicked shut behind them, and silence crept back in.

Heather let out a shaky breath. "They're intense."

"They're enforcers," Player said simply. "That's their job. But they're good men. They'd die for the club."

The unspoken part hung heavily in the air. *And now, maybe for me too. I'm not worth it.* Heather swallowed hard and tried to ignore the weight of that thought.

* * *

Sitting on the edge of the twin bed in the room Player gave her, Heather still wore her jeans and hoodie. She sat staring at the photos on the bookshelf of what had apparently been Margot Donner's childhood room. The framed pictures showed Margot in her softball uniform, beaming in a cap and gown at graduation, and holding up a shiny new deputy badge with pride. There was even a photo of her sparring in a dojo, fists taped, a look of pure determination on her pretty face.

She looks like someone who always knew who she was. Who she wanted to be.

Heather sat curled in on herself. Guilt felt like a rock in her stomach, and she knew there was no way she'd be able to sleep. Her mind kept latching onto fears and doubts, spinning on everything. Brick's betrayal, the cartel, and the danger the Hounds now faced because of her.

A soft knock at the door pulled her out of her head. It creaked open slightly, and Player's large silhouette appeared, lit from behind by the warm hallway light. "You okay?"

She nodded, even though it wasn't true. "Yeah. Can't sleep."

His boots were quiet on the hardwood as he stepped in. "Didn't figure you could." He glanced at the photos on the bookshelf, then back to her. "Yeah, Margot's a badass. You'll meet her at some point."

Heather let out a shaky breath. "I wish I was more like her."

Player crouched in front of her, his gaze meeting hers. "Don't sell yourself short. Yeah, Brick's dumb ass left you. But *you* told the truth when it counted."

She shook her head. "I… I feel like this is all my fault."

"It's not," he said firmly. "You didn't ask for this. Brick made his choices. You're living with the mess he left behind."

Heather dropped her gaze. "I appreciate everything you're doing. All of you. But I don't know how I'm supposed to lay down and pretend I'm safe while you and your people are out there risking your lives for me."

There was a pause before his response. "You're not pretending. You're surviving."

Heather didn't answer. She had no idea how to.

Player rose and extended his hand. "Come on.

I've got an idea."

Heather's gaze met his. "Where?"

"You said you can't sleep, right?" he asked, a faint smile playing at the corners of his mouth. "Then let's do something else for a bit."

Despite everything, she slid her hand into his and let him lead her out of Margot Donner's childhood bedroom.

* * *

Player

The basement light flickered on with a soft hum, casting long shadows across the cool concrete floor. Heather stepped cautiously behind him, her gaze darting toward the windows above ground level as if they might hold ghosts. They didn't, but he understood why she looked.

"This help?" he asked, nodding toward the low ceiling and the solid brick walls. "The windows down here aren't big enough for anything but a squirrel to squeeze through."

She gave a small nod, her body relaxing. Her shoulders lowered slowly.

Player stepped aside to let her take in the room. It was one of his favorite hidden corners of Mercy, both a part-time capsule and a clubhouse hideout. One wall was lined with old wooden shelves stacked with mason jars. Some still had handwritten masking tape labels, half-faded: Apple Pie, Blackberry, Fire Cider.

"Margot's mom used to do all her canning down here," he said as he moved toward the shelf. "Pickles, jams. That kind of thing. Her dad…" He gestured at the jars with a grin. "Let's just say he took a different approach to preserving fruit."

Heather's brows raised. "Is that moonshine?"

"Sure is." He reached for a jar and gave it a swirl. "He made some of the best in the county. We come down here sometimes. Club planning, private talks, cards."

She squinted at the battered table in the corner. A deck of cards sat unopened on top next to a small bowl of poker chips, all of it waiting like it had been placed there just for them.

"So… you drink moonshine and make plans?" she asked.

Player smirked. "Nah, the drinking's for the nights we don't get anything done."

Grabbing two mismatched glasses from a dusty shelf above the sink, he rinsed them off and poured himself a shot. Then he held out the jar to her.

Heather took a cautious step back. "I don't really drink. And I'm not playing strip poker, if that's where this is going."

He tried to keep a straight face. "Do I look like that kind of guy?"

She hesitated. "Yes."

His laugh echoed off the concrete, a rich sound that eased her nerves even more. He shook his head and set the jar down, still grinning.

"Damn. Harsh." He raised his glass in mock offense. "Don't worry, sunshine. Just cards. You win, you pick the next playlist. I win…" He winked. "I keep the last cookie."

Heather cracked a smile. Barely there, but it was real. With the weight of the world finally lifting a little, he felt something else settle between them. It was quieter than panic and warmer than fear.

Safe.

Player shuffled the cards slowly, one-handed, to show off.

Heather sat across the table, a furrow between her brows as she watched the deck move. The tension was still here, but her eyes had lost their glassy panic. Now they held something else. Focus. Maybe even fire.

He dealt two cards to each of them, then set the deck aside.

"You play?" he asked casually, leaning back in the metal folding chair and downing his shot.

Heather shrugged. "My mom liked to play. She taught me the basics when I was a kid. We didn't have a lot of money, but we had poker nights."

"Sounds like a smart woman."

"Yes."

No hesitation, just quiet truth. He saw sadness there, tucked just beneath the surface. Something that still ached. He knew the feeling.

They played a few hands, and by the fourth, he realized something that made him grin. She was *good*. Not lucky or bluffing her way through. She read the cards, read *him* as easily. Every twitch, every delay, every attempt at distraction, she clocked it. *Damn*. Most people underestimated him because he smiled too much and didn't talk like a man who'd seen blood. Heather hadn't underestimated him for a second. She watched him, figuring out the angles, trying to decide if he was worth trusting.

He liked that. Way more than he should.

Truth was, Player knew how people saw him. He'd always been the guy who got bored too quickly, always keeping things light so no one got close enough to see through the cracks. But Heather? She *saw* him. And instead of running from it, she sat across from him in borrowed clothes, her hair pulled back, not a smidge of makeup, and still looked like a punch to the chest.

The little lady was gorgeous and smart. But underneath, she was wounded. Brave, even if she hadn't seen it yet.

He pushed two chips into the pot and glanced at her cards. "You gonna raise or fold?"

Heather narrowed her eyes. "You're trying to bait me."

"I mean, Player *is* my name."

She shook her head, her lips twitching at the corners.

That half-smile? That look? It was worth every cartel mess they were dealing with. He was in trouble, and he knew it. Not because he was falling too fast, but because for once, he didn't mind.

Player leaned back and whistled low as Heather laid down a winning hand. *Again.*

"Damn, girl. You're hustling me," he said with a grin.

Heather only raised her brows in response, reaching for the jar of moonshine on the table. Without a word, she poured herself a shot and knocked it back straight. No hesitation.

"Well," he said slowly, "I didn't see *that* coming."

She coughed, then smiled through the burn. "Didn't say I *never* drink. I said I don't… usually."

"You waiting until you felt like you'd earned it?"

"Something like that." She leaned her elbow on the table, chin in her hand. "Besides, if I'm about to be the reason half your MC ends up in the hospital, I figure one drink is fair."

His smile faded. "Hey, don't."

"What? Joke about it?" Her voice stayed light, but her eyes gave her away. "You know it's true."

"You're not the reason for any of this. You're

caught up in this mess, like us."

She gave a noncommittal shrug but didn't argue. Not out loud, anyway.

Player watched her carefully, then softened his tone. "So, besides poker and mystery shots, what else don't I know about you?"

Heather arched a brow. "Is that your go-to line?"

"Only when I'm trying to make a pretty girl feel better."

She laughed once, a short, breathy sound, but it made him grin anyway.

"I already know about *you*," she said, pointing her finger at him. "Player. Club flirt. Serial one-night stand. Razor made it *real* clear, and your friends don't exactly defend your reputation."

He chuckled, hands up in surrender. "Okay, yeah. That tracks."

She narrowed her eyes at him playfully. "So why me?"

He looked at her for a long moment.

"You saw me," he said, voice quieter now. "When I stepped in front of you with the cartel watching… you didn't run away. You stayed right there. That took guts."

She smirked. "Still sounds like a line."

He grinned again, the kind of look that made girls laugh and lean closer. "Yeah, well… might be. But it's also true."

As she poured another half-shot, eyeing him over the rim of the glass, Player knew he was in trouble. The kind of trouble you don't walk away from.

They played a couple more hands. She won both. She wasn't just lucky. She knew what she was doing. Cool-eyed, even after three shots of moonshine left his own tongue a little heavier in his mouth. He couldn't decide if she was naturally good at poker or if she just read people like a damn open book. Either way, it had him watching her with more interest than he'd planned on tonight.

After her third win, she poured herself another shot and tossed it back like a pro. But this time, when she set the glass down, her eyes didn't hold the same fire. They were softer.

Was it wrong that he wanted to see her smile again?

"You're dangerous with a deck," Player said lightly, watching her carefully.

Heather surprised him by answering in a quiet voice. "I used to deal for tips at the bar when it was slow."

"That where you met Brick?" he asked.

Heather stared at the cards in her hands, but he knew she really wasn't seeing them. "Yeah," she finally said. "Dive bar in Mississippi. I was working doubles, barely getting by. He started coming in, flashing that dumb smile. Telling me I was too pretty to be stuck there. Said a girl like me deserved more."

Player leaned back in his chair, keeping quiet, letting her talk. Listening was an art most men didn't appreciate. Sitting still in the moment without the need to fix things, explain them, or talk over someone else's pain. He'd learned that skill the hard way, watching women in his life shut down when their voices were ignored. Sometimes silence said more than words ever could.

Heather wasn't only talking. She was peeling herself open, layer by painful layer. It was probably the alcohol, but he'd take it. And he'd be respectful. The last thing she needed was him jumping in with some half-assed sympathy or worse, a joke to ease his own discomfort. No, he wasn't going to make this about him.

He'd give her space. It was obvious to him how hard it was for her to admit her part in the mess she found herself in. She still blamed herself for trusting a man who saw her as a convenience, not an actual fucking person.

Heather wasn't dumb or weak. She was trying to navigate an awful situation. If it took all night, he'd keep sitting there and letting her remember what she'd been carrying alone for too long. It was what he literally signed up for, right? He'd told the cartel she was his old lady. He had nowhere else to be.

"At first, I thought he was simply trying to sleep with me," she continued. "He was real persistent, but never pushy… nice. Asked me to help out with little things. Run errands. Drop off envelopes. Pick up packages. Said he'd make sure I didn't have to sling drinks every day."

"And you didn't ask what you were delivering?" Player asked gently.

"I was too stupid to," she admitted, her voice hitching. "I liked the money. Liked not having to scrub blood off bar floors or deal with drunk assholes groping me for singles. Brick made me think I was finally doing something right." She shook her head and laughed, but it wasn't a happy sound. "Turns out I was only useful."

Player didn't touch her. But God, he wanted to. Not in the way she'd expect, with hands or heat. No, with understanding. He didn't want to be another man who used her up and moved on. "You weren't stupid, Heather," he said finally.

"Sure feels like it now."

"You were doing the best you could," he said

after a moment. "There's a big damn difference. Brick either stole money from the cartel or lost it. My money's on the first option. He either knew what he was doing, or he was fucking stupid." Player leaned forward. "Do you know exactly what he did?"

Heather shook her head slowly. "No. I don't. I asked once. He just said the less I knew, the safer I'd be."

Player exhaled sharply, leaning back again. "Classic bullshit. What did he say to get you to go with him?"

She hesitated. "He told me they'd be looking for me too. That I was part of it now. That if I didn't come with him, I'd be left behind to deal with the fallout. He said... he'd protect me."

Of course he did. Fucking coward. "And after that?"

Her voice got quieter. "Then there were *expectations*. Rules. Things I was supposed to do. How I was supposed to act. What I wore. Who I talked to. If I didn't..." She shook her head again, like she could rattle the memories loose. "The bruises started."

The silence between them tightened. Player fucking knew it. But hearing her say the words, raw but without asking for sympathy, burned through him like moonshine going down wrong. So, she had to fuck him, do what he said, and when she didn't, Brick smacked her around.

Turns out, surviving wasn't all she'd done. Heather carried everything that had happened, and Brick had robbed her as much as he had the cartel. Yet, she still sat across from him and looked him in the eye.

Oh, he hoped his brothers found the asshole and brought him back. He wanted to kill Brick himself.

"Then he just... left me after all." Her voice finally broke. He watched her burying her face in her hands, tears coming on. "I guess I was... a down payment or something."

Player couldn't take the sight of her breaking down anymore. Her shoulders were shaking, her face buried in her hands as if she WERE trying to hide the shame someone else had put there. It cut much deeper than he was ready for. Shoving back his chair, he walked around the table and dropped into a crouch by her side. He wrapped his arms around her and pulled her in.

Heather stiffened for a second before giving in, leaning into him as if she'd been holding herself up for too long. Her forehead pressed against his shoulder, and her fingers curled into the fabric of his shirt. He didn't like the way she was shaking. "I've got you," he murmured, low and rough against her temple. "You're safe now, all right? They can't get to you here."

She didn't speak or move, just clung to him. Slowly, she lifted her head. Those gorgeous green eyes were glassy; her cheeks wet with tears. For a moment, she looked at him, her gaze moving over his face.

Then she kissed him. He could tell it wasn't planned. Hell, it wasn't even careful. It was desperate, trembling, and full of everything she didn't know how to say. He tasted guilt and fear on her lips. He felt her need to feel anything else but broken.

Player froze, startled. It wasn't because he didn't want it. He did, but he didn't expect it as an exchange for comforting her. When he kissed her back, he was gentle, no pressure. He savored the warmth of his mouth against hers. He held her steady.

She pulled back first, her eyes wide, like maybe she regretted it already. "I'm sorry," she whispered. "I shouldn't have --"

"Don't," he cut in softly. "Don't apologize." He

didn't regret it at all. The taste of her on his lips was so sweet.

Heather didn't let him go but kept her arms around his broad neck. Something shifted in those wide, green eyes, like she'd quietly made up her mind about something. In the span of a heartbeat, her lips were back on his. She was soft fire against him as she moved closer.

Player did his best to balance them both from where he crouched on the floor next to her chair. Her enthusiasm tipped him over, and he hit the cold concrete floor hard with her arms around his neck, her lips dancing with his. His gaze locked with hers as he glanced up at her, now sprawled on the floor next to her chair.

"Darlin'," Player whispered. "I like where this is going. I can't believe I'm saying this but, are you *sure*? I don't want to take advantage of you with all the shit you're going through."

Maybe it was the alcohol talking. Maybe it was her truly her wanting him. Heat flashed in those beautiful green eyes as she hovered above him. "Is this the ladies' man of your club having second thoughts?"

Player grinned up at her. "As much as I'd like for this to play out," he said carefully, "I need to know this is really what you want tonight."

Heather didn't appear to be backing off. "What would it take to convince you?"

"Kiss me like you mean it," he said, holding her gaze.

Then she did.

Chapter Five

Heather

Heather hadn't planned on the night going in this direction. She couldn't even blame the moonshine she had poured into a mostly empty stomach. She'd known what she was doing when she climbed into his lap and slipped her arms around his neck. She'd slid her fingers under the collar of his shirt so she could feel the warmth of his skin. Right then, everything had been her choice. Player wasn't making demands of her in exchange for keeping her safe. For once, the moment belonged to *her*, not to Brick or the chaos of the storm he'd pulled her into.

After all, it was easy to see why Player was a ladies' man. He was impossibly gorgeous, his broad shoulders giving way to long, muscular limbs. The intensity in his blue-green eyes took her breath away as she continued the kiss, pouring herself into it. She liked the scratch of his beard against her skin as his lips blazed a trail down her chin to her throat. She loved the rough texture of his hands as they began skimming over her back and arms.

She wanted this. *Him*. Even if he was the club's so-called ladies' man, she wasn't looking for anything lasting. Just tonight. The present.

Her heart raced as she reclaimed his mouth with her own, careful at first and uncertain. And he let her, his patience surprising, but exactly what she needed in the moment. He wasn't pushing her or grabbing her. Player let her come to him. God, that wrecked her.

"Is this okay?" she whispered, fighting back the doubt trying to creep in.

Player's hands stopped, resting gently on her hips. "Yeah, darlin'. It's more than okay."

His voice was warm and solid. Not nearly as cocky as she'd expected.

Heather kissed him again, harder this time, needing to believe this was real. This was her choice, not her being manipulated or threatened. She was using him for comfort and validation, and she knew it. She needed to feel wanted again in a way that wasn't transactional or laced with danger.

But something about the way he held her, careful and slow, made her pause. Player could easily use her back. Most any man would, right? But he didn't kiss her that way. That wasn't how his touch felt.

"I'm not doing this because of your reputation," she said, brushing her lips along his jaw. She wanted him to understand what this was even though she was still trying to come to terms with it herself.

"I'm here," he said, his voice gravelly now. His pulse was clearly kicking up as her lips teased that vulnerable point at his throat. "You can take what you need."

"Tonight doesn't mean I'll expect more," she lied. Well, half-lied. "I… I need this to be mine, okay?"

Player stilled for a breath, easing back to cup her face, his thumb grazing under her eye. "Then it's yours. Whatever you want, okay?"

Her heart squeezed in her chest. It wasn't the words so much as the way he said them. He'd chosen his words carefully, implying no pressure or expectations. He wasn't giving in to her, but he was handing something over, even if neither of them realized exactly what in the moment.

All she was sure of was the feeling of hard muscle beneath her hands as her hands skimmed over his torso. With care, she pushed his cut off his shoulders, and he let her. Before he'd shrugged out of it, her hands were reaching for the hem of the T-shirt he wore, which had to be two sizes too small judging by the way it stretched across the broad expanse of his chest. Reaching behind him, he grabbed the back of the shirt and roughly pulled it off for her in one sexy movement that showed off his heavily muscled arms and the impressive display of muscle covering his torso. There was a light dusting of hair across his chest, a shade darker than what was on his head.

A slow grin spreading across his face told her he was putting on a show for her, and he *knew* she liked what she was seeing. *Gorgeous bastard.* Her hands trailed over his chest and arms as her lips returned to his. When was the last time she'd felt *real* desire? Her last two relationships in as many years had been more friends-with-benefits situations, and she hadn't seen a lot of benefits from either. Her relationship with Brick, if one could call it that, had been transactional. An obligation she'd never wanted. Heather resented her obligations to Brick, with his soft, sagging flesh and the firm mound of his middle. Now, when presented with a man who could have easily been the cover model of her hometown's annual sexy firefighter calendar, she allowed her desire to rise and take over, if only for a few hours.

She wasn't trying to rush through it but need pushed her on. She enjoyed kissing him because the man knew how to kiss. Since he was letting her set the pace, she was one who stopped and pulled off her hoodie. It wasn't nearly as sexy as his slick move, but eventually she worked her way out of it, showing off the lacy purple bra she wore beneath it. *That* got his attention. She loved the way his eyes moved over her upper body. She didn't have large breasts, but she knew how to show off them off. When she stood up to work off her jeans, Player was full-on grinning, not even pretending he wasn't enjoying the show. But he stayed put and resisted any urge to either help or hurry her. His intent gaze stayed on her as she worked the tight denim over her hips and down her thighs. She was grateful they came off easier than the hoodie had. And if her panties matched the bra? Not intentional. It was her preference. Right now, she had no regrets as the man's gaze unapologetically roamed over every inch of her as she moved back into his lap, wrapping her legs around his waist. She could feel the heat rolling off him as she went back to kissing him, pressing herself into all that heated muscle.

Heather wasn't sure if she turned up the heat on their kiss or he did. Honestly, she didn't care. Wrapping her arms around his neck, she ground against his cock. The wet fabric of her panties and the rough denim covering him didn't stop her. But it was affecting him. His breath rushed as if he'd been running, his arms tightening around her slimmer form.

"You feel so damn good," he muttered into her neck, his hips working against her now to pick up her rhythm.

She hummed. "I could feel better."

Player's breath huffed against her neck. "What am I allowed to do here, darling?"

Well, since he'd asked…

Reaching behind her, she worked her bra open and shrugged out of it to toss it to the side. She didn't get to enjoy his heated gaze long as it moved over her breasts because Player dove for her with his mouth and hands, and God, did he know what he was doing. Those rough hands felt good on her breasts, and he was confident, knowing how to squeeze without hurting her. His lips and teeth on her nipples felt sinful, and she loved every minute of it, continuing to grind her center into him as he teased her.

A gasp pulled out of her after he stopped, because a beat later he'd grabbed her hoodie and pushed her back onto the floor, placing her garment under her head as he did. His gaze locked with hers and he pulled her flat on the floor beneath him, keeping his movements slow. When his hands went for the sides of her panties, she didn't try to stop him, although he moved slowly enough, she could have. Once he'd pulled them free from her body, he moved over her. He was broad and muscular, his shadow swallowing her.

His kiss was careful when he leaned down to claim her mouth with his own. "Can I taste you?" he whispered against her lips.

Was he kidding?

Since she was as breathless as he was at this point, Heather nodded wordlessly, watching him drop kisses across her breasts, then the plane of her stomach. He pressed a careful kiss to her mound, almost innocent in its speed and pressure. She had been making an extra effort to keep herself well-groomed, even though her life had been pure chaos the last few weeks. The extra effort was paying off now.

Watching a man of his size lower himself onto the concrete floor between her legs was something to see. He was careful as he pulled one of her thighs over his shoulder and breathed her in. One large hand settled over her tummy while the other curled around her thigh. The small smile he flashed her had her core tightening in anticipation. Hopefully, he was good at this.

She soon realized good didn't even begin to cover it. A ragged gasp pulled from her as he got his mouth on her. Heather's back arched, her hands sliding down to his head as he worked her with his mouth in ways that couldn't be entirely legal. When he moaned into her soaked flesh, she could feel it everywhere. Her thighs tightened around his face, but he doubled down, working her clit with his tongue, making her lose her mind, but not giving her the pressure she needed for release either.

Player held her there, drowning in need, on the floor with his face between her thighs. Her fingers clutched the short strands of his hair as he worked her with his mouth. When she tried to move her hips, his hold on her tightened like a vise. She pulled at his hair, hoping he'd give her more, let her come, he didn't respond. The man was perfectly content keeping her there on the floor and holding her in place for his sinful torment. He kept at her until all that sensation and heat gathered there in her core. Pleasure started rising fast, and she wasn't in control of the sighs and cries he pulled from her as he kept her dancing on the tip of his tongue.

When he slid a finger inside her, her walls tried to clench around it. She was so *close.* His tongue ruthlessly teased her clit as a second rough finger slid into her, and her lower body ached with need. Her hips moved now, and he allowed it. It took her a moment to realize she was basically fucking herself on his fingers, but she didn't care. She needed release in the worst way, her hips moving with his fingers and tongue, silently begging. His fingers turned and curved, the change causing her to lose a little momentum. She whined before she could stop herself. She'd been right *there.*

But then his fingers curled inside her, brushing against a spot that lit up her entire body, an unexpected electrical shock. It was the only warning he gave her. Heather panted, trying to hold onto his head. Her body twitched in need on the cold concrete floor. She would have done anything for him to finish her, to end her torment.

Then he did. His fingers curled again, stroking her just right and staying there. Her body exploded. Heather screamed as she came, currents of pleasure racing through every inch of her body as she shook and twisted beneath him, a slave to his touch. She was loud, and she didn't doubt the twins, outside keeping watch, could hear everything. But she couldn't bring herself to care as wave after wave of bliss shook her like a fierce storm. Her entire body was shuddering in sensation when the storm broke, and his touch gentled, allowing her a moment's respite.

"How are you, beautiful?" Player whispered.

Heather shivered at how close his voice was. When he lowered himself over her, so strong and warm, she wrapped herself around him with shaking limbs. She could smell her excitement on him. She tasted it when he smeared her juices across her lips in a slow, lusty kiss. While the release he'd given her felt wonderful, she wanted more. Her body craved more.

"I'm… pretty good," she managed, slitting her eyes open to see him above her, looking way too pleased with himself.

"You want more?" the bastard asked.

Since she was still trying to get her breathing back under control, she answered him with a nod. Speech was impossible.

With an impressive efficiency, she watched him lift from her only long enough to push his own jeans down. Of course he was commando under there. He paused to fish his wallet from his pants, pulling a small foil pack from it. With a speed that was truly impressive, he had the condom extracted and expertly rolled on in what had to be under ten seconds. And what he was packing…

Yeah, I want that.

Heather should have been embarrassed, but she spread her thighs for him as he draped himself over her again. Player didn't hesitate in lining himself with her entrance and pushing in. She sucked in a breath because he was significantly bigger than Brick and the feeling of him stretching her walls was intense. But he was careful and took his time. The feeling of fullness was the best kind of sin and when he slid home inside her, he paused to give her a moment to adjust.

All she could do was clench around him. *Holy fuck, he feels good.* Slowly, she started moving her hips.

Player took the hint. Balancing most of his weight on his forearms, he started moving in her, with slower strokes at first. Heather loved being stuffed so full, wrapping herself around his strong, firm body. The concrete floor wasn't the most comfortable place, but she wasn't complaining as their bodies moved together, chasing the same bliss.

When he stopped abruptly, the impatient huff escaped before she could stop it.

Player was panting above her. "This ain't going to work, darlin'."

What? Was he serious right now?

Before her mind could start spinning all the reasons for them stopping were bad, the man pulled free of her before scooping her off the floor like she weighed nothing. Heather hung on as he placed her on the table with more care than she'd ever expect from a rough man like him. Without missing a beat, he slid back inside her and started fucking her again.

Wrapping her arms and legs around him, she hung on until he carefully wrapped a hand around her throat and eased her onto her back. He slid in and out of her with ease, and all the while he watched her for any signs of distress.

"This better?" he whispered with a hint of a cocky smile playing around his lips.

Heather moved her hips with him, craving more speed. More of everything. "You stop again, and I'll slap the shit out of you," she warned, smiling. It wasn't entirely a joke.

That had him laughing as his hands gripped her hips tightly and he began to thrust into her harder. "Threaten a man with a good time."

If she hadn't been so blissed out, she would have laughed. The man was a damn menace. But in his defense, he knew what he was doing, and she was back on that uphill climb in seconds as he started giving her what she wanted with power and speed. She moved a hand to her clit, gently stroking herself the way she liked, to get there faster. She didn't miss the heat in those blue-green eyes as he watched her, mesmerized by how her fingers moved. He thrust into her like he was punching the air from her lungs.

Her breath came out in a rush when release came for her. Her fingers worked desperately, and he sped up his movements to match until she came, her cries echoing around the basement as he worked her through it. Spasms were still racking her body when he grabbed her hand and began sucking her juices from her fingers. Her heart raced in her chest, and her pussy rhythmically squeezed him as she rode it out, thrashing on top of the small table.

"You come beautifully," he whispered when her body slowly eased.

Player was still going, still hard and driving into her like he was born to do it. Slitting her eyes open, she watched him chase his own release. All his muscles worked as he held onto her hips and fucked her for all he was worth. When she slid her hand back down into her folds, his gaze darted after the movement. His lips parted in a way that told her he liked what he was seeing. Out of curiosity, she slid her hands over her breasts, started teasing her nipples with her fingers. Little pinches had them tightening up into peaks, exactly the way she wanted, needed.

Now his mouth hung open as he watched. She wasn't sure he knew his thrusts were speeding up, but she kept up the show, licking her lips as she did.

Player swore long and loud as he came, his thrusts harder as he pounded into her. Watching him throw his head back and growl as he pumped into her was something to see. Once he was spent, he moved his hands from her hips to the table. Leaning over her, he dropped his head, trying to catch his breath. Carefully, she smoothed a hand over his head, threading her fingers through the short locks of his hair.

Player glanced up at her after a moment, one corner of his mouth curving up. "You liked that, huh?" he managed to say.

Heather was grinning, the only answer he was getting. She wasn't going to feed his ego.

He carefully pulled himself out of her, sliding off the filled condom as she somehow managed to sit up, wrapping her arms around herself. She felt weak as a kitten, shivering as her skin cooled. Player walked back to the table and began grabbing their clothes off the floor. They started dressing, sneaking peeks at each other as they did.

"What time is it?" she asked, pulling her panties back on.

Glancing at his watch, he muttered, "Just after three."

Her mind was still fuzzy from the moonshine, but the anxiety wasn't as bad now. She yawned as she grabbed his T-shirt and pulled it over her head. She felt like she could sleep now, and being surrounded by his scent was something she very much wanted.

Player grinned. "We done with poker night?"

Heather nodded. "I'm sleepy."

"Okay. We'll head back upstairs."

"I don't want to sleep alone," she said before she could stop herself. In all honesty, she'd never liked to sleep alone. Tonight, she *wouldn't* be able to sleep alone. Her mind would see to that.

Player nodded. "Works for me," he muttered with a soft smile. "I was going to take the couch, but we'll move into the master bedroom. It'll be comfortable."

Perfect.

He took her hand in his as he led her up the basement stairs, turning out the light when they reached the top.

* * *

Player

Player woke up warm. Heather was curled up against him, sound asleep, her breath soft against his chest. His arm was still tucked around her waist like his body hadn't wanted to let go. The long spirals of her shiny black hair draped over his arm, over the soft white bedding.

Hell.

He lay there for a second longer, trying not to

think too much about how she'd looked at him last night. She'd touched him like she had something to prove, maybe to herself more than to him. For whatever reason, he didn't want to cheapen it by calling it sex, but he knew better than to let himself think it meant more either.

Heather had told him last night didn't mean she'd expect more. Except now *he* was. That one sentence had carved something clean and cold right through his chest. Heather didn't expect more. She wasn't holding her breath for promises or pillow talk or forever. She'd made a choice, and she owned it. And for the first time in a long damn while, Player wasn't sure if he liked being the one not chosen.

What the hell is wrong with you, he thought, dragging a hand through his hair. *Since when do you catch feelings because a woman didn't fall apart over you*?

But it wasn't quite that simple. He heard a floorboard creak in the front of the house, pulling him out of his thoughts. Instantly alert, his instincts snapped into place. He carefully eased his arm from beneath Heather, moving slowly so he wouldn't wake her. She stirred, then settled again with a soft sigh that twisted something in his chest.

Barefoot and shirtless, he grabbed his jeans from the floor and tugged them on. The morning air was cooler than he expected, and the hall was dim with light beginning to creep through the curtains. By the time he stepped into the living room, he found Axel and Ryder standing near the front door, looking as casual as ever.

"You girls sleep well?" Axel asked with a knowing smirk.

Player scratched his chest. "Fuck off."

Ryder chuckled. "We're heading out. Got some

things to handle back at the garage."

"Appreciate the backup last night," Player said, voice low but genuine.

Ryder nodded. "Hero and Malachai are heading over. They'll take perimeter. No eyes last night, no movement."

"Razor send them?" Player asked.

"Snow did," Axel said, tossing a nod toward the kitchen. "He's stopping by later, too. Said he had some updates."

Player nodded, glancing back down the hall. He didn't want Heather to wake up alone and wonder where he'd gone. Not after everything she'd spilled last night. But this was business.

"Text me when you get back to the shop," he told them. "Let Razor know she's good here."

Ryder gave a mock salute, and the twins slipped out the door like shadows, leaving the house quiet again.

Player stood there for a long moment, listening to the silence. Then he turned and headed back down the hall to her. As soon as he took a step, he found Heather standing behind him. Without say anything, she gave him a sleepy, sideways glance before she slipped into the bathroom and shut the door.

Running his hand down his face, he let out a breath. She was up now, and he knew damn well she wasn't going back to bed. Not with everything circling her mind like vultures.

Guess I better make myself useful. Heading for the kitchen, he hoped there was something in there to scrape together some sort of breakfast. To his surprise, the cabinets still held a few supplies. There were eggs, a pound of bacon, some butter, and a loaf of bread. *Jackpot.* Tucked on the counter like a gift from the gods was a container of ground coffee and a basic drip machine. He almost smiled.

Hell yeah. I really need that.

He set the machine to brew first, because priorities. Then he got to work on a simple breakfast. It was nothing fancy, scrambled eggs, toast, and bacon. But it was the kind of morning routine he hadn't done in too long. It felt good to do something quiet and normal. He cracked the eggs into a bowl and whisked them with a fork, the sizzle of bacon already starting in the skillet. The smell drifted into the air, warm and familiar. *Comfort food.*

If he was honest with himself, Player wasn't sure what this morning was supposed to be. Just breakfast? Last night was fun, but back to business?

For once he had no idea. This was usually the part where he started to make his excuses. He'd crack a joke, flash a grin, start laying the groundwork for an easy out. It wasn't out of cruelty, just habit and self-preservation. It was how he kept things simple. Keep it light, keep it fun, keep it moving.

But this? This wasn't simple. This was pretty fucking far from simple.

Then again, he knew he didn't have to figure anything out right now. As soon as his brothers got their hands on Brick and dragged his sorry ass back to Mercy, the heat with the cartel would hopefully die down. Razor would handle the rest. Heather would be safe. Case closed.

Then it would be easy, right?

So why did his chest feel tight even thinking about it? Why did the idea of this ending, with her walking out of that room one day and never looking back, bother him more than it should? He didn't like that feeling, not one bit. It was the kind of emotion that

Chapter Six

Player

Player's phone buzzed against the table, the vibration sharp enough to rattle his half-finished mug of coffee. He glanced down at the screen. *Snow.*

"Showtime," he muttered, pushing out of his chair.

Through the front window, he caught sight of Hero's black Jeep pulling up to the curb. Margot's truck slid in behind it with a wreath hanging crookedly from the grill. A second later, the front door swung open, and Snow's tall figure filled the frame, his white hair slicked back from his shower. The intensity in his gray eyes told Player there might be some news. Hero was on his heels, and Margot brought up the rear with her deputy's badge catching the morning light. She carried a small paper bag in one hand.

Heather froze in the kitchen doorway, watching them walking in like the floor might open beneath her.

Snow didn't waste time. His gray-eyed gaze moved to Heather, then back to Player. "Our guys are still on him. Brick's slippery, but he ain't smart. They've got eyes on someone who might be helping him. Can't confirm that yet. If our guys get him, they'll bring him back. Razor wants him breathing so *we* can decide what happens next."

Player nodded. *Good. About damn time.*

"In the meantime, sit tight," Snow went on. "Mercy's being watched, and not just by us. Maybe by Salazar's men too. That means neither of you so much as set foot on that porch without backup."

Heather's shoulders tensed, guilt rolling off her so heavily Player could almost taste it. She wrapped her arms around herself like she could hold the feeling in.

"All right," Snow said, tugging at his cut. "Malachai's on his way. Until Brick's in hand, you two don't move. Understand?"

"Understood," Player said. He didn't need the reminder, and Heather wasn't leaving his side.

Snow's gaze moved to Margot. "Ladies, give us a minute."

Heather's tension spiked sharply. Player could practically feel it from across the room, watching her hands twist in front of her like she was bracing for a verdict.

Margot noticed and stepped close, laying a steady hand on her arm. "You have coffee on?" Margot asked gently. "I could use some."

Nodding, Heather motioned to the kitchen, trembling now.

Player gave Heather one last look before following Snow and Hero down the narrow stairs to the basement. The air was cooler, still carrying the faint tang of the moonshine they drank last night. The table and metal chairs sat where they'd left them, the box of cards shoved to one side.

Snow didn't sit. He leaned against the table instead, crossing his arms.

"What's *really* going on?" Player folded into one of the chairs, elbows on his knees. "Beast, Outcast and Crash have been my best friends for year. Beast is good at finding people. They should have been able to grab Brick by now."

Snow's gaze locked with his. "They're chasing circles. Brick hot-wired a car and ditched it at an old truck stop in West Virginia. They thought they had him cornered, but it was diversion. Bastard's buying time."

Player's gut knotted. *For what*?

Snow's gaze locked with Player's. "You know what I think? He's not carrying the money. If he had it, he wouldn't be dumb enough to try pawning Razor's gun. He left Heather because she slowed him down, not because he was done with her. He's headed somewhere he thinks the stash is waiting. If there's a third party in this, and we think there is, that's the person who got the money out of Biloxi for him."

"So, he's headed there," Hero added. "Trying to keep them off his trail as he goes. But if the money's gone, Brick's a dead man walking."

"Didn't you say you had eyes on someone who might be trying to help him?" Player asked.

"Yeah," Snow replied. "A woman. We don't know much about her yet, but Outcast is on it."

"A woman, huh?" Player shook his head. "What's Brick going to do if the money's gone?"

"If that's the case," Hero said, "he's going to point the finger at someone else and try to run."

Player's blood ran cold. *Heather*.

"They know where she is," Snow pointed out. "How much you want to bet he told them Heather knows more than she really does?"

Player scrubbed his hand down his face. "So, he used her as bait, then doubled down by making her the excuse."

Hero nodded, his expression grim. "Exactly. That's the only reason he'd circle back here. Every day they don't have her he's still on the line for what's owed. If he doesn't have the money, be ready. He'll come back to make sure they find her to get them off his sorry ass."

Snow's gaze cut to Player. "Which means we've got two problems. One, Brick's probably lost the money. If he had it, he wouldn't still be lurking around. Two, he told the cartel Heather's the key. They won't back off until someone proves otherwise."

The basement went quiet for a long beat, the faint hum of the shop lights buzzing louder than they should in Player's ears. All he could see was Heather's face this morning, trying so hard not to look terrified when she asked if the club resented her being here. She had to know Brick had put her in the crosshairs again.

Player exhaled slowly. Inside, he was on fire. "Then we find him first. When we do, he's the one who pays."

Hero spoke up, his voice low and even. "Crash got word through one of his old contacts. Outcast followed up to authenticate it. What he took wasn't pocket change. We're talking six figures, maybe more."

Player's stomach dropped, though he didn't let it show. *Six figures. Jesus Christ, Brick. No wonder El Cuervo showed his face.*

"If Razor gets Brick back in one piece," Snow explained, "he'll hand him over. No hesitation. Razor's not about to put Mercy in the crosshairs over a dumb fuck like Brick. Especially not one who stole from a cartel. He'll wash his hands and let Salazar have him."

Cold, and exactly Razor's style. He had no room for sentiment.

"But if Brick slips through Crash, Beast, and Outcast's hands?" Snow's voice was rough as gravel. "Salazar won't stop. He'll keep hunting, and every Hound with a patch in Biloxi and Mercy is fair game until the debt's paid in blood or cash."

Shaking his head, Player felt the weight of it settling on his shoulders.

"You picked one hell of a fucking time to take an old lady," Hero told him, a corner of his mouth curled up into a half-smirk.

"Razor'll make his call," Snow said. "But you've already forced his hand by claiming her as your old lady. That means she's not going with Brick. Razor might be pissed, but he won't put her in Salazar's hands. He'll fight first." Uncrossing his arms, Snow stared him down. "You know why? 'Cause the *second* he lets cartel muscle take a woman off our porch, the Hounds look fucking weak. Doesn't matter if she was Brick's girl, doesn't matter if she's got no patch on her back. If we give her up, it tells every enemy out there we'll trade flesh to keep the peace. You don't come back from that."

Player listened, knowing he was right.

"The Hounds' name means protection. Brotherhood." Snow continued, "You break that once, it's done. Nobody trusts you, nobody respects you. If Razor's got to choose between war and looking weak? He'll bleed every man in this chapter dry before he lets the club's reputation die."

Trust went a long way between Player and Snow. They'd built it working side by side at Snow's security business, running wire and installing cameras in half the county. But this was much bigger than business. This was the kind of mess that burned whole chapters to the ground if it wasn't handled right.

"Let's hope we can catch this son of a bitch alive to face his own shit," Snow finished. "'Cause if he gets away clean, we're all in the fire. You, me, Razor. *Everyone*."

Snow wasn't wrong. Razor would cut Brick loose without blinking, but if the bastard slipped the noose entirely, they were all screwed. That was the reality of their situation, plain and simple.

But for once in his life, Player didn't give a damn

about the cold math of it. He wasn't thinking about percentages or what Razor would or wouldn't do. All he could see was Heather upstairs in the kitchen, the haunted look in her big green eyes. She was scared out of her mind and still blaming herself for a mess Brick created.

Maybe he was out of his depth on this one. Hell, maybe he was making the biggest mistake of his life. But something in him had already decided. If standing in the fire meant keeping her safe, then let him fucking burn.

* * *

Heather

Heather's mind was a wild jumble of guilt and fear.

Last night had given her a few brief hours of respite while drinking moonshine and sleeping with Player. She had no regrets there.

In the light of a new day, she was still in the middle of cartel hell and running for her life. God, she couldn't even string her thoughts together.

Margot moved through the kitchen on her own. This had been her house once, and she knew exactly where every mug, drawer, and switch was. She set a small paper bag on the counter, her deputy badge catching the light, before pulling a mug from one of the kitchen cabinets and pouring herself a cup of coffee. Like Heather, she didn't put anything else in it. She drank it straight.

"Emily sent these," Margot said, blowing over the top of her coffee and sliding the bag toward Heather. Her dark auburn hair was pulled back in a no-nonsense way, like she didn't have time for frills. Her warm brown eyes, set above a spray of freckles, made the sharpness in her tone easier to take. "She owns Whisk & Whimsy. It's a bakery a couple of blocks down from here. She's Snow's old lady. Best Christmas cookies ever, with cinnamon, the whole works. They're a big deal each year at Christmas. They're usually sold out by noon each day."

Heather stared at the bag, the smell of sugar and spice rising out of it. That small token of cheer was completely at odds with the dread sitting heavy in her chest.

"Thank you," she said, pulling out a chair at the small kitchen table and taking a seat.

Margot left the counter to join her at the table, placing the mug down in front of her with the kind of confidence Heather had only ever faked. She seemed like the kind of woman who looked like she belonged anywhere, even standing in a room full of rough bikers.

"You're with Ryder?" Heather asked after a minute.

Margot nodded, smiling. Only the mention of someone Margot cared about could come close to messing with the other woman's composure. Even then, it would be out of love, not weakness.

What would it be like to live with that kind of certainty? To move through the world so steady in who you were? To know nothing, not even a cartel breathing down your neck, could shake it?

"How do you do it?" Heather asked finally, voice low. "You're a sheriff's deputy *and* you're with a biker?"

Margot shrugged. "Same way you do anything that matters. Clear communication lines, trust. Knowing who's worth standing next to when things get bad."

Heather looked down at the table, her throat tight.

"Look, I know you're scared right now." Margot's tone softened. "But Player claimed you. That means something. The Hounds will fight before they hand you over." She took a sip of coffee, her dark eyes steady. "See, clubs like this? We run on loyalty, not convenience. You wear a patch, you're a brother. A man claims a woman as his old lady, she's under the same protection as him. That patch covers her too. It doesn't matter if it's been a week or a lifetime. Once he put you under his wing, every man in the Hounds is bound to stand with him."

She listened, trying to take it all in. She knew some things about the MCs, but there was a lot more she didn't know.

"Now, don't get me wrong," Margot went on, her voice lowering. "Some guys throw that claim around easily. But not in this club. Player sure as hell didn't do it lightly. Not when he's never had an old lady before. That line he drew out there in front of Salazar? It wasn't only words. It's a promise. It means the club would rather fight and bleed than hand you over. If they did that, it wouldn't just be about you. It would tear down the whole club's name. And Razor? No way he'd ever let that happen."

The words should have been comforting. Instead, Heather's stomach knotted so tight she almost doubled over. Men like Beast, Outcast and Crash were already risking themselves chasing Brick, and now the club would fight for her too. She hadn't meant for any of them to bleed because of her, but that's exactly what could happen.

Margot's words rang in her ears. *The Hounds will fight before they hand you over.* That meant every man wearing their patch, every woman tied to them, would bleed because of *her*. All because of the choices she hadn't made carefully enough. She hadn't asked the right questions and had allowed herself to be dragged along in Brick's wake. She'd never wanted anyone else to be caught in the mess she and Brick had made. But now Player had drawn a line for her, and the whole club stood behind it, willing or not. The guilt was cutting her open.

When she finally lifted her gaze, Margot was still. Heather knew what she was doing. Margot didn't know her. She was weighing every word, every twitch of expression, searching for cracks. The woman was watching for the faintest sign Heather might be lying. If she was, if this was all some kind of trick, then Ryder, Margot's man, would be putting himself on the line for a woman who wasn't worth it, and Heather understood exactly why Margot had to be certain.

Heather swallowed, her throat tight. "I swear I'm not lying to you," she said, her voice steadier than she expected. "I was so *stupid*. I let Brick talk me into things I should've questioned, but I never lied about what I was doing. I didn't even know what it really was until it was too late." Her gaze met with Margot's, the intensity of those watchful brown eyes pinned her in place. "I swear to you, if I'd known I was dragging anyone else into this, I never would have come here. I'd have run the other way. At least I would have tried."

The silence stretched, thick and heavy. Heather's hands twisted in her lap until her knuckles ached, but she didn't look away.

The tension in Margot's shoulders eased slightly. It wasn't forgiveness, but it was something. Enough for Heather to breathe again, even if her chest still burned with guilt.

"You know," Margot said, "Ryder has never been a saint, but I fell for him. Hell, I'd been in love with that man since high school, and he managed to work his way through almost every woman in Mercy except me." A wry smile tugged at her lips, touched with something older than amusement. "We didn't come together until years later, when the Mafia came for Axel's old lady. That's a tale for another time. Point is, Ryder had a reputation too. Ladies' man, heartbreaker, the whole damn package."

Heather hadn't expected *that* confession. "The Mafia?" She remembered Player saying something about the club facing off against them.

Margot nodded. "Yeah. Next to the Mafia, the cartel doesn't seem so scary. The Hounds made it through that. They'll make it through this too." Warmth bled into her brown eyes. "What I'm getting at is if you're doubting Player because of who he's been? I get it. I never thought I'd see the day he'd stick his neck out for one woman. But he did. For *you*. Men like that don't do it unless something's different."

Heather searched Margot's face for even the smallest hint of doubt, but there was none. Only the kind of conviction that came from someone who had lived it herself. Heather's chest tightened, like the air had shifted. A man like Player, who'd had every reason to keep her at arm's length, had chosen instead to claim her in front of killers. Not because it made sense, not because it was safe, but because… he had. Suddenly, all the cracks in her defenses felt a little harder to hold together. Maybe Margot was right, and something *was* different here.

Then again, she'd only known him for three days. Why did he put so much at stake for someone he barely knew?

Margot went on, eyes steady. "The difference is, Ryder was honest with me from the start. He didn't sugarcoat anything. He didn't lie to make me feel safe. He gave me a choice of being in this world."

"You're also trained in law enforcement," Heather pointed out. "He knows you can handle yourself."

Maybe it was the way it was worded, but Margot's chin lifted at those words. Pride flashed in her eyes. "It's more than that." Margot shook her head. "Choice matters. Brick took that from you. That says more about him than it does about you."

All of the tension, the burning guilt, loosened in Heather's body at those words. For the first time since Mercy, she didn't feel she was being quietly measured and found lacking.

Heather wanted to believe, to let the warmth of those words in. But the echo of Brick's promises was still too raw. *I'll keep you safe. You're with me now*. She'd heard that kind of vow before, and it had turned to chains around her neck.

So why did it feel different when Player said it? Why did the thought that he might actually mean it scare her more than comfort her? Heather moved her hands onto the table in front of her, trying desperately to calm herself.

"Why should I trust him?" The words came out quieter than she meant, raw enough to sting. "Why should I believe Player's any different from Brick? Or any of the others who only said what I wanted to hear?"

Margot seemed to be considering her answer. She studied Heather, steady as stone, as if she were wondering how she could actually reach her. Then her lips curved, not quite a smile. It was more like a truth laid bare. "When a man like Player puts his reputation on the line, it's more than words. It's about what he does next. Brick claimed you and used you. Player claimed you and stood between you and a cartel enforcer without hesitation. That's not talk. That's action." Margot tilted her head as she spoke, her auburn hair catching the light. "Actions count for everything."

Heather wanted to argue, wanted to cling to her fear because it felt safer than hope. But Margot's words lodged deep anyway, nagging at the wall she'd built around herself to keep people out, to keep them from hurting her.

"Thank you," Heather murmured, her voice so low it almost disappeared between them.

"Don't thank me yet," Margot said quietly. "Save it for when we get you through this."

Heather gave the smallest nod, but it was enough. For the first time in weeks, she didn't feel like she was standing alone.

* * *

Player

The house was quiet after everyone had left. It was the kind of quiet that made every tick of the clock sound louder. Player had straightened up the basement room downstairs, unclogging the sink there. All of them knew it needed doing but they hadn't done anything for the last couple of months. It gave him something to work on while they waited for his friends to grab Brick and drag his sorry ass back to Mercy. While they waited for the cartel to start some shit.

Yeah, waiting fucking sucked.

Once the sink was fixed, he noticed the silence

and realized he didn't know where Heather was or what she was doing. Player headed upstairs, finding her in the living room, sitting curled up in one corner of the couch, staring out the window.

He dropped down in the chair across from her, his elbows braced on his knees. "You look like you're trying to solve world peace."

Her faint laugh held no humor. "I don't even know who I am without the fear," she admitted, words tumbling out before she could stop them. "Every choice I've made for months has been about survival, about staying one step ahead of what's chasing us. Every day Brick told me what to do, and I… I let him. Now he's gone, and I don't even know what to do or what I want. Or if I *deserve* to want anything."

Her honesty hit him harder than he expected. Most people wrapped their pain in barbed wire. Heather laid hers right out, fragile and real. Still, Player appreciated a woman who knew what was wrong and told him, not asking or expecting him to fix it for her.

Player leaned back in the chair, the leather of his cut creaking as he shifted. "Maybe that's the point," he said in a low voice. "You don't have to know right now. You don't have to have some big, shiny life plan. You get to… be. For a while anyway. Eat decent food, get some sleep, talk when you feel like it, tell me to shut the hell up when you don't." He shrugged, trying to make it sound lighter than it was. "Surviving's good. But you can't exist like that. Not for long anyway."

Brick was an asshole, and he'd done this to her. He'd picked her apart and made her dependent on him. Made her afraid. And Player, for once in his life, didn't feel the itch to make a joke or look away. He let her see he meant it because he truly did. Normally, that sort of honesty felt too close to intimacy, to belonging.

Normally, it would have scared the shit out of him.

Somehow, with Heather, it didn't.

Her gaze slid away from his, and he caught the way her shoulders tensed like she'd already said too much. Then, softer than a whisper, she asked, "Do you think your friends are okay?"

Player could see the guilt behind her eyes, the burden she carried for things that weren't hers. He wasn't about to let her sink deeper into it. "They're fine," he said, letting a grin curl at his mouth. "Hell, no one on this planet can track a bastard down the way Outcast can. The man's a damn bloodhound when he sets his mind to it. You know he once found a girl off a picture he lifted from some asshole tied up in a gun deal gone wrong. He didn't have a name, didn't have an address. Just a snapshot. And he found her."

That got her attention. Her head came up, her gaze catching his with something that wasn't fear. Player leaned forward on his elbows, warming to the story. "Outcast had been looking for her since they were teenagers. He never stopped. Tracked her all the way to Louisville." Player had to laugh, though part of it was awe. "The son of a bitch climbed into a cage with a huge fucker named Goliath. To hear him tell it, the guy looked like he could break a man in half. Outcast went in swinging anyway, came out the other side alive. That's the kind of stubborn motherfucker he is."

He let the words hang a second, then softened his tone. "If I had to place a bet? I'd put money on Beast, Outcast and Crash dragging Brick back here to face his own damn mess. They've got this. You don't need to carry it on your shoulders, okay?"

Heather blinked at him, like she wasn't sure if she believed it, but *wanted* to. "I can't believe Outcast really found her."

Player's mouth tipped into a grin. "Yeah. He did. Name's Anya. She's his old lady now. He'd kill anyone who looked at her wrong."

Heather nodded slowly, like that part she could understand. Her gaze stayed on him though, sharp and searching. "But none of you know me. Why would you do this… for me?"

Player took her in, really *looking* at her. She was drowning in fear, in guilt. She honestly looked like she was still waiting for someone to decide she wasn't worth the trouble.

Finally, he leaned forward again. "That's what we do. We don't have to know you, Heather. You're under our roof, you're wearing our protection now, and that means you're one of ours until Razor says otherwise. Me?" His grin flickered, softer this time. "I claimed you. I don't need a reason. You're mine to stand for, whether you believe it yet or not."

It seemed his words landed heavily. She stared at him like she wanted to argue, but all that came was a shaky breath, and for once, she didn't push.

* * *

Heather

Heather froze when he said the words. *I claimed you.*

No one had ever said anything like that to her. Not Brick, not anyone. With Brick it had been all about survival, a transaction wrapped in threats. With Player… it sounded like a choice. Protection without a price tag. What would that be like?

Her throat tightened. She really wanted to tell him not to say things like that. He didn't know her. If he really saw the mess she was inside, he'd take it back. But, God help her, she couldn't. The look in his eyes, so steady and sure, made the protests catch and burn on the way up.

Instead, she turned her face slightly, pretending to focus on the glass in her hand. Her fingers were trembling, but not from fear this time. More from the quiet, dangerous seed of something she didn't dare name. *Hope*. She'd forgotten what it felt like to hear someone claim her, not because of what she could do for them, but because they *wanted* to. That terrified her more than the cartel ever could.

"It's so hard to… not panic about all of this," she said with a voice that sounded much calmer than the storm inside her mind. "I can't keep myself from worrying. What happens when one of your friends is killed? Or the cartel comes after us here because Brick snuck off? Having someone put themselves in danger for a stranger, for me, I…"

His blue-green eyes were soft on her. He studied her for the longest minute. Probably trying to figure out how he'd saddled himself with such a pathetic excuse of a woman.

"Stop," he said after a moment. "Who the fuck convinced you you weren't worth fighting for, Heather? Was it Brick?"

Tears stung the backs of her eyes, and she hated it. She couldn't remember the last time she'd cried so much. For a few days, leading up to their arrival in Mercy, she'd chalked it up to spending the holidays on the road with Brick. Normally, she would have spent the holidays in her hole of an apartment, with a tiny fake Christmas tree near her television and a long string of Hallmark Christmas movies if she was lucky enough to be single. Otherwise, she spent them with her latest emotionally unavailable boyfriend, waiting in vain for him to make the holiday special for her in any way. Hell, a greeting card would have been monumental to her, but she'd never even gotten one of those. Not from a man she was in a "relationship" with.

What was she supposed to think? Brick was just the latest guy to use her for his own selfish purposes, dumping her here in Mercy with a biker club that could have handed her over to the cartel. But they hadn't. They were sheltering her, and she didn't understand why.

Blowing out a sigh, she shook her head. She'd already revealed too much to Player as it was. And she'd slept with him previous night. Considering his reputation, she knew that didn't necessarily mean anything. It had been physical release. A nice bubble of moonshine and endorphins that helped her sleep for a night. Helped her escape the guilt and the hope someone like Player…

No. No, she wasn't going to let Player's words, or Margot's, convince her this was anything more than business as usual. It wasn't. *Everything* was a transaction. She'd trusted Brick who had promised her a way to make more money, a way to maybe climb out of the desperation she'd always lived in. It ended the same way it always did. When trouble found Brick, he pulled her into it. Then he made her pay for the protection he offered. The price was always the same. Her body, her loyalty, even when she received nothing in return.

She never really received anything in return.

Realizing Player was still waiting for an answer, she met his gaze. She shrugged, and gave the only answer she had to give. "I'm not."

In the span of a heartbeat, he was on his feet and

walking in her direction. Player dropped heavily on the couch next to her, the intensity of his gaze on her just as intent. His jaw flexed, the muscle ticking hard as he studied her. "Bullshit," he said, the word low but steady. "You don't get to decide that. Not after Brick left you holding the bag, not after you stood your ground out there when Salazar was staring holes through you. You're here. That's enough. More than enough."

Leaning closer with his elbows braced on his knees, his gaze remained locked on hers. "You keep telling yourself you're nothing, you're gonna start believing it so deep you won't ever crawl back out. But I *see* you. I'll be damned if I let Brick or anybody else write the rest of your story for you." For a second, the words hung there between them, sharp as barbed wire. Player eased back, gentler now, the edge in his voice giving way to something else. "So, no. You're not nothing. And don't you fucking tell me you are again."

The venom in his words would have her recoiling, but the emotion flashing in his eyes stopped her cold. No one had ever spoken to her like that. No one had ever defended her that way, when she couldn't even defend herself. Her heart ached in her chest as she thought about what his words meant, how the intensity of his gaze on her made her feel.

Leaning closer to him, Heather planted a hand between them on the couch. Her other hand lifted to his face, her palm smoothing against his cheek while she sent up every prayer she knew he wouldn't notice she was shaking. Wouldn't notice how close she was to coming apart. All she knew was she wanted that peace she'd experienced the night before, wrapped in his arms with his body on hers, inside her. All the warmth, the pleasure, felt like a glimpse of heaven she'd never reach, safety from the storm, even if it was only for a little while.

Player let her kiss him. He just held still for her for the longest moment while she kissed his mouth, while she closed the distance between them on the couch. When she deepened the kiss, he allowed it. When she pressed herself against him, one muscular arm wrapped around her like a band of steel to hold her in place.

When he scooped her off the couch, her heart slammed in her chest. But her need outweighed the fear. She let him carry her out of the living room, down the hall to the room where they'd spent the night together. Player didn't drop her onto the bed as much as he followed her down, his weight pressing her into the mattress. She wrapped herself around him, wanting his strength and desire, wanting to feel something besides guilt, panic, and fear.

Last night had made her feel beautiful, worth something. She was greedy enough to want more.

Player was already panting. She wasn't in the mood for much in the way of foreplay. Like two horny teenagers in a backseat, they worked off their shoes and jeans. She'd barely had time to part her thighs for him when he speared into her, drawing a gasp from her that was pure relief. Their kisses were heated, their hands skimming over each other's bodies, needing to know the other was real. He didn't move at first and while she appreciated the courtesy, Heather needed him in the worst way. Circling her hips under him, she tried to draw him into that timeless rhythm. Lowering himself onto his elbows, planted on either side of her head, Player took her head in his hands as he began to fuck her, giving her what she wanted, fast and careful all at once.

Heather hung onto him, willing to give him anything to make the pain pause. When he broke the kiss, and his gaze met hers, she could almost feel like he could see her heartbreak. He dropped kisses over her face, along the column of her throat. His breath was hot in her ear, had her shivering around his cock.

"Not going to let anything happen to you," he swore, his movement in her body growing in speed and strength. "I will show you… you're worth something… worth it to me."

Their bodies strained together, a quick, lusty dance. But her heart was caught up in the strings of that lust. As Player moved within her as if she were precious, something he needed more than air, she could almost pretend he felt something for her too, even though her heart whispered it was impossible.

Heather reached her release a heartbeat before Player did. Her own cries were drowned out by the roar of his, and it was a sound she could hear every day. Every single day if she was ever given the chance.

Player claimed you and stood between you and a cartel enforcer without hesitation. That's not talk. That's action.

Margot's words drifted through her mind as Player collapsed and rolled to her side. Pulling her into him, she ended up with her head on his chest, her hand over his pounding heart.

Chapter Seven

Heather

Heather draped the folded blanket on the back of the couch, smoothing it flat as if the little chore could somehow pay her way. Margot's house wasn't hers; none of this was, and every moment she felt she was living on borrowed time someone else was paying for. Every creak of the floor reminded her she was a problem the club had to carry as she walked to the kitchen.

From the kitchen doorway, Player leaned his shoulder against the frame. He watched her with a steady half-smirk. "You planning on alphabetizing the spice rack too?"

Her hands froze on the dish towel. God help her, even his teasing felt like a spotlight, warm and heavy all at once. That was Player's thing, wasn't it? The easy charm, the cocky humor that came to him as easily as breathing. She'd seen it at *Sackett's*, the way women leaned toward him without even realizing it, drawn in like moths to a flame.

She wasn't immune. Not even close. Part of her bristled at it. *You don't get to look at him that way, not when you're already trouble dropped in his lap*. But another part of her, the part that had been starved for anything that wasn't fear or manipulation, ached for what he was offering. She craved his attention and the way his eyes lingered, like she was *worth* looking at. She knew it was foolish because she was his girl of the week at best. Once this drama was over, his interest in her would likely go with it.

Forcing her gaze away, she folded the towel too neatly. "Trying to make myself useful," she muttered, hoping her voice didn't betray the way her pulse skipped at nothing more than his grin.

"You already are." His tone was casual, his gaze lingering too long.

Heather folded her arms, her pulse racing. *He regrets last night,* she told herself, *and the night before. Of course he does. I'm baggage he's stuck with.*

"Is that supposed to be hospitality?" she asked, forcing a little bite into her voice. Inside, though, her stomach was a huge knot. Player, leaning there with that easy half-smile and steady gaze, had her off-balance. *Of course he's charming,* she thought bitterly. *Men like him always are.* She'd seen that look before. Brick had had his own version of it when he wanted something from her and so had every man she'd ever mistaken for a safe place to land. She wasn't sure if Player's attention meant protection, pity, or another game he was good at playing.

Her words slipped out like armor, a thin layer of sarcasm to keep from showing how unsettled she felt under the intensity of his look.

Player's grin widened a fraction. "Baby, if I was showing you hospitality, you'd know it."

The words had heat flooding her face. She looked away on that note, and his low chuckle followed, threading under her skin.

But it didn't settle her. If anything, it made the tightness in her chest worse. Restlessness wouldn't allow her to keep still, as if she had to keep moving to earn her place in the room. Every dish she washed, every blanket she folded felt like proof she wasn't a total burden. Still, the thought circled in her mind like a vulture. *They must resent me being here.* These men were risking their lives, their families, their town, because she'd been stupid enough to fall in with Brick.

The guilt pressed heavily in on her, but she

straightened anyway, lifting her chin so Player wouldn't see how much it weighed.

"Honey, you're exactly where you're supposed to be right now."

Heather's gaze caught his. He was still in the doorway, but his voice was steady. No, he wasn't joking this time. For a second she couldn't breathe.

Player watched her as if it was the simplest truth in the world, and she didn't have to scrub dishes or fold blankets or prove herself useful to anyone as far as he was concerned. The warmth of it hit her harder than she wanted to admit, and she fumbled for a response, anything to push back the sting in her eyes. Why would he say that? Why would he care?

After a long moment, he lifted one shoulder in an easy shrug. "Razor doesn't keep dead weight under his roof. If he had some problem with you, you'd be gone already. So quit trying to prove something that's already settled."

Heather's lips twitched despite the knot in her stomach, and she couldn't help feeling that it was exactly what he'd been aiming for.

"See? Knew I could get a smile out of you," he said, pushing off the doorframe and strolling past her like he owned the room. He plucked the dish towel from her hands, tossed it onto the counter, and shot her a look that was half-teasing, half-serious. "Relax a little, darlin'. Nobody here's keeping score."

She shook her head, trying to bite back another smile. "Easy for you to say. You don't feel like a stray somebody left on the porch."

Player turned, his gaze locking with hers again. This time his smirk softened into something that felt more like a promise. "Nah. You're not a stray. You're under our roof, and that makes you ours. End of story."

Why did it feel like the way he said "ours" really meant "mine?" Warmth bloomed in Heather's chest before she could stop it, curling right up against the doubt she carried. She wanted to tell him to stop saying things like that. She was so afraid to believe him. But the words stuck in her throat.

His grin slipped back into place, lighter this time. "Besides, if you keep fussing over every corner, I might start expecting turn-down service and breakfast in bed."

Heather cut him a look on that note. "Do you ever take a break from being a lady charmer?"

Player gave her a lopsided grin, letting the silence stretch long enough to make her squirm. "Why would I? It seems to be working."

But he didn't press further. Instead, he jerked his chin toward the back of the house. "I found a box of decorations in the basement earlier. No tree, but if you want one, I can get someone to haul one over. Make the place feel less like a hideout and more like Christmas."

The offer caught her off guard. A tree. Decorations. *Christmas.*

For a heartbeat, she didn't know what to say. It was too normal, too gentle, in a life that had been nothing but running and fear for weeks. The idea of someone hauling a Christmas tree into this house for her, especially considering the shit they were in *because of her* during the holidays, hit her sideways.

Don't believe it, she warned herself. *Don't start thinking this means more than it does.* Brick had promised to take care of her too, hadn't he? *And look where that ended.*

But the warmth of the offer lingered, slipping

past her defenses. For the first time in a long time, she caught herself wondering what it would feel like to wake up to twinkling lights and the smell of pine instead of fear and loneliness. That scared her most of all. *Yes, she wanted that.*

She covered the ache the only way she knew how. She forced a half-smile and said, "I'm not exactly the decorating type."

Player's mouth curved, slow and knowing. "Guess it's a good thing I am, then."

The answer stole her breath. She didn't argue. She watched him fish his phone out of his pocket, then heading back down the hall as he called someone.

* * *

Player

Player was halfway through stringing lights along the fireplace in the living room when Ryder's shadow outside the window caught his eye. Then he stepped into view, Axel trailing behind him. The twins were too still, too sharp-eyed, for it to be anything good. Player set the lights down and headed out the front door to join them.

"Walk to the fence," Ryder said, tipping his head in that direction.

Player followed them, his boots crunching over frosted grass. The twins didn't waste words. They never did. But the look they traded before Ryder spoke was enough to set his gut churning.

"There's a fresh scuff on the fence," Ryder said flatly, pointing it out. "Like somebody slipped over and back."

Axel opened his palm, and sitting there was a cigarette butt. "It wasn't there long next to the fence. The embers were warm when we found it."

Player swore under his breath. His stomach sank, ugly and cold. It sure felt like Brick's style. In the ten damn years he'd know Brick, the fucker always had been sloppy, arrogant, and convinced he could circle as close as he wanted without paying the price.

"You tell Razor?" Player asked.

Ryder nodded. "He's having Snow bring over motion lights and cameras. We'll keep eyes on the place. But you need to know, someone's already been close."

Axel's gaze stayed fixed on Player, reading him. "Who do *you* think it is? Cartel?"

Player shook his head. "No. Cartel wouldn't waste time creeping around fences. If it was them, we'd already be picking glass out of the walls. They'd hit hard, fast, and loud. This? This is sloppy." He exhaled, the sound edged with frustration. "Feels more like Brick. Fits him too."

The twins exchanged a quick glance, both grim. Ryder tilted his chin.

"You heard anything from Crash, Beast and Outcast?" Player asked.

Axel shook his head. "Not today. They'll check in soon, though."

Player scrubbed his hand over his face. The silence of his brothers sat heavy. Too heavy. Brick slipping past them once was bad enough. If he was circling back toward Mercy and Heather, it meant trouble was closer than they all wanted to admit.

If Brick was watching Heather? That was a whole new problem.

As they walked back to the porch, Ryder crossed his arms over his chest. "If it's Brick, he's not just sniffing around. He's watching *her*. Don't let that claim blind you, brother. You're in it now, and Razor's watching you too."

Axel's expression was sharper, his eyes narrowing as he studied Player. "Yeah. You've always been the one who could walk away clean, but this isn't one of your flings. If Brick's circling, it's not just about money. It's about her. You've got to be ready."

"You sure about that?" Player asked. "If he's got the money, why is he back here?"

Axel seemed to consider that. "It made sense he left her behind when he was about to get to the cash. Beast, Outcast and Crash think it's where? West Virginia? But if it's gone…"

"Exactly," Player told him. "If the money is gone, he could be trying to grab her and hand her over to the cartel to save his own ass."

Heat rose in his chest. Player didn't need them to tell him what he already knew. Besides, Heather wasn't a game, not anymore. But he swallowed down the quick snap of temper. None of them knew the entire story yet. But they would soon.

"To answer your question, I'm ready." Player straightened, meeting Axel's stare head-on. His words came from somewhere deeper than he'd planned. "And don't give me that look. You didn't know Sadie either, not when she showed up in Mercy half-dead. But the club went to war for her anyway. Took on the whole damn Mafia to make sure she lived through it. Heather's no different. She didn't ask for this, and I'll be damned if she pays Brick's bill."

Silence fell between the twins. Axel's brow lifted a fraction, Ryder cutting him a quick glance. That flicker of surprise, like they couldn't quite believe what they were hearing. It was all the answer Player needed.

"If I catch Brick's dumb ass *here*," Player added, "he won't walk away breathing."

* * *

The familiar scents of the garage, the oil, rubber, and exhaust fumes, didn't do a damn thing to soothe Player's nerves. Cutting the engine, he swung off his bike. His boots crunched against gravel as he reached the door. Hero had an SUV up on a lift, working on its underside. He was running the shop solo while the twins were at the safe house. He nodded to Player who was headed for the back office.

Razor was back there, his forearms on the desk. Snow was already there, scrolling on his phone, looking like he'd aged a year since Player had last seen him. Neither was a good sign.

"Sit," Razor said, not bothering with greetings.

Player dragged a stool over, settling in, every muscle coiled tight. "What've we got?"

Razor leaned forward, his hands clasped on the desk like a man bracing for impact. "Beast, Outcast and Crash found the woman. The one they suspected was helping Brick."

"Found her?" Player asked.

"Dead," Snow said. "Her apartment was torn to hell. Apparently, she's the one who got it out of Biloxi for him. But she didn't sit on it. She blew through it before he could get there."

"They think he killed her?"

Razor nodded, his expression grim. "Left her body behind and ran like the fucking coward he is. Crash, Outcast, and Beast picked up his trail again, but he's running lean. He could already be back in Mercy."

The air in the garage thickened. Player leaned back on the stool, his boots planted wide as his brain worked the angles.

"He left Heather to make a run for his stash," he said slowly. "But when it was gone, he doubled back.

After killing the woman. And you know he didn't cover his damn tracks. He'll have cops on his ass now."

"Yeah," Razor replied.

"He's looking for her," Snow added. "Outcast got intel from Vendetta in Oak Grove. People have been asking around at gas stations and truck stops about a woman who fits Heather's description."

Player's hands curled into fists. "People? Or the fucking cartel?"

"Exactly," Razor said. "He's probably told the cartel she knows where the money is. Now it's gone, they're breathing down his neck, and the dumb fuck's panicking."

Snow looked up from his phone, his stare hard. "So now it's a matter of who can grab her first, him or the cartel. We've got to lock this down, fast."

Player shook his head. "Based on what Axel and Ryder found over at the house, I think Brick knows exactly where she is."

Snow muttered a curse, dragging a hand through his hair. "So, what's the play? Wait for him to make a move and hope we're faster?"

Razor's mouth was a tight line. "We don't wait. That's what Brick's counting on. He's a coward, but he's not stupid enough to walk through the front door. He's watching, circling, looking for an opening."

Player leaned forward, jaw tight. "Then we give him one."

Both Razor and Snow looked at him.

Player nodded. "Ryder and Margot's place. We make it look like we're moving Heather there to lay low. A quiet house in the country, far from town, fewer eyes."

Snow leaned back in his chair, arms folded. "If Brick's watching, he thinks it's his chance. Small escort, remote area. Just two women."

Razor smirked. "But Margot's not a club girl. If Brick shows up thinking it's an easy grab… Well, he's dead fucking wrong."

Player let out a slow breath. "He wouldn't know she's a deputy. The last time we had the Biloxi Hounds up, Ryder and Margot weren't together. He'll think she's Ryder's woman. He'll think he's got the upper hand." His gaze shifting from Ryder to Snow and back, waiting on any objections. He could see the beginnings of approval in Razor's face.

"He tries anything," Snow said, "and she'll put him down before he ever gets close enough to touch Heather."

"All right," Razor said. "We'll build the move. One SUV, nothing flashy. An old lady helping another get to safety."

Snow added, "We're not dropping any hints either. If we're right, and the son of a bitch is already watching, he'll play. Hell, he can't afford not to."

The office went quiet.

Player pushed off the stool, and the adrenaline was coursing through his body. "Then we make damn sure it's a game he loses."

Razor nodded. "We'll roll this out carefully. I'll get word to Ryder and Margot."

"Good," Player said. "I'll talk to her."

Snow's gaze narrowed. "Think she'll go for it?"

Player didn't hesitate. "She's scared. She's been used, lied to, and pushed into corners she didn't deserve. But Heather's not stupid. She's smart enough to know Brick's not finished, not until he gets what he wants or someone stops him. I'm done waiting for that fucker to make a move."

Razor's voice cut in, low and steady. "But do you

think she trusts you enough to play along?"

Player's eyes didn't waver. "I'll make damn sure she does."

The weight of his promise settled between them. Player wasn't protecting Heather only because he'd claimed her. He wasn't doing it out of guilt or obligation. He'd seen the fear in her eyes and the fire still flickering underneath it. He *wanted* her to trust him because he knew what it'd cost her to trust the wrong man. he'd be damned if she ever paid that price again.

He turned toward the door. His voice was gravelly and filled with conviction. "I'll talk to her tonight. If she agrees… we set the trap."

Razor's final words followed him out the door. "Then let's make it one he doesn't walk away from."

* * *

Heather

Margot had been in the living room with her for maybe five minutes when the sound of a car door slamming outside drew Heather's attention to the window. A moment later, the front door swung open without a knock. In breezed a woman who looked like she could set the whole room alight just by walking into it. She was gorgeous, purple hair falling in waves around her shoulders, her black boots clicking confidently on the hardwood. Her smile carried more spark than warmth.

Wrapping her arms around something beyond the door, she managed to carry in a tree that was bigger than she was. It was a potted evergreen, the kind you replant after the holidays. Player had made good on his idea of decorating for Christmas.

"Where do you want it?" she asked Margot.

Heather was glad she hadn't asked her. Was she

a delivery person? Was she with the club?

"This is Deva," Margot explained with a half-smile. "Razor's old lady."

Heather's jaw nearly dropped. Razor, the older, sharp-eyed president who carried himself like every decision could be life or death, was with her? The age difference wasn't an issue for Heather. But the tiny young woman with all that sass wasn't what she'd imagined when she thought of a club president's old lady. She was louder, brighter, and far more likely to bite first and ask questions later.

Deva shifted the tree into the crook of her hip and stuck out her free hand, nails painted a festive red that looked wicked against her pale skin. "You must be Heather. Heard you've had a hell of a ride lately."

Heather shook her hand, caught between awe and intimidation. Up close, Deva radiated a kind of fire she didn't know how to measure herself against. It wasn't just confidence. It was command.

"Don't let the emo chick fool you," Margot said wryly. "She's one of the voices the rest of us listen to. Keeps the boys in line too."

"Somebody has to," Deva quipped. She set down the little tree by the window, then dusted her hands.

"There. It will add a little life in here," she went on as her gaze moved to Heather, sharp as a blade but not unkind. "Now, I'm gonna give it to you straight. If you're gonna stay under our roof, you need to stop looking like you're waiting for the guillotine to drop."

Heather stiffened, heat climbing her neck. "I'm not --"

"You are," Deva cut in, her purple hair catching the light as she tilted her head. "Your shoulders are around your ears and you look like you want to sink through the floor. I get it. I'm sorry as hell for the situation you're in." Blowing out a breath, Deva continued, "But I've seen it before. Every man with power wants women to fold small. That's their game. But you're standing in our house now. That means you don't fold."

Margot watched from the couch, her smile edged with amusement. "Told you she's fire."

Heather tried to find her voice, but Deva wasn't done. She stepped closer, lowering her tone to something that burned hotter for its quiet. "Let me tell you something. Razor runs this club, but don't think for a second the old ladies don't hold their own. We fight our own fights, and we keep our men sharp. You wanna be around bikers? You need to decide if you're gonna be baggage or backbone."

The words landed like a gauntlet dropped at her feet.

"What she's saying, Heather," Margot added, "is you've got more fight in you than you think. The rest will come."

Deva's smile finally softened, though it still carried teeth. "Exactly. And don't get it twisted. I'm not asking you to swing a bat in the yard. Just don't forget that even in the middle of chaos, you've got a choice. Don't let Player make you think otherwise."

Heather swallowed hard, realizing the two women were watching her closely. One was sharp and fiery, the other calm and assessing. Both were measuring her, yes. Both, in their own way, were also giving her permission to be more than the frightened shadow she felt like.

Heather wetted her lips, the words tumbling out before she could think better of it. "I'm not really his old lady. He… he only said that so the cartel wouldn't take me. It isn't…"

Deva snorted, one perfectly arched brow lifting. "Sweetheart, you don't have to pretend right now with us. Men don't go making declarations like *that* unless they mean to stand on 'em. Razor would've had his ass if it was just talk."

Heather felt heat rush up to her face. She opened her mouth to protest again, but Margot cut in.

"I've seen them together," Margot said, eyes steady on Heather. "Player's different with you. I'm not making any predictions here because Player is Player. But…"

The room went quiet, the soft tick of the kitchen clock the only sound. Heather's heart sank. She wanted to deny it. But Margot's observation made her think about something she wasn't ready to admit she wanted.

Deva smirked. "Guess we'll see."

Heather couldn't find her voice. She sat there with her heart thundering, wondering how on earth she'd gone from Brick's shadow to being told she might be somebody's choice. She stared at the little living tree catching the afternoon light like it belonged there. Like *she* belonged there.

Awkward. She should've laughed or shrugged it all off and made some kind of joke about how wrong they were. But the words wouldn't come. Instead, she sat there with her chest tight and her throat aching, too full of feelings she didn't trust enough to name.

Heather wasn't used to being seen. Brick hadn't seen her. None of the men before him had. They didn't look at the girl who always tried to be helpful nor the woman who cracked jokes when she was nervous. They didn't see the heart underneath it all that was still bruised and learning to beat for herself again. But these women? They saw something. And worse… they weren't trying to talk her out of it.

Maybe Heather wasn't Player's old lady. Maybe she never would be. But for the first time in a long time, she wasn't running. Maybe someone like Player wasn't either.

Margot stood and stretched. "I can run down and dig out the rest of the decorations from the basement if you want."

Heather shook her head quickly, her voice a little too fast. "Player already moved everything upstairs. It's all on the kitchen table."

Margot arched a brow. "He did, huh?"

Deva grinned like a cat who'd caught a mouse. "Then what the hell are we sitting around for?"

Heather blinked. "Wait. Now?"

Deva pushed back from the table and gestured toward the tiny tree like it was a sacred mission. "Absolutely now. We've got a Christmas tree, decorations, and about fifteen minutes before one of these boys comes back and ruins my aesthetic with a skull ornament or something." She looked at Heather with a wink. "Come on. Not every safe house comes with tinsel and trauma."

Heather laughed before she could stop herself, and something warm cracked through her nerves. She didn't know what tomorrow would bring. Hell, she didn't know what the next hour might bring.

But for now? She could put a ribbon on something or hang a star. She could be a part of this, whatever this was.

* * *

The tree twinkled in the corner of the living room. It was small but cheerful, lit with soft white lights and decked out in a hodgepodge of ornaments Deva claimed were "charmingly tragic." Margot had taken her family's more sentimental ornaments for the tree at the home she shared with Ryder. But there was some leftover, generic ornaments they'd bought one year when her father Clyde brought home a bigger tree than they usually had. Margot had rigged an angel out of coffee filters as they worked. The whole thing really shouldn't have worked, but it did.

Heather sat on the couch, a beer in hand, with Margot and Deva on either side of her. The laughter had come easier than she'd expected. There was warmth too. It was the first time she could remember feeling like this, like she belonged in a room with these women. Hell, had she ever known women like them? Both were capable, loyal, sharp-edged, and unapologetically themselves.

She didn't realize how much she'd needed this. Needed *them*.

The front door opened, and Heather's heart jumped before she even turned to look. Player stepped inside, boots heavy against the floor, brushing snow from his leather jacket. When his gaze landed on her, tipsy and smiling on the couch, he stopped in his tracks.

"Damn," he muttered with a crooked grin. "I didn't think you'd make this place look like a holiday card, sunshine."

Heather's breath caught, and for a moment she forgot how to move, how to think, how to breathe. God, he was handsome. The man was so rugged and real it almost hurt to look at him. The cold had brought ruddy color to his cheeks. His tall, muscular frame filled the doorway like a shadow she never wanted to outrun.

Player looked like something out of a movie, dangerous, magnetic, and impossible to ignore. His lazy half smile, the gravel and heat in his voice, the glint in those blue-green eyes that could melt her with a single glance. And right now? He was all of that just for her.

It was insane, really. To want someone like him, someone so far outside the kind of life she'd ever known. But right then, it didn't feel insane at all. It felt inevitable.

She could never hold onto a man like Player. But God, she wanted to.

Deva stood and handed him a beer. "We did all the work. She supervised."

"I'm a known taskmaster," Heather deadpanned, and Margot snorted into her drink.

Deva winked at her. "Well, boss lady, we'll leave you two to it."

"Wait, already?" Heather sat up straighter, but Margot and Deva were already collecting their jackets.

Deva grinned. "Trust me, you want us to go."

"Don't start," Player warned, but his tone was lazy, amused.

Margot gave Heather a quick hug, warm and tight. "You're good," she whispered near her ear. "Stop wondering if you are."

Then they were gone. The silence that followed wasn't awkward. It was charged. Warmth still lingered in the room, but now it was a different kind. The kind that had Heather's pulse quickening as Player leaned back against the door after locking it.

She swallowed hard, suddenly far too aware they were alone again. "They're… really something."

"Yeah, but so are you." His voice was low, sure. "Didn't even get a chance to miss you and there you are, flushed and buzzed and lighting up the place up."

Heather laughed, looking down at her bottle.

"It's the beer."

"No, it's not." He crossed the room and sat beside her, close but not crowding her.

He smelled like the winter air he'd just come from, mingling with the spicy aftershave he wore and his own unique scent. She let it go to her head.

"It's you," he went on, pinning her there with the intensity of his gaze. "It's what you look like when you're not bracing for disaster."

Heather's breath hitched. He was right. God, he was right. For the first time in what felt like forever, she wasn't curled up in a knot of dread, waiting for the next thing to go wrong. There was a Christmas tree glowing in the corner. Laughter still lingered in the air from the women who had, somehow, let her belong. Her muscles weren't clenched, and for a rare, fleeting moment… she felt okay. Not safe, not secure, but okay. And it was a revelation.

She didn't know if she deserved it. Relief, joy, and softness were emotions that always felt like things reserved for someone else. But tonight, with the beer dulling her anxiety and the glow of the tree in her periphery, she wanted it. She wanted to hold on to this sliver of peace a little longer. To stay right here, in the warmth of his presence, before the storm inevitably found them again.

Her smile faded slowly. "Don't get used to it."

"Too late." He met her eyes, steady and unflinching. "You're a beautiful woman, Heather. But when you smile that way… damn."

Did he have to say things like that? Like it cost him nothing? It was just another smooth line from a man who probably had no idea what it did to a woman like her. Her heart kicked harder in her chest, heat blooming beneath her skin, equal parts flattered and panicked. She wasn't used to compliments, not real ones. Especially not from a man who looked like him.

She didn't know how to handle it, how to take it, except to glance away as if his words hadn't melted something deep in her gut. She wanted to believe it. But wanting and trusting weren't the same thing. Not when men like Brick had taught her exactly how cheap sweet words could be.

And yet… when Player looked at her, she couldn't shake the thought that just maybe, he meant it.

She decided on the coward's way out.

"Did anything happen while you were gone?" she asked.

He hesitated, but only for a beat. "Nothing we need to worry about tonight."

Heather didn't believe him entirely, not with that flicker behind his eyes. But for once, she didn't press. Maybe she didn't want to know right now.

Right now, all she could think about was how badly she wanted to stay. Not just tonight, or until the cartel or Brick got tired of chasing shadows. She wanted to stay here. With him. She wanted to believe this warmth could last. "You sure?" she asked softly.

Player reached out and tugged gently on her flannel sleeve, coaxing her closer. "I'm sure about you."

Before her brain could interfere, Heather kissed him. It wasn't light or lusty. No, it was her sharing the fragile peace of the moment with him, the soft press of her lips to his. That's all she meant it to be, at first. But slowly, as the kiss continued, her hands smoothed up the muscular wall of his chest. His hands slid up her arms to cradle her face as if they had found something rare, something they wanted to hang onto. She deepened the kiss, and he allowed it. Player didn't pull her against him, but she moved closer, seeking his warmth.

No, she wouldn't think about later tonight or tomorrow. She wanted to enjoy this moment with him. Maybe it would be one of few memories she'd have of him. She gave herself to the moment, her arms winding around his neck as the kiss grew heated.

She whined a little when he broke the kiss, but then she didn't expect him to scoop her off the couch as easily as he did. Heather pressed heated kisses to his throat as he carried her out of the living room, back into the quiet of the master bedroom. It was shrouded in shadows when he dropped her onto the bed, and she reached for the lamp on the bedside table. She didn't want memories of the dark. She wanted to see everything, to burn it into her mind.

Player shrugged out of his jacket as he climbed on the bed, the too-small T-shirt that stretched across all those muscles she wanted to get her hands on. Heather pulled off her flannel shirt, the camisole she wore beneath. She hadn't been wearing a bra, and his gaze went straight to her breasts. Heather laughed as he lunged for her then, his larger frame pressing her into the mattress. When his lips met hers this time, currents of heat and desire raced through her body.

They rolled until Player was under her. Breaking the kiss, she grinned at him as her hands went to the front of his jeans, impatiently working them open, pulling them down and off along with his boxers.

He started laughing, scrambling to pull off his boots. "Okay, now. Give me a minute."

She watched him pitch each boot off the side of the bed as she helped strip him bare. Once he was, Heather got her hands on him. He was hard in her hands as she stroked him, watching him relax on the bed with a wicked smile. Since he didn't take issue with that, she put her mouth on him.

This Heather was confident about. As she teased the head of his cock with her lips and tongue, his hands sank into her hair. He wasn't guiding her movements. Not yet anyway. He looked so good above her with his lips parted, eyes shining with lust as he watched her. Enjoying the taste of him, she worked him further back into her mouth. She loved the way his hips moved with her, the sexy little sigh he released when she got her hands on his balls to see what he liked there.

"Goddamn." His voice was low and rough. "That's fuckin' amazing."

She winked at him with a mouthful of cock, taking him further until he reached her throat. The way he gasped when she did that had her libido growing fangs. When she doubled down on him, his fingers clutched in her hair until her scalp stung a little. But she didn't let him slow her down. She kept going, enjoying the control she had over the handsome devil's pleasure. The way his face and chest darkened, the way his fingernails started lightly scraping her scalp as she worked him.

Player sat up in a hurry, startling her enough to stop. Carefully, he pulled her in to him for a kiss that set her nerve endings on fire. She knew he could taste himself, and it only made her want him more. He burned her down with that kiss, rolling them until she was on her back.

"You're too fucking good at that," he told her, sounding winded as he stripped her jeans and panties off in a hurry. "I want to revisit that… But right now, I need you too damn much."

He left the red fuzzy socks she wore on as he slotted himself between her thighs, and she was grinning about that. Not so much when he took himself in hand and positioned himself at her entrance, where she needed him right now.

Player slid into her in one smooth thrust and held long enough for her to hang onto him. Then he hit the gas pedal, taking her as if he wouldn't survive if he didn't.

Heather loved how she disappeared beneath him, the way he powered into her over and over until she couldn't remember anything else. His thrusts came fast, hitting all the right places until her body tightened around him, until the release that was running her down had her raking her nails along his back. He took the hint, thrusting harder and faster, fucking her into the bed with abandon.

When she came, Heather's cries filled the room. But it sounded distant as waves of pure bliss crashed in her lower body and spread out from there. It took her breath away as he continued to ride her, to draw her orgasm out until she saw stars, until her grip on him eased a little.

She was still recovering when he rolled them again, and Heather ended up on top, straddling him. She tried to catch her breath. The gorgeous devil was grinning at her, his expression pure mischief. "You gonna ride me, cowgirl?" he asked with that shit-eating grin that drove her crazy.

Well, she was going to try. Her arms still shook, and her thighs too. When she didn't spring into action, he grabbed her hips and began thrusting up into her. After a moment, she moved with him but kept control of her lower body. Planting her hands on his chest, her body moved with his, their movements gaining speed.

Player threw his head back, growling when he came. His grip on her became almost painful as he bounced her on his cock, working himself through it.

Her heart was racing when she collapsed over him, struggling as he was to catch her breath. Player held her there in the peace of the moment, and for once her mind wasn't scrambling to come up with something she should be panicking about.

"We need to figure out something to eat for dinner," he said after a moment.

Yeah, she could stay in this happy little bubble for a little while longer.

Chapter Eight

Heather

The kitchen was still and quiet with the kind of silence that felt temporary, like the calm before the storm. It was the day before Christmas Eve.

Heather stood there, waiting. The silence settled around her like a too-heavy coat. *Christmas.* It was a holiday built on warmth and nostalgia. A time when you could pretend the world wasn't as broken as it was. In the situation she was in, that level of pretending felt impossible. Something big was happening today, she knew.

But she was tired of the anxiety and the hopelessness. Maybe she could go on a little faith for a change. Player and his brothers had gone to such lengths to keep her safe to this point. They were likely about to face even more danger. Maybe if they could do that for her, she could be stronger for them.

The sun hadn't fully broken through the gray morning yet. There were hints of pale light stretched across the frosted yard. It looked so peaceful here. But it was a kind of peace she didn't trust, not with the dark energy she felt lingering beneath it. Not with a cartel out there somewhere, and Brick hiding like the coward he was. Not with everything in her life hanging by a thread.

She wore one of Player's hoodies, the sleeves swallowing her hands. She tried to keep the memory of last night with the tree, the lights, and his voice in her ear, first and foremost in her mind. But the memory almost felt like it belonged to someone else. A dream, sweet and fleeting.

But this morning, reality was cold and dangerous. She could continue to cower and worry. Or she could face it all, stop being a coward.

She recognized the sound of Player's footsteps behind her.

"You're up early," Player said, his voice rough with sleep.

"So are you."

He crossed the room slowly, brushing a kiss to her temple before settling beside her. For a moment, neither of them spoke. Heather kept her eyes on the yard, fighting to keep her anxiety at bay. She could feel the shift in him too, the burden that had been weighing on him since last night. She turned to him. "Something is happening today, isn't it?"

Player nodded. "Yeah."

He looked tired, but steady. Always steady somehow when it came to her.

"We're moving you," he said quietly. "Making it look like Margot is taking you somewhere else. It'll be somewhere out of town. We want Brick to think he has a shot at you. Like you're an easy mark. But it's a setup."

Heather went still. *Like you're an easy mark…*

She knew he wouldn't let anything happen to her. Yes, she was bait again. But this was different. Brick was the one who'd made her life part of some high-stakes game. This time Player and his brothers were using her as bait. But the intention was different. It was meant to protect her.

If Brick was back, something had gone wrong for him. Was he going to sell her to the cartel to help pay his debt? Or was it something worse? "So, I'm the shiny thing you're using to lure Brick in?" she asked, somehow keeping her voice steady. "For maybe the cartel?"

Player didn't try to soften it. "You're the reason

we're doing this at all," he said. "We need to get our hands on him before the cartel does."

"That's what this is about," she whispered. She was right. "It's not just Brick."

"No," he said, steady as stone. "It's not. We think he told them you knew where the money was. That you lied to him. Now they want answers."

Heather's blood ran cold. Of course Brick would do exactly that. He'd spin it around, sell her out, point the cartel straight at her to save his own worthless skin. They weren't chasing a rumor anymore. They were chasing *her*.

She stared at him, fighting to stay calm. "What happens if they get to me first?"

Player stepped closer, his gaze never leaving her as he took her hands in his. "They won't."

Heather looked away, taking a deep breath. God, she hated how familiar this felt. It reminded her of the time she'd spent with Brick being used and leveraged. As if the only time anyone gave a damn was when she was useful or at risk.

But this wasn't Brick manipulating her, nor the cartel.

This was *Player*. And the way he was looking at her, the intensity in his blue-green eyes, made something inside her wobble. "You can't promise that."

"I can promise I'll do whatever it takes to stop it. That's why this trap has to work." He held her stare. He offered no lies. No reassurances he couldn't back up. Just the blunt, brutal truth from a man looking at her like she mattered to him, actually meant *something*.

She dragged in a breath. *Stay steady*.

"I'm scared, Player," she said, her voice barely above a whisper.

"I know," he replied, squeezing her hands gently. "That's why we're not leaving anything to chance." Slowly, carefully, he pulled her against him until she was safe in the circle of his arms. "I'll be watching," he said, his voice low by her ear. "And when he shows up? We end this. No more running."

Despite everything, despite the fear curling in her belly, she believed him. She *needed* to believe him.

Easing back from her, he reached into the inner pocket of his jacket and pulled out a slim, battered burner phone. Holding it out her, he said, "You press this, I'll find you. No matter where you are."

She took it slowly, fingers brushing his. "If you're going to be there, why would you need to find me?"

He watched her take the phone from his hand, then his gaze returned to hers. "I don't know what's going to happen out there. If something goes sideways… I need to know I can get to you fast. No guessing."

Player's voice dropped, low and rough. "I'm not letting anyone take you from me. Not Brick. Not the cartel. No one." Leaning down, he pressed his forehead to hers. "I'm not putting you out there alone. Margot's a deputy sheriff and a good one. You'll be right there with her. I'll be close, and so will my brothers. Beast, Crash, and Outcast are back now too."

Wait. His friends were safe? "They're okay?" she asked.

He grinned at her. "Honey, I told you. All of 'em are tough bastards. That's why they're my best friends."

It was hope, and something she yearned for. There was also fear, yes, but she could push that back long enough to do this. She nodded, voice catching.

"Okay. Let's do it."

* * *

The winter air was cold and crisp. Heather tightened her coat and shoved her hands deeper into her sleeves as Margot unlocked the driver's side door of her truck. It was quiet outside of Margot's childhood home, the house she'd been staying in for safety. But it was no longer peaceful. No, there was a charge in the air, and it felt like everyone was holding their breath.

Glancing back, there was no sign of Player. Ryder was chatting with Axel, who was doing a good job of looking bored as he leaned against his bike. It was all an act, of course, for the benefit of those they now knew were watching. Heather could feel the coiled tension in every glance, every nod.

She was the one in the spotlight. The bait.

Even though Player claimed that part wasn't true, it felt that way to her.

Margot hefted a duffel into the bed of her truck like it weighed nothing. "You nervous?"

Heather huffed. "Is that a trick question?"

Margot smirked, warmth in her dark eyes. "You're doing great. You haven't tried to make a run for it yet."

Her laugh came off more nervous than she'd hoped. "Give me time," Heather said.

Deva drove up to her surprise, parking just beyond the driveaway. The gray sky didn't even take the edge off the sharpness from the old lady of the Hounds' president. Deva strutted, there was no other way to describe it, heading straight for Heather. Her vivid purple hair was pulled back in pigtails, and she was dressed like she was going to a death metal concert next.

Heather opened her mouth to speak, but Deva

got there first.

"You look scared shitless," Deva said, stopping just shy of touching her. "I get it. But we need to sell this, okay?"

Heather's stomach flipped. "Okay."

Deva grinned, unbothered. "You're here, and you're *doing* it. I'm here to remind you. You're not hiding. You're walking into the fire with your head high. Yeah, your knees might be shaking, but guess what? So are ours. We'll keep moving anyway."

Heather swallowed hard. "Thank you," she said somberly. She wasn't one of them, but she appreciated the other woman's encouragement.

Deva stepped in a little closer, lowering her voice, the edge gone now. "You don't have to be fearless, Heather. You have to be braver than the asshole chasing you. And you've got a whole damn club at your back. Player's already half out of his mind worrying about keeping you safe. So don't waste that. Own it."

"Player?" She hated how quiet his name came out. "I don't know why he's --"

Deva grinned now. "I know why. It's not for a piece of ass. He can get that anytime, anywhere. He's serious about you, darlin'. That makes you one of us. Now, make me proud."

Heather didn't know how to respond. Her throat tightened, and she had to look away, pretending to focus on Margot, who was clearing clutter out of her passenger seat in the truck. Her fingers curled around the strap of her bag, her knuckles white. "One of you," she echoed softly, the words tasting foreign and dangerous on her tongue.

She'd never really belonged anywhere before. Not without strings or secrets or someone waiting to use her. It almost felt like too much to hope for.

But now she had someone betting his life on *her* safety. A woman like Deva calling her one of their own, and a choice staring her in the face: keep running or stand her ground.

Meeting Deva's gaze, she nodded, steeling herself for what was to come. "I'll make you proud," Heather said, trying to sound confident, but missing it by a country mile.

Deva winked. "Damn right you will." Then she motioned to Margot's truck. "Go on."

With a reluctant smile, Heather walked around and climbed into the passenger seat. Her anxiety was escalating, knowing it was all real. Her gaze tracked Deva as she headed back for her SUV. Then she scanned the rearview mirror automatically, watching as the first decoy vehicle pulled out ahead of them, just like they planned.

As Margot settled behind the wheel, she threw Heather a wink. "Relax. I brought in a 200-pound, methed-out guy last week who was running around naked right off Main Street. Someone like Brick doesn't scare me."

Heather had to ask. "Does it bother Ryder at all? What you do for a living?"

Margot smirked as she backed her truck out of the drive. "He says it makes him sleep better at night knowing I can break someone's nose with my pinky. Besides, Ryder knew exactly who I was when we got together. He's never tried to dim that down. That's love, right? Someone who doesn't just put up with your fire but likes getting burned a little."

"Love?" Heather asked. "I don't have a lot of experience in that department." She watched the road ahead as they got on their way. "You're lucky, you know. To have someone who really loves you and doesn't want to change you."

Margot cut her a look, but it was kind. "Yeah," she said after a moment. "I know." She didn't elaborate, and Heather didn't push.

The silence settled in again, and it was so much heavier now. After a moment, Margot broke it with her signature cool confidence Heather couldn't help but envy. "All right, listen up," she said, tapping the steering wheel with one finger. "This ride may be quiet, or it may not. If anything feels off, you stay in the truck unless I tell you otherwise. You don't argue, you don't try to play hero. You stay close, do exactly what I say, and we both go home in one piece."

Heather nodded, her pulse kicking up a little. *This is serious.* Brick hadn't just betrayed her; he'd thrown her to the fucking wolves.

If Brick got his hands on her, he wouldn't hesitate. He'd hand her over to the cartel without a second thought, just to buy himself a little more time and distance. It was like she was nothing but a pawn in the mess he'd made. Honestly, she had to realize that was all she'd ever been to him anyway.

Unease sat on her chest, and the cold air outside the truck felt like it had seeped straight into her bones. When she'd been running and hiding with Brick, trying to outrun the cartel for reasons she barely understood, it had been about survival. But today's plan, or mission as Player had called it, felt like it was upping the ante. Her anxiety was climbing as she sat huddled in the seat next to Margot.

Her instructions played on a loop in Heather's head now. *Stay close, do exactly what I say*. Deva's order echoed there too. *Make me proud*. She felt the burner phone she'd tucked into her pocket as if it were a lifeline, a promise from Player she'd be kept safe as the road stretched ahead. She wasn't alone. To hear him tell it, there were Hounds in decoy cars, planted around Margot and Ryder's house out in the country and the road leading to it.

You press this, I'll find you. No matter where you are.

She believed him. God help her, she did.

"I know you've been through hell." Margot's voice pulled her out of her thoughts. "I know this is a lot. But I need you sharp, okay? Not scared. There's a difference."

The truck cruised through the outskirts of Mercy, its headlights glowing on the frost-laced pavement. Her nerves climbed with each mile. Heather's grip tightened on the phone she'd dumped in her pocket, and it was becoming an effort to stay still on the seat.

The silence stretched until Margot broke it. "Are you okay?"

"I think I might puke," Heather admitted.

Margot snorted. "There are some plastic grocery bags in the glove box if you need one."

They shared a small, tense laugh. It was enough to soften the edges of Heather's fear. That's when she saw it. They passed a dark pickup truck parked at an odd angle just off the shoulder of the road.

Nothing unusual, except for the steady puff of vapor trailing from the exhaust into the cold afternoon air. The truck wasn't just parked. It was idling.

A few miles later, a silver sedan fell in behind them. It stayed back for a while, almost too long for Heather's racing heart. When it finally turned off onto a side road, Heather let out a breath she hadn't realized she was holding.

Margot clocked it too. "They're watching," she said quietly. "Just like we wanted."

Heather's fingers tightened around the burner phone. She tried to focus on breathing slowly, in and out, as her fear started to escalate.

"I wonder if it was him," she said quietly, eyes still on the side mirror. Margot had never met Brick, so she probably wouldn't know what he looked like. "Or the cartel?"

Chapter Nine

Player

The house was too quiet considering how many people were inside.

Ryder's place sat on the edge of a wooded ridge. Axel's house was a mile down the road, and both were built on the land their parents left behind. Ryder's house was remote, quiet, and nearly impossible to find unless you knew exactly where to look. The isolation made his place secure, but tonight, it felt less a home and more a bunker bracing for a storm.

The trap they'd laid earlier hadn't gone to plan. Brick never showed. Worse, the ones who did show were cartel muscle, sent by El Cuervo himself, and they came with more force than the Hounds expected. He'd given the cartel enough reason to try and hunt her down. The fact Brick wasn't with them said *he* was running from them too.

Still, the decoy plan had given them insights into what was going on. The Hounds had been careful and ran enough interference to be sure no cartel soldiers followed them back. Eyes were posted at every approach, and no unfamiliar vehicles had come within shouting distance of Ryder's place. For now, at least, the women were safe, but no one was pretending it would last.

Player tried to keep the weight of failure sinking into his gut. He was fucking furious -- not at his crew or even at the cartel, but at himself. He'd gambled on a controlled move and came damn close to losing Heather. The second he saw those blacked-out SUVs crest the ridge, he'd felt the bottom drop out. It didn't matter that they'd prepped, planned, and covered every angle. The cartel still came within inches of taking her. That was on *him*.

There was shame underneath the anger, sharp and personal. He was the one who swore she'd be safe. The one who told her *they'd never get close*. Now Heather sat there in the middle of this debrief, shaken and quiet, because he couldn't stop what happened. She trusted him with her life, and he nearly handed her over to the very people they were trying to protect her from.

He felt like he let her down. But it was a feeling he refused to carry into tomorrow. Next time, there'd be *no* mistake. No close call. No mercy. Only the end of the line for Brick and anyone who came with him.

Leaning against the kitchen counter, Player folded his arms as he scanned every face in the room. The house had an open layout. The kitchen bled into the living room with nothing but a stretch of polished hardwood between them, no walls to soften the tension. Despite the weight of the meeting, the space still bore the fingerprints of Margot's warm, offbeat charm. A modest Christmas tree stood near the front window, strung with mismatched ornaments and soft white lights glowing against the glass. A handmade wreath hung on the inside of the front door, and on the mantel above the fireplace, a selection of Christmas cards was displayed in various positions.

Heather sat on the couch beside Margot, her legs curled up, a thick hoodie swallowing her frame. Her eyes were steady now and focused. She was still here, and that counted for something.

Beast, Outcast and Crash flanked the doorway. Razor paced near the front window, muttering under his breath. Hero sat on the stairs, with his head tilted, listening. Margot had a steaming mug of coffee in her hand, and one bare foot tapping a silent rhythm on the floorboards. Ryder had his arm around her shoulders but said nothing.

Snow had to return to town for Mercy's annual kids' Christmas party, which they held for those who didn't have much. It was his second year running as Santa Claus. The event was being held at *Whisk & Whimsy*, his old lady's bakery. Deva had gone to lend a hand, mostly to make sure the frosting didn't turn into a food fight.

Even with all that going on, Snow kept his ear to the ground. His voice came through Razor's phone on speaker, slightly staticky from wherever he was patched in. "Okay, got it. Surveillance shows Brick circling familiar spots. Old haunts, bars, pawn shops. He's looking for her."

Player didn't need confirmation. He'd felt Brick's presence like a change in pressure. "And the cartel?"

Snow's voice tightened. "Burners are pinging towers from Mercy to the county line. Somebody's driving dark. They're watching travel hubs like gas stations, cheap motels. Anywhere someone might bolt from. But they're getting sloppy now. Desperate."

Ryder shook his head. "Local law's not gonna touch this. Not with cartel in play."

"Sheriff Sawyer?" Player asked.

Margot snorted. "Leave my boss out of it. Randy's a good man. He's not for sale. But he's not suicidal, either. If we try to loop him in, he'll pull his deputies, including me, off the streets."

Razor's phone crackled on the counter. From the other end came Deva's voice, amused and distant, like she was multitasking. "Santa's got to go right now. Talk to you later."

There was a faint rustle before the call disconnected. Razor lit a cigarette with steady fingers, exhaling slowly.

"You ever think about callin' the Feds?" Margot asked. Ryder cut her a look from where he sat next to her. "DEA could drop the hammer on all of them in one sweep."

Razor snorted. "You mean the same government that let a cartel set up shop here in the first place come clean it up? You got more faith than I do."

Player said nothing. He didn't want the DEA involved either. They wouldn't see what Brick had done or how scared Heather was. They'd see a girl with cartel ties and a pile of missing money. If the cartel flipped the narrative on her, she'd be trading one cage for another. That wasn't happening on his watch.

Razor's voice dropped lower, smoke curling from the corner of his mouth. "You sic the Feds on a cartel like that, it doesn't end. It escalates. They retaliate. Next thing you know, Mercy's on fire and every Hound in the whole fucking state's got a target on his back."

He looked at Margot then, the weight of years in his eyes. "We handle this our way. The cartel gets their rat. Heather's safe. We don't go invitin' another war when we just survived this one."

Player gave a slow nod. Razor wasn't wrong.

Razor's voice cut through the room like a blade. "The cartel showed their hand. Next time, we *break* it. I knew the minute Brick's sorry ass turned up here we'd be dealing with *something*. But the cartel? We need this shit done yesterday."

A beat of silence. No one argued.

From where he stood in the kitchen, Player saw the way Heather flinched. Her shoulders drew in, her chin dipped low, and her hands curled tighter in the sleeves of the hoodie she hadn't taken off since they left the safe house. He knew she thought *she* was the problem. He'd told her that none of them were blaming her for this. Not for Brick, nor the money he lost. Not for the cartel threatening to crash their town.

Player nodded. "This time, let's give them what they want."

Ryder sat forward on the couch, unfolding a worn paper map of the county on the coffee table like it was wartime. Coffee mugs got pushed aside. Everyone leaned in.

"They think she has the money," Ryder said. "That she's scared and trying to run. let's give them what they expect."

Margot leaned forward, her eyes scanning the roads and highways. "We need what? A bus ticket, cash-only motel? All of it is easy enough to fake. We need enough to make her trail look hot."

Crash stepped in, tapping the route toward the state line with a gloved finger. "We could have somebody at a gas station drop a rumor she was crying. Left in a hurry. Paid in cash for a burner phone. Real shaky."

"Now there's an idea." Margot tapped a spot on the paper map with two fingers. "We do it at *Cowboy Pete's*."

Player's brow lifted. "Seriously?"

Cowboy Pete's wasn't some random gas station. Not long ago, it was where Sadie, Axel's old lady, had first turned up, beaten and on the run from her Mafia-connected ex. It was also where Elsie Damron, the woman who'd helped her, and Margot's own father, Clyde Donner, were both gunned down. The place wasn't just unlucky. It was haunted by loss, soaked in the blood of people Player respected.

Margot nodded. "It's perfect. The new owner's

shady. Hell, he might already be on cartel payroll. If they've got anyone sniffing around, they'll pick it up."

Crash whistled low. "Wasn't that where…"

"Yeah," Margot said flatly. "My dad died there. So did Elsie Damron. I was hoping they'd tear the damn thing down. I've been keeping an eye on it ever since."

Razor nodded. "That might work."

"Heather walks in there looking spooked," Margot replied. "She flashes some cash and buys a burner phone. When she asks how to get somewhere like the community center, I'd be willing to bet the cartel will know within the hour."

"So she comes in," Player reiterated slowly. "She looks scared. Spouts some crap about where she's going, flashing cash…" He trailed off.

Margot nodded. "Exactly."

Player looked toward Heather, who hadn't spoken yet. She watched and listened, her lips pressed together while she tried to stay composed.

"Someone will tip off Brick or the cartel, maybe both," Player said. "They'll think she's holed up near the center."

"Or meeting someone there," Margot added. "Maybe getting a fake passport or something."

"They'll come," Ryder said, his voice low. "They'll *all* come."

"Then we make sure we're ready to meet them," Player said.

Player's gaze drifted to Heather on the couch. She was absorbing every detail. He caught the subtle shift before anyone else did. She wasn't trying to hide her fear anymore. But she also didn't look like someone on the verge of a panic attack either. She knew what they were doing and why. He could see it on her face. She was in.

Player shook his head. *This was a story,* he told himself. *A trap. But she was the one carrying it on her back, and she knew it.*

Hero, quiet until now, looked up from his spot on the stairs. "When they come?"

Silence gripped the room for half a second.

Razor stepped in closer, his eyes hard. "We'll be waiting, ready to cut off any escape routes. This time, we reach an agreement, or they won't walk away." His gaze swept the room, holding each gaze long enough to make his point. "We end this. Publicly, if it has to be."

Player nodded. "We make them believe she's vulnerable, all alone. Brick will bite first. The fucker knows she doesn't have *his* money. But he'll want what he thinks she has. The cartel won't be far behind him. We might need backup. Just in case things go loud."

Razor's eyes met his. No hesitation. "I'll make the call." He stepped out, pulling the door shut behind him.

The air shifted, heavier without Razor's presence. Margot scribbled some names and intersections on a notepad she pulled from a drawer, murmuring something to Ryder about camera angles and line-of-sight. Crash and Outcast were already deep in debate about where they'd set up a secondary intercept. Axel stood near the window, watching the drive like something might roll in any second.

Player focused on Heather. She looked like a woman who had resigned herself to the fact that she was being sent to the gallows, and she'd made peace with it.

Pushing off the counter, he crossed to her without a word. He crouched in front of her, his arms resting on his knees, so they were eye-level.

"You good?" he asked her quietly.

Heather hesitated. Then nodded. "Yeah. I'm good."

It was a lie, to make him feel better. It was the kind people told to get through something hard. The kind you said when people were counting on you, and you weren't ready to fall apart yet.

Player didn't call her on it. But he held her gaze a moment longer and said, "I'll be with you the whole time. All of us will. You're not doing this alone."

Behind him, he heard the door open, Razor's boots approaching. Everyone looked up.

Player stood first. "Well?"

Razor gave a short nod. "They're in."

"The Cottonmouths?" Ryder asked.

"Vendetta's coming, and bringing five more," Razor said. "They'll be ready to back us up. No questions, no price. Just said, 'Tell Outcast and Player we ride.'"

Outcast grinned. "That sounds like him."

Crash cracked his knuckles. "Then let's build something worth riding into."

Razor moved toward the map, rejoining Ryder and Margot in plotting it out. But Player took Margot's seat on the couch next to Heather, draping an arm over her shoulders. He was proud of the fact she wasn't shaking like a leaf.

* * *

Heather

After the meeting broke up, Heather slipped away quietly, climbing the stairs to the guest room Margot had given them for the time being. The hallway floor creaked beneath her feet, the old farmhouse quiet now except for the low hum of voices downstairs and the occasional groan of the heating system kicking on.

She pulled the door shut behind her but didn't turn on the light, crossing the room to sit on the edge of the bed instead. Her hands rested in her lap, caught in a dim beam of light from the pale moon outside tonight.

She understood what they were planning and what it meant. She knew they were protecting her, even though she hadn't earned it from them. Brick didn't have the money he stole from the cartel, so he'd come back to hand her over. Assign her the blame. The cartel had already come for her, and it was scary how close they'd been to doing that.

Now, the Hounds of Hell were going to make her a ghost. A shadow with a purpose. It was a smart enough plan. But no matter how ruthless and controlled it was, her life was still on the line.

The door eased open a few minutes later. Player stepped inside, quiet as ever. He didn't say anything at first. He shut the door behind him gently and leaned against it, watching her. "You all right?" he asked finally.

Heather looked up at him. "No, but I can do this."

He crossed the room and sat beside her. She felt the heat of him even before his arm wrapped around her shoulders, and she welcomed it.

"I know you can," Player said. "And you're allowed to be scared."

"I just want this to be over," she whispered.

"It will be soon," he said with a note of determination in his voice. "We're going to play this out on our terms. Not Brick's. Not the cartel's. You've got everyone downstairs riding for you. We've also got

Cottonmouths coming. I'll be there for you most of all."

She let herself lean into him a little. "They're going to believe I'm running away with money I never had. I never even saw it. I don't even know how much it was."

"They're going to believe exactly what we want them to believe," he murmured, pressing a kiss into her hair. "When they come… they won't be leaving."

His hand found hers. Callused fingers, warm and sure. Her grip tightened. "I'm glad you're here," she said softly.

He turned to kiss her temple. "I'll be here till it's done."

She hated the thought, but she had to wonder how long after that he'd still be with her. She exhaled slowly. Her breath felt tight in her chest. "It was real today. They weren't bluffing."

"No, they weren't," he agreed. "But we were ready. We cut them off. Now we know exactly what we're up against. This time we *will* end it."

She turned then, enough to look over her shoulder. "This is going to work?"

Player nodded. "It is."

"But what if they catch on? What if --"

"They won't." He lifted a hand to brush a lock of hair from her forehead. "I fucking hate we're putting you in this position, Heather. I need you to know that. But I think you can do it. And when Brick tries to crawl out of his hole because he thinks you must have something, and he *knows* you don't have the money he fucking lost, we'll be there. We'll be ready to take him down. If the cartel is stupid enough to buy his bullshit, we'll take them down too."

Heather stared down at their joined hands. She

knew he wanted to keep her safe. All of them did. Maybe they weren't the ones she didn't have faith in.

"What if I panic?" she asked. "What if I freeze up or I say the wrong thing or --"

"You won't." He turned, cupping her face with his other hand. "You don't see how fucking brave you are, do you? You didn't run today. You *stayed*. You let us fight for you."

Her throat felt thick. She swallowed hard. "Because of you."

His gaze locked with hers, his thumb gently brushing across her cheek. "Heather, I'll hunt every last one of them to the edge of the earth before I let them touch you." He leaned in, resting his forehead lightly against hers. "You've got *all* of us. Razor. Margot. Ryder. Beast, Outcast and Crash . No one here is going to let anything happen to you."

"I still don't understand why any of you would go to war for me," she whispered. "I'm --"

"Don't you dare fucking say you aren't worth it, Heather." She didn't miss the heat in his tone. "If you value my sanity," he said with all sincerity, "just don't."

She smiled then, moved by how dedicated this man was to making her feel like she belonged here, with the Hounds. With *him*. "In my defense," she said slowly, "I've never been in the center of a war before. You know?"

He broke into the kind of smile that could undo a woman in seconds -- the charming, irresistible one he'd probably used a hundred times before, but somehow was starting to feel it was hers. "Feels weird, huh?"

Heather nodded. "Yeah."

"You'll get used to it."

She leaned into him. For once, the silence didn't

feel heavy. "I'm scared," she whispered.

He kissed her temple. "Good. That means you're paying attention."

She curled her fingers into the front of his shirt, grounding herself in the solid weight of him. "Don't let me disappear for real."

"Never," he promised. "You ghost long enough to draw 'em out. Then you come home."

Her breath caught. *Home*? The word sank deep, hitting something she hadn't let herself feel in years. Slowly, she lifted her gaze at him, searching his face for what he meant.

Player didn't look away. His thumb brushed her jaw, gentle but sure. "Yeah, home," he said quietly. "Right here. With me. With the people who'll bleed before they let anyone take you away from me."

His words were more than a promise. They were an anchor. For the first time in a long time, she let herself *want* to believe.

He didn't give her a lot of time to think. Player's kiss started off slow and seeking, a warm press of his lips against hers. His hold on her was light, like he was giving her an out if she needed one.

Heather wanted him. She wanted to lose herself in him and forget all the craziness dominating her life, at least for a little while. She kissed him back, her hands clutching in his shirt.

It didn't take him long to get the hint. His arms tightened around her, and he changed the angle of the kiss, deepening it. One large hand slid up to the nape of her neck, the other pulled her against him and held her there. Player was a good kisser; there was no denying that. But this was the first time she felt like he wasn't trying to dazzle her with his skill, to make her feel amazing, to show off what he could do.

No, tonight what he poured into each touch and every caress was patience and reverence. He broke the kiss long enough to kick off his boots and pull off hers. He didn't drag her up the bed. He scooped her up as if she weighed nothing, which was impressive considering she was a taller girl, and then placed her in the center of the bed like she was something precious. The tender way he gazed at her had her heart fluttering with hope and need.

Tomorrow, she was going to be bait in a plan to try and free herself and the Hounds of Hell in Mercy from the watchful eye of El Cuervo and his cartel. They needed to end Brick's selfish little drama before he got someone killed. If everything went the way they wanted, would it mean her home would be Mercy? Would it be with Player? For a little while?

Climbing onto the bed with her, his gaze locked with hers. Again, that smile she loved. "Surely you can turn off that brain long enough for me to rock your world, can't you?"

She winked at him. "Maybe."

"Maybe is all I get?"

She sat up and her fingers raced through the buttons of his flannel shirt as he shrugged out of his cut. He didn't even wait for her to finish unbuttoning the shirt before he was stripping it off, grinning when she got her hands on the tattooed wall of his chest. All that warm muscle felt so good under her hands.

"Your turn," was all he said before he grabbed her hoodie and stripped it off in one easy motion.

Grabbing her chin with one hand, he pulled her into him for a kiss. Gone was the tenderness, the seduction. Now he meant business.

Her back hit the mattress, and she found herself pressed into it by two hundred pounds of muscular biker. His mouth still claimed hers, his hands were everywhere. He stripped off her bra, made quick work of her jeans and panties. He climbed back up to her, scorching her lips with a kiss full of need.

As much as she loved being under him, literally disappearing beneath him, Heather somehow got him to roll with her. Now she sat astride him, gazing down into his handsome face, her hands planted on the broad wall of his chest. She kissed him, but at her own pace. She wasn't ready to step on the gas pedal just yet. She wanted to take the lead. She enjoyed dropping kisses over his jaw, down to his neck. He brought his hands up to cover her breasts, but he wasn't trying to take over. *Yet.*

Heather stopped to tease his nipples with her lips and tongue, feeling his intent gaze on her the entire time. Pleased he was squirming a little, she moved down, working open his belt with her hands, pulling his jeans open. He was all on board helping her pull the heavy denim off him, along with his boxers. His face flushed as he watched her excitedly, knowing what she was about to do.

Heather had to stop there, laughing. "Don't look so excited."

"Christmas came early," he said, dropping his head back onto the pillow as she got her hands on him.

Running her hands all over him, she explored him, taking her time. When she nuzzled her face against his cock, she almost laughed at the way he was fighting not to reach for her, his big hands clutching the homemade quilt on the bed beneath him. When she got her mouth on him, she was curious as to whether he could be quiet for her. Half of the Hounds were still downstairs, and while he might enjoy putting on a show for them, that was the last thing *she* wanted.

Other than a couple of manly sighs, Player was quiet. His hips jerked each time she pressed her lips to the head of him. When she pulled the top of his cock into her mouth, a low groan rumbled in his chest. It encouraged her, invited her to do more. Player was a good boy for her as she pulled him in deeper, angling for the back of her throat. She bobbed on him a few strokes before coming up for air, getting her mouth on his balls then. Everything she did was random, with no patterns, what she wanted to do. Player's back began to arch, his hands finally wandered up, sinking into her hair.

It didn't take long until he had her head in a tight grip, face fucking her as he started chasing his release. His grip wasn't tight enough to hurt, and his thrusts had her eyes watering, but she didn't mind. There was something humbling to her, being able to take apart a man as gorgeous and rugged as Player. She knew even if this didn't go the way she hoped, even if she didn't get to keep him in the end, she'd remember this. How he looked under her on the bed, the taste of him in her mouth.

When he came, she swallowed him down, staying with him as he jerked in her grasp. The low growl wasn't too loud. His fingers clutching in her hair stung, but it was a good pain. His breathing was labored, his eyes closed when she released him. Smiling, she moved up closer, resting her head on his shoulder. The moment she did, his arms closed around her, and she basked in his warmth, getting comfortable there on his chest.

She could still hear voices downstairs, but it sounded like people were making their way home. She tried not to think about that or tomorrow. She focused on the steady beat of his heart, his warm, damp flesh beneath her cheek.

Player sat up abruptly, but only to get them under the quilt, to cover her up. She lay there with her eyes closed, relaxed. He bounced her on his chest as he laughed.

"Don't get too comfortable, darlin'," he said, "I'm not done with you yet."

Heather smiled.

"Tomorrow is Christmas Eve, isn't it?" he asked as they lay there.

"It is," she replied.

"What would you like for Christmas?" he asked, his fingers tracing random shapes on her lower back.

"I already have everything I want," she murmured. *Will I get to keep it*?

His hold on her tightened. "So do I."

"No matter what happens tomorrow," Heather said, not able to look him in the eye as she said it, "thank you for this. All of it. I never had a man act as if I were worth a damn. Until now."

Again, the slight bounce as he chuckled. "We're going to kick ass tomorrow. You'll get used to it, being with me. You're my old lady. It was official the moment I told El Cuervo. So don't think you're getting rid of me that easily."

Heather didn't have anything else to add. She snuggled closer, allowing herself to believe what he said was true.

Chapter Ten

Heather

The sky was pale, winter gray, low and heavy with the promise of snow, probably the kind that waited for nightfall to make its move. But she didn't have that kind of time.

Heather stepped out of the small white SUV, her boots crunching against the brittle gravel as she slammed the door shut with a little more force than necessary. It was a nice vehicle, but it wasn't hers. She was borrowing it from Vendetta's old lady Dylan. The scuffed-up backpack slung over her shoulder was Margot's, meant to help sell the illusion.

It needed to look like she was hitting the road. She hadn't slept much last night so she probably *looked* like hell. Inside, she had enough adrenaline to run a marathon. But her hands weren't shaking anymore. Somehow, she managed to stay focused. She mentally reviewed the plan.

"In, out. Don't linger. Pull the cash out of the bag like you're panicked and dumb. Get the burner. Look over your shoulder. Act nervous," Player had said last night, his voice low in the dark.

"Looks like you really won't have to act," he added, brushing a kiss over her knuckles.

He wasn't wrong.

She parked the SUV at the edge of the lot, crossing the pavement slowly to head for the store. *Cowboy Pete's* was a rundown gas station not far from the interstate. Its signage was faded, and it had a dinged-up ice machine by the door. The windows were dirty, and there was a bullet hole in the glass to the right of the door. Was that from the day Margot's father and another lady were shot and killed? Why hadn't anyone replaced the glass? That day had ended in blood. Heather hoped this one wouldn't.

The loud chime overhead startled her as she stepped inside. Her gaze swept the store quickly, taking in the clerk behind the counter. He was a younger guy who looked like he wanted to be anywhere but there. *Good.*

Margot had confirmed they were still selling prepaid phones, and Heather made her way to the back wall where the locked rack hung above the scratch-offs and nicotine pouches. Her boots echoed dully on the stained linoleum, the overhead fluorescents buzzing faintly above her like flies. When she reached the phones, she slid the backpack off her shoulder and let it drop with a loud, deliberate thud. The sound cut through the quiet store like a shot.

The young guy behind the counter looked up from his phone, startled. Early twenties, maybe, with dark, shaggy hair and a wrinkled Mercy High hoodie. His gaze met hers like he was hoping she didn't need any help. Heather made sure she looked uneasy, keeping her shoulders tight and glancing over her shoulder just a beat too long.

"You need something?" he called over, not quite rude but not exactly friendly either.

She gave a little nod, eyes darting to the side like she didn't want to be overheard. "Yeah. Uh… yeah, I need a phone. One of the prepaid ones."

The clerk stepped around the counter with a ring of keys and unlocked the case when he got there. "A phone?" he asked, side-eyeing the backpack on the floor.

Heather hesitated. "Yeah. Just the phone."

Let him assume what he wants, she reminded herself. *Let him think it's sketchy.* That was the whole point.

He nodded toward the display. "Any one in particular?"

Heather didn't meet his gaze. "Don't care," she muttered in a tight voice. "I just need it to work."

She crouched, unzipping the front pouch of the backpack, and made a show of digging around like she was in a rush. She felt her shirts, the small handgun. Then her fingers brushed the envelope Player had packed in there. It was worn and overstuffed, aged enough to look real. Exhaling a shaky breath, she yanked it free and held it in her shaking hand. The trembling? *That* was real. The thick envelope half-flopped open, flashing a fat stack of neatly banded hundred-dollar bills.

The clerk's eyebrows lifted, and he hesitated for half a second before pulling one of the mid-range models from the display.

"Uh… all right," he said slowly, glancing toward the window like he suddenly realized they might not be alone in the store.

Exactly what she wanted. "I'll ring you up at the counter," he said, carrying the phone to the front of the store.

She hauled the bag up onto her shoulder and with the envelope still in her hand, she followed him. Heather turned enough to glance out the front window. And froze.

A figure leaned against a dark car parked across the street at a local sandwich shop. He was half-shadowed, his posture casual. She couldn't make out his face, but she didn't need to.

It was Brick.

Her heart lurched in hope and fear. Well, the plan was working.

If Brick was here, the cartel wouldn't be too far behind. That meant it was almost time.

She paid for the phone with one of the bills from the envelope and kept her head down. She hunched her shoulders a little. Just enough. "Excuse me," she said to the clerk as he handed her the change from her purchase. "Can you tell me where the community center is? I'm supposed to meet someone there but… I have no idea where it is."

The clerk's gaze flicked toward the window again. He saw the car.

Hook set.

The clerk frowned, shoving a paper receipt into the small plastic bag with her phone. "Community center?" he repeated, thinking. "Uh… yeah, it's out past the post office, left on Miller. You'll see the sign."

But his eyes weren't on her anymore. His gaze shifted out the front window again, fixing on the dark sedan across the street. "You, uh… waiting on someone?"

Heather followed his gaze but didn't turn fully. Brick was getting into the car, and once he had, the tinted window lowered by a couple of inches.

She swallowed. "Yeah," she lied softly, forcing a weak smile. "Something like that."

The clerk hesitated a beat, then nodded, clearly eager to get her out of the store. "Be careful out there. The weather is supposed to turn nasty later. Ice and snow."

As she walked toward the door, her heart still pounding, she caught her reflection in the glass. Her face framed by gray sky and flurrying snow, and she looked properly terrified. She had every right to be.

The sharks were already circling.

* * *

Player

The cold clawed at his throat, feeling like he was breathing in the edge of a blade. The dead grass was covered in frost and Player could almost feel the snow coming. The old community center sat on its hill under the moody sky like a forgotten relic. Its windows were dim, and its cracked pavement was already dusted with snow.

Player crouched low behind the skeletal remains of a storage shed along the fence line. Through the scope of his rifle, he could see everything, especially Heather.

She sat alone in the idling SUV, in full view of the lot. Her hoodie was zipped up; her dark curls were pulled back and held to the back of her head by a clip. The backpack was on the passenger seat where it was supposed to be. Her fingers gripped the steering wheel like it was all that tethered her to the earth.

Player was proud of her. He knew how scared she was, but she was playing her part perfectly. Even if every second of fear she experienced made Player's blood burn.

They were locked in.

Every Hound and every Cottonmouth was in place, and the tension coiled tight as wire. Ryder and Axel had taken up position behind the maintenance building across the street, crouched low with a clear line of sight on the south road. Their view was narrow but critical. No one was coming in that way without being seen.

Crash, Outcast, and Snow were dug in near the tree line, camo jackets making them damn near invisible in the dimming light. Their scopes swept slowly, methodically, tracking every inch of the perimeter for movement. Snow hadn't said much since they got into position. Outcast barely restrained the fury behind his trigger finger. Next to him Crash was calm and calculated, as always.

Hero and Malachai had the rear alley covered, their spot tighter and more confined. Close quarters and tighter angles meant no room for mistakes. Razor, always the strategist, ran point from Snow's nondescript van down the block. The windows were tinted, the engine off. Inside he watched the monitor feeds, one hand on the comms, the other on his weapon. He was calm and cold, calling the shots.

Margot positioned herself inside the center itself, posted behind a curtain on the second floor. She'd secured the high ground early, radio in hand, her eyes never leaving Heather. Her voice, when it came over comms, was low and even.

Beast had taken the north side solo, and no one argued. The man was a human wall with nerves of reinforced steel. He hadn't spoken since they rolled in, but knowing he was out there, silent and waiting, was enough to raise the hairs on the back of Player's neck. He was probably the only Hound big enough to ever try and take Beast on, and he hoped it never came to that.

The Cottonmouths moved like shadows in between. Vendetta, the president of the Oak Ridge chapter, had brought Shade, Ripper, and three more riders. All of them were quiet, armed, and ready to kill. No chatter, no showboating, just cold, lethal focus.

The other MC hadn't always been that way. Back when Eli Crizer was still alive and wore the president's patch, the Cottonmouths had been loud and reckless, all swagger and short tempers. They'd roll into a job half-cocked, arguing over who got credit before the dust even settled. Razor used to call them "mouthy bastards with more ego than aim." But now under Vendetta's leadership, that swagger had hardened into precision. There were no wasted words or unnecessary movement. Every man knew his place and his purpose there.

Player had to give credit where it was due. The Cottonmouths were born again hard. Now they moved as a single machine, disciplined and dangerous. They were a crew that didn't need to posture to prove how deadly they were. Tonight, that was exactly what the Hounds needed beside them.

This wasn't a stakeout. It was a war table with live bait. Heather was the spark in the center of it all. He caught a flicker of movement down the road, heard tires crunching over frost. Player dropped his head, steadied his breath. *Here we go.*

A black Dodge Charger crept around the corner. It had a scraped up fender, and its passenger side mirror was missing. No plates. The driver's window lowered, and he saw exactly who he expected to see. Brick parked at the edge of the lot like he fucking owned it.

Player shifted in place, sighting him in the crosshairs. From this distance, he watched Brick take a moment, light a cigarette, then toss the match out the window and onto the snow-dusted asphalt. He scanned the lot, his gaze landing on the SUV.

Heather looked up.

Even from here, Player saw it. The way her body stiffened. The way her head tilted slightly in confusion first, then realization. She knew Brick had shown up. Player just hoped she could handle him.

Brick smiled. His smug, snake-slick grin made Player want to pull the trigger and end it right then and there. But he stayed put, watching the bastard get out of the car and start walking. He crossed the parking lot slowly, one hand loose at his sides, the other holding his cigarette. Brick moved as if he thought he'd already won.

Player's comm crackled softly in his ear.

"We got him," Razor's voice murmured. "Nobody moves till I say."

Brick reached the driver's side window. He tapped once, then leaned in what they expect he was about to offer Heather a deal. Like she *owed* him something.

Heather didn't roll the window down, but she didn't bolt either.

Player blew out a breath. Every instinct in his body screamed to move, to act, to *end* the man.

But this had to look real. Brick had to buy it.

Before he could take another breath, Malachai's voice snapped over the comms.

"Two SUVs just passed the corner store. Blacked out, no plates. Tinted windows. Southbound. ETA three minutes."

Player exhaled once, low and steady. This was it. The cartel had entered the chat.

Razor's voice followed, low and final. "That's them."

Across the line, every man shifted. Safeties clicked off, rifles adjusted, tension drawing tight like a coiled spring.

Player's eyes never left Heather.

They were about to walk straight into hell, and she'd lit the match.

* * *

Heather

The cold wind cut through the cracked driver's side window, but she really didn't feel it. Her grip on the steering wheel was tight, her knuckles bone-white against the black leather. She took a deep breath, trying to ground herself for what came next.

She was fighting with everything she had to keep her composure. She couldn't let that old fear back in. Not when she'd made it this far.

Heather had one task left and that was talking to Brick, at least long enough for the Hounds to deal with him. She'd stashed the envelope full of hundreds right where Player told her to, behind the rusted-out electrical box near the back of the building. Margot would have recovered it by now. That way, even if Brick searched her or the car, he'd come up empty.

A tap on the window made her jump. Brick was standing next to her SUV, staring right at her. She didn't look up or roll the window down, just stared straight ahead, pretending she didn't notice him.

Seconds passed.

She heard the crunch of gravel as he circled the front of the SUV. The passenger door creaked open and Brick climbed in like he belonged there, moving the backpack down by his feet.

Heather's stomach turned, but her face stayed still. She was in it now.

"Hey, baby," he said, his voice sounding like syrup over broken glass. "You look good."

Heather didn't move. *Baby? You look good*? Brick had dragged her into his shit, manipulated her, abandoned her, and now here they were. Her fear finally started to fade, slowly replaced by something stronger and not as familiar to her. *Anger*. But she played her part. *Focus now*. "I wasn't sure you'd come back for me," she murmured, keeping her voice small.

Brick leaned back in the seat, giving her a long look. "Nah. I… had to regroup. You know how it is."

Like you weren't the one who left me behind to be killed. She nodded, letting him think she was still spinning in his orbit. He'd underestimate her, as he always did.

"I've come into some money," she said quietly. "Thought maybe we could" -- she shrugged --"start over? Or hand it over if the cartel is still on your ass."

Brick's eyes lit up. It was greedy and stupid and obvious, and for once, it worked in her favor.

"Well, depends on how much we're talking about, baby. I always knew you were clever," he said, reaching across the console like he might touch her. She shifted out of reach, and it made him laugh. "Still mad, huh? That's okay. You'll get over it. I did what I had to do. I got double-crossed if that makes you feel any better."

His face turned hard for a second, then soft again. Now the manipulation was as plain as day to her. Why hadn't she recognized it before?

"You think I liked leaving you?" Brick asked. "I didn't know who I could trust. I didn't even know if you were still here until I heard you'd been seen around town."

She sighed. "You didn't say anything to me. I woke up, and you were fucking gone."

"I know," he drawled, shaking his head. "Razor was being a dick. The cartel was breathing down my neck. I fucking panicked. That's all, baby." His gaze roamed over her. "But you… you landed on your feet. I know what you probably had to do." His lip curled. "Sleeping your way through the Hounds in Mercy? Fucking your way to safety?"

Heather calmly met his gaze. "You think so?" she

asked, her voice cool now. "If I did, I learned it from you."

She caught him off guard. "You don't mean that. You care for me, baby. I know you do."

For a heartbeat, Heather almost laughed. God, he still thought she was the same woman he could push around, demean, and pull back in whenever it suited him.

But sitting there, watching him make that stupid mock-wounded expression, she knew he'd picked her, *used* her, simply because she was convenient. She made him feel big when he was really small. That's all he really was. All he'd ever been. Small. So small.

Her anger burned low and steady now. She'd spent so long thinking she was weak because of him. But she'd survived him. Maybe she was stronger than she thought, like Player said. "I meant every word," she said, sharper now. "And I just realized something. I'm not scared of you anymore."

Before he could react, the low growl of engines rose in the distance. Then headlights swung into the parking lot. Two blacked-out SUVs slowly drove up. Heather froze, realizing it wasn't the Hounds.

The color drained from Brick's face.

"What the fuck!" He twisted around in his seat, reaching for the door. "You fucking brought *them* here?"

Heather was done pretending, shaking her head. "They're here for *you,*" she whispered. One SUV screeched to a halt, doors flung open. Two men stepped out. They were cartel muscle, masked and armed, sweeping the lot.

Brick scrambled out of the car, ducking low, as panic set in. "Fuck, fuck, fuck!"

Heather stayed right where she was. The

earpiece she'd tucked into the neckline of her hoodie clicked to life, Razor's voice steady. "Showtime."

Then all hell broke loose.

* * *

Player

The cold gnawed at Player's knuckles where they gripped the butt of his gun, and his breath was visible in the fading light. The tension was fucking tangible around them. The fading light grew shadows on the snow-slicked pavement, and every biker around the lot waited stone-still, their hearts thudding behind Kevlar and leather.

Ryder and Axel were off to his left, flanked by Vendetta's Cottonmouths, Shade, Ripper, and three more riders. All of them were ghosts in dark layers and deadly quiet. Beast stood at Razor's right shoulder, massive and unmoving as always.

Across the lot, the cartel made their entrance. Now a sleek black SUV crept in, and Player didn't need anyone to tell him who it was. The doors opened and two men stepped out first, rifles ready, eyes dead.

Then *he* climbed out. El Cuervo. Salazar. Smooth as sin in a long coat, his black hair glinting under community center's lights, that same calculating calm on his face. He smiled faintly, not warm or polite, as if this was a business meeting and not a powder keg ready to blow at any moment. His mouth curved at the corners, his smile that of a man who'd watch others beg and still walked away without a second thought.

Salazar spoke first. "We both know why we're here."

Player didn't respond. Razor did.

"You got your rat," Razor said evenly. "He's the one who stole from you. He's what you wanted if I remember right."

Behind Salazar, two more cartel men dragged Brick forward. His face was already a bloody mess, and one of his arms was twisted at an unnatural angle. He wasn't walking so much as being hauled. His boots dragged through the slush.

Heather, still sitting in the driver's seat of the SUV, stared straight ahead with her chin lifted. She was holding her own, not broken yet.

Salazar raised a brow. "He stole from us. Then he lied about it. That part is easy, my friend. But the girl…" The man's gaze slid to Heather. "She helped him hide. We have damages we need to collect."

Razor didn't flinch. "I've already told you once. She's non-negotiable."

Salazar's smile didn't move. "She is. If you want peace."

Player stepped forward, his voice like steel dragged across gravel. "She's *mine*."

That got Salazar's attention.

Player's tone sharpened. "She's my old lady. And I'll fucking bleed any man who says otherwise."

The air went still. Cartel rifles lifted a little higher. Crash spat in the snow. Beast cracked his neck like he was ready to rip someone's spine out. Vendetta was in his line of sight, a few yards behind the cartel, smirking back there. And for a second… the balance of power teetered.

Salazar's gaze swept the field, cold and calculating.

Brick whimpered something about loyalty, that they were supposed to protect each other. That Heather *owed* him.

Player took another step forward. "You lay one hand on her, and I promise you, Salazar… you won't walk away from it. None of you will."

A whisper of movement from behind Salazar caught his eye.

Heather.

She'd slipped out of the SUV, silent as snowfall, and now stood eight feet behind the cartel boss, the handgun Player had slid into her bag held in both hands, aimed steady at the back of the cartel leader's head. Her jaw was set, her breath fogging the winter air, her eyes sharp and unreadable.

Player almost forgot to breathe. *Jesus, sweetheart.*

Her stance and calm told him she knew exactly what she was doing with the 9mm he'd given her.

The cartel noticed a beat later, their rifles twitching her way with a sudden, rippling alertness. Muffled Spanish snapped through the air. A half-dozen barrels pointed at her heart.

Salazar stilled and then, to Player's disbelief, laughed. He didn't look threatened, he was amused. Like the girl with the gun proved something he'd suspected.

But Player didn't find it funny. Edging forward again, his tone was low and final. "I said… she's mine. You so much as breathe wrong, and we both know how this ends."

Another long pause.

Salazar waved his hand. "Take the rat."

Like it didn't matter. Like Brick was a receipt being returned.

The rifles lowered. The cartel grabbed Brick by both arms, wrenching him toward one of the waiting SUVs. He screamed something about being set up, about how he could make it right, but no one was listening.

Salazar turned just before stepping into his SUV.

The door hung open, his men flanking either side, Brick gagged and shoved inside like cargo. His gaze met Player's across the snowy lot, perfectly calm, before shifting to Heather. "You got lucky tonight, *chica*. But luck runs out. When it does, I'll be there to collect." Salazar glanced at Player one last time. "Enjoy your holiday, *hermano*. I'm a patient man." Then he stepped inside, and the door slammed shut. The convoy of cartel vehicles vanished into the night, taillights bleeding red into the darkness, swallowed by the winding road out of Mercy.

Heather didn't lower the gun until they were out of sight.

Player exhaled and moved to her fast. She allowed him to take the gun from her hands, slide into the waistband of his jeans at his back. "You okay?" he asked, wrapping his arms around her before the adrenaline could catch up.

Heather nodded into his chest. "Yeah. Now."

He pressed a kiss to her temple, his voice low. "First you turn out to be a seasoned poker player… now you know your way around a gun? Gotta say, sweetheart, you're full of surprises."

Her breath hitched. Her fingers curled into the back of his cut. "Tonight, I surprised myself," she whispered. "That felt… good."

Player grinned. "Fuck yeah, it did." He meant to steal a quick kiss, but his lips lingered, and he really didn't care what anyone else thought.

Around them, tension started to bleed out like steam after a firefight. The brothers of the Hounds and the Cottonmouths stepped from the shadows, weapons holstered but eyes still sharp. No one was fully relaxed yet, but the shift had begun.

Ryder gave Player a long look, then smirked.

"Well, shit. Guess I owe Razor twenty."

Player raised an eyebrow. "What for?"

"For betting your rotating bedpost days were numbered."

Outcast barked a laugh, shaking his head. "Player's settling down."

Crash pointed toward Heather, who was still wrapped up in Player's arms. "The man's done. That's it."

Margot stepped into the circle, cutting Ryder a look. "You bet against it? You used to be just as bad, *and* you fell for a cop."

Ryder flipped her off before stepping up to wrap an arm around her. "And survived it."

Margot snuggled into his side. "Barely."

The air shifted then, the banter not just a release, but a return. They'd made it through the night.

"Let's clear out," Razor ordered. "Deva's going to keep texting me until she knows everything. And this cold ain't doing shit for my back."

"I hear you, brother," Vendetta said, the Cottonmouth president walking up to shake hands.

It was time to go home.

* * *

Heather

The truck idled in the drive, heater running, windows slightly fogged. Heather sat with her hands in her lap, still wrapped in the hoodie she'd practically lived in these past few days. She watched the front door of Ryder and Margot's house, expecting Player to wave her in.

But instead, he jogged back out with her tote bag in one hand and his own duffel in the other.

When he opened the door, her brow knit. "We're

not staying?"

He slid the bags behind her seat, leaning in close. "Margot made it clear we're very welcome," he said quietly. "But tomorrow's Christmas. I want ours to be something else."

"Something else?" she echoed.

"Something real," he said. "Not with ten people crashing on couches and dogs barking. Just… us. You. Safe. Me not looking over my shoulder every five seconds." He kissed her temple like punctuation, then slid into the driver's seat.

Heather didn't say anything, just reached for his hand across the console and held it tightly the whole way back.

They drove into Mercy. The house Margot grew up in was the way they'd left it. The second they stepped inside, Heather felt the quiet sink into her bones. *Safe*. The first thing she did was turn on the Christmas tree lights.

He carried their bags to the main bedroom. She sat down on the couch, her eyes stinging as she looked at that tree. She didn't look at Player when he walked back into the room. "I didn't think I'd get a Christmas," she said softly.

"You got this one," Player replied. "And every one after, if you want 'em." He joined her on the couch, and she wrapped her arms around his waist. Her head found its usual place against his chest.

"You don't have to say things like that," she told him. "I don't expect anything."

He tipped her chin up, cutting her off with the barest smile. "I don't say anything I don't mean. And I do have expectations. I told the Hounds, the cartel, and half the Cottonmouths you're my old lady. You're not going to make me look bad now, are you?"

While he'd spoken in a teasing tone, the look in his gorgeous blue-green eyes was dead serious. The sheer emotion she read there threatened to take her breath away.

"No," she whispered.

She'd expected his kiss. She hadn't expected it to scorch her, burn her down until she was twisting in his arms, trying to get closer. His kiss was greedy, his hands already sliding up under the hoodie she wore. He'd unfastened her bra with the flick of a wrist, his hands skimming up to cover her breasts as she allowed him to deepen the kiss.

For a moment, she thought he'd press her down on the couch. But then he released her, grabbing a throw from the back of the couch and tossing it onto the carpeted floor in front of the Christmas tree. His grin was pure mischief. "What do you think?"

Heather nodded. Making love next to the Christmas tree sounded like a good time to her. They both climbed onto the throw, peeling off layers as if their clothes were on fire. Somehow, he ended up lying on the floor, holding her hips as she rode him, running her hands over the muscled wall of his chest, stealing kisses from his lips as their bodies worked together, seeking bliss.

Player looked up at her, smiling. Her heart skipped a beat at the sight, her body clenched around him.

"What?" she asked softly.

"You have no idea," he whispered, "how beautiful you look right now." His thrusts were slowly gaining in strength as he kept staring. "The lights from the tree are shining off your beautiful black hair. You don't even look fucking real."

Heather gasped as his movements sped up, as he

worked up into her a little faster.

"Want to burn this into my memory," he said, lifting a hand to wrap around the back of her neck. Pulling her down, he whispered against her lips, "Want to remember how you looked, our first Christmas together, for the rest of my life."

His kiss was demanding, his body more so. It didn't take long for him to bring her off, and he reached his climax right after. They ended up tangled around each other beside the tree. Player covered her with the throw while they recovered.

Heather had found her courage today. Now, in his arms, she could almost believe she deserved to be happy. "Thank you," she whispered. "For everything. For tonight. For not giving up on me. I don't know where we're going from here, but --"

He tipped her chin, making her meet his gaze. "Yeah, you do."

The look in his eyes took her breath away. Her gaze searched his, full of hesitation. "You sure?"

"I've never been more sure of anything in my whole life, Heather," he said, brushing his lips over hers. "We'll figure it out. You and me."

As the tree lights blinked quietly before them, and the snow finally began to drift past the windowpane, Heather finally let herself believe.

This wasn't the end. It was the beginning.

Jamie Targaet

Jamie Targaet is the author of the Hounds of Hell MC. She's anxious to introduce you to this club of gorgeous, dominant men and the lucky women who surrender to them. The ride is going to get wild at times, not going to lie. But there's thrilling action, scorching hot sex scenes, and all the feels.

Jamie writes erotic romance for Changeling Press, a little fanfiction on the side, and she's an aspiring horror writer in another life. She enjoys time with her family (including the fur babies). She likes good horror movies and shows, emo metal and classic rock, and time spent in other worlds writing and reading. She loves hearing from readers and is looking forward to hearing from you.

Hounds of Hell MC is part of the Hounds of Hell MC Multiverse.

Jamie at Changeling: changelingpress.com/ jamie-targaet-a-227

Changeling Press LLC

Contemporary Action Adventure, Sci-Fi, Steampunk, Dark Fantasy, Urban Fantasy, Paranormal, and BDSM Romance available in e-book, audio, and print format at ChangelingPress.com -- MC Romance, Werewolves, Vampires, Dragons, Shapeshifters and Horror -- Tales from the edge of your imagination.

Where can I get Changeling Press Books?

Changeling Press e-books are available at ChangelingPress.com, Amazon, Apple Books, Barnes & Noble, Kobo, Smashwords, and other online retailers, including Everand Subscription and Kobo Subscription Services. Print books are available at Amazon, Barnes and Noble, and by ISBN special order through your local bookstores.

ChangelingPress.com

www.ingramcontent.com/pod-product-compliance
Lightning Source LLC
LaVergne TN
LVHW020530100826
845148LV00010B/1407

* 9 7 8 1 6 0 5 2 1 9 5 8 5 *